Thomas Sweterlitsch has a Master's Degree in Literary and Cultural Theory from Carnegie Mellon. For the last twelve years he has been a Reader Advisor with the Carnegie Library for the Blind and Physically Handicapped. He lives in Pittsburgh with his wife and daughter. *Tomorrow and Tomorrow* is his first novel.

Praise for *Tomorrow and Tomorrow*:

'Thomas Sweterlitsch is a superstar. Right out of the blocks, he's managed to achieve what most authors never do: the creation of a world so complete – so sensually rich and emotionally authentic – that it reduces the real world to a pale impression. *Tomorrow and Tomorrow* is a brutal, beautiful book. Read it' Jesse Kellerman

'This book has the sci-fi X factor – the ring of awful truth' *Sunday Sport*

'A must-read for lovers of tech noir' Yangsze Choo

'*Tomorrow and Tomorrow* is literary sci-fi, focusing on the picture, like Henry James' *Wall Street Journal*

'*Tomorrow and Tomorrow* is a delicious dystopian mystery . . . *Blade Runner* meets *Minority Report*' *Kirkus Reviews Blog*

'Weird, hypnotic, and lovely' Django Wexler

'Fans of William Gibson and classic noir will love how the styles intersect here' *Library Journal*

'Vivid and compelling' *Publishers Weekly*

'A mesmerizing, genre-mixing sci-fi, noir mystery . . . I could not put it down' Wayne Gladstone

'Thrilling and thought-provoking, *Tomorrow and Tomorrow* is a most intriguing and original read' www.forwinternights.wordpress.com

'Thoma[illegible] is so bleak and shallow [illegible] rdpress.com

'An en[illegible] rishes' www.theeloq[illegible]

TOMORROW AND TOMORROW

THOMAS SWETERLITSCH

headline

First published in Great Britain in 2014 by HEADLINE PUBLISHING GROUP

First published in Great Britain in paperback in 2015 by HEADLINE PUBLISHING GROUP

1

Cataloguing in Publication Data is available from the British Library

ISBN 978 1 4722 1486 7

Offset in Dante MT by Avon DataSet Ltd, Bidford-on-Avon, Warwickshire

Printed and bound by CPI Group (UK) Ltd, Croydon, CR0 4YY

Headline's policy is to use papers that are natural, renewable and recyclable products and made from wood grown in well-managed forests and other controlled sources. The logging and manufacturing processes are expected to conform to the environmental regulations of the country of origin.

HEADLINE PUBLISHING GROUP
An Hachette UK Company
338 Euston Road
London NW1 3BH

www.headline.co.uk
www.hachette.co.uk

For Sonja and Genevieve

There is a pain – so utter –
It swallows substance up –
Then covers the Abyss with Trance –
So Memory can step
Around – across – opon it –
As One within a Swoon –
Goes safely – where an open eye –
Would drop Him – Bone by Bone –

—EMILY DICKINSON

· PART I ·

WASHINGTON, DC

8, 23—

Her body's down in Nine Mile Run, half buried in river mud. Time-stamped late April, the rains must have exposed her. Or maybe the rain-swollen river rose around her, the current rinsing away the foot or so of silt that had covered her. Time-stamped 6:44 p.m.—shafts of sunlight slant through the woods, dappling the mud in the clearings. The water's a mossy green where the sunlight hits, but outside the direct sunlight the water's a sooty brown, almost black. I think of the earth here, the history of this place, how accustomed it is to burning—the hillsides running steep to the riverbed were once slag heaps for the mills, rolling landslides of molten ash—but by the time I knew this place, everything was reclaimed and greened. It was a city park.

When the time stamp's reached 7:31 p.m. it's grown too dark to see so I adjust the light filters. The woods and the body brighten with the sickly pallor of digitized light. I can see her feet now, white like white mushrooms grown bulbous in the soil. Bookmark the body. I leave her, finding my way back through the woods along the jogging path in the utter dark.

At the trailhead parking lot I reset to 6:15 p.m., a half hour before I will find her body. The night reverses to a bluer shade of dusk. I follow the jogging path that runs serpentine through the woods before scaling down a tangle of roots and bramble, holding on to reedy branches to keep my balance. I've been this way before. Scan the underbrush for footprints or signs of struggle, scraps of clothing, anything, but I don't find any tangible traces until I find the white lump of her body—a pallid curve I take as her back and a spray of hair much darker from mud than the honey-brown I know from photographs of her. I kneel near her. I study her, trying to piece together what happened—trying to understand. At 7:31 p.m. it's grown too dark to see.

I retrace my steps. At the trailhead parking lot, I reset to 6:15 p.m. and the night reverses. Her body's down there, half buried in mud. I start along the jogging path, scanning the woods for traces of her. I'll find her in about twenty minutes.

10, 21—

People often ask us how their loved ones died, expecting extraordinary circumstances or wondering whether they suffered terribly, and I'm reminded of Auden's "Musée des Beaux Arts" because, with rare exception, the deaths we research are banal—someone eating, opening a window or walking dully along. Nothing extraordinary—though often survivors remember how fine a day it was, how perfect for autumn, how almost like summer. The end occurred quickly, that much is verifiable—no one suffered except the ones who lived. Five hundred thousand lives ended in the blinding white flash. Shadows elongated and became like charcoal smudges, the City became like snowy ash and in a breath of wind vanished. Other than details, all we really answer about their loved ones is that they likely did not suffer and they likely died as they had lived. Even this dreadful martyrdom ran its course.

October twenty-first—

Ten years since the end.

Tuesday's the last I used brown sugar. I'd even pinged Kucenic that morning to be courteous, to tell him I'd a touch of the bug and wouldn't be coming in—but he informed me I'm already out of sick days and vacation days and some of the other archival assistants were tired of covering for me. That I would be docked pay and may face probation. There'd been complaints, he said. He voiced a few minutes later, his profile pic all snowy beard and kind blue eyes, his Adware left gaudily exposed like a crosshatch of silver wires threading his skull beneath his wispy hair. This was over at Tryst Coffeehouse, on their Wi-Fi to take the call. My Adware's shoddy, running a skittish frame rate that augments reality with a shitty split-second delay. Kucenic's image hung in my eyes like a transparency overlaying café menus, displays of lattes, Red Eyes, mochas, velvety coffees hovering wherever I looked, Fair Trade and Organic info scrolling over every bag of beans. He asked if everything was all right, but his lips weren't quite synched up with his words.

"Everything's fine," I told him. "My sinuses, I think, just a sinus infection—"

"You're researching homicide," he told me.

"I'll be better tomorrow—"

"I've trusted you with potential fraud and homicide," he said. "There's a schedule we have to follow, there are reports—"

"Her body was tampered with—"

Self-conscious discussing the body in a crowded café, but everyone at the nearby tables was immersed in their own Adware streams, chatting to unseen companions or slumped over their coffee lost in private fantasies—no one paying attention to me.

"RFI #14502—Hannah Massey," said Kucenic. "You've written that the Archive's corrupted around her—"

"Whoever's trying to cover up the killing is sloppy," I told him. "All those corruptions in the Archive are like fingerprints, but there are a million fingerprints and it will take time to make sense of them all—"

"You're burning yourself out," he said. "I understand this is a difficult time for you, and I'm sympathetic, I am, but I need to know if you can handle this report right now. It's been months since you first found her. I need you to wrap this up. Do you need help? We can work out a leave of absence. We can reassign your cases—"

"I don't need a leave," I told him. "I can't afford a leave—"

"What does your doctor say?"

"Leave personal shit out of this," I told him. "Don't turn this personal—"

"You're doing taxing work," he said, easing off a bit. "You're always thorough in your approach, but there are gaps in your presentation. Significant gaps. What about the victim's parents? Her friends? You haven't even filled in her last hours—"

"There are no last hours, not yet," I told him. "I've tracked her to the point of her disappearance, but that's not when she died. She was on campus, a psychology lecture about human-computer interaction. After class she cut through campus and entered the lower level of a parking garage on Fifth Avenue, near Morewood. No security cameras down there. That's when she was taken—"

I minimized Kucenic and stared into my coffee, at the nutrition facts appearing there like legible shimmers of light. There's a gap in the Archive from when she entered the parking garage to when I found her body near the river. Security cameras were installed in that garage in the weeks after she vanished—there's plenty of footage of the garage's lower levels' time-stamped weeks and months following her disappearance, of security guards making their rounds on golf carts, but all too late.

"We need to trim the scope of what you're working on. State Farm just wants proof of how she died," said Kucenic. "A documented cause of death—that's all. A one-page summary. And when we're certain we're dealing with homicide, I'll have to register her death with the FBI—there are legal implications if we don't handle this properly. We need to stick to their timetables. I can't go days or weeks without hearing from you—"

"I found her body," I told him, thinking of spring rains sluicing away her shallow burial. "No one else would have—"

"Look, Dominic," he said, "if you're going to work in this field, you have to understand the bigger picture. You can't just hole up in the research, block out every other consideration. You have to understand that when I meet with State Farm, their reps will be excited by what you've found, the work you're doing, but their first question will be *Why haven't you told us how she died?* That information means money to them—they care about the money, not the girl. You have to think like they think if you want to be effective in this line of work—"

"They don't care who killed her, just that she was killed," I said. "Isn't that right? You want me to ignore what happened to her? I can't do that, Kucenic. For the past few weeks, whenever I close my eyes I see her—"

"All these images aren't real," he told me. "You immerse into the Archive and if you're not careful, you forget that it isn't real. You spend so much time watching people die, it can affect you. It's okay if you can't keep up right now, if you can't work like this—"

"What do you mean, 'forget that it isn't real?' It was all real—"

"Log some hours," he said. "Work through this. I'll need an update by this afternoon—"

"Fine, fine," I told him, but skipped work that afternoon anyway. I immersed at the Mount Pleasant Library, accessing their public Wi-Fi from a wingback chair in the gov docs room that's hidden from the reference desk librarians. Private back there, no one to bother me. Brown sugar comes in blister packs—taupe heptagons—cut for use as a study aid. I dry swallowed the pill. I closed my eyes when the sweetness hit and my breaths grew deeper. I loaded the City. I was with my wife then. For a solid ten hours, at least, I was with her. The librarians kicked me out at closing so I slept the night in their parking lot, half hidden by a hedgerow. Still connected when I woke, but the City had timed out—the morning feeds blaring *Cash Amateurs* and looped promos for season 4 of *Chance in Hell* and the *Voyeur Cam* pay streams and *Real Swingers of DC* and groupons if I opinioned who was hotter between last week's murdered Fur girls on *Crime Scene Superstar*, blonde versus redhead, dead teen bodies displayed in crime scene streams, *Look here to vote, look here—*

Dr. Simka has diagnosed me with major depressive disorder, substance abuse disorder and secondary traumatization. He's prescribed Zoloft and suggests I should exercise more, that jogging through Rock Creek Park when the weather's nicer or training for the National Half Marathon will cleanse toxins from my bloodstream. He says I'm putting on weight and it worries him.

"Maybe we should try to lose some weight together," I've told him, but he just pats his belly and laughs.

Simka's offices are over in Kalorama, near 21st and Florida, in the building with the bright red door. He's filled his waiting room with furniture that he's made—black cherry Mission-style chairs, a magazine table, a matching bookshelf filled with his early editions of Lacan. After our biweekly hour I feel I've pawned damaged goods to him, that my case is certain to hurt his success rate. I mention this to him while he's signing my EAP paperwork, but he just smiles and nods and strokes his bushy mustache and says, "You don't need style points to win—"

I've learned to trust Dr. Simka. I talk with him about Theresa, about my memories. We discuss the amount of time I spend in the Pittsburgh Archive visiting her. We try to set limits, boundaries—we try to set goals. Simka doesn't believe in VR therapy, preferring face-to-face contact with his patients, so I relax on his cushy leather couch and have conversations with him—about anything, anything at all, whatever's on my mind, whatever thoughts I'm trying to exorcise. I talk with him about my work for Kucenic, about the archival research I'm assigned—the information's confidential, but I unburden myself to Simka. I told him about RFI #14502, the woman whose body I found.

"There was a dispute," I told him. "The policyholder's beneficiary—her sister, in Akron—filed life insurance claims for the woman and her three children, but State Farm contested the claims to avoid part of the payout, contending that only two of the woman's children could be verified as dying as a direct result of the bomb—"

"So, your firm was contacted to confirm their deaths," said Simka.

"Kucenic won the case in a batch bid and assigned it as part of my caseload," I told him. "We were contracted to find evidence to bolster State Farm's dispute, or if we found that all three children did die in the blast, to provide recommendations for a settlement—"

"Either way, you're searching for a dead child," said Simka.

"I found the first death easily enough," I told him. "A boy at Harrison Middle School. Plenty of security cameras in the school, plenty of footage to reconstruct his life. I made sure I was with him in the classroom as he died, marking when the white light streamed through the windows, marking when he burned. The second child was only a few months old. Another boy. I logged several hours in the house with the policyholder, the mother. She spent almost every afternoon watching *The Price Is Right* while her boy cried in the bassinet. Sometimes I picked up the boy to try and soothe him, I don't know why—I knew it didn't matter, that the boy was long since dead, that the crying was just a webcam recording re-created there. I just held him, sang to him until he calmed, but the moment I put him down the Archive reset and he was back in his bassinet crying. He was crying in his crib when he died. Each child earned a separate report—"

"And the third?" asked Simka.

"Hannah," I told him. "Nineteen years old. She'd been tampered with in the Archive, huge chunks of her life deleted. State Farm keyed in on the deletions when their researchers first examined the claim, which is why they put it up for bid, but they couldn't track her—"

"And you could?" asked Simka.

"I can be obsessive about the research, is all," I told him. "State Farm doesn't have the manpower. When something's been deleted from the Archive, it generates an exception report because the code falters. If you isolate time frames you can print thousands of pages of exception reports and slog through them, try to stitch back what's happened. Clever hacks replace whatever they've deleted or changed in the Archive with something else, something similar—if you're careful, you can delete something and insert a forgery without generating an error message at all. Whoever deleted Hannah, though, wasn't skilled or very careful—I could reconstruct her life by following the exception messages, reading the code; it just took time. I imagine it's like following a boar after it crashes through the underbrush—"

"Where did you find her?" asked Simka.

"I found her body in the river, half buried in mud over in this reclaimed slag site called Nine Mile Run. Academic footage of the watershed taken by Carnegie Mellon's Environmental Science department. Her body had been buried there, but the rain washed away the mud that had covered her. Whoever deleted her didn't think to delete JSTOR footage or didn't know it existed as part of the Archive. By the time I found her body, she was swollen. Hard to even recognize—"

"You seem particularly upset over her death. You deal with this type of work on a regular basis—"

"You would have liked her," I told him. "She was a psych major. An actress in a comedy troupe called Scotch 'n' Soda. She was a head turner, vibrant—but I couldn't even recognize her body when I found her in that footage. Only a few minutes of white in the mud, a partial of her back and her feet. I had to prove it was her through the exception reports—"

Nearly every death is contested, nearly every property damage claim. Billions and billions of dollars in lawsuits. My research is handled like a spreadsheet, but I told Simka those three children still troubled my sleep. Simka listened attentively—he always listens to what I have to say like he's hearing essential news. I told him I replay those children's deaths so often I can't tell if I'm reliving their deaths in the Archive or if I'm just remembering what I'd seen. I ask him to help me stop remembering. He jots down notes on a yellow legal pad. He doesn't interrupt me with too many questions. He lets me speak. When he does talk, he spends a lot of our time together asking about the Beatles—what certain lyrics mean.

"The Beatles dropped acid and ate psychotropics when they wrote," I tell him, "so as a mental health professional, you're in a better position to interpret their lyrics than I am—"

"True, true," he says, "but I might miss literary aspects that you're trained to find. You know, I picked up on a lot more of Baudelaire by talking with you than I did through the apps, so maybe between the two of us, we can make some sense of *Abbey Road*—"

He suggests I should keep a journal. Just write the date at the top of the page and continue from there. Just be free with it, it will help. He gave me an ultimatum—that I'd have to at least try journaling or he wouldn't continue signing my EAP paperwork. I don't believe the threat, but he actually bought me this notebook—real paper, I think—and presented it to me with a download called the Progoff Intensive Journal method. He says I should write in longhand, that it will help my concentration—that dictation apps don't have the same calming effect as penmanship. Simka is holistic—he believes the building blocks to a healthy, productive lifestyle already exist within me but that I have to learn how to stack the blocks in a new way. He suggests I listen to classical music to improve my sustained concentration skills. Feeds and streams contribute to the fracturing of our consciousness, he says. Try John Adams and listen through—at least twenty minutes a stretch, without augments, without shuffle. He hums a tune the Adware eventually identifies as "Grand Pianola Music"—*click to add to iTunes library.*

I take my Zoloft every night, but every night I wake up dreaming of my wife. 4 a.m. 6 a.m. The clock radio plays HOT 99.5, crap pop, but I lie deadened and listen, wishing my bed were a sinkhole and that I'd somehow die. The clock radio plays into the afternoon before I bring myself to shut it off, before I bring myself to climb out of bed. I indulge in Pop-Tarts and Mrs. Fields. I've been eating Ho Hos. Gavril swung by late Friday afternoon to see how I was feeling and found me eating an entire box of Ho Hos for breakfast with coffee. "No wonder you're sick all the time," he said, his breath like espresso and cigarettes mixed up with those blueberry Coolsa strips he chews.

A few years ago, Simka ended a session by saying, "Dominic, a fish rots head first—"

He suggested I rediscover personal hygiene—that no matter how bad I feel, I was sure to feel worse if I didn't shower. So, I shower—and that has helped. I shave every morning. Long strokes with the razor, over my neck and jaw, over my skull. It's bruised up there—black splotches, violet. Labyrinthine ridges of Adware like a street map of a foreign city embossed on my skull. I look in the mirror and follow the lines of wires as if they might lead me somewhere—anywhere other than where I really am.

Simka says to find someplace comfortable to write. He's described his home office to me, out in Maryland, with its oak desk and a picture window overlooking a woodland backyard. My apartment's public housing, but there's a fire-escape terrace with a view of the surrounding rooftops—air-conditioning units and service entries. It's chilly out here. The neighboring terrace's potted plants died weeks ago in the first frost but are still outside, brown and brittle. I sip my coffee and bundle in my robe and sweatpants, a gray hoodie and slipper-thick socks. The sunrise pinks the sky—beautiful. Quiet. Wi-Fi's included in the lease, or should be, but the router's been broken going on three years. I hear a wet click whenever my Adware tries to autoconnect—like a popping knuckle just behind my right ear—and have to dismiss the low-signal warnings again and again, even though I've asked never to be alerted. Every five minutes, click—the network connection icon in my peripheral spins and the low-signal warning pops up again like a floater in my line of sight. "Dismiss," I tell it. Five minutes later, click. I can only take so much.

So, here it is: A Day in the Life. A chronicle for Dr. Simka.

Theresa. Theresa Marie.

Even writing her name feels like scratching a phantom limb.

I take the bus these days because I sold my Volkswagen for cash years ago. Seats are occupied, so I sit behind the driver, near a scratched glass poster looping commercials for Mifeprex and TANF and YouPorn. Closer to Dupont Circle my Adware autoconnects to wifi.dc.gov and the feeds tingle my skull—blacking out a few seconds before my vision reboots with a shitty display of augs and apps, freebies mostly, looming when I notice one, the others receding, my profile bundled with so many pop-ups and worms that my vision strobes while it loads. GPS info and route maps and Metro schedules hover midbus—real time supposedly, but the bus schedule's off sync by a half hour or more and the map's of a Silver Spring route that doesn't even exist. The passenger across the aisle stares at the ceiling, giggling—he's drooling down the front of his raincoat, utterly engrossed in the streams. He's spamming indiscriminate friend requests, but my social networking's locked so no one bothers me—I stare out the window and concentrate on the CNN Headline feed:

BUY AMERICA!!! FUCK AMERICA!!! SELL AMERICA!!!

The *Buy, Fuck, Sell* feed's leading with a new leaked sex tape of President Meecham, the ten-year anniversary of Pittsburgh demoted to postjump news. *PRESIDENT MEECHAM REVEALED AS*

DORM ROOM SLUT! MEECH'S PEACHES EXPOSED IN TEEN SEX SCANDAL!

Headaches from news torrents and commercials overloading my secondhand Adware, shit I picked up on Craigslist years ago from a U. of Maryland kid who'd already fried some of the wires without telling me. Hilfiger, Sergio Tacchini, Nokia, Puma. President Meecham from her days as Miss Teen Pennsylvania kneels in the aisle of the bus. *Real footage,* says CNN, *not sim, not sculpt.* She touches herself and the talking heads comment: *Everywhere, Americans have been given the choice between Love and Filth, and they have uniformly chosen Filth.* Al Jazeera America's the only stream covering Pittsburgh as a lead, posting satellite imagery captured on that first sunny day after the end, of the scorched earth like a black harelip on the mouth of the Appalachian Mountains. Pull for a stop.

Gavril lives in Ivy City, a renovated loft on the corner of Fenwick and Okie—warehouses and abandoned tenements, a Starbucks on the corner, a Così. Gavril's building's slashed with graffiti and slathered with wheat-pasted handbills for Qafqa concerts long since past and photocopied pics of the Pittsburgh mushroom cloud and offers for sex with male models and cheap rates on love hotels. Spray-painted: *One who is slain in the way of Allah is a martyr.* BBC America loops the "Star-Spangled Banner" over aerial views of the way Pittsburgh was and the way it is now: radioactive weed growth and the black guts of buildings—but the stream interrupts and reloads, bothered by all the vandalized and nonlicensed Tags setting off my Adware's net security. *Are we any safer than we were ten years ago?* I ring the buzzer.

"Kdo je to?"

"It's Dominic—"

"Moment, please—"

Every time I'm here, the place is filled with girlfriends and bumming students, poets I've met around, politicians scoring cocaine, models passed out on the couches, editors, business associates of some sort waiting aimlessly, actors fixing sandwiches for themselves in the kitchen—who knows who all these people are, but the place is like a social lounge and there's never anywhere to sit. Cousin Gav—my mother's sister's son. He grew up in Prague, a scene-star installation artist by the time he was seventeen, a college dropout once featured at Art Basel, but after Pittsburgh he gave up that momentum to be with me in the States. I love him for that, for everything. Since coming here he's abandoned art but gone freelance with fashionporn and photography—he's done well for himself.

One of Gavril's women opens the door—this one a willowy blonde almost as tall as I am, so pale and thin it's like her skin's translucent. Twenty? Twenty-one? She wears a XXL Manchester United jersey belted like a dress but nothing else, the pink saucers of her nipples clearly visible through the sheer fabric.

"What's with all this Frost bollocks?" she says.

"You're English," I notice and she rolls her eyes.

Her profile's an obvious fake—*Twiggy*, it says, born *19 September 1949*. Occupation: *IT girl*. The American Apparel sponsorship's real, though, her profile displayed in arcs of copyrighted font.

"I asked a question," she says. "Frost? Are you trying to be fucking funny?"

"You must be the poet," I tell her. "Gav mentioned you might be around—"

"He says he's reading Frost to find inspiration for his Anthropologie shoot. I told him if he wants pastoral imagery, then Wordsworth's a better bet than Frost, but you have him reading all the wrong stuff anyway—"

"Wordsworth? Christ, don't pollute him like that. Are you a student?"

"Georgetown," she says. "Ph.D. 20th-Century American Modernism. I'm a Plathist—"

"'Mad Girl's Love Song,'" I tell her. "I like that one."

"She should have used Adware," says Twiggy, "to distract her from all that shit she obsessed about. She was a gorgeous girl, would have been brilliant for the *Mademoiselle* app—"

"I shut my eyes and all is born again," I tell her, misquoting the lines.

"Gavril expected you'd like me—"

The never-ending party is spare this morning, only a quartet of scenesters shuffling cards at the kitchen table, smoking cigarettes and eating eggs. Twiggy joins another young woman, a brunette, playing Mike Tyson's Punch-Out on the VIM, the furniture pushed to the edges of the room, Tyson prancing bullish. The brunette's in spandex and thigh-high tube socks, jabbing and kicking riotously, so model thin and gangly she's like a spastic female skeleton raging in fits of laughter.

"You suck," says Twiggy, readying herself for Tyson. "You've got to, like, sidestep the uppercuts—"

BBC America talking heads hover in my sight: *Executions in the terrorist courts, a stroke of Meecham's pen beheads a thousand jihadists, a thousand thousand—*

Gavril's in the back bedroom, the room he calls his darkroom even though he doesn't develop anything, preferring digital work on his iMac even over imprints or holograms. Oversize prints of his static photography decorate the walls—young women he finds on the street, impossibly gorgeous the way he shoots them, catalog ready. Gavril's in a tracksuit and smiles when he sees me. Jockish, when it comes down to it—his hug ends in a double fist bump handshake that I blunder and he laughs. The room smells like him—apple-scented Head & Shoulders, Clive Christian cologne. Cigarettes smoldering in emptied coffee mugs. When he first moved to the States he was wiry, but now he's filled out from fine food and smiles easily, his physique rock hard from all the soccer and sex. He only wears pajamas or a tracksuit—I've never seen him in anything else.

"John Dominic," he says.

"Gav—"

"What the fuck, man? Are you translate me? Can you understand what I'm saying?"

"I'm translating," I tell him, the app keeping up well enough as he speaks in Czech, but making him look like poorly dubbed cinema.

"I tell you I want to learn English to be inspired, to read Robert Frost in the original—"

"I'm teaching you Robert Frost—"

"I'm expecting trees and snowing woods and bullshit like that, but what do I get? Some kid cutting off his fucking hand with a saw and no one gives a shit—"

"They get him a doctor," I tell him.

"For Christ's sake," says Gavril, "I want horses and trees and snowy fields and barns, and shit like that—"

"I know what you want—"

"Yeah, man, the road less taken," he says, poets.org spam fluttering at the fringes of my sight—*free credit scores, click here! FREE! FREE! FREE!*

"We'll get to it. How's business?"

"Business," he says. "Is good. Listen, if you want some work, I could use some copy for a few things—"

"Sure," I tell him. "E-mail me—"

"I'll also send you the contact sheets for Twiggy," he says. "What do you think, eh? You let me know what you think—"

"About the girl out there? Christ, Gav—"

"Listen," he says, "I was in preproduction for the Anthropologie winter catalog, up in New England, when American Apparel pings me out of the blue. They tell me they have a rush job, some last-minute interactive campaign they want to launch but their photographer pulled out, some guy I'd never heard of, and they wanted to know if I could do the work. They offered double what I usually get, so I told them, sure, sure, I can fit it in. The only condition is that I have to use the girls they send me. They want to use amateurs and Twiggy out there won an Internet modeling poll, a 'Real Girl Next Door' click-to-vote. You let me know what you think, okay? Built like a fucking—twenty-one years old, her tits point straight up. Vivian's her real name, from England—hey, Dominic, that's the job for you, cousin. Model scout—"

"No, no. Not for me—"

"I could hook you up, Dominic. Cure your depression better than all this bullshit therapy you go through. Get you with an agency. They'd fly you to Iceland or Brazil and all you'd have to do—You can work a camera, can't you?"

Anthropologie and American Apparel portals in the Adware. Young women in flower prints in the Parisian countryside, farmlands, abandoned barns—the Anthropologie summer catalog portal so paradisiacal I can almost let myself forget I'm in this apartment, in this city, this life. I peel off ten bills and lay them on the desk. Gavril counts and pockets the cash, handing me a blister packet of brown sugar. We do this casually, almost as an afterthought, without words.

"What do you think?" he says. "You tell me about Twiggy. She told me she wanted to meet some poets, so I mentioned you were the best I knew. She's interested—"

"I don't think I'm all that interested—"

"Pittsburgh was ten years ago," says Gavril. "That's an eternity, cousin. You wallow in Pittsburgh, but you need to forget. You need distraction—if you want, I can let you be the stand-in while I film those two girls. I'll film you in a threesome—"

"How's my aunt doing?" I ask him.

"I'm serious, Dominic," he says. "You need to clear your mind. Have some fun with life. It's not too late to live—"

"I can't," I tell him. "I can't—"

"Anyway, your aunt is good," he says. "She spends all her time in her studio making wood-block prints—she's very happy, but she worries about you. I showed her a picture from the other night and she said you look like a bear ate you. A bear, Dominic. She wants you to take a vacation, spend some time in Domažlice, out in the country. Relax a little. She misses her nephew—"

"I'll visit," I tell him. "Maybe going out to the country for a while is a good idea. Get away from everything—"

"Cuts off his fucking hand and no one gives a shit. Barns and horses, man. I want barns and horses next time. My Anthropologie concept is to channel Robert Frost. Barns, horses—"

"When are you free for dinner?" I ask him.

"I'll hit you up," he says in English. "My schedule's a bit harsh this week. I'll take you to Primanti's for a sandwich—"

"Not there—"

"Keep your network open—"

"Out, out," I tell him, leaving.

In the living room, Twiggy's faring better against Tyson, landing combination punches—making tweety birds flit over Tyson's eyes. When she sees me, she breaks off from the game.

"Can I talk with you?" she says.

She pulls me aside and asks if I'm using.

"No, nothing much," I tell her. "Just some brown sugar, nothing hard—"

"You like uppers, then?"

"Just to help me concentrate sometimes," I tell her.

"I want to give you something," she says. She opens her purse, a gold tube hardly big enough to carry lipstick and car keys, and fishes out a heart-shaped pill wrapped in a plastic baggie.

"What is this?"

"A valentine," she says, slipping it between my lips. "Let it kick in and then take the brown—"

I bite down—the pill tastes like cherries. Twiggy friends me, pushes her contact info into my address book.

"If you like it, I can get you more," she says. "If you ever want to talk Plath sometime, or dig into Sexton—"

I watch her a heartbeat too long after she returns to her game, her jersey dress rising with every punch, and my Adware fills with pop-ups and redirected streams to escort services and live companions, to cam girls in lingerie who coo they want to meet me. Whatever she just gave me kicks in. I hurry from the apartment, illegally opaque sex ads blotting my sight and I almost tumble down the stairs, the advertisements showing girls so realistic in the streams I stand aside on the landing to let them pass, but they're just images, mirages, all just light. "I don't want any, I don't want them," but the ads are better at knowing what I want than I am and ranks of girls march for my approval, all slight variations of Twiggy, blonde hundreds in the apartment lobby until I'm out on the street and they fill the sidewalk, lockstepping in unison, like a mirror image of a mirror, a thousand Twiggies receding into space everywhere I look.

There's a KFC in Dupont Circle, a two-tier restaurant. Crowds in lines, the place is swamped. Menu apps hijack my attention with flashing extracrispy breasts and thighs. *Original, Cajun, Buffalo!* Relax—the last thing I need is for some plainclothes KFC cop to think I'm jumpy and call for a drug sniffer. A two-piece extracrispy box from the menu kiosk and a restroom token from the cashier. They have semiprivate stalls here, on the second floor—I leave the chicken and hit the restroom. Someone's washing his hands. A few stalls are in use. I lock myself in the far stall and peel apart the packet of brown sugar, swallow the pill. My tongue's filmy with the aftertaste—chalky, bitter. *JESUS CHRIST SAVED MY SOUL* knifed into the door. Someone's drawn Colonel Sanders shooting rainbows from his massive cock. A tightness in my eyes. Combined with the valentine Twiggy slipped me, the burn hits my nerves like a current—like everything I see is etched in light. The stall and the toilet pulse. Colonel Sanders looks *real*—absurdly real, textured, with volume, his hair like a spool of cotton, his rainbows shimmering as the most beautiful colors I've ever seen. Infinite streams of flushing toilets and washing hands. I wander from the stalls, wander from the KFC—I'm in Dupont Circle, in the street—picking pebbles from the crosswalks. I concentrate on the City.

Pittsburgh.

I concentrate on Three Rivers Net and the Archive app swims into focus, the icon an image of the golden triangle cradled by its rivers. I load the City-Archive and my vision blacks out, replaced by the gold and black crest of an eagle-stamped shield topped by castle parapets.

Log in.

"John Dominic Blaxton," I tell it, struggling to enunciate. Allow auto fill-ins, "yes." Remember password, "yes." I seem to remember traffic in Dupont Circle and the noise of horns and screaming. Someone asking if I'm all right—of course I'm all right—and when they try to help me out of the street, through the crosswalk, to safety on the sidewalk, I shrug them off and panic. I may have fallen to the concrete. There are other sounds, other voices, the noise of Dupont Circle as the City-Archive crest fades, as DC fades, as the City surrounds me, western Pennsylvania in summer twilight as real as any dream.

376, the Parkway from the airport—roads the gray of moondust, the surrounding hills dense with trees grown dark in the gathering dusk. The Parkway was like this at the end—congested lanes too narrow for the volume of traffic. The glare of onrushing headlights, taillights like lines of rubies. I'm here. I remember. Shopping malls and gas stations and restaurants illuminate the peaks of the shadowy hills. I've shopped in these malls. I've eaten in these chains. Beneath the rusted Norfolk and Western trestle, the road rises and finally cuts in lowering arcs, descending, gutting deeper through the hills until the tunnel. The tunnel, a square of burnished light cut into the mountainside. And through—a concrete blur of fluorescent light and ceramic tiles, the reverb whoosh of engines, wind, and when the tunnel ends the City bursts around me in riotous blooms of glass and steel. I plunge through the skyline. The light of skyscrapers floats on skeins of interstate bonded by golden bridges, a ghost image of the City reflecting in the black mirror of the rivers, my God, my God, I remember, it's everything I want, it's everything I've ever wanted, it's everything I want to remember.

I'm here.

I'm here:

"Pay when you leave—"

The bus driver, an older black man sipping from a thermos. Port Authority sweater-vest and slacks. I almost want to touch him, to touch his arm to feel him, to see how real he feels, but I sit toward the rear, thankful to smell the layering of body odor and stale air, the vinyl seats. This was the 54C—South Side to Oakland. There are others on this bus, others visiting the Archive—we're different from the illusions, somehow lighter. We all look at one another, wondering what we've lost.

The driver takes us along Carson and several of us disembark to walk among the lights and people, to remember what it felt like to be on the South Side on a Saturday night. There are more people in the Archive than usual today, because of the ten-year anniversary—survivors enveloping themselves in these memories. The bars teem with faces basking in the bluish glow of a Steelers game on the flat screens. Reruns, but they can still cheer as if the games were new, as if they didn't already know who lost. The crowds are thick on Carson, just as they had once been, but I stay on board the bus to look at the streets scrolling past, to see the places I'd known, places I could walk into and still see everyone I once knew as if nothing had happened, as if they were still alive, still here. Nakama, Piper's Pub, Fat Head's. Near 17th the bus stops and more people climb on. Real people, other survivors. We look at one another, wondering.

I ride the 54C loop farther eastward, between the brackets of the rivers, until the edge of Shadyside. I walk to Ellsworth Avenue down streets of mansions and tended lawns—these are houses of the dead, everyone who lived here is dead. Tree shade, a row of cars idling up ahead at the light at Negley—and just beyond the intersection, a sign for Uni-Mart. I used to buy milk there. Overpriced cereal's on the shelves, and instant coffee, and Twinkies, Slim Jims. Antacid and aspirin behind the counter. They used to sell *Playboy* magazine there, and *Penthouse*—long after you couldn't easily find actual magazines, but Uni-Mart sold them on a wire rack along with fashion magazines and *Us Weekly* and magazines with pictures of girls and trucks, all shrink-wrapped. I'd love to look at those. I'd love to wander the aisles, to smell the ammonia-clean of the bathrooms and the hot dogs juicing on their rollers and watch a Slushie gush bright cherry red into a waxy paper cup—but not now, not now.

The Georgian Apartment with its black iron gates. This is where we lived. Layering, the scent of mown lawns, of car exhaust, of fried food from the restaurants a few blocks away on Walnut. I'm here. Layering, every tree marked with a SmartTag: *American Elm, White Poplar*, special highlights on a *Cutleaf Weeping Birch*, and along the ground, *Lily, Tulip*, every flower—with links to Wikipedia, JSTOR, the Phipps botanical database. Moving SmartTags on insects, an annotated anthill with journal references about fifteen feet away.

I'm here—

On Ellsworth, the ginkgos have shed their leaves, carpeting the sidewalk with a vomit-sour sludge of crushed berries. I run through the Georgian's courtyard, stone benches line the walk and columns flank the double front doors. Layering, the scent of the fuchsia peonies overflowing the Grecian planters. The apartment lobby's tiled black and white, with brass mailboxes for the tenants and a carved mantel over an ornamental fireplace. It's all so real. My reflection's in the mirror above the fireplace but I can't stomach to look. The paisley carpet on the central staircase is threadbare and stinks of cigarette smoke. The stairs and floorboards creak. Fire doors and ill-lit hallways. An Exit light at the far end of the hall, a window with gauzy curtains. I'm here. Room 208.

I'm here—

Just outside the room door, a section of the apartment wall's been repainted as a SmartTag, scrolling through faces of 208's previous tenants—the pictures pulled from driver's licenses and student IDs, the census, or linked through cached Facebook profiles to the names on the leases.

Blaxton, John Dominic and Theresa Marie—

The SmartTag vanishes, loading my profile. I step into the foyer of my old apartment. The walls are cream and the floors are a gleaming blonde hardwood. The kitchen is a galley, the bathroom small—cracked tiles and a sink with separate handles for hot and cold. The radiators cough and clank. I take my coat off, my shoes. We didn't have much furniture, but what we had is here—the seafoam Ikea couch in front of the bookshelves, a set of wooden Ikea chairs we'd painted red. The bookshelves sag with stacked poetry books and poetry manuscripts sent to me to consider, books and manuscripts I never read, never will read. Railroad tracks cut through the busway gully about fifty yards from the building. We'd hated the trains when we first moved in, but grew accustomed to the swaying iron lullaby as they rushed near our windows each night. I miss them, Oh God, how I miss them. Our bedroom is spare—a futon with pillows and comforters, the sheets tangled like we'd left them. A set of dresser drawers bought cheap in the children's section of Target. A television with a DVD player. I undress. I lie in bed with her, holding her, waiting for the trains to sing us to sleep. I breathe in the scent of her hair. Night falls.

11, 17—

"Dominic—and I'm here because I've had problems with Adware, that sort of thing. I'm a survivor of Pittsburgh. I tweak to enhance immersion, so I'm here for substance abuse, too, but that's considered a secondary on my paperwork—"

"Hello, Dominic," they all say.

The leader sits beneath the clock. Sickly green walls. A chalkboard: *What lies behind us and what lies before us are small matters compared to what lies within us.—Ralph Waldo Emerson.* The others slouch on folding chairs in a semicircle staring at me, fluorescent tubes carving their faces in white and shadow. A few twitch for a fix—cigarette packs and lighters already in their sweaty hands.

"Dominic, you have the floor—feel free to speak your mind. Tell us about your grieving. What are you struggling with? You don't have to stand—"

"Brown sugar, mainly. I've also done MDPV, Adderall, Dexedrine and LSD, but they don't work as well, sometimes they kink the immersion with paranoia—"

I've casually become an expert of stimulants, the paraphernalia of attaining highs vivid enough to make the streams real, and I hate myself for it—I hate how easily I recite the litany of shit I've used and how quickly I can catalog their range of effects. I was never like this, I was never like this before—Theresa wouldn't recognize the man I've become.

"I had an episode the other day," I tell them. "Heroin in my system from a pill called a valentine when I dropped brown sugar at a KFC and lost control. I can't even remember—the police picked me up wandering Dupont Circle. I'd stopped up traffic—a public nuisance, my fifth disturbing the peace charge. They arrested me and checked me into an Urgent Care clinic. They cleaned my blood. Dialysis with dopamine stims and a pack upgrade to the Adware that's reconditioned my cravings—"

"Involuntary Assistance," they call it: two dozen beds, male nurses with heavy hands used to subduing violent patients. Nylon straps, buckled down. The patient next to me retched crystallized blood—Christ. They laced me with tubes, plugged me into the machine. I gave up, stopped struggling. Intravenous fluids coursed through me. I didn't feel the dialysis, but heard the whir, chug, whoosh of the machine cleaning my blood and rushing it back to my heart. I wondered where I was—*The hospital. Did something happen to me?*—savoring the last wisps of Theresa and Pittsburgh as Twiggy's heroin valentine was filtered from my body. The Adware downloads completed and my personality numbed—fucked everything up, all my account settings. The nurses flashed visuals of drugs and measured my responses, tinkered with my Adware until I fell within the normal range. My addiction was cured.

"A clean bill of health?" asks the leader.

"A clean bill of health, but I was convicted on a drug abuse felony because of the heroin and sentenced to eight years of prison, but the sentence was waived in exchange for a correctional rehabilitation program. I lost my job—"

"What happened?" asks the leader.

"My boss's hand was forced because of the felony charge," I tell them. "But I think he was losing patience anyway. He voiced and told me that my employment status had changed, that I would no longer be working for him. I tried to argue—"

"And now you're here with us, a grief support group for men affected by Pittsburgh-related PTSD—"

"The Correctional Health Board mandates I change treatment providers and go through a year's worth of correctional health counseling before my case will be reevaluated. The clinics are overcrowded so I was enrolled in outpatient therapy—"

"I hope we'll be able to help you make progress toward your goals," says the leader.

"I never had headaches like I do now," I tell him. "I can't focus anymore—"

"That's from the wiring," says one of the others—Jason, maybe. Jayden, or something. I can't quite remember his name. "If you don't have that Lux shit, you burn it out and fry your head," the guy says, rubbing his own surgery-pocked scalp. "Your brain sprouts tumors—"

"Thank you, but no crosstalk this meeting," says the leader, a petite man, soft, sallow, with a thinning patch of hair gelled into wispy spikes that doesn't quite hide the wormy white lines of his own Adware scar tissue. The men here obey him. When he smiles, his eyes remain dispassionate. His voice is soft. No Adware during the sessions for privacy—the leader runs a firewall fob to disrupt network connections. We can trust one another, I'm told.

"Dominic, tell us a little about yourself," says the leader. "Where were you when you heard?"

It's hard to talk about this—especially here, surrounded by strangers, all men, their own problems brimming in their eyes. One man yawns, and it's disrespectful, disrespectful to her. It happens like this—overwhelmed by memories. The linoleum tile floor of the classroom, the ceiling lights—I don't want to think about the end, I don't want to think about her. Not here, not with these people.

"Shit . . . Oh, shit. I'm sorry—"

"It's all right to cry," says the leader. "Let it out. Talk with us, share your story. Hearing each other's stories helps us to understand we're not alone. We were all away from friends and family when it happened. We've all lost everything. We haven't been uniquely chosen to suffer—"

"I'm sorry," I end up saying.

"Please, tell us what happened," says the leader, older than me by a few years, maybe ten years or so, but he has a boyish face and bright, condescending eyes that seem to diagnose me even as he pities me. He purses his thin lips. I cry and feel the others losing what patience they might have had with me. I meet the leader's eyes, wordlessly begging him to let me off the hook, but he just watches me, waiting, his head cocked like a parent prepared to believe the lies his children will tell. The others in the group watch me, too—some do, anyway.

"Columbus, when it happened," I tell them. "I was at a conference, at Ohio State—the Midwestern Universities Conference on Literature. MUCOL, it was called. I presented a paper on John Berryman's *Dream Songs* and the notion of Subjectivities and Dialogism and the changing nature of the Speaker—I forget the specifics. We went out for lunch following the morning panels. On High Street, at a sports bar when we heard the news. I think I may have screamed and just collapsed. I remember screaming. I remember the scent of the carpet at the restaurant—like beer and cigarettes and stale fabric. The others, these colleagues of mine I'd met just the day before—they all just looked at me. Everything was confusing, I remember. Not knowing exactly what had happened, but within fifteen or twenty minutes as the news rolled in—no one was left alive, I knew that. No one in Pittsburgh was left alive. I don't know what I would have wanted them to do, but they just sat there, looking at me—"

"And you visit the Archive of Pittsburgh through your Adware, to relive your life there, and you use stimulants to heighten your experience of the City—"

"The drugs help," I tell them.

"And you immerse to see her?"

"My wife—"

"What was her name?"

"Theresa Marie," I say, her name unnatural in my mouth, like chewing on a foreign phrase. I don't want to speak her name for others to hear—she doesn't belong here, not in this place, not with these men.

"What happened?"

"Nothing—nothing happened," I tell them. "I was in Columbus and couldn't get home. There was no home. I drove as far as I could—until the checkpoints in West Virginia. I was put up in temporary housing. FEMA. Someone told me I should head back to Columbus, where I at least had a hotel room booked, but I thought I'd be able to get through to Pittsburgh. I just couldn't comprehend that it was no longer there. I tried calling Theresa all night. I could still leave her voice messages—"

"Brown sugar is a variant of methamphetamine," says the leader. "Dominic, it's killing you—"

"It helps make her real—"

"I understand," says the leader, "but it's killing you—"

"What does it matter if I die?"

"You don't want to die," he says, like he's explaining simple math. "You want to see your wife again, you want to relive all the years you were blessed to have with her, and you want to somehow compensate for all the years you aren't able to spend with her. You're here because you want to remember your wife through healthy immersion. You want to live so you can grow old with the memories of your wife. You want her to live on through you. You don't want to die."

"You don't understand," I tell him, knowing that he does understand, that they all understand.

A fifteen-minute break with the smokers on 13th—we're like derelicts out here, milling around in front of Walker Memorial Baptist, bathed in the light of the church's video board: *Do less Facebook, Do more Faithbook*. A phalanx of DC police armored trucks pulls to the red light, the cops in riot armor looking our way, their eyes hidden behind black visors. What do they think of us? We're all tagged, so they must know not to bother with us—they must see our blinking records proclaiming we're being rehabilitated. The light changes and the armored trucks rumble on. Shop lights in the dusk—the Rite Aid at the intersection with U Street looks like a pool party over there. Jangling my Adware, that's all. Women in bikinis overlaying the street, splashing and frolicking and sunbathing—every time I glance over, there are different faces and different bodies, different swimsuit styles, slight variations searching to find my ideal, to force my implied consent. What are they selling?

Pineapple Fanta! Coconut Xocola! Join the party! $5.50—

No, no—I don't want any. Not now. I don't want to buy—

Ogling white bathing suits and golden skin until Xocola gives up on me and I'm staring at nothing but the Rite Aid, the sidewalk, cars caught at the red light, mildly aroused and my brain still tingling from the failed sales pitch.

Ten o'clock. The leader encourages us to hold hands and

pray—"Our Father, who art in Heaven . . ." We mumble through. The leader reminds us about the sign-in sheet and distributes plastic cups and asks us to fill them.

"We went through a thermos of coffee, tonight. No excuses—"

We file into the bathroom. We're orderly, quiet. We're all just checking boxes, putting ourselves through the paces. Share to prayer. Fill the cup. No one talks to each other—we just take our turns at the urinals, the words of the Lord's Prayer already distant as we piss into our cups. We file back into the meeting room. The leader's wearing latex gloves and collects the samples in a cooler. They hand him their plastic cups, they sign the sheet, they collect their coats and leave. When I hand the leader my cup, he says, "Stick around a few minutes—"

The last donut's a sugar coated—I eat it, and pour another Styrofoam cup of coffee. Once everyone's gone, the leader snaps his cooler closed.

"One of the more unpleasant parts of the job," he says. "Collecting the samples. But outpatient therapy's better than the detox ward. I'd much rather collect urine than deal with detox—"

"I've been through detox," I tell him.

"A few times, I understand," he says. "Don't want to go back there again, I suppose?"

"Urine samples after every meeting?"

"I'm afraid so," says the leader. "It's part of the deal. You won't clear your conviction until you test clean for about a year, give or take, although they'll put you on probation after a few months if your tests remain clear. By the way, outside of group I'm not Dr. Reynolds. Call me Timothy—"

"I didn't talk too much, did I? I hope I didn't interrupt the group with my story. I didn't mean to cry like that—"

"No, no," says Timothy. "That's not why I wanted to see you—

you did fine, actually. You were very courageous tonight. Sometimes newcomers don't like to share and it takes time to draw them out. I was actually hoping to talk with you about your work status for a few minutes, if that's all right. You worked for the Archive, didn't you? Your file says you worked for the Pittsburgh City-Archive—"

"Not exactly for the Archive," I tell him. "The Archive's run by the Library of Congress. I worked as an archival assistant for a research firm called the Kucenic Group, so I used the Archive quite a bit. Insurance claims, some genealogy—"

"Do you think you'll be given your job back once you complete therapy?" he asks.

"I'm not sure—I guess I don't think so. Not this time—"

"You're not interested in the work anymore?"

"It's not that—I'd take my job back," I tell him. "I loved the work, but I fucked up. Mr. Kucenic has shown a lot of forbearance with me over the years, but he'd trusted me with something important and I failed him—"

Timothy packs up his papers in a leather satchel. A few moments pass before he asks, "What were you working on? If you don't mind my asking—"

The question jolts me—the dead girl in the river mud, her bone-white feet spattered black. Her body flashes in my mind as clear as any memory.

"I research people who have died in the Archive," I tell him.

"That sounds like difficult work," he says. "Emotionally difficult. Who were you researching? Someone close to you?"

"I can't—I don't think I want to talk about it," I tell him, but the silence deadens around us so I ask him, "Well, then—is that all you needed?"

Timothy considers me a moment. "It's not so much what I need from you, Dominic. This is more about what you need. I think

I can help you—if you want the help. No more of this 'I want to die' business, though. You'll need a new attitude about your life and your recovery. I think I can accelerate this entire process for you if you're willing to work. And recovering your physical and emotional well-being is work, don't think otherwise. Reviewing your file, though, I just don't think you're an optimal candidate for group therapy—"

"I don't understand," I tell him. "Dr. Simka was specific in what would be required—"

"Dr. Simka and I disagree about your treatment," says Timothy. "Please don't get me wrong—I'm sure Simka's a good doctor. He has an excellent reputation—"

"He's been good to me—"

"You're in my care now," says Timothy. "I've been looking over your file—Dr. Simka's compassionate, but lacks imagination. His knee-jerk reaction was to prescribe Zoloft and sign off on pharmaceutical app reconditioning. There's plenty of published evidence to support the short-term effectiveness of pharmaceutical apps. I've seen them help. I've seen full-blown heroin addicts off the habit in about an hour following the right download, but I've also seen those same men and women using again weeks or even days later, because the underlying causes of their addictions were never treated—that's what these RN techs don't understand. They think a brain rewire will solve everything, like a miracle cure. Change is possible, Dominic, but it has to be a total change, body and soul—a reawakening. You, for instance. You're clean, but nothing's stopping you from using again. Tonight, even—"

"I want your help. I just don't understand what you're trying to tell me—"

"Are you hungry?" he asks. "I'll treat. Or we can just grab some coffee if you'd rather. I'm starving, myself—"

Timothy erases the chalkboard and rearranges the chairs, pulling them from the circle and tucking them back into the desks. I help him. He's like the teachers I had back in high school—slacks and a sweater-vest over his shirt and tie, hopelessly rumpled. He shuts off the lights and locks up, leaving the key in an envelope and sliding it under the office door. We leave together—it's started to snow.

"Dr. Simka's recommendation went a long way in influencing the Correctional Health Board's conclusion following your episode the other night," says Timothy, "but I believe they fit you into an incorrect treatment program. I feel so strongly about this that I personally requested your case slotted to my group—I don't know if you realize that. I want to oversee your treatment, so you aren't pushed in a counterproductive direction. I don't believe group therapy will help you. I don't believe Zoloft is a responsible long-term solution. These methods are a foundation built on sand, meant to treat symptoms, not the underlying causes. Once we find the correct treatment for your depression, I believe your other lifestyle choices will change. You'll become healthier. I believe we'll be effective in your case—"

"Good news," I say.

"You're placating me now, but in ten years when you're trim and happy you'll remember this conversation. It is good news," he says, smiling—genuinely smiling for the first time, I think, this entire evening.

Timothy drives a powder-blue Fiat, twenty years old at least, parked crooked and scraped along the passenger side. He stashes the cooler of urine samples in the trunk while I climb in, these European cars cramped and awkward for my height. My knees hit the dash. The top of my head touches the roof—I'd be crippled if we wreck, my face windshield-kissed and my knees shattered.

He pulls into traffic, cutting between cars. I brace myself, the feeds kicking in with traffic patterns and weather reports on the windshield display, a snow front rolling in with little to no predicted accumulation. An eruption of nightingales—a flock swarming outside the windshield despite the wintry night: Twiggy's ringtone, it looks like. Her avatar's a webcam selfie in black-rimmed glasses and an *All Things Considered* sweatshirt, her hair a feathery halo. Her face hovers, but I let her nightingales sing as we pass through Dupont Circle, every building facade a fashionporn billboard, every storefront a video from Unwerth and Testino and Gavril—paradise after paradise. Every storefront tempts me—it looks like there are parties behind the show windows, rooms filled with models in slinky skirts sipping martinis and laughing, but there aren't parties in there, it's all Adware marketing, illusions. Twiggy gives up—she sends a text, asking for poetry recommendations. Her profile blinks out and the nightingales fly away.

"My wife and I were visiting her family in Atlanta," says Timothy, Rhett and Scarlett cartoons breaking through the pop-up filters to offer discount packages to the American South, *Gone with the Wind*–themed tours.

"You're a survivor?" I ask him.

"I'm a survivor in the same sense that you are," he says. "We left Atlanta late, passed through Birmingham around midnight, and the highway just tapered off. Country roads overgrown with trees. Pitch-black two-lane interstates. I've never seen such darkness—the headlights reached out but I couldn't see. Just the center line when there was a center line and the trunks of trees and dumpy roadside gas stations, long closed. We thought we were lost. We looked for a hotel, but never found one. Lydia fell asleep and I just drove, thinking I could push through until morning. My eyes would close, would close a little longer. I felt like I was dissolving. I was—

depressed, Dominic. I was so sick of life—I know you understand. Headlights approached and I could see them from a long way off and I'd imagine swerving into the oncoming lights, at the last moment just twitching the wheel toward them—but the headlights would rush past and once the taillights disappeared in the rearview we were alone again in that utter dark. I was cheating on Lydia—my wife. More than just cheating on her. I was a terrible husband, very selfish. We'd grown bored and I think we were blaming each other for what we were losing. Two in the morning, three. It was just after three in the morning when I noticed the road change. There was something coating the road—it took time to realize it was blood. The road was covered in blood. I saw a deer's body in the headlights, and then another two or three bodies, and soon I saw dozens of deer. I must have shuddered or made a sound because Lydia woke up. Their carcasses were torn apart and spread over the asphalt. I don't know what could have happened. I imagine a big rig in that vast black night tearing through a herd as they crossed, but I don't really know what could have killed so many. The meat came into our headlights and we saw heads and hoofs and torsos, the road just blood and torn meat and fur. Bones. It took a solid minute to drive through, a solid minute before our headlights lit nothing but the blacktop road—a minute is a long time. I think I laughed once we were out of it and Lydia wondered if she'd been dreaming, but laughed too a little—wondering where in the hell we were. Alabama. We checked into the first respectable hotel we came to, around five in the morning—this was all the way in Tupelo, Mississippi, by that point. We slept. We woke up late in the afternoon. We heard the news about Pittsburgh—no one at the hotel thought to wake us up to tell us. No one from our families or friends knew where we were staying or how to reach us. Lydia just turned on the TV while I was in the shower and screamed—"

"I'm so sorry," I tell him, never knowing what to say.

"We've all lost," says Timothy, smiling without his eyes smiling. "That's my enduring association with Pittsburgh—when people ask where I was, I see that hotel room shower and hear my wife screaming—"

"I hear 'Pittsburgh' and my mind flashes to that sports bar in Columbus. Ohio State Buckeyes—"

"God created us with the ability to move on from overwhelming grief," he says. "Coping involves understanding our own innate worth, understanding that if we're the ones surviving tragedy, death, divorce or change, then we're the ones ultimately responsible for sorting our complex emotions in order to fulfill God's plan for us—"

"Is that what you believe?" I ask him.

Kramerbooks & Afterwords for dinner—a café and bookstore, a haunt of students and the chic intelligentsia, young professionals, writers. I've been here before, several times. We're seated among the books, at a corner table. We order pasta—butternut squash ravioli and parmesan cheese. Hungrier than I realized.

"Lydia and I—our marriage wasn't strong enough," says Timothy. "After Pittsburgh I confessed everything about Emily—"

"Emily must have been the woman you were seeing?"

"Emily was there for me when my wife wasn't," says Timothy. "She was a beautiful, bright young woman, but she had self-esteem problems and before I fully realized what I was doing, I was taking advantage of her. We met through the clinic. I'm not proud. I still miss her. Of all the people I lost that day, I still think of Emily the most—I wish things had been different. I'm telling you this because I understand how you're suffering—"

"Letting go's difficult," I say.

"Well. It is difficult," says Timothy. "Lydia and I tried to work through it, but never stood a chance. Healthier for both of us, I think, when we separated. I moved out here to work in the psychology department at Georgetown—I was listless. I bought into a full suite of Adware—top-of-the-line stuff, at least for back then. I used to come home from campus and lie down on the basement couch and lose myself streaming the Victoria's Secret catalog, that sort of thing—the *Sports Illustrated* swimsuit issue. Agent Provocateur vids. Soft stuff, promotional kink—there was a scenario where two girls went to a country manor wearing nothing but lingerie. I streamed it so often that even now I could close my eyes and lead you through that manor house room by room, telling you everything that happened to those two girls. I didn't do anything else with my life—I didn't go out to eat, I didn't have any friends, I'd just eat cereal or SpaghettiOs for dinner and stream this stuff. I'd spend entire days searching for perfect faces in the streams, trying to find the perfect model, the perfect scenario, and I'd snap from the Adware dehydrated and aching, my eyes bloodshot—"

The waitress delivers the check and Timothy pays for both of us.

"I was once like you," he says, "drugs to realize the streams, my brain hardwired to pornography, secretly photographing girls in my classes with my retinal cams, girls I'd see on campus. I sank very low, Dominic—you wouldn't believe what I was capable of. Think of the worst type of man—that was the man I *was*. I need you to know it's possible for a man to change. Do you believe that a man can change, Dominic?"

"I don't know," I tell him.

"A man can change—"

"The scales fall from our eyes, is that it?"

"I'd spend twenty, twenty-one hours a day streaming pornography, but I bottomed out—I blacked out in Georgetown Cupcake, of all places. I just collapsed. I woke up in the back of an ambulance, hooked up to an IV. Familiar?"

I nodded that it was familiar, yes, "Numerous occasions," I tell him. "But you pulled through—"

"I didn't pull through. I was saved, Dominic—"

"Saved?" I ask him.

"I experienced grace—"

"Look, I appreciate your interest in me, I do, but I'm not religious. I'm not looking to be saved. I don't think I'm interested in this pitch—"

"I know better than to evangelize to my patients," he says. "This is about finding the light within you that has gone out and flipping the switch so it comes back on—"

"Responsible immersion techniques, that sort of thing? How you get along with the streams?"

"Matthew 18:9," says Timothy. "'And if thine eye offend thee, pluck it out and cast it from thee: it is better for thee to enter into life with one eye, rather than having two eyes to be cast into hell fire.'"

"I don't understand—"

"I plucked it out, Dominic. I cut at my scalp with an X-Acto knife and pulled out the wiring. You can peel it right off the skull plate and just yank it out of your brain. I was in the hospital for three months recovering, but I was saved. Corneal laser surgery for the damage pulling out the lenses, but I was saved. Even if I would have lost my sight or lost my life at that moment, I would have gained my soul. When I recovered, he was there waiting for me—"

I glance at him and notice now that the scar tissue showing through his thinning hair is different from the usual Adware scars, not the grid ridges most people have, but an ill-healed white tangle.

"You've got to be kidding me if you think I'll tear out my Adware—"

Timothy laughs. "My story—my *personal* story—is that I accepted Jesus Christ as my Savior and my faith in Christ gave me the strength to overcome my addictions. I don't know what your personal story will be, Dominic. I'm hoping to help shepherd you to that crisis of change, and I'm hoping that you'll come through that crisis a new man. I have a proposal for you—"

"I'll just complete the group sessions, Dr. Reynolds. I really don't want to get involved with any of this. No offense, I can tell you feel strongly—"

"Waverly," says Timothy. "The man who was waiting for me in the hospital was a man named Waverly. He had a business proposal for me—a partnership. He needed my expertise for the work he was involved in and I believe he'll need your expertise as well. Not everyone gets an opportunity to meet a man like him, but you came along at the right moment, Dominic. Dumb luck, in a way. If you work with Waverly, you won't need to worry about Correctional Health Board regulations or completing therapy; you won't need to worry about your arrest records, the felony charge, about money, your future employment status. He can release you from all these restraints, freeing you to take care of your own health, find your own change, pursue your own happiness. Waverly's an influential man, Dominic. I think he can help you—"

"Let's leave this stuff about happiness and change on the table for a moment. This man Waverly can clear my felony charge?" I ask him. "Is that what you're telling me? Get me out of therapy, offer me work?"

"I just want you to meet him," says Timothy.

Timothy offers a ride home, but I need to be alone. I need time to clear my thoughts—to Google Waverly, if nothing else. I take the bus. Empty at this hour, the rear seat's vacant so I stretch out, unwelcoming to anyone who might board and find their way back here. Scan for signals—the bus's router's exceptional, Metro.net a stronger signal than the citywide Wi-Fi, so I switch connections even though it's only good for a half-hour slot. New Hampshire to M, hoodie pulled low to block the city lights and the flash of passing ads. *Waverly + DC* nets hits—Theodore Waverly, Ph.D., head of something called Focal Networks, a consultancy firm it looks like. Adware marketing. His client list includes multinationals, the Chinese government, the European Union, the United States. A press-release bio's repeated on every site he's mentioned: a survivor of Pittsburgh, chair of the Human-Computer Interaction program at Carnegie Mellon, work in artificial intelligence and cognitive psychology for DARPA. Developer of something called precognitive bypass communication. Deep roots in DC—an adviser to the Republican Party, a donor to the Washington Ballet, the DC symphony. He sits on the Kennedy Center board of trustees. Not much personal information, nothing specific—not even a picture of the man.

Timothy mentioned *happiness*—that he wants me to pursue my own *happiness*. I can't fathom what *happiness* might mean anymore—it seems like luxury to someone whose life feels like a lead-lined discomfort, something that Timothy in his Christ buoyancy doesn't seem to understand. I don't seek out happiness, just pockets of alleviation—a drowning man sipping at bubbles of air. I load Three Rivers Net, the City translucent against the bus like a tissue paper overlay, thinner without brown sugar but I close my eyes and see more clearly: the stretch of Parkway through the hillside as the Archive loads. Happiness was Theresa. The City opens around me, the layers of architecture, the lines of rivers, steel bridges and curving brick streets that twist like tendrils of dreams.

I'm here—

Room 208.

The Georgian.

Gauzy curtains, paisley carpets, cream walls stained the color of tea from years of previous tenants' cigarette smoke. Our apartment. I'm here—scrolling through the faces of past residents until I come to us: *Blaxton, John Dominic and Theresa Marie.* I can unlock the dead bolts with a key. I can feel the polished wood of the front door. We had one of my aunt's wood-block prints of the White Rabbit in the foyer that's re-created here—quirky decor once but grossly appropriate now, the illustration receiving me as I make my way through the longish, claustrophobic front hallway, falling back into everything I've lost.

Theresa. In this first glimpse of her, she's edged with light—sculpted from a video when my retinal lenses were new, before I knew how to use them properly or understood the settings and light filters.

Theresa, Theresa, oh my God, Theresa—

I kiss her, but the moment I touch her, she's no longer her—she becomes the VR sculpt I'd commissioned, nothing more. I remember Theresa too specifically for the cheap RealPlay engine I'm using—specifically what her skin felt like or the feathery feel of her hair or how she breathed or the tickling shivers when she placed kisses on my ears. If I'd had more money, the designers could have filled out the illusion using sense impressions from my memories, but all I could afford was to choose something from their catalog of ready-mades, scrolling through mannequin figures in their studio until I settled on the body model closest to my wife. Touching this body is close to my wife, but it's not my wife—it's not quite her—it's as close as fantasizing about my wife while holding another, similar, woman. I step back and look at the woman I've been kissing and Theresa returns to focus. She's standing in the foyer, hazed by a corona of overexposed light. It's her, it's her—

"Is this the camera?" she says, noticing the new lenses in my eyes, but the scene shifts—our first Christmas in the apartment, the tree in our living room, the glow of Christmas lights reflecting from the hardwood floors and casting us in a white dim. When I kiss her, I feel the warmth of her body. Holding her, I can smell her hair, or an approximation of her hair, the licensed scent of the Aveeno shampoo she used, the approximation of her body. Wrapping paper crinkling as I crumple it into balls for the trash bag. Ornaments ring as I touch the fir boughs. The creak of the hardwood as I step. She's opening my gift, a set of Nina Simone vinyl—she's excited, I remember, and says she's wanted them, that she almost bought this set just the other day. She plays the first record and fills our apartment with "Lilac Wine."

We have dinner at the Spice Island Tea House in midwinter. Snow blankets Oakland and strings of holiday lights still illuminate the barren trees. The darkness of the restaurant interior is pierced with candlelight. Glasses of Thai iced tea. Samosas and vegetable rolls on small plates. She's wearing her beige skirt and leather boots, a violet cardigan over a halter top embroidered with calla lilies. Layering, the wax and flame. Layering, the smell of basil curry. Candlelight reflects in her eyes.

I have something to tell you, she will say.

"I have something to tell you," she says.

"No wine?"

"I love you," she says. "I'm glad we're here tonight—"

I was at the doctor's today, she will tell me. I thought I had thc flu—

"I thought I had the flu this morning," she says.

As it turns out, she ran some blood work, she will say.

"And, Dominic, we're going to have a little girl," she says. "She ran the advanced amino test and we're going to have a little girl—"

"Oh, my wonderful, dear God—"

Home through snowfall—the car parked, stepping through slush. Thrilling in my belly, wrapping my mind around having a daughter—another chance at having a daughter, trying not to remember the earlier disappointment of unexpected blood. We'd been trying to conceive since the miscarriage—something was wrong, we'd thought, sure there was something wrong with us, that we wouldn't be able to have biological children, but now—a daughter. My daughter. Theresa already describing outfits she'd seen at Tots and Tweeds, already letting herself remember again the Strawberry Shortcake bike still in her parents' basement. We're genuinely happy—in the Archive, at least, we're happy—but I remember we were trying hard to be happy, trying to push away whatever apprehension had bred in us, trying not to acknowledge that a second miscarriage was entirely possible, trying instead to re-create the innocent excitement we'd felt the first time around. Layering, ice water from snow soaking through my shoes. Layering, tires and wet asphalt. Window lights in upstairs rooms. In our bedroom, her body softer, even softer somehow, and Theresa removes her cardigan and unties her halter and I'm holding her, kissing her shoulder, please don't let it end, but it ends. It always ends.

My half hour of Metro.net expires. The wet click of autoconnection to DC's Wi-Fi, but it's too spotty to reload the City. A message from Timothy's home phone blinks in my peripheral—he's set up a meeting with Waverly.

"I'll be there," I respond. "Tell him I'll be there—"

Others have boarded the bus since I've been under, commuters heading home after long shifts, I guess, or students late from the library, standing in the aisles—giving me a wide berth. I respond to

Twiggy's text asking me for poetry recommendations by suggesting she track down a copy of *Ouroboros* by Adelmo Salomar—one of my favorite writers, a Chilean poet. Passing near Fur Nightclub, police have cordoned off New York Avenue. Everyone on the bus rubbernecks the scene. Club kids huddle near the police cruisers, mascara running in smears from their eyes and blackening their lips. What's happened? I search *Washington City Paper* for news, but the streams blare promos for the next episode of *Chance in Hell*, season 4, and *Candid, Homemade Personals* of middle-aged women masturbating into webcams. Gazing out the window at a heavily armed cop talking to a boy with eyebrow studs and lip piercings. The club kid's girlfriend wears fishnets and a denim G-string, her hair in wild shocks of blue tube-thick dreads that quiver in the wind. What's going on? The boy's profile lights long enough for me to scroll his Twitter feed, @MimiStarchild—*Body in the bathroom,* it says. *Joanna,* it says. *Found her,* it says. A twitpic of the mess: the victim stripped, the remnants of her dress binding her ankles. Blonde, but her face is ruined. She'd been bent over the toilet, hands tied to the pipes, breasts down in the water. "Jesus Christ," I say, and close out Twitter, but the *Washington Post* feed's already picked up the story, knocking *Chance in Hell* from the top DC trends: Joanna Kriz, a student at George Mason, found dead in Fur. Pics of her flood the streams, discovered by tabloid Facecrawlers that hacked private accounts. A gorgeous girl—a student of architecture. Jesus Christ. The *Post* feed displays 3-D renderings of her school assignments, buildings she'd designed, architectural models. Pictures flash of her high school graduation and with her family at Thanksgiving, but I'm watching her life unspool, and now I'm watching sexts she'd sent to boyfriends, found by the Facecrawlers, nude selfies posing in front of mirrors, drunk tongue-kissing a girlfriend while a crowd cheers her—within minutes the feeds are only interested in Joanna Kriz if she's fucking or mutilated, they've reduced her to the essence of what the viewing public will click on and trend. I ring the bell and leave the bus, the feeds saturated with Joanna Kriz. Hail a cab, slump in the backseat—I just want to go home. Within minutes the murdered girl's family signs with *Crime Scene Superstar*, grieving but ready for their opportunity to share their daughter's beauty with the world and collect royalties. #Kriz trends in the feeds, critiques of the dead woman's body—face too horsey but nice tits—rating her fuckability based on crime scene photographs. I reach my apartment, out of the range of the public Wi-Fi. Everything in my apartment is silence and the only thing I can do to fill it is cry.

11, 21—

The District of Columbia in late November—a golden afternoon, another round of sleet predicted for tonight. Sunlight dapples the Potomac, tourists swarm the National Mall. We share an outdoor table at the Café du Parc, at the Willard InterContinental. Everything's burnished crimson and copper in the autumn light—stone surfaces of government buildings, cherry-red double-decker tour buses, what leaves remain in Pershing Park. Clusters of tourists chase guides waving neon pennants—desperate to see the White House through the wrought iron gates, the house set back on the chemically lush lawn, the alabaster columns and the world-famous gardens that obscure the views, the tropical fauna engineered to live even through winter, so flower-swollen it's as if the air itself had ruptured into blossoms. They've come to imagine they're closer to President Meecham here. They've come to imagine her life in those distant rooms—to maybe even catch a glimpse of her, or at least view the landscape she views as if the land itself is already a relic or somehow infused with her. Meecham shimmers through everything here—every tourist advert, every set of "White House China" sold from souvenir stands, every police shield, strip club pop-up, every fashionporn ad for DC couture—a mass hallucination, an ineffable vision, as if the northern lights had been captured bodily. "America's Queen," they call her, and they come to her like supplicants at Lourdes, carrying signs and posters depicting Meecham as the Virgin of the Seven Sorrows, seven knives piercing her porn-perfect breasts.

Waverly smokes. Blue eyes, disconcertingly blue—the color of Windex or antifreeze. A white sweep of hair. He's like a publicity photo of a poet—stentorian, craggy and wrinkled, pausing in the conversation to savor his cigarette, or to gaze over the throng of tourists while he collects his thoughts. I'm bedraggled beside him in my hoodie and sweats. He's wearing a suit, an Anderson & Sheppard that my Adware informs me is from Savile Row, London. Every other table is filled, I notice, except the ones contiguous to ours—like he's arranged a buffer of empty plates around us, a bubble of relative quiet and privacy.

"New York," says Waverly, when the conversation comes around to where he had been when Pittsburgh ceased to exist. "A fund-raiser at the Museum of Modern Art. You know, I swap stories with survivors all the time and love trumping them by saying I was staring at *Guernica* when it happened. I remember everyone in the gallery falling silent for a few moments—Pittsburgh must have sounded as distant to them as West Virginia or Alabama—until the notion hit that Manhattan might be the next to go. There was an unseemly panic—"

Adware overlays our table with adverts—Travelocity gnomes pitching Manhattan, Wheeling, Birmingham. Animated George Washingtons hawk cheap tickets to symphonies in the National Cathedral. I ignore them, try to concentrate on Waverly, but the George Washingtons morph into slutty Marthas in white wigs and low-cut gowns with powdered white breasts jiggling for my attention, seating charts nestled in their cleavage, *buy, buy*.

"I understand you work with an outfit called the Kucenic Group?" he says.

"I do. Or did—"

"Research, I take it? Insurance claims, that sort of thing? An impossible thicket of litigation—"

"Everything's contested," I tell him.

"You'd think it would be easier, having the City-Archive at your disposal—"

"It could be easier. Governments used to have the authority to issue mass death certificates," I tell him, the patois of my job flowing mechanically, "but a case called *State Farm v. the State of Pennsylvania* changed all that. Since the Archive exists, the insurance companies argued they should be given the chance to verify every individual insurance claim, every property damage claim, everything. The checking takes years, slows down the payouts—"

"Are you good at your job?"

"I was dedicated, and interested—"

"You're underselling yourself," says Waverly. "I already know how good you are. I've talked with Mr. Kucenic and he tells me you were one of the best researchers he's ever had, if not the best. Intuitive, efficient. He said your skills are far above your pay grade, but your personal difficulties hold you back from assuming greater responsibilities. He wonders if you have a fear of success—"

Waverly takes a drag on his cigarette and lets the smoke rise from his mouth. He's reading something in his Adware while we talk—I watch his eyes twitch as they scan text. Why has this man bothered Kucenic? I don't want him talking to Kucenic about me, I haven't agreed to anything.

"Different priorities," I tell him. "I don't have a fear of success—"

"After talking with Kucenic, I realize your work must have been nerve shattering," he says. "Watching people die, studying how they died, determining if their deaths are legitimate or somehow fraudulent, and all the paperwork. You must feel like you're tracking ghosts sometimes—"

I've watched hundreds of people burn alive, but the woman buried in the river mud hangs over me like a burden of conscience. They haven't left me—no one I've researched has ever left me.

"They are like ghosts," I tell him.

"I want you to track a ghost for me," says Waverly.

The usual nervous churning of butterflies when new opportunities present themselves—or at least distaste for stirring from my comfort zones. A fear of distraction from the things I care most about, maybe. I finish off my cappuccino. "You don't need to waste your money on me, Mr. Waverly," I tell him. "Accessing the Archive is free, if you sign up through the Library of Congress. There are plenty of actual librarians who are looking for research opportunities. Real professionals—"

"My daughter," says Waverly.

A manila folder—an 8 × 10 of a woman that dissipates the Adware. Crimson hair the color of blood, languid eyes like emeralds. The photograph must have been for a fashion ad: the woman's posed in a stylized hunch, her black gown exposing bone-white shoulders.

"This is your daughter?"

"I thought you'd be interested once you saw her picture," he says. "Her name is Albion—it means the 'white cliffs.' Albion O'Hara Waverly. I've mourned her for ten years—just out of college when that picture was taken. Long after the end, I clung foolishly to the hope that she might have somehow escaped—but I'm sober now."

"I'm sorry for your loss—"

Waverly dips a biscuit into his cappuccino. Illy pitches espresso in the Adware—I consent and soon our waiter brings a fresh cup and biscotti on Waverly's tab.

"I schedule regular times to visit my memories of Kitty in the Archive," he says. "Kitty was my wife of thirty-nine years. Katherine. There are certain memories I have—taking her to Mellon Park on Sundays for brunch, pastries and strawberries and champagne, and to the Frick in the afternoons for high tea. I commissioned designers to sculpt these moments so they would be more real for me than even my own memories of her. My daughter used to be there with us, but recently I haven't been able to visit Albion—"

"You can't bring yourself to it?"

"No, no, it's not that," he says. "She's somehow vanishing from the City. Deleted. Someone's deleting all her files—the public files and even my own private files. The job's been thorough. The librarians—I've tried the librarians at the Library of Congress, and they've been sympathetic but haven't been very helpful. They have too much work to do, building the City, maintaining it. I've filed police reports—but the police don't have the resources. Besides, they don't prioritize this as a missing persons case or anything of the sort but rather a data mismanagement claim or at worst cyber-vandalism or a hacking charge. Digital graffiti, that sort of thing, if they even want to entertain the notion that something like this is in their jurisdiction. I've searched on my own, but she's vanishing. I have photographs—I know she exists. Existed—"

"Have you tried the Kucenic Group or one of the other research firms? They're set up for work like this—"

"I trust Timothy about you," he says. "When I talked with Kucenic, he wanted to transfer me to a sales rep, someone who handles accounts. He rattled off the names of awards and bragged about his *U.S. News & World Report* ranking, but when I asked if the person assigned to my case would be as skilled as you, he told me that he has a capable staff that can handle any query. He went on to tell me that your drug habit ruins you as a worker—"

"I'm clean," I tell him.

"Good—"

"But it's not difficult work. This is the type of research grad students are doing all over the country, that librarians are doing—"

"The cream rises to the top, Dominic. I don't want 'capable staff.' I don't want salesmen, I don't want account representatives, and I certainly don't want graduate students. I want someone with your skills, someone working for me. Someone with discretion—"

I scan the photograph of Albion, save the image to my Adware. Maybe the caffeine's strafing my nerves but I feel sick and want to run from here, to hole up in my apartment and powder myself into oblivion, but something Timothy said snags my thoughts—*you don't want to die.*

"You want me to find your daughter? Recover the files?"

"I want you to restore her to the Archive," he says. "I want you to track down who is doing this to me, to my family, so that I can prosecute them to the fullest extent of the law, or at least protect us from similar future threats. I want you to find out who has deleted her so that I can have my daughter back. Please. I've already lost her once—"

"I'll help you—"

Qualia Coffee on my way home. Checking e-mail: Gavril's written several times—all marked "high importance," of course. Attachments of photos from fashion houses he wants me to caption—Anthropologie, House of Fetherston, Tom Ford—and his friends' artist statements to translate into colloquial English, the usual odd jobs he lets me do. I mark them all as unread.

I ping Kucenic and when he doesn't answer, I text him: *Met with Waverly. Hard sell. What's this all about?*

A new message from Waverly's secretary pops up as I'm pouring creamer into my coffee—he's set up a per diem for direct deposit and negotiated with Kucenic so I can retain access to my archival security codes. I respond with my checking account number and PIN and within seconds the first deposit's made—a rate substantially higher than Kucenic ever offered. Another file hits my in-box—a brief dossier about Albion.

Kucenic texts back: *I'm sorry, Dominic. Please don't contact me—*

The heat's off in my apartment again. Kucenic's reply stings, but I try to understand—all the trouble I've caused him. Getting colder, so I wrap up in my comforter and watch a doc called *A Round of Fiddles* about Objectivist poetry but my mind wanders. Waverly's daughter, Albion. By evening, another storm front's dusting DC with snow and I shut off my lights and watch the encroaching winter—the weather here's an odd mix of extremes, like Pittsburgh once. Warm enough in the afternoon to walk without a jacket yet snowing by nightfall. What would Gavril make of that photograph of Albion? What would he make of the clothes she wore—would he have recognized the gown? Maybe the whole production was something local to Pittsburgh, something amateurish. Scanning the dossier: Albion was twenty-four when she died, just shy of graduating from the fashion design program at the Art Institute. Images of her designs: tweeds and plaids, a prep fantasia. Other images of her: I've never seen a woman in real life who looks like these photographs, and I wonder how much of this imagery is false—camera tricks to make her seem tall, postproduction effects on her green eyes, coloring to make her hair that particular shade of blood red?

"Theresa Marie Blaxton—"

I say her name out loud, using her name the way Flagellants would have lashed themselves to remember the Passion of Christ.

"Theresa Marie Blaxton—"

I may be the only one on earth who remembers her, who remembers to speak her name.

11, 25—

Paperwork for Simka to sign, to transfer my care to Timothy. Visiting him, this morning, I actually wear a suit—to impress him, I think, even though it's been years since I've worn this suit and the fit isn't quite right anymore. Out of style now, or just too tight over my waist and rear, the jacket shoulders pinched, the collar like a stranglehold. Up the central stairwell to where his secretary, a cousin of his, a plump woman with a thatch of cranberry-red curls and heavy blue eye shadow, buzzes me into the reception room.

"Domi!" she says, "I don't recall having an appointment for you today. Here, have a brownie—"

"It's just a social call," I try to explain, but take a brownie anyway. And another.

Nervous. Twenty minutes or so, drinking a complimentary Keurig. Simka escorts a patient from his office, a teenage boy—fourteen, maybe fifteen—studded with a Mohawk of pins and pierced with chains through his face. They're talking about woodworking, Simka going on about his Zen theory of the lathe. He has the boy working on a project, a chair it sounds like.

"Excellent, excellent," says Simka, "but remember, too, that you had trouble making picture frames at first, but now—"

Simka gives the boy his full attention—he asks about something the boy was to have read, *The Woodworker's Guide*, Amazon portals linking *Add to cart*, but when the boy fesses up that he hasn't yet read the chapters, Simka smiles and nods and says, "Next time, next time—"

Simka's secretary mentions that I've been waiting. He's surprised to see me, saying, "I didn't recognize you in the suit!" He shakes my hand and asks how I've been. He tells me I look suave, stroking his mustache and grinning, asking if the suit's new, complimenting the fabric. I tell him the last time I wore this suit was when I eulogized my wife.

"Well, you look good," he says.

He invites me into his office—the familiar room—and I take my usual sofa seat. Simka doesn't sit in his usual seat, though, a leather recliner near the sofa, but rather wheels around the ergonomic chair from behind his desk. There's a potted ficus, but otherwise the room's bare. Comfortable, though. The furniture's oversize leather—I've been so tired recently I feel I could curl up on the sofa and sleep. He asks how I am and I answer. He offers me more coffee. He asks about Timothy and I tell him everything's fine. Awkward gaps stud the pleasantries until I realize I'm hesitant, that I've been waiting for him to pick up his notebook and pen, the usual signal that our session has started. I'm not his patient anymore—

"I just brought some paperwork for you to sign," I tell him.

"Oh, yes," he says, and I hand the sheets over. "You know, you didn't have to hand deliver these forms—"

He takes them to his desk, flattens out the creases I've made in them and reads them over. Everything's standard, I've been told—but Simka is thorough. He removes an ink pen from a small box he keeps on his desk, shakes it twice, then signs in his looping official script. One page and the next. The third. He looks over what he's done—ending an almost eight-year relationship with a few swipes of his pen.

"Since you're here, though, I wanted to show you something," he says, pulling a file from his desk. "When you transferred to Dr. Reynolds, I went through your old paperwork to pass along anything relevant and found some drawings you made. Do you remember these?"

He folds open several sheets of sketch pad paper—of course I remember these drawings, but haven't thought of them in years. Drawings I'd made during our first sessions together, when I was defensive, cautious to talk with Simka about anything personal. I'd been sent to mandatory counseling by the Employee Assistance Program when the depression and drugs began to affect my work—my case was slotted to Simka. At first, our sessions were largely silent on my part, businesslike—Simka asking questions about the nature of my work, my work environment, wondering if I got along with my coworkers, with my boss, fishing for reasons why I might be having so much trouble. I rarely answered, or was vague. One afternoon several sets of crayons and a few pads of newsprint were spread out on an activity table in his office.

"I didn't bring these for you," I remember him telling me when I noticed the art supplies. "I run an art therapy group for teenagers. After-school stuff—"

I remember I told him that my wife used to do some art therapy as a volunteer at a place called the Manchester Craftsmen's Guild. It was the first time I'd mentioned Theresa to him.

"We've been making memory maps," Simka explained. "You draw the house you grew up in and write in everything you can remember about it, every detail. You'd be surprised how much you remember when you're filling in a memory map, the specificity of the details. The kids never have enough room to write everything they want, so we journal, too—"

"What's the point of all this?" I think I asked him.

"It helps you remember," said Simka. "It helps you to understand yourself. The memory maps help people understand what is important to them, what they're passionate about—it helps them remember significant signposts that they may have ignored, it helps them recover. Then you start drawing in the neighborhood you grew up in, sometimes on a separate sheet of paper. Everything you remember—"

I don't remember how, exactly, he coaxed me into picking up a crayon to draw—I may have even suggested it, or maybe I just started drawing—but that's how we spent our sessions for quite some time. Here's the house in Bloomfield where I grew up, a brick three-bedroom row house, the building almost a hundred fifty years old when I'd lived there, my handwriting on the map impossible to read now, but I remember describing the crab apple tree in the back lot; the plank of wood my father had nailed between the branches to serve as a little bench up there; the shells of locusts left on the bark of the cherry tree; my dog, Bozworth—a German shepherd. Here's my drawing of Bozworth—noodles of black and brown crayon, hardly recognizable as a dog if I hadn't labeled him in pencil. I used to walk him down by the tracks and we'd stand aside on the gravel slopes to watch trains trundle by. Fourteen years old when we put him down. Simka hadn't even known I was from Pittsburgh until I drew the rivers.

"I do remember these," I tell him. Here's one of Phipps Conservatory, where Theresa worked in the education department—I tried to draw in the walkways through the gardens, the vanilla bean trees, the butterfly forest and the café where we used to meet. Another map, labeled *The Georgian—Room 208*. Our shelves filled with vinyl records and books, our cupboards filled with exotic ingredients for Theresa's cooking. Boxes of poetry manuscripts people had sent for my fledgling poetry line, Confluence Press, all unread when they burned. A few programming books, when I was studying coding to make Confluence Press viable as an e-book enterprise. Here's the second bedroom, converted into Theresa's office. I opened up to Simka through these drawings, and eventually I could talk freely without them. Simka had helped me immensely those early years—I used to collect things, back then. Hoard things. I used to buy crates full of old newspapers—anything printed from before the bomb. Simka helped me realize I couldn't hold on to the past in that way, that I indulged in unhealthy obsessions that were bankrupting me and contributing to the squalor I lived in. "Let go," he'd told me. He stabilized me.

"You can keep these drawings," he says. "Otherwise, I'll keep them tucked away in your file—"

"You should keep them," I tell him.

Simka smiles. He carefully folds up the drawings and returns them to the file folder.

"And how are you handling your dreams?" he asks. "The last time we spoke, you were having some difficulty sleeping. You were thinking deeply about the young woman—Hannah, I believe her name was. Do you still think about Hannah?"

Horrified by the notion that I may have abandoned her, but for some reason I don't want to tell Simka the truth—that I think about Hannah whenever I try to sleep, that I see her body and sometimes imagine her voice, so I say, "I stay busier now than I used to. Kucenic has her case now, he'll take care of her. I don't have much time to think about the past—"

"Well, then. Here's your paperwork," he says. "Good luck. I'm very proud of how far you've come. I know that it's been hard for you recently. I should have realized that you might have needed some extra attention right now, and I'm sorry I failed you in that regard. The ten-year anniversary. I should have anticipated how hard this would be for you—"

"I'm healthy," I tell him. "All's well that ends well—"

"That's fine, very fine," says Simka, but tells me recovery rarely happens in one gulp, and that it's a fine idea to still journal—that I'm still suffering from depression and anxiety, even if I'm feeling better and have been distracted by some exciting new changes.

"I'm still writing," I tell him, and show him this notebook. He flips through, his Adware overlaying my poor handwriting with Verdana typeface. He reads a page. "Good," he says, "good detail. Consider using some of the Progoff prompts . . ." I remember an early session when I showed him my poetry, the poetry I used to write. He'd read them attentively, twice over, three times over, and had said, "These are beautiful."

"So, now we're talking purely as friends," he says. "Addiction and recovery from depression are difficult. There isn't a quick fix—even complete dialysis and Adware reconditioning don't treat the underlying causes of your addiction. You'll have to work at this, Dominic. As they say, 'You're gonna carry that weight—'"

"Timothy told me a very similar thing but said you'd disagree. At any rate, I feel like maybe I can become happy again—"

"Hm," he says. "Just so you know—indulge me, here, Dominic: you are still eligible for further substance abuse treatment through the District system. Dr. Reynolds pursued your case file once the Correctional Health Board determined you'd have to switch out of my care. I'm not sure why he pursued you, Dominic—but it makes me wonder if he has a predetermined treatment schedule in mind. If you find that your current therapy isn't helping you meet your goals, and if you decide to sign up for further substance abuse treatment, Dr. Reynolds wouldn't even have to know. There are confidentiality requirements if you apply directly to the Correctional Health Board. Keep that in mind, anyway. Once the novelty of switching treatment methods fades, you may search out substances again to bring clarity. Old habits die hard—"

"You know, Dr. Simka, bringing up substance abuse clinics with me is counterproductive. I'm beyond that. I'm with Timothy now—"

"I can't argue with success," he says.

We're interrupted—his secretary doesn't buzz but knocks discreetly, poking her colorful head into the office to announce his next appointment's ready in the reception room. Simka shakes my hand and asks me to dinner, to talk further when we have more time, in a different setting, over cognac, but I'm noncommittal.

Timothy finds me as I'm leaving Simka's office. He pulls over in the Fiat, rolls down his window.

"Nothing you're doing is more important," he yells to me. "Come on with me. Get in—"

The lingering cigarette stink of the interior, the lack of legroom. Timothy inches through a throng of pedestrians crowding the boulevard, laying on the horn, and peels away once he's clear.

"How did you find me here?"

"You mentioned you'd be over this way," he says. "Kalorama, at Dr. Simka's office. I figured I'd take a chance, try to spot you—"

Again the exhilaration of potential death in wreckage as Timothy drives—he cuts off a garbage truck at the intersection, running a stop sign he claims never used to be there. He's wearing a suit and tie, a wool overcoat. He's a slight man but flabby, and when he smiles his face blossoms into double chins.

"I have meetings today," he says. "Actually, you're on the docket. I'm recommending to the board that they withdraw you from group therapy. Waverly will be your sponsor, if that's all right with you?"

"That's great news," I tell him. "Absolutely. I have the paperwork you needed from Simka—"

"I'll take over your case as a private therapist, because there are treatment requirements we have to keep up with. Red tape. I'll keep the talk therapy to a minimum, though, so we don't waste your time. I will hold you to staying clean, however. This isn't a Get Out of Jail Free card—"

"I understand."

Timothy folds into traffic. I ask him where he's taking me.

"A clinic Waverly uses from time to time. He has a gift for you, a sort of welcome to the company gift—"

"The company?" I ask. "Focal Networks? Is that who I'll be working for?"

"You've been doing some research about him, I take it? You won't be working for Focal Networks, not officially, but you'll have some of their perks—"

"What is it, exactly, that Waverly does?"

"Psychology applied to business," says Timothy. "Algorithms. Think of it like this: You see two advertisements. You pick one to pay attention to. Waverly figured out why you pick one and not the other—he can predict it. He can predict which images hold your attention in the streams, which ones you'll remember. His work is mostly academic theory. I've tried reading his papers, but they're all math—"

"So . . . Marketing?"

"Marketing consultancy, maybe, but you don't quite understand. His company goes beyond marketing. Marketing is irrelevant once you hire Waverly—"

"Then why all this shit in the Adware? If he's figured it out—"

Timothy laughs. "All that shit in the Adware *is* Waverly figuring it out. He's programming you," he says. "Every time you look or click or fantasize, you give him the key—"

A private Panda Electronics clinic in Chevy Chase. The showroom fills with spots for Panda Electronics, hallucinations of Chinese girls wearing cosplay lingerie and panda bear ears, cuddling with panda bear cubs, offering deals on personal devices. The clinician is dressed in Ralph Lauren, a polo shirt and white slacks—simple, but she's a stunner, black hair and pale, high cheekbones and vivid violet eyes. A plastic surgeon must have installed her Adware because the scarring cresting her forehead resembles the veins of a leaf rather than the haphazard gridding most people have. Her profile's set to public—*Agatha Kramer*, a biocommunications major at Georgetown, a cheerleader for the Redskins, vids of her in mustard and yellow spandex, doing high kicks on the sidelines. Her profile pic's one of Gavril's "Street Fashion" series—so she'd been one of his impromptu models for the blog. She smiles as we approach.

"Mr. Waverly?" she says.

"Yes, the Waverly appointment," says Timothy. "This is Dominic. He'll be yours this afternoon."

Mannequins line the wall displaying the latest Adware—implants, SmartMed fashion, URL codes for upgrades and free app downloads. Timothy points out a mannequin with demo wiring—the iLux is beautiful, a net of gold wires set on a bioinorganic plate that rests on the skull, wire points that will grow naturally with the brain.

"This is what Waverly picked for you," says Timothy. "I hope you like it—it's already bought and paid for—"

"You can't be serious," I say. "The iLux? That's too much—"

"Think of it as a show of support for the good work you'll do," says Timothy. "One of the perks I mentioned. Think of the iLux as your company car—"

I sign in, fill out the consent forms—in prouder days I may have balked at a gift like this, wondering at the quid pro quo, but now I accept iLux like I'd accept air to breathe. Agatha asks if I'm ready and leads us down sterile halls into a rear room. A dentist's chair. I relax my weight into it, Agatha lowering the seat cushion and reclining me backward until I'm looking up at her, the ceiling lights like bright saucers in my eyes, the smell of her breath mints and makeup wafting down to me. She drapes a paper bib over me, tucking it into my shirt collar.

"Please turn off password protect for the transfer," she says, and when I do, an alert surfaces about our mutual friend—Gavril. Agatha smiles, friends me. "You know Gav?" she says and I tell her he's my cousin.

"He's amazing," she says. "I'm such an obsessive about his work. This one time he actually stopped me on the sidewalk and asked to take my picture—I almost died. The girl I was with couldn't believe it—"

"He's a good guy," I tell her.

Timothy sits on the couch, settling in with paperwork on his tablet. Agatha shaves what stubble is left on my head, then preps me with an alcohol rub and applies a local anesthetic. As my scalp numbs it feels like my consciousness lifts several inches above my body, that I'm still aware of my legs and arms, but everything feels below me, *down* on the chair.

"Are you comfortable?" Agatha says.

"Very much, yes, thank you," I tell her.

"Can you feel this?"

"What?"

"Any pressure of any kind?"

"No," I say.

"Good—"

She leaves the room for a moment, wheeling in the surgeon arm when she returns—it's chrome with a multipronged hand that she positions over my head. She flips a switch—glaring light—and lowers goggles over her eyes.

"Ready?" she asks.

"I'm ready—"

Her profile vids blink out as she cuts my current Adware. Unplugged. I feel pressure now—or imagine I can, hearing the quiet rotors of the surgeon arm operate. I feel the wick and whir when the arm slits me open and feel the liquid rush like a distant tickle and the towels Agatha holds against my neck to catch blood. Timothy's watching the procedure, interested. Grinding, a spritz of something cold—an ice water bath or a chemosuture. The surgeon arm spools out the old Adware from my brain like winding spaghetti onto a fork, the old wires slipping out easily with only minor tugs and nudges, pinching a bit. Nothing to cause pain. It's an odd sensation but not entirely unpleasant. Agatha makes a comment and laughs, but I miss what she's said over the sound of the machine.

Agatha changes out my paper bib and dabs up more blood. The arm's swiveled to a different needle, perforating my skull—I understand how this works, what's happening. Jostling from the pressure and soon the arm begins stitching in the iLux, Agatha feeding the surgeon arm the gold netting like threading bullets into a machine gun. The surgeon arm replaces my scalp and sutures the wound with its heat needle—new scars from the operation, grids of scar tissue cutting across the scars already up there. The Adware boots. I lose my vision. The blindness is temporary but disconcerting—this total blindness is always disconcerting. I feel the surgeon arm swipe out the old retinal lenses and replace them with the Meopta lenses.

Timothy says, "Looks good."

Agatha's moving—a sink turns on. She's talking, removing each tool from the surgeon arm—click, click. My hearing diminishes, but soon *iLux* appears in gold cursive on a field of black. The Adware welcomes me and begins transferring my account settings, using Focal Networks as the default for hosting information. When the progress bar fills, I open my eyes.

"How do you like it?" says Agatha.

Definition higher than reality—I understand what that pitch means, now—yes. The world was low-res and fuzzy before, like I'd been viewing the world through Vaseline goggles until now, everything suddenly so clear. Agatha's face—glistening lips, wisps of hair, long mascara-thick lashes.

"I love it," I tell her. "This is incredible—"

The world is designed—orderly apps, housed in spherical graphics. The augs are accessible but unobtrusive: date, time, weather, GPS mapping, social networking. Agatha's profile populates my vision—her cheer vids spooling in half-light, but when my thought shifts to one it becomes opaque. The retinal cam is already autostoring imagery of Agatha, placing her in my address book, autodictating where and when we'd met, autocopying pics and vids from her profile that had caught my attention in the split second I'd scanned through them. FaceRank interprets my vitals, tracks changes in my baseline, places her near the top of recent looks, just below my memory of Twiggy. When I look at Timothy, the Adware captures his face but autocell populates info because he lacks a profile, the iLux interacting smoothly with my thoughts before they've even become my conscious thoughts.

Timothy signs that I've been successfully discharged and that he's taking me home. He lifts my arm around his shoulder and helps me from the clinic—it's difficult to walk, like my numbed consciousness floats a foot or so in front of me. Wide steps, unsure of where my foot will land and constantly surprised at the suddenness of pavement. Timothy eases me into the Fiat. He tells me to close my eyes so I don't get motion sickness and vomit in his car. I close my eyes. He turns corners tightly, my body swaying in the passenger seat—I'm clutching the seat belt harness for support, nauseous from the heightened sense perception.

"Go ahead and try to sleep," he tells me. "You don't need to stay awake—"

I try to relax, consider sleep, but instead of sleep I load the

City—the load time's negligible, the processing speed of the iLux incredible. The Parkway East, the iLux defaulting to the highest resolution, rendering the City indistinguishable from reality, through the tunnel—

A rain-murky evening. The Starbucks at the corner of Craig and Forbes, a bare-breasted mermaid logo on glass. People drift through the café, once captured inadvertently on security cameras or retinal cams, their profiles pulled from cloud storage, archived in the City because of the Right to Remember Act and used to populate these places, even these minor corners of the City. Ghosts living their scant bit of electronic existence in a perpetual loop, ordering coffee forever, sitting at café tables forever, repeating the same conversations forever, trying to hurry home through the rain but ending up back in line for coffee. They seem to look at me, interact with me. I watch them through the rain-streaked windows holding umbrellas, their skin absurdly white in the failing light, like deep-sea fish swimming through the depths. They'll disappear from existence as soon as they're out of my view, until someone else is here to see them. Students from the Catholic schools and Carnegie Mellon and Chatham wait in line—the sound of steam in milk, of shouted orders, *May I call?*—every table filled, faces illuminated in the pale blue of laptop glow. Hannah Massey is here—she's here, waiting in line to order a drink. Archived here from when she was still alive.

"Hannah," I say, and she turns her head as if she's heard me.

"Earl Grey," she says.

I watch her leave Starbucks, tea in hand. I watch her cross the intersection in the rain. The moment she's gone, she seems like a dream, like maybe I hadn't seen her here at all. Across the street, the Carnegie Museum is shrouded in fog, graced with iron-black statues of angels that always reminded me of the angels of history sent to transcribe the end of time. What did these angels see when the end of time finally arrived? Were they burned? Maybe they melted or maybe survived, iron corpses ready for excavation. Everything's re-created here—every detail. Corporate Starbucks feeds trademarked *Sense* details to the City—the trademarked smell of Komodo Dragon Blend. The trademarked taste and mouthfeel of an iced pumpkin scone.

I was working on a poem, I remember, waiting for Theresa.

What would our lives have been like? Never sure, but I try to be realistic with my regrets, memories like these affording me a window, I think, to my life as it was never lived. Theresa meeting me, wearing a rather expensive maternity dress she picked up from Nordstrom the week before—a Maggy London crepe de chine with indigo and gold. She looked stunning. I remember her carrying the weight of our child like someone burdened with secret good news. Reservations at the Union Grill up the street. We met friends of hers that night, Jake and Bex from the Arts Council—I remember feeling hopelessly out of my depth, unable to contribute to the conversation, really, beyond a dirty joke here and there and some talk about a poet I'd been reading that no one else had heard of. Impressed with Theresa—how quick she was, how she carried the conversation. I remember she chatted about sustainable horticulture and a set of adult classes she'd received grant funding to offer at the Conservatory—a community garden project she was eager to start in East Liberty, a greening initiative. We left that evening with plans to attend a young professionals networking happy hour the following week—and I assume this is what our lives may have been like, mundanely glamorous, new dresses from Nordstrom to attend fund-raising parties and cocktail hours, meeting new people important to Theresa's work. I would have finished my Ph.D., I imagine. I would have gotten Confluence Press off the ground.

Who knows? It would have been fun, though. Our lives together would have been fun. We walk to our car, parked a few blocks away near the Greek Orthodox church—drenched by the rain, but laughing. All the buses that pass by are filled with ghosts.

Timothy drops me at my apartment.

"How can I see Waverly? I want to thank him—"

"Soon," he says. "He's actually having a little get-together in a few months, if you can make it—"

"I'm free," I tell him. "I'm always free—"

I undress upstairs, learning my new system: the iLux suite from Panda with Meopta retinal lenses. The old SIM transferred over. Global Connect on Waverly's account—no more hunting hot spots. My skull's more valuable now, like it's been gold-dipped and diamond-studded—horror stories of thugs breaking heads, stripping expensive tech, I'd make a much better victim now. The pain's a residual ache—a discomfort, really—through my shoulders, behind my eyes, a chemical itch across my scalp.

Concentrate on Albion to dull the discomfort. The dossier Waverly's secretary had forwarded me is titled *Albion*—but it's just a thin profile listing her Pittsburgh addresses, the make of her car, the names of a few friends. An insubstantial résumé—he hasn't even included samples of her design work, no portfolio. No places of employment listed, no personal details—no suggestions of where I might find her, where she spent time when she was alive. Wouldn't Waverly know more than this? Attachments of a few other images, candid photographs unlike the glamour shot Waverly initially showed me, but the effect is still the same—Albion's beauty is unreal, like a Pre-Raphaelite stunner even when she's just lounging on a sofa or posing on the overlook of Mount Washington, the city skyline framed behind her. I run her name through the obvious databases—the *Post-Gazette* Archive, the *Tribune-Review*

Online, the U.S. Census Historical Register and the Bureau of Labor Statistics—but the name "Waverly, Albion O'Hara" results in zero hits. I want to find her.

There is a certain pleasure I take in this work—the speed it takes to find my query, the forethought needed to cover every angle. Naked and bundled under comforters, my ceiling gridded with coupons and logos, *Café de Coral, Ben's Chili Bowl, Little Sheep Mongolian Hot Pot,* the streams flash President Meecham's beach body, spring break wet T-shirt sex, the Madonna Centennial, a new slate of Japanese hard-core torture games—but the streams dissipate as I slip back through the heart of the City.

Polish Hill. The Immaculate Heart of Mary Church. Hillsides coppered with autumn leaves and crosshatched by dream-twisted narrow streets, alleyways, forks and switchbacks, the Immaculate Heart's green domes and cream brick facade surrounded by ramshackle row houses faded, sagging, worn. Gooski's is nearby, flashing neon Duquesne Pilsener ads in grime-streaked windows. Albion lived here at the end—down on Dobson, 3138, third floor. Layering, the soaked-clothes damp of drizzle and wind. Polish Hill was one of the artist enclaves by the end, artists too poor to afford the gentrified properties down in Lawrenceville so they moved up the hill, buying cheap properties no longer needed by the dying last remnants of the neighborhood's original stock, generations of Pittsburgh families with Old Europe still in their blood. Art spaces, open studios, cheap bar after cheap bar.

Albion's building is a corner property, boarded windows tagged with stenciled graffiti of lingerie models who have the heads of pigs. The door's password protected, its green paint flecked and scraped revealing rotten original wood and rusted hinges. Rainwater puddles at my shoes. Override with the Archive code and I'm in—so Waverly's right, Kucenic left my old codes active. A dank lobby. Piles of unopened mail scattered on the stairs and window ledges. Tags hover in the foreground and I scroll through the tenants that had lived here before the end—there aren't many, but Albion's not listed among them. The stairs are bowed, the walls blue with several coats of rancid paint that sweats and glistens in what little light there is. I'm out of breath climbing the two flights of stairs. Dates of Albion's lease—her door's also password protected, but before I can enter the override code, I hear the dead bolts falling away, the chains, and a young woman opens the door, an Asian woman. She looks as if she's readying herself for a night out, her mantis-green dress unzipped at the back. She's holding the front of her dress to her breasts, barely concealing herself, her shoulders bare. She's lovely, and I stammer for something to say. She looks at me as if she were expecting someone else.

"I'm sorry," I tell her, without thinking.

"John Dominic Blaxton," she says, recognition dawning over her. "Focal Networks—"

"I'm sorry?"

She smiles—her profile's blank. "You live in the public housing in Columbia Heights. Room R-17. Washington, DC—a temporary residence, previously of Pittsburgh and Virginia. Husband of Theresa Marie Blaxton. No children—"

"Excuse me?"

"You aren't welcome here," she says, shutting the door. I enter the archival override code and the door opens, what should have been Albion's door, but the space is empty now—a small apartment, just a one bedroom, with one corner converted for use as a kitchen. The floor is unfinished hardwood. The walls are a generic cream, even the light fixtures are painted over. There's no furniture here. There's no woman. There's nothing here.

"Hello?" My voice echoes in the empty room.

12, 14—

"Was this a dream?" asks Timothy.

"Parts of it were a dream, but I'm not sure what was real—"

Timothy's office is cluttered, unlike Simka's—stacked papers overflowing from plastic bins, bookshelves piled with true crime paperbacks and sets of leather-bound reference works, the *DSM-IX* in multiple volumes, dictionaries, thesauruses. His desk is clean, only a blotter, a pen and a leather-bound Bible. The chairs are mid-last-century, set around his desk as if for a meeting.

"Would you like some coffee? A drink?"

"I'd love some coffee—"

"I worry talk therapy will be counterproductive," says Timothy. "When I look at the improvement you've made in this short amount of time—with a support system, supervised immersion, no drugs—it's inspiring. Dominic, I don't want you to identify yourself as someone who's sick, as someone who needs to talk to a therapist. That sort of self-identification can often create problems. That's not who you can become. Dominic, you're healthy—"

An identity issue, he tells me. If I think that I'm sick, I will be sick. If I think I'm well, I will become well. Timothy believes in positive thinking—that physical health follows the *belief* of physical health, that the power of the spirit can heal the body. He tiptoes around calling his system the "power of prayer" but he quotes studies and clinical trials stating that God helps recovery much more effectively than medication. *What is your identity?* he asks. *Do you want to be ill? Or do you want to be healthy? Who are you?*

"How did you start working in the Archive?" he asks. "Were you always interested in this kind of work?"

"I was still thinking of pursuing my graduate studies after Pittsburgh," I tell him. "Everyone was very accepting of survivors—it was easy to transfer programs. I chose the University of Virginia, moved to Charlottesville. I'd been studying Klimt and Schnitzler and Freud—"

"You aren't a graduate student now?"

"No. Not anymore—"

"Why give it up?"

"Why?" I wonder. "Truthfully, I was already giving up on that sort of work years before. I think I know the exact moment I gave up—in my second year of classes at Carnegie Mellon, I presented a paper about Lacan. The shifting nature of desire. I showed projections of Egon Schiele's work, some of the more pornographic stuff, and theorized in front of the class about female masturbation. I was beginning to think of myself as a sort of intellectual provocateur of the department—"

"You're cringing," says Timothy.

"I'm still embarrassed," I tell him, "even after all these years, I'm still embarrassed. I used to wear a bowler hat, if you can believe that. So, there was a woman in class with me, she—I remember she used to be a ballerina, a real, professional dancer, but gave it up for French theory. After my presentation about Lacan, I was cutting across campus and she called out to me. I remember what she was wearing—this gingham dress. She told me how excited she was that I had talked about Schiele, that Schiele was one of her favorite artists. She said our areas of research were strikingly similar and she wanted to talk with me more about it. She invited me to dinner at her apartment. She said she was an excellent cook and told me that she had invested in a catalogue raisonné of Schiele with giclée reproductions of his work, but she didn't know anyone else who might appreciate it. I was—actually, I was terrified of her. I'd always been intimidated in classes with her because she seemed to understand all the readings we were assigned. I didn't think I could legitimately spend more than five minutes talking to her without exposing myself as a fraud. I didn't know much about Lacan other than a few essays I'd read. Derrida was incomprehensible to me. I couldn't figure out Bourdieu. I mispronounced all their names. I'd never bothered to read Foucault. She'd left the top few buttons of her dress undone so you could see the edge of her bra—this black, lacy thing. Imagining her apartment, imagining all the dog-eared paperbacks of theory and philosophy I knew she must have read, imagining sitting next to her looking at Schiele, the book spread open across her legs, scared me. I felt like she was playing a very adult game with me. She was very attractive, very intimidating. After that afternoon I felt like a poseur, studying Freud and Schnitzler. Schiele, for Christ's sake. I never took her up on her offer. I stopped wearing my bowler—"

"And this was before Theresa?"

"Oh, yes—Theresa wouldn't have . . . not if I was wearing a bowler hat. By the time I met Theresa I'd already given that up. I'd already talked to my adviser about switching to 20th-Century American Modernism. Wallace Stevens. T. S. Eliot. I was more interested in an MFA in creative writing, to be honest—I thought I might transfer departments. I'd already started Confluence Press. A contemporary poetry series. That was always my real passion, to publish other people's poetry—to curate a line of poetry books. I started taking classes in the computer science department, figuring out some coding so I could theoretically maximize e-content for the poetry press. I've tried to write poetry since. It's odd to me—if I read a line by, say, Philip Larkin, I'll be struck by how beautiful the line is, how perfect or how true. But if I write that line—that same line—just seeing it in my own handwriting sickens me and I'm overwhelmed by the depthless stupidity of the words. I don't write poetry anymore—"

"Weakness," says Timothy.

"Maybe," I admit. "I was a disappointment to everyone at Virginia once I showed up. I didn't go to classes. I didn't research. I just spent my time buying used books at Oakley's and Daedalus—just absolutely hoarding books and newspapers, burying myself in my apartment. I was—suicidal isn't the right word. I was taking this class about the *Decameron* and was failing—the professor noticed I was in a tailspin, I guess. She invited me out for coffee and I told her how unhappy I was. She thought I might be able to use more structure than a graduate student life provided—maybe work for a few years, then come back to the program. I told her that sounded fine but I didn't know what to do with my life. Her cousin owned a research group in DC and she thought what little I'd picked up about coding would make me a perfect fit with that kind of work. She got me an interview. It turns out her cousin wasn't hiring, but he knew a guy who was. An entry-level job with the Kucenic Group—"

"And under Simka's care for drug abuse?"

"My boss, Kucenic, placed me in the Employee Assistance Program and that program connected me with Dr. Simka—"

"The entry-level job was an archival assistant?"

"It provided enough of a salary, and my cousin Gavril helps me quite a bit. Blog writing, copy, blurbs, that sort of thing. It's not much of a living, but it's all I need—"

"Have you ever had this dream before?" he says.

"No—"

"What parts are you sure were a dream?" he asks.

"The dimensions of the apartment," I tell him. "The interior was too large—"

"Tell me about the interior of the apartment," he says.

I tell him. I'm on Dobson, in Polish Hill. It's grown dim—twilight in the late afternoon. House windows burn orange and the bells of the Immaculate Heart are ringing. Timothy's interested now.

"Did you intend to visit Albion's apartment?"

"Yes—yes, I did. I'd gone to look for her—"

Lucid, at first. The shallow sleep Adware exploits for deep-penetration product placement. I'd bookmarked the entrance to Albion's apartment building the first time I was there so that whenever I enter the City I'm loitering here, waiting for her. The green door, rotten around the edges. Windows boarded, spray-painted with the stenciled graffiti of lingerie models with the heads of swine. The pigs' heads are goofy, grinning and slobbering, with razor blade teeth—the lingerie they wear is made for fetishists, eighteenth-century frills in the lace. I try the door to the apartment building and find it's unlocked. The foyer, the unopened mail on the windowsills. Paint-flecked walls and the hardwood moaning as I climb upstairs—this is when the lucid dreaming stops and I fall into deeper sleep, I think, my attention drifting, the scene shifting, but not asleep heavily enough to engage the automatic offs. Upstairs to the third-floor landing, to her apartment. Is this when I woke? I'm not sure—I may have still been asleep. I scroll through past residents looking for her name, but Albion isn't among them. This is typical. I type in the dates she'd lived there. The door opens. I step inside.

"You sound like you've been to her apartment before," says Timothy.

"Many times—I've been trying to find her for Waverly," I tell him. "But one of two things has always happened when I visit Albion's apartment. Most often, the apartment is empty—just an empty space, just a place holder. I can walk through the rooms, but I might as well be studying a blueprint of the space. Every so often, though, a woman will open the door—a young woman, younger than I am, Asian. She seems to know who I am—she rattles off my name, information about me—but that could just be the AI pinging my profile. She's always polite, but always tells me that I'm not welcome and always shuts the door before I can slip past her inside. The apartment changes. But that's the nature of the City—the City changes. The bones of the City are facts but the flesh is memory, mutable. And with iLux, or any of the newer suites, the City pulls from memory and imagination and fills in with details that were never, strictly speaking, true. It makes an archivist's job much more difficult—trying to find the truth through all that muck of fantasy. But this time, once I typed in the dates and opened the door, the apartment is different again. It's decorated. Sparse, just a few pieces of furniture—but it's furnished, lived in. I'd never seen the apartment like this. The furniture's mismatched, all secondhand pieces, repainted. The walls are hung with paintings—large canvases, like Rothko color-fields the shade of bruises—and sketches of fashion designs. Bolts of fabric and dyes and a sewing machine. A lavender dress pinned to a mannequin—"

"Albion's apartment," Timothy says.

"It must be Albion's apartment. I'm assuming that whoever deleted Albion is substituting information to make it harder to track—"

"Was she there?" asks Timothy.

"Albion? No, she wasn't there. That same woman was there.

That young woman. She always seems like she's readying herself for a party. She welcomed me in this time—"

Examining herself in the mirror in the living room. Inky hair bundled high, held in place by two sticks. The woman's tall—almost as tall as I am, I realize. She applies her makeup. I watch her darken her lips to the color of wine. She's pale. She wears high heels—black, patent leather heels that reflect the faint apartment light. The dress catches my eye, something Gavril would be interested in—a damask print, black on a green the color of pale emeralds. She walks across the living room, her dress unzipped in the back so I see her white skin and the black strap of her bra. She enters the bedroom but returns a moment later, adjusting a pearl earring.

"Who are you?" I ask.

"Zhou," she says. "Who are you?"

I tell her I'm looking for Albion, and when she turns from the mirror I see a reflection of red—for just a moment, a flash of red hair in the mirror.

"Oh, of course," she says, "John Dominic Blaxton, of Pittsburgh, Virginia, and Washington, DC. Temporary residences." She returns to her own reflection. I search the apartment—the kitchen, her bedroom. In the bathroom I find curly red hairs on the porcelain of the bathtub and know I'm in the right place.

"Were you still dreaming?" asks Timothy.

"I don't think so although I don't know—"

"Is that why you mentioned the woman from your class? The woman who liked Schiele? You described what she wore, earlier—you were detailed when you told me about her, about her undergarments. You mentioned specifically that you could see the edge of her bra. Were you dreaming and pulling details from your memory through the iLux?"

"No—I don't think so, though maybe the woman in the apartment made me remember the woman from my class." I think I was awake when I saw Zhou, when we spoke, but think I'm dreaming as I explore her rooms. A hallway I hadn't noticed branches out from the main room, a corridor—it's narrow, with half-opened doors leading to other rooms, unfinished rooms. It dawns on me that the rooms are repeating, that I'm wandering through previous incarnations of the finished room. I come to another bathroom, but the red hairs are no longer on the porcelain.

"Go on," says Timothy.

"The corridor continues and this is when I believe I was dreaming, because the episode has the hallmarks of a dream—I'm frustrated, lost, and can't remember how I get back to the living room, to Zhou. Another corridor, and I see him—"

"Who?" says Timothy.

"This—man, I don't know who. I've never seen him before, I don't recognize him. I figure I'm dreaming or that the barriers between Albion's apartment are blurring with another person's private account, that maybe this man is a previous tenant of the apartment—another survivor come back to visit his space, or just another recording inserted from the cloud. I figure I'm interrupting something private.

"'I'm sorry,' I tell him. 'I didn't mean to—'

"But he just looks at me, almost as if he's not quite sure I'm even there with him—"

"What did he look like?" asks Timothy.

"Sitting in a wingback chair, the upholstery striped like a piece of hard candy, a cup of coffee near him on a low table. He wears slacks and a blazer over a T-shirt. The T-shirt says *Mook.*"

"How old?"

"Fifties, maybe early sixties. Or maybe late forties, but tired. I remember his eyes the most clearly—sad eyes, like his face was drooping. Like Droopy Dog? Do you remember that old cartoon Droopy Dog?"

"What else about him?" asks Timothy.

I tell him that I remember the color gray. Undefined. I don't remember the man clearly. Gray, drooping, rumpled, sad—but arrogant in a way. I don't like him. He sips his coffee, considering me. I apologize again, saying something about visiting a friend, that I'm lost here. He doesn't move or speak with me, but I turn around to leave and he's vanished. I'm sure I'm awake, now—but he's gone so I figure he was part of the dream. I return to Zhou.

"How did you return to her? You were lost—"

"The program was like a Möbius strip—"

I turned away from the man in the Mook shirt and saw a door I hadn't noticed before, and when I went through the door I reentered her apartment. This is a loop. Now I understand—things have changed since first entering her apartment. Zhou is dressing for a party. I watch her. I hear the shower running—there's no one else in the apartment. I can no longer find that corridor with several doors—no, now there's just the short hallway that leads to her bedroom. I open the bathroom door and find Zhou in the shower. I watch her through the fogged curtain. She seems pleased when she notices me watching her, and lets me watch, rubbing soap over her breasts and dousing herself with shampoo. She asks if I want to join her, but I ignore the question and she laughs. Zhou dries herself and walks nude to her bedroom and there I watch her dress in an elaborate set of lingerie. She steps into the green dress that she doesn't bother to zip. She makes her way to the living room mirror—this is where I'd first seen her, applying makeup in the mirror. There—the flash of red, Albion's hair, flickers in the reflection and disappears. Here's where it loops: She goes to her bedroom, returns adjusting the pearl earring, but once her earrings are on, she takes them off. Zhou unzips her dress and lets the fabric slide from her body. I watch her reach up and unlatch the front clasp of her bra. Very beautiful, the kinds of perfection women's bodies have in dreams, uncanny and vivid. She undresses and makes her way to the bathroom, starts the shower and steps in once the water's warm, lathering herself. I tell Timothy that I watched the cycle several times that afternoon, and that's how I realize the loop is without variation.

"Whoever's erasing Albion uses the entity Zhou as a place holder," I tell him, "a forgery inserted into Albion's deletions so the code doesn't fold in on itself and generate anything traceable. The work is seamless, absolutely beautiful—"

"Waverly may be interested in that bit about the red hair in the mirror," says Timothy.

"Sure," I say.

"And the hair in the bathtub," says Timothy. "I think, especially—"

He asks whether I'm craving drugs and I tell him I haven't thought of drugs since being cleaned out, certainly not since receiving iLux. I just don't need them anymore. He asks about Theresa, if I've seen Theresa. Yes, I tell him. Yes. He tells me I look fine, that I'm progressing nicely.

12, 27—

Grid the Archive like a crime scene and walk it, checking each grid square for changes through time. I clocked my fair share of this type of tedium when I first worked for Kucenic, when the firm assigned me all the shit cases—sometimes spreadsheets help. Grid Albion's apartment building and scan the months before her lease and the few years she lived here, pausing in each grid square to watch time flow past in fast-forward, a miasma of daylight and night. Albion's apartment building is a story of decay—windows break, replaced by plywood, the plywood rots, is covered by graffiti. A cornice breaks from the roof, shatters on the sidewalk—the roof is never patched or repaired. Bricks deteriorate, the mortar receding. Detritus gathers on the sidewalk and is swept up against the building but never cleared away until fire consumes everything and the landscape turns to ash.

Rewind. Grid the Archive a second time, check the grid perpendicular to my first search—I notice an accumulation of graffiti concomitant with where I've bookmarked the start date of Albion's lease, a quick spray of color covering the plywood windows of her building. So, someone started tagging the apartment once Albion moved in. Zoom on the graffiti: a pig's head appears amid the scrawl of illegible signatures and obscenities and tags—a grinning swine with razor blade teeth.

Fast-forward and the tag becomes elaborate: a skull-faced doyenne walks two swine-faced women on leashes like they're dogs. Cross-reference my copies of Kucenic's "handwriting samples"—detailed records he's kept of vandals we've encountered over the years, sample images of graffiti styles, bits of telltale code—but there aren't any documented instances of pigs' heads like these. Lasso and copy the image and run a Facecrawler in the universal image cache—the results pour in, near matches of women holding prize-winning pigs at state fairs and young mothers encouraging little girls to touch pigs at petting zoos, of the Arkansas cheer squad huddling around their razorback mascot. Thousands of images of women and the faces of pigs. *1% finished . . . 2% . . .*

Albion drove a '46 Honda Accelerant, forest green—but a search for the make/model, limiting to "Polish Hill" and the years of Albion's lease, yields zero hits, a *No results found* message suggesting I should ease the parameters of my search.

Zero doesn't make much sense—even if Albion parked off-site or if the dossier's incorrect and she never actually owned a Honda, the Accelerant was popular enough that someone's Accelerant should have appeared in the search results. Impossible to believe zero Accelerants were archived in Polish Hill for that year set—even someone just cutting through the neighborhood should have appeared, zipping down the hill from Oakland to the Strip.

I ease the parameters—search for the Accelerant but not the specific make, still limiting to "Polish Hill" and the years of the lease, but again come up with nothing.

I ease the parameters further—search only "Accelerant" in the entire City-Archive and the results hit every Honda dealership, every model year, every truckload of new makes, every used Accelerant, every advertisement, every Accelerant parallel parked on every street, every car in every driveway, too many hits even to consider, but still nothing in the particular blind spot where I'm trying to see.

Pepsi helps me think, so do Ho Hos—I uncap a fresh two-liter and open a new box, take a five-minute break before immersing again. Think. The Archive's still Java based, so I set the parameters to "Polish Hill" and the years of Albion's lease, but I don't search for the Accelerant—rather, I search for a "TimelineException," the telltale error in the code that means that something's not historically accurate, that someone's been tampering. I run the search, expecting to find a few hundred or even a few thousand hits, but the search locks up my iLux with an untraceable mess of TimelineException results—nearing a million exceptions before I kill the process. Christ—

Scanning the error report—whoever's erasing Albion's car intentionally mangled the code, it looks like, must have deleted or swapped out or tampered with just about every car archived near her apartment to crash searches with errors. I've seen similar with insurance scams—but whoever's deleted Albion is especially thorough. There's nothing I can use to track this mess. I can't help but admire the work.

Think through the methodology—a reflection of red hair in the moment Zhou turns from the mirror. Nothing traceable in and of itself, but that leftover reflection is at least one slip—maybe the work isn't quite as seamless as it seems.

Real-time hours loitering outside of Lili Café on the corner of Dobson and Hancock, the same building as Albion's apartment, watching cars, or rather watching the reflections of cars in the café's picture windows. When a car passes on Dobson, I note the make/model, then note the car's reflection on a separate spreadsheet—sometimes only registering a blur of color. The cars that pass rarely match their reflections and I'm hopeful I'll catch a trace of Albion's Accelerant reflected in the window glass. Dull work, but something to slog through, a start. I recognize the barista archived here—Sandy, I think her name was—petite, with a cloche hat and black-framed glasses. She was a screen printer, I remember, her neon and pastel posters for Pittsburgh bands and the Steel City Derby Demons decorate the café. Theresa used to work with her—booked her to teach art workshops with the high schools, making prints using plant materials. She steams milk, pours leaf shapes onto the skim of lattes. Her customers are vaguely familiar to me, too, some of their faces—people I might have seen around. Another car passes and I note its reflection. Scanning over four days' worth of footage until a silver Nissan Altima passes but casts a reflection of a green hatchback Accelerant on the café window and I know I have her.

Time-stamp the reflection, bookmark it.

I run another Facecrawler, limiting to "Polish Hill" and the years of Albion's lease, but instead of searching for Albion's Accelerant, I search for this substitute car, the '53 Altima sedan. Ready to kill the process if I hit the same flood of errors, but the hack's slipped up: whoever deleted Albion's car used the Altima as a universal substitution, probably with something as simple as Find and Replace All. The Facecrawler brings manageable results—I pin the results to a map of Polish Hill and the pins cluster around two locations like a trail of bread crumbs: Albion's apartment on Dobson and the underground parking garage of another nearby apartment, a high-rise just a few blocks away tagged the Pulawski Inn. I save my search, reset the Archive to a date when the Altima should be parked at the Pulawski Inn, and walk to try and find the car.

Every floor of the Pulawski Inn is quartered into lofts, every loft expansive with picture windows and sliding glass doors that lead to slim balconies. The lobby's the color of champagne, with wingback chairs and couches candy-striped in pale gold. A mahogany table centers the room, topped with a vase of orchids. The building manager receives visitors at a front reception desk. She's reading Camus—her brunette hair matches the mahogany table, her skirt and blouse match the walls. She smiles when I approach, says, "How may I help you?" but when I ask if she's ever heard the name Albion, she searches through her database of recorded conversations and says, "No results found—"

"Can you tell me how to get to the parking garage?"

"The elevator's just off the lobby," she says, pointing my way.

I take the elevator to P1 and pace the narrow lanes of the garage, scanning cars, cross-checking with the results of my Facecrawler, and find the Altima parked in a row of spaces reserved for guests. I save the image, but everything about the car's been wiped—no license plate, no VIN, no garbage or stuff in the backseat or the floors, nothing but a generic sculpt of a Nissan, probably ripped from a dealer stream, nothing unique to Albion.

I loiter by the car, hoping for Albion to come. Waiting, disoriented by the odd angles of the garage sculpted from fish-eye security cam footage, I focus on the elevator and bookmark the moment when the doors slide apart. Zhou. A navy peacoat, her hair tucked down inside her collar. She wears a white knit dress, her legs luminous in the elevator light. She's with a blonde, another stunner—taller than Zhou by a few inches, in tailored blue jeans and a crimson paisley halter that shows off her shoulders and neck, her hair in a loose braid that hangs well past her belt. The blonde's features are pure Scandinavian, with sharp cheekbones and almond-shaped blue eyes. Her left shoulder to elbow is inked with a tattoo sleeve—a complex pattern of red roses and calla lilies. She lingers with Zhou in the elevator, laughing at some remark Zhou's made, their fingertips touching, and before Zhou leaves, the blonde reaches beneath the collar of Zhou's coat and untucks her hair. I follow Zhou from the elevator to the Nissan, but the moment she steps inside the Nissan she disappears, a red spot hovering in her place to let me know a TimelineException has occurred.

Follow the blonde. We ride together to the tenth floor and although the blonde and the elevator are illusory, I can smell the floral scent of her shampoo, the fabric of her clothes. I touch her arm and feel her muscles and skin—she responds to my touch. Someone's sculpted her here—her specifically, layering in her scents and reactions. She doesn't have the generic flesh feel that others have in the Archive. At my touch, she leans close and parts her lips, expecting me to kiss her, it seems, but I keep to myself and she eventually resets, watching the ascending floor numbers. Someone programmed this scene to relive intimate moments with her. When the doors open, I follow her. The hallway is the same champagne color as the lobby with wall sconces that emit a pale glow. She unlocks her door, Room 1001, steps inside and closes the door behind her. When I try to follow, the door is locked.

"Override," I say and a keypad hovers in the wall. I enter my access code and the door swings open, but the room's been replaced with a generic sculpt, nothing but the model floor plan for this type of room, generic furniture and generic decor, nothing else, nothing of the blonde.

I return to the lobby. The building manager tips a cup of water into the vase of orchids. I ask her for the name of the woman who lives in Room 1001, and after a quick search she responds, "Peyton Hannover—"

I note the name.

Checking the results of my image search for the pig's head graffiti—nothing conclusive, but an interesting string of hits that's surely the inspiration for the image: an etching and aquatint from

1879 called *Pornokrates,* by a Belgian artist Félicien Rops, of a woman nude except for stockings, opera gloves and a blindfold. She's walking a pig on a leash. I find a hi-res version of the image and save it along with the graffiti on Albion's apartment. Not sure what this all is supposed to mean—

12, 29—

The old houses here in Polish Hill feel like they're sinking into mud or sluggishly collapsing downhill toward the riverbeds. Row houses with wood siding, the siding unpainted or the paint long since peeled away, the wood blanched silvery gray but gone to rot near the foundation and gutters. The gate in the chain-link's padlocked but the fence is waist level so I climb it. Mud-swamped stamps of yards studded with dog shit and toys, the porch a slab of concrete that's cracked apart. I've been working in the end unit. The screen door hangs on loose hinges.

I open the front door. I step inside.

The hallway's dim from a mass of dead flies and gnats never cleaned from the fixture glass. "You're in Steelers Country" in needlepoint, framed. Hardwood, the tap-scratch of claws and the wet suck-breath of a large dog. It turns the corner and I yelp—embarrassed by the start of terror at yellowish eyes and teeth the color of buttermilk, but it's all so real, the guttural apparition of a pit bull pushing against my legs and nosing into my crotch, sniffing. The dog's all muscle, its social profile glowing: *Oscar, beloved of the Stanleys.* I touch his ears, rub the folds of his velvety head. I know he's not real—it's not real—but iLux pulls memories to fill out the gaps of the sculpt, the smell of wet dog and the feel of dog's slobber and moist nose. Hot breath and smooth tongue. "Okay, boy, it's okay," trying to push the bulk away from my knees.

Oscar doesn't follow up the stairs. He watches me and sneezes a rope of snot that he shakes from his face. Carpeted stairs, a length of pipe for the rail. The Sacred Heart of Christ hangs on the landing. Other pictures clutter the upstairs hallway, of the owners of this house, Edith and Jayden Stanley, their friends and family, all dead—dumpy women with dull hair in scrunchies and wiry earnest-eyed men, baggy T-shirts and Steelers jerseys, nurses' scrubs and bright white sneakers.

There's an attic entrance in the hallway, a trapdoor in the ceiling. I pull the leather strap and lower the ladder. A single bulb lights the attic, low wattage. Hot up here—stifling. Boxes, Christmas decorations. Windows bracket the room, one looking over the street out front and down to the torn shingles of the porch roof, the other looking over the fenced-in backyard, the coiled dog chain in the grass and the kiddie pool filled with an inch or two of rainwater. Beyond the backyard, the broad face of the Pulawski Inn rises over the neighboring rooftops. The mustard-yellow bricks darken to ochre in the rain. There's a folding chair already set up near this window. I sit. I watch.

Three windows from the top, on the eastern corner—Room 1001. Auto zoom ×3, ×9—scanning the windows, looping fast-forward and reverse in time. Peyton Hannover was a student at Chatham University, studying literature, and a part-time model in local commercials: Pirates season tickets, Mattress World, Shop 'n Save. I've watched Peyton Hannover's commercials and have watched her dine with friends, have watched her walk alone through Frick Park and have watched her die—waiting in line at a CVS in

North Oakland to buy a bottle of chocolate milk, squinting at the blinding flash before her skin caught fire and turned to ash, blown apart in the same scouring wind that blew apart the CVS as easily as if it were made of newsprint.

I watch her now, on a Thursday evening in late July, as she prepares dinner in her kitchen—a dinner I've watched her prepare several times now: slicing strawberries for the salad and scooping chicken from the bag of marinade. I'm able to watch her now, as she lays out each chicken strip in a skillet and waves smoke away from the alarm, because for ten months before the end, Jayden Stanley ran a Canon HD webcam with 27× optical zoom pointed toward her windows. He'd filmed her from his attic, recording to a password-protected 10-terabyte pay account from JunkTrunk that the Right to Remember Act rendered accessible using my archival override codes. He had filmed Peyton Hannover as she undressed after classes and on weekend mornings as she ate grapefruit and drank coffee in her pajamas on her balcony. He filmed her in spandex, practicing yoga in her living room. He filmed her having wine with friends and filmed long hours of her empty apartment while she was out. He filmed her through the picture windows that must have been appealing to her at the time she signed her lease, affording sweeping vistas of Polish Hill and the downtown skyline beyond. The view from the Stanleys' attic window to Peyton's apartment is unobstructed: I can see her apartment's exposed brick interior walls from here, a poster of polychrome Warhol flowers, everything. I can see it all clearly. I've reviewed all ten months of Stanley's footage, most nights watching Peyton doing nothing more interesting than watching HGTV or *America's Next Top Model*—but there is one evening that interests me, this Thursday in late July.

For most of the evening, Stanley's filmed the wrong room—

hours of useless footage of Peyton's darkening bedroom, polygon shards of sunset receding from the wall above her bed. He must have checked his camera at 7:42 because the frame adjusts. Peyton in the kitchen cutting strawberries and rinsing lettuce. She's wearing spandex shorts and a long-sleeved T-shirt, one shoulder exposed. Plastic basins and metal tubs line the short hallway leading to the bathroom—but Stanley's zoomed in too close, cutting off the view of the rest of the loft. I imagine Stanley hurrying here, maybe his wife calling him down from the attic, maybe Oscar moaning to be let outside, adjusting the video to capture Peyton in the kitchen, but keeping him from adjusting the shot the way he would have liked—but I'm guessing. Almost twenty minutes filming these washbasins. Albion steps into view nearing eight o'clock, carrying bolts of fabric. Her crimson hair's lifted in a tight bun twisted together with pencils. Her skin is cameo white—I'd call her swanlike but that might sound like I'm falling in love with her. She's not wearing much in Stanley's video—a sports bra, spandex shorts, tennis shoes. She's athletic despite her height, handling the bolts of fabric without goosey awkwardness. Maybe she'd once played volleyball. Or tennis. I watch as Albion measures and cuts the fabric and as she submerges lengths of cloth into each tub.

I imagine now they're eating dinner together, but the table is out of view. I watch the basins. Peyton returns to the kitchen sink after nine. Albion returns to the frame nearing nine thirty. She kneels, pulls cloth from the tubs—it's dyed a rich violet. She hangs the fabric dripping from a makeshift line, dye raining over painter's plastic. Her hands and forearms are purple, like she's been strangling grapes for wine. I watch her. Peyton crosses into view—briefly. Albion laughs. A few minutes later, Albion yawns and stretches, raising her arms above her head, cracking her shoulders. I finish out the view of her. This trace ends when the fabric is hung and she carries the basins into Peyton's bathroom. That's the last I see of her. I've looked forward in time, but Stanley misses filming when Albion takes down her fabric, misses the rest of the cleanup, or any other time Albion may have visited Peyton—or the footage may have already been deleted. I loop back. I sit in the folding chair in Stanley's attic, watching out the attic window to the apartment building and wait for Albion. Peyton's slicing strawberries and scooping chicken from the marinade. Albion enters the frame, carrying bolts of fabric. I watch her.

1, 8—

The graffiti on Albion's apartment doesn't stem from *Pornokrates*, like I'd first thought—but appropriates an image from an Agent Provocateur printbook called *Manor House*, one of those limited-run narrative catalogs fashion houses distribute to investors each season. I found a *Manor House* reproduction on kink.torrent: the copy's shit quality, but I can tell what the image is—three women, two on leashes. The auteur of the printbook, a photographer named Coudescue, must have used *Pornokrates* as inspiration for his image—I pinged Gav with an attached thumbnail, wondering if he knew the work. He responded that I could see it in person whenever I could make it out to his place.

The printbook I'm hunting is several seasons old already, but Gavril collects this stuff: photography monographs, printbooks, catalogs, file folders stuffed with printouts of fashionporn editorials that have caught his eye over the years. Everything's kept in a walk-in closet he calls his "reading room"—the only place Gavril separates from the ongoing party filling out the rest of his apartment. A cushioned folding chair's crammed in there and an end table with a green-shaded lamp. A notebook. He's nailed boards on every wall for shelves and has catalogs stacked three deep and in teetering stalagmite stacks on the floor. He's excited to show off his collection, "the true art of our age," he says, lighting a joint as he explains everything to me, running his palm over the stubble of his head like a baby discovering bristles, saying, "There's no reason our age shouldn't be defined by fashion imagists like La Havre, Coudescue, Smithson—"

He finds the printbook I came for, but says, "Look at this one, here—Gucci. This is Teenie Mizyuki's breakout book—fucking political commentary, right here. He took the Gucci fall line and brought it into these bombed-out Palestinian villages following the civil war. Didn't hire models, just used the girls he found. Brilliant, fucking brilliant stuff—"

"How long have you had this?" I ask him about the Agent Provocateur printbook I came to see—it's thick, three hundred or so pages, all full color, glossy, promoting a line called *Upstairs, Downstairs*.

"Shit, brother. I don't know. Ten or eleven years? The higher-end lines put out high-fucking-quality printbooks. There's a collector's market for these. I unloaded a spare copy of La Havre's *Gucci* a few months ago and bought dinner for a month. The one you want isn't worth as much, but don't bend the corners—"

The catalog isn't anything special as far as I can tell, a rambling narrative of a blonde and a redhead seduced by everyone they meet during a weekend at a country manor—stable boys, kitchen staff, the mistress of the house. Timothy described this to me—this might be the very scenario he said he streamed when he was going through his depression, before he tore out his Adware. Maybe this is a companion book to the stream he was obsessed with. Soft-core de Sade, every page slickly produced and shot like a fairy tale, the porcelain-skinned girls ravaged in various states of undress, the lingerie different for each scene. Page 136, I say, "Oh, shit, there it is—"

"What? What is it?" says Gavril.

The house mistress nude in stockings, opera gloves and a blindfold, the girls on hands and knees tethered by leashes. I scan and save the image, letting my thoughts clack against each other. "I keep seeing this picture," I tell him. "There's an image made from this picture, only with pigs' heads on the two girls. It's painted on Albion's apartment—"

"Who's Albion?" he asks. "Domi, are you seeing someone? *Zkurvysyn*—"

"I'm tracking someone named Albion in the Archive. She was a model, you might know her—"

I flash him the picture of Albion to see if he can place her, but Gavril says whoever she is, she's strictly small-market amateur. "A nice shot," he says, "she's a good-looking girl, and could have modeling work easily," but says that for her to even blip on the professional databases she would have to be a careerist—really work to promote herself. "There are all sorts of do-it-yourself bullshit sites you might find her on," he says, "but it would take a lifetime scrolling through homemade glamour shots made by every deluded high school girl who thinks she has a shot at fame in the streams—"

"She died in Pittsburgh—"

"Oh shit," he says. "Shit, I'm sorry. Let me think a minute. Well, even if she'd been pro or semipro, the networks didn't exist then like they do now. This picture was a small-market campaign, otherwise you'd have found a reference to it—the people who are into fashion history are fanatical. So this is a one-shot. Something indie, something local. No chance you'd find her through this picture—not with current resources. No chance. The image isn't even signed. There's no augment to it. Nothing to reference. Tell me about the pigs—"

I tell him I'll catch him up over dinner. He wants to take me to Primanti's. I suggest somewhere else, maybe that Thai place he'd found, but he insists. He drives. He finds the Beach Boys on the radio and sings along, fucking up the words, and I laugh.

He parks in downtown Silver Spring and we walk to Primanti's, a gaudy Pittsburgh-themed restaurant next to an indoor amusement park. The smell of grease and alcohol waft from the restaurant, the outdoor tables full of people drinking East End Brewing, gorging on French fry–laden cheesesteaks. A souvenir shop almost as large as the restaurant fronts the place, loaded with key rings, postcards of Pittsburgh in spinning racks, magnets, porcelain beer steins. There's a wall here called the Pittsburgh Wall where people have written the names of the deceased—I think it was meant to be like the Vietnam Memorial, a sober monument to the dead, but the wall's a thick tangle of Sharpie ink and pocketknife engravings, utterly illegible. I wrote Theresa's name here years ago, but it's been long since buried over. Even now there are people scrawling more names while they wait for tables—most people just write their own names now. How many of us are true survivors? There were only a hundred or so people documented to have actually survived the bomb—people protected from the blast by odd flukes of coincidence, people who dug out of the rubble and were eventually saved by rescue crews. And there are many more people like me, saved through a quirk of scheduling that took us out of town for the afternoon—I don't know how many people are true survivors, but I've read that the survivors of Pittsburgh are like splinters of the True Cross, that if you were to gather us all together, you'd have three or four times the amount of the peak population of the entire city. Adware flashing to the "Pennsylvania Polka" begs me to buy limited-edition We Will Never Forget clocks of the Golden Triangle beneath a waving American Flag, porcelain Hummel Steelers babies or commemorative Barbie Pittsburgh Girls, in Penguins jerseys or miniskirts made from Terrible Towels. We're seated in a wooden bench beneath a picture of Franco and the Immaculate Reception. The waitress asks, "What're yinz havin'?" Gavril likes hops but I go for a chocolate stout.

"So, who's this Albion?" he asks.

"I'm working for a man named Waverly," I tell him. "Private work. Albion's his daughter. I'm searching for her in the Archive. I have iLux now—"

"How'd you come across that?"

"A perk," I tell him. "You ever heard of a company called Focal Networks?"

"Of course I have," he says. "Wait, is that the Waverly you're working for? Theodore Waverly?"

"Where have you heard of him?"

"Jesus fuck, Dom, he practically invented Adware. He invented how we use Adware, at any rate. NPR talks about him. That Focal Networks is a think tank for the Republican Party. They write policy for Meecham—"

"Shit—"

"Shit's right, cousin. Big shit—"

"I'm not involved in any of that," I tell him. "Like I told you earlier, I'm just tracking Albion—"

"That's an odd name," he says. "Beautiful, but odd—"

"She's been erased from the City-Archive. I checked the Pittsburgh Project, the Department of Labor and Statistics, cached Google and Facebook pages, Twitter, LinkedIn, and ran wildcard and hashtag searches using InfoQuest and Three Rivers Net. Nothing. E-mails to the librarians at the Map Institute and the Steel City Memorials here and Johnstown and a formal letter to the City of Pittsburgh Citizen and Corporation hard Archive in Virginia—"

Our cheesesteaks arrive and Gavril asks why a man like Theodore Waverly would want me for the job—he wonders why out of so many programmers and researchers in the workforce, a man as rich as Waverly would bother to pull me out of a rehabilitation program to handle something like this.

"What's that supposed to mean?" I ask him.

"Dominic, don't take it the wrong way—it's a real question," he says. "Theodore Waverly could hire Kucenic's entire firm, if he wanted to. He could probably call in a favor from the NSA, you know? But he chose you, you of all people, my cousin Domi. It doesn't make any sense—"

"He talked with Kucenic, but Kucenic told him that I was the best researcher," I tell him. "Cream rises to the top. Now, listen to this: when I first started searching for Albion, I ran a Facecrawler on her picture, and the Facecrawler yields almost thirty thousand hits—but they're all hits with less than two percent probability, so I figure it's a wash—"

"Cream rises to the top? Bullshit rises—"

"Listen: I scanned through the results, and sure enough, Facecrawler found redheads, that's all—not a single definite match for Albion. Well, one of the hits hovered around a seven percent probability, so I checked it out. It was this fuzzy, dim image captured in a dark corner of this place in Pittsburgh called the ModernFormations Gallery, at a poetry reading. The face I was looking for was totally obscured, so I couldn't tell whether or not it was Albion, but, Gav, I was one of the readers that night. I was onstage, waiting my turn to read. I saw myself—"

"Oh, that's creepy—"

"I was wearing a shirt and tie—I was skinny back then. I looked like I was twelve years old—"

Gavril pays—he's prearranged the bill so I didn't even have a chance to split with him. He promises he'll poke around about that picture of Albion I showed him, see if he can find anything about her modeling or fashion work, but he's doubtful. He offers to let me keep the printbook, but once we're back at his place I take a few minutes to look at and scan every page, saving a digital file. Gav wants me to stay for drinks, but I tell him I'll be working, that I won't be around for a while.

Sixteen-hour immersion shifts, eight hours off—to piss, shit, sleep, shower, eat, drink and ping Gav or Timothy so someone knows I'm still alive. General Tso's takeout and two liters of Pepsi. Instant oatmeal for breakfast and lunch. Sleeping fitfully for three or four hours before waking up to immerse again. My clearest lead to Albion is through Peyton Hannover, so I try to re-create her life, find where else she intersects with Albion. I've tracked Peyton to when she lived in her previous apartment, at the Cork Factory Lofts on Railroad Street, when her ink sleeve was colorless, only the beginnings of an intricately lined floral pattern, and even before that, to her freshman year at Chatham before she had tattoos at all, when she lived in the dorms and her hair was cut short, a boy's cut she wore parted slick like T. S. Eliot. I follow her. Peyton bikes mornings, strapping on a pink helmet she keeps in a Schneider's Dairy crate belted to the back of her seat like a basket. She keeps to main streets as she rides so she's re-created in the mapping—security camera to security camera, traffic cams, dashboard cams, cams in everyone's retinas who noticed the blonde as she passed. Railroad Street to Smallman through the Strip District to Lawrenceville. I follow. Faces in passing cars are only blurs—petals on a wet, black bough—impressions inadvertently captured in Peyton's background and sculpted here as part of the environment. These faces unnerve me. Faceless. I feel like they try to catch my attention. I feel like they want me to notice them, to notice them specifically, to turn my attention from Peyton and fill in their features with some streak of memory, but there's nothing to remember about them, no details or memories I have that can flesh them out. I've never known these faces and they pass away in the peripherals.

Before Peyton accrues successes with her modeling, she works as a waitress at Coca Café. She wears skinny black jeans and tight T-shirts screen-printed with the names of retro bands—Centipede Eest, Host Skull, Lovebettie, Anti-Flag. She serves French toast with lemon sauce, mixing lattes behind the counter, busing dishes between orders. I watch her—she slides gracefully through narrow gaps between tables. Theresa and I used to come here for brunch on Sunday mornings, and iLux coaxes my wife from my memories, cozy in the back booth with coffee, sharing warm banana bread, trading sections of the *Post-Gazette.*

"I don't think I've told you about my new friend at the Conservatory," Theresa tells me. "Mind if I have the last of this?"

"No, go ahead—"

"So good," she says, spreading wild berry cream cheese on the heel end of the banana bread.

"Your friend . . . ?"

"Right, so after the Flowers of Thailand workshop, this guy comes up to me—probably in his forties, I'd guess. I'd noticed him from the tour—sweatshirt all disheveled, these giant holes in his jeans. He hangs around until everyone else is gone and asks me if we grow weed in the greenhouse—"

"Was he serious? You're kidding me—"

"He tells me he'd be happy to show me better growing methods than the ones we're currently using. So I told him that we don't grow weed, but he might want to get in touch with the Pittsburgh Cannabis Society. He says, 'What's cannabis?' I tell him, 'Cannabis' is another name for weed. You know what he told me?"

"Are you making this up?"

"He says, 'Damn! You mean they smoke weed *and* eat people?'"

Theresa and I lingered over coffee these mornings—she was working on a book, I remember, combining her dissertation with a travelogue she'd kept about time she'd spent in Thailand when she was in graduate school, about ecology, farming and local cuisine. Or she'd polish up her grant proposals or press releases about the community gardens she'd created—she wanted to turn her work into her own nonprofit someday, to establish sustainable urban farming practices in the neighborhoods.

"Do you mind if we take a walk?" she asks halfway through brunch, looking up from what she'd been writing. She dresses up to come here—almost equestrian this morning, a white blouse and beige slacks tucked into knee-high boots of reddish leather. The iLux is flawless loading around my memories, loading the underside of Theresa's hair like the color of wet sand and the top the color of straw in sunlight.

"I'd love to take a walk," I tell her.

We saunter down Penn, Lawrenceville an eclectic mix of boutiques and cafés before the end, tree-lined boulevards and renovated townhomes. The trees are in bloom. We hold hands, looking through shop windows, swinging into boutiques. Sugar, Figleaf, Pavement, Pageboy. In Pageboy, Theresa skims through the racks, scoping for vintage. At the time, I was slightly bored waiting while Theresa looked at clothes—I'd lean against the wall reading something I'd brought along with me, but now I'm sick at myself for having wasted those moments—

A billboard mars the early afternoon—a King of Kings anti-abortion image of a fetus, a burned and bloody coil. The billboard had been there for years, long enough that the image had faded. "Poor taste," Theresa used to say, but the image was intolerable after she lost our child, who wasn't yet our child, I remind myself. Cramping in the restrooms of Heinz Field, confused, wondering if this was early labor until she saw blood in the toilet water, returning to our mustard-yellow seats weeping, wanting to stay at the game, to stay for the fourth quarter for my sake because the tickets were expensive and hard to get and I'd always wanted to see a game, pleading with me to stay in our knit hats and waving towels, but hysterical. "What's wrong? Tell me what's wrong." This had been our first try. Allegheny General, the ER overflowing with patients that night. We waited hours for follow-up tests once the doctors explained what had happened. I lay with her in the hospital bed, eventually too worn and shocked numb to cry, holding each other while the end of the game we'd left played itself out on the television bolted to the ceiling, telling each other that we'd try again, we'd try.

"Intolerable," Theresa says about the billboard. She's shaken and apologizing to me for ruining our morning by becoming upset, telling me that it's silly to feel this way, but the billboard's bothering her, that it suddenly got to her, that fetus she'd seen dozens of times before. I tell her it's all right, I tell her that they shouldn't have billboards like that in the city, that it's all right to cry, it's all right—I told her that at the time, comforting her or trying to, but I want to tell her what I know now, that in a few years we will try again, that it will be a surprise to us both, that she's going to tell me over dinner someday that we're having a daughter, but I can't finish the thought because I know her second pregnancy will end in light. We duck into Pavement so she can find a restroom and dry her eyes. Bamboo hardwood floors, folded cotton shirts on tables, sparse racks of sundresses. Facecrawler alerts me—the default tone that something I've searched is nearby—and the memory fades. I follow the alert to the boutique's front door, the window collaged with handbills and posters for Mac Miller and Kellee Maize, Chinese language tutorials, Schoolhouse Yoga classes and glossies for the local fashion lines they carry here: Penny Lane, Zeto, Raven + Honeybear. It's the Raven + Honeybear ad that Facecrawler's hit, Peyton Hannover modeling as a prep school sexpot in a leather-cushioned library. She's reaching for a book on a high shelf, exposing the long white parallels of her thighs between her powder-blue plaid skirt and powder-blue argyle knee-highs. In cursive: *Just a little higher.*

A quick search: Raven + Honeybear's referenced on a number of archived sites and listed on the Pittsburgh Business Registry as a fashion line, but the company's cached home page is corrupted and every direct link's been fouled. Filtering the Facecrawler to *image plus text* finds other Raven + Honeybear handbills posted on boutique tackboards, almost all featuring Peyton, waves of white-gold hair and eyes so blue they're like a doll's glass eyes. The line specializes in an aesthetic of polo matches, collegiate tenures, private girls' schools and gentlemen farming; young women sipping tea at the Frick or playing croquet, Peyton in tweed slacks and plaids, tailored blouses and neckties, men's clothes if such care wasn't taken to flaunt the model's figure.

I've found Peyton's picture in other archived ad campaigns and fashion editorials, spreads for *Maniac* magazine and *Whirl*, even a few spots for American Eagle but she's too ethereal to fully meld with the AE girl-next-door vibe. This Raven + Honeybear campaign feels different somehow, Peyton's other modeling work capitalizing on her surface look, depicting her almost as an ice goddess or as unapproachably beautiful, but the Raven + Honeybear feel much more homemade, like I'm looking at a set of personal photographs rather than a slickly produced ad campaign. The images remind me of the style of the first image of Albion I'd seen. Thinking of Peyton and Zhou together in the elevator, every gesture of Zhou a forgery of a gesture of Albion, thinking of Peyton and Albion in the apartment dying fabric, imagining Albion taking these pictures of Peyton, dressing her up in plaid skirts and asking her to pose.

The Archive lists Peyton Hannover as arriving in Pittsburgh from a place called Darwin, Minnesota—population 308. Peyton's parents are still alive in retirement in Florida. They've set up a VR memorial at remembrance.pit—Peyton their youngest daughter of five, but I've only spent a few minutes with her childhood pictures displayed at the memorial, videos of her first Halloween, pictures of a knockout at prom too perfect for the meathead kid in a tux who grapples with her corsage. I consider contacting her parents, to ask if Peyton ever mentioned a woman named Albion, but I'm too closely acquainted with loss to bother whatever memories they've let heal over. Leave well enough alone.

Peyton's first appearance in the Archive is as a freshman at Chatham University. Cutoff jean shorts and steel-toed boots, a Chatham hoodie. She's at the 61C Café, outside on the patio surrounded by blooming sunflowers, reading a Penguin Classics edition of *Jane Eyre*, oblivious to the attention her legs attract when middle-aged men sit with their coffee at nearby tables. When she speaks, you hear Minnesota in her voice. An eighteen-year-old shaking off small-town dust in what must have seemed like a big city. I track her: parties most weekends, girls on ratty couches sipping from red Solo cups, basements smoky and crowded with scruffy men holding cans of Pabst Blue Ribbon. Peyton's like an orchid in a vegetable patch, smoking cigarettes in holders, occasionally sporting a monocle, aggressively flirting up other girls who don't seem to quite know what to do with her. She led a wild life at first, destructive—sloppy drunk and sick at parties, passed out by the early morning, striking out with straight girls so letting random guys take her to bed. She laughs everything off—but spends most of her time alone, friendless until she gathers with people to party.

Tracking her life, I find Peyton in Schenley Plaza, at a WYEP summer music festival. She's with a group of her acquaintances, sharing a blanket spread on the lawn. Peyton's begun to grow her hair out by now, no longer the T. S. Eliot slick but a wavy blonde—it makes her look younger, somehow. She's also started the tattoo that will eventually sleeve her arm, just a few flowers, lilies and roses, near her shoulder. We've gathered together at the concert, too, other survivors. I see their faces in the crowd—somehow lighter than the others. We notice one another and sometimes smile, but more often than not we simply ignore each other, knowing that the more we acknowledge one another, the more we ruin the illusion that these summer nights might never have ended. I take off my shoes and feel the grass on my feet. Donora's headlining and Peyton's enjoying herself, laughing, but by the time moths swarm the park lights, she's moved away from her friends. I follow her and find Albion sitting alone on one of the benches edging the park. Her hair's tucked beneath a knit beret. She wears a linen skirt and a suede jacket. She's older than Peyton by a few years, but they're comfortable together. Peyton slips her arm beneath Albion's suede coat, and the intimacy—like Peyton's fingers touching Zhou's in the elevator—flusters me, races in my blood. They're ignoring the concert, ignoring Peyton's friends. By the time the concert ends I've seen the two women kiss, a short kiss but unmistakable that they're lovers, discreet, but nevertheless drawing attention from the men around them, men with their families, playing with their children in the lawn but unable to keep their eyes away from two women kissing. Peyton and Albion leave together and I try to follow, but the footage runs out and I'm looped back into the crowd.

1, 19—

I've only seen two traces of Albion, once dying fabric in Peyton's apartment, once kissing Peyton in the park. Hours might pass without thinking of Albion, but then the thought of her overwhelms me, at first just a recollection of what I'd seen but growing into a compulsive urge to see again, and again, the pull stronger than any drug I've used—I load and reload those traces of Albion and watch her, memorizing everything about her, every detail, perfect, so perfect. I watch until my mind's like a worn rag and my eyes so strained they feel like they're still open even when they're closed. The rest of Albion's life is a hole I'm filling in by the edges, like I'm figuring out the shape of an object by studying the shadow it casts. Obsessive about the research—my life's become Albion. I reload the stream of Albion kissing Peyton in the park—

Never stray far from Peyton, because Peyton leads me to Albion—as Peyton reads Camille Paglia at an outdoor table at Panera, yoga classes at the Athletic and Fitness Center, cutting across Chatham's campus to a class on Blake and British Symbolism. Occasionally, I find Peyton with Zhou and know that Albion's been replaced in these moments—Zhou's a forgery, so when I come across her in the Archive, I study her, trying to understand the original: Peyton's quicker with a laugh than Zhou, Zhou much more serious, sober. At the Carnegie Museum of Art, Zhou stands back to study paintings, she'll point something out to Peyton, give a quick rundown of the artist's life or talk about materials. Zhou is Albion, I remind myself. They stand in front of a John Currin painting of two nude women, their bodies in illusory angles, awkwardly posed. Zhou's mentioning that Currin spent time in Pittsburgh and Peyton listens but she mugs a bit, she poses like the women in the painting. She causes a scene until Zhou laughs along with her. Peyton's in complete control of her effect on men—Zhou's much more reticent, almost like she wishes for invisibility. Peyton draws her out, forces Zhou to pose along with her, gets one of the security guards to snap their picture in front of the painting.

I find an early reference to Raven + Honeybear as a participant in a couture show, a joint fund-raiser for Gwen's Girls and Dress for Success Pittsburgh. The models are listed, "Peyton" by first name only. The Gwen's Girls website is still cached, with a dozen untagged pictures of the fund-raiser on their Pinterest board, some showing Albion. If anything, Albion outstrips the models, her hair in crimson cascades, wearing a tweed three-piece suit I'm assuming is of her own design. Albion's in the background of another image, suit jacket unbuttoned, hands in pockets, casually leaning against a column watching the catwalk—reserved, just as I've come to know her through Zhou. There's a series of pictures showing designers' studios—they're all untagged, but I recognize Albion's tweed and plaid designs in one of the images, the successive picture an exterior of a brick building that looks a lot like a Lawrenceville row house storefront. I run a Facecrawler match on the building and, sure enough, it pins a location: just off Butler Street in Lawrenceville, on 37th, but the location tag's been corrupted. Someone's been tampering with this place.

I follow Peyton as she leaves her shift at Coca Café and walks the few blocks to 37th—scant footage as she makes her way down side streets from Butler, but I pick her up again at the row house, a decrepit building bordered by a gravel lot, wild brush and weeds delineating one property from the next. Peyton must have been filming this footage herself—a POV shot taken with retinal cams as she types the key code and enters. The interior's been redone—hardwood laminate flooring, an office and showroom on the first floor, decorated by a bird and bear mural, Raven + Honeybear in gothic script. This is Albion's studio. The workroom's upstairs, the second floor a loft-style space with picture windows and exposed ceiling beams. I find Zhou sitting at a sewing machine, working a pair of trousers. She smiles as Peyton enters the room.

"This is what you'll be wearing," she says.

Sifting through footage of the studio—there isn't much, most days either already deleted or simply not filmed. I search the Archive's timeline and find random hours of Zhou working at a sewing machine, or working with clothes pinned on cloth dummies, but finally come across an untagged series of events that haven't been tampered with. Rather than Zhou, I find Albion documenting the preparation for a show, maybe with a flip cam on a tripod. She wears a sweatshirt and yoga pants, a Steelers knit hat. The footage is time-stamped September twenty-ninth before the end, at nearly three in the morning—Albion marks fabric before she sews. Peyton stands on a pedestal wearing a pink floor-length skirt like a spill of roses. Her breasts are uncovered, her corset top laid out on the worktable. An unusually heavy rainfall freezes into soft flakes that drift down outside the studio windows. I remember this snow, actually, waking up startled to see everything coated in thick, wet white. Three inches overnight. I remember Theresa and I walked to breakfast at Crêpes Parisiennes that morning, wondering if the snowfall was a fluke or an early start to winter. It would warm up again, though—by later that afternoon, in fact, the weather warmed and the snow melted. We'd have less than ten more days together. But tonight, while Theresa and I would have been sleeping as the rain froze and the snow dropped softly, Peyton stands on a pedestal bathed in the glare of studio lights while Albion brings her the corset.

Looking out the window at the snow, I notice a man standing outside in the lot—he's wearing a wool overcoat, black or charcoal gray. His hair is white. He's watching me as I watch him, snowfall accumulating on his shoulders and the top of his head, but it's too dark to see his face. When I turn back to the two women, Albion has been replaced by Zhou. Outside, the man has disappeared—footprints in the snow lead to the building. He's coming. I try to disengage from the City, but the system's locked. I'm paralyzed. My Adware net security's flashing red with warnings, alerting me to impending system failures but I can't escape.

The studio door opens and he enters, shaking snow from his shoes and removing his coat.

"Who are you?" I ask.

"I'm Legion," he says. I recognize him, the man in the wingback chair I'd seen in Albion's apartment who wore a Mook T-shirt. I should be able to push my way past, but he has me in his complete control—I can't move.

"Dominic, isn't it?" he says. "John Dominic Blaxton, isn't that right?"

"Are you working for Waverly?"

Mook smiles.

"I figured you were another of Mr. Waverly's junkies," he says. "Disappointing—"

"Who are you?"

"Who are you?" he says. "John Dominic Blaxton, of 5437 Ellsworth Avenue, Pittsburgh, Pennsylvania. Ph.D. candidate in Literary and Visual Theory at Carnegie Mellon University and the University of Virginia, recently an Archival Assistant for the Kucenic Group. Drug abuse problems. Constant rewiring for Adware upgrades. A dull life, but you were in love. You spend an awful lot of time immersing to visit a woman named Theresa Marie Blaxton. Your wife—"

"Don't say her name. You don't ever say her name—"

"I'm correct, aren't I? You log more hours reliving the same bits of memory than anyone I think I've ever had the pleasure to know. Most people visit the Archive for quick visits, to relive some happiness or indulge in a past normalcy or visit loved ones on birthdays or the anniversaries of their deaths. Most people like the convenience of paying their respects once or twice a year, but you're different. This is an obsession you have. Over and over again, you have dinner with your wife at the Spice Island Tea House so you can hear her announce her second pregnancy, what a shame about the first—"

"Don't you ever fucking talk about her," I scream but my voice mutes when Mook whispers, "quiet."

"I watched your wife die the other day because I was curious about her," he says, "curious about what, exactly, you saw in her—have you ever watched your wife die? What was she, eight months pregnant? Nine? She was in Shadyside, window-shopping—all those cameras in Shadyside, her death is very well reconstructed. You don't visit her death often, though, do you? Too painful, I assume?

There's a window of T-shirts at a store called Kards Unlimited. Obscene, dumb T-shirts. Your wife was reading obscene T-shirts when she died. I wonder if the baby kicked when the bomb went off. I wonder if it knew it would never be born. Mr. Blaxton, what was it? Boy or girl?"

He allows me to move and scream and so I shake him, but touching him is like touching a sack of sand—he's heavy, too heavy to be real and I realize he's not real, we're not real, of course we're not here, there is no here.

"Your child would have been a girl," says Mook. "I know about you. You're easy to track. Your drug habits, your stints in and out of hospitals, therapy. All that paperwork. Your death is very well documented, just like your wife's—only your death is much slower and is dragging out over years. You're a simple man, Mr. Blaxton. No mysteries to you. That very simplicity is why I'm giving you a second chance that I might not usually give—"

I'm too bewildered by what's happening to quite understand his threat. I try to ping his socials, to find out his name, but his profile display is nothing more than a grinning pig's head with a lolling tongue that repeatedly speaks the word *Mook* in a Porky Pig singsong.

"Are you the one who's deleting her?" I ask.

"I think I understand your motivation here," he says. "You're acting here because you've had some trouble with the legal system and you're looking for a clean record, some gainful employment. On top of that, you're emotionally compromised because of this business with your wife. I pity you, actually. I'm not unfair, Dominic, but I have an agreement in place that I need to honor above all my other considerations. Nevertheless, I think we can come to an understanding. Are you listening?"

"Yes," I tell him.

"Quit looking for this woman you know as Albion. Stop immediately. Find other ways to make a living. Terminate your employment with Waverly, let this go. Otherwise, I'll take action against you—"

"What action?"

"Look at this young woman—Peyton Hannover, this bright young thing," he says, guiding my attention to Peyton as she lifts her hair for Zhou to fit her for the corset top of the gown. In an instant, Peyton's image corrupts and her body scrambles, her mouth ruptures outward, her teeth and gums splayed in flowering wet rows that sink through her neck to her chest, her face sinks, nipple-eyed, her body hunches, patches of blonde hair sprout in tufts, her genitals open and spill like water to the floor. A layer of dissonance—a spoiled body. I try to withstand this, to look at Peyton, to prove Mook's threats are meaningless, but I can't endure. I flinch away.

Mook says, "Imagine your wife—"

"Oh God," I say, his words pounding me like a hammer striking meat. "Please don't do that. Please—"

"It's okay to look," he says, and when I look again, Peyton's been deleted, the space she occupied replaced by a smudge, like Vaseline swiped over the air.

"There's a program I have access to called the Reissner-Nordström worm—do you know what that is?"

"No—"

"It's a modified Facecrawler," he says. "In the time it takes your heart to beat, I can desecrate every memory, every instance of your wife in this City. I can corrupt your presence here so that not even your iLux can access the moments you cherish with your wife. I run the worm, and she's gone. Do you understand?"

"Yes," I tell him. "Yes. I understand—"

"Ask yourself: Is losing your wife a second time worth your loyalty to Waverly? I'm guessing not—"

"Why are you doing this?"

"You're not listening," he says. "If I perceive that you haven't let this matter with Albion drop we will take action against you. I will, Mr. Blaxton. Are we clear?"

"Yes," I tell him. "I'm through. Through—"

"I think you know your way out," he says.

Vertigo as I'm shoved from this location, the Archive a blur but re-forming—I'm in the parking lot, looking up to Albion's lit studio windows. The snow's sticking now, falling in soft flakes that crunch beneath my footfalls as I run, squalls kicking up that blow blinding veils of snow from the branches of pines. Home—home to Room 208, the Georgian. I take off my wet clothes in the foyer. I find her asleep and crawl into bed beside her. Theresa. I put my arm around her and press close, feeling the simulated warmth of her body, the simulated rise and fall of her chest, trying to hold her, to keep from losing what I've already lost.

2, 1—

Whenever you visit this place, there are others here—too many survivors in mourning to get a sense of what we actually used to be like here. Katz Plaza, it used to be called—centered by a Louise Bourgeois fountain and benches shaped like laconic, watchful eyes. We come here to view the end. We stand like we're in a gallery, ringing the plaza. We know it will happen at thirty-seven past the hour, and as the time nears we watch for him—there, the truck pulling up on 7th, the man climbing down from the cab holding a steel suitcase. Some of us begin to cry, but most of us have seen this before, many times before. We can't stop him, we can't rewrite history even as we pass through it, so we simply watch: the man kneeling in the center of the plaza, raising his arms in some sort of prayer. Some of us think we hear the name Allah. We watch the man unlatch his suitcase. The man pauses, and we wonder, millions of us have wondered if in that pause he was reconsidering, if he might have turned back. We watch as the man opens the suitcase. Light—

She loved walking here. On Walnut Street, in Shadyside. She loved window-shopping here—the Apple Store, Williams-Sonoma, Kawaii, e.b. Pepper—but her favorite place was an upscale general store called Kards Unlimited. Theresa died there—wearing blue jeans tucked into riding boots, an oatmeal-colored cardigan draped over her pregnant belly. I've stood with her outside of Kards Unlimited's picture window as she sipped an iced mocha from Starbucks, looking at the T-shirts on display. *My Other Ride Has a Flux Capacitor. Llamacorn. The Folding Chair Parking Authority. A Clockwork Orange.* I've watched her many times looking at these shirts, and have come to believe that at the end, at the very moment the world ended for her, she was reading a Mr. Rogers T-shirt, *It's a Neighborly Day in the Beautywood.* The sky burns. Cameras record. Theresa squints. Her hair catches fire at the tips, then flashes like a diadem across her head. She dies too quickly, I believe, to have felt any pain. I'd always assumed that our child simply perished in the womb, but now Mook's taunt thorns in my mind, and as I watch Theresa cocooned in fire, I imagine that our child may have known, may have kicked and squirmed as her mother died around her, may have understood and suffered.

Gossip heads and tabloids speculate on who she'll wear, but Gavril's already tipped me off that President Meecham's tapped Alexander Porta this year, the Natalia Valevskaya protégé, and that tonight's executions will feature at least seven full costume changes to coincide with the fall couture shows. I've scanned the League of Women Voters app—the U.S. Communist Party, the Greens, the Teas, the Army of God and the Mid-Atlantic Socialists aren't even participating—show trials, they call them, a spectacle. Nine men will be executed tonight, federal criminals: alleged jihadists, traitors, multistate spree killers. I've accepted Timothy's offer for a ride to Waverly's for his viewing party. Standing in the rain, the streams exceptionally vivid in the overcast light—rioters in San Francisco are already burning city blocks in Hunters Point, rioters in Chicago are already burning police cars in Millennium Park. Timothy pulls up in the Fiat and tells me to get in before I catch pneumonia.

Timothy listens to light jazz, stuff like the Fontainebleau Quartet and Slim Vogodross. He asks how I've been and I tell him I've been busy searching for Albion, but I don't mention Mook, nothing of the threat against my wife. I'm planning to tell Waverly myself, when we meet about his daughter—I'm planning to collect what I'm owed and quit. Timothy merges onto the Beltway and pushes the Fiat, weaving through congestion at eighty, eighty-five miles an hour until he takes an exit about forty-five minutes outside DC.

Virginia. An hour-and-a-half drive, Timothy exits the interstate and once off main roads, we drive through woods. Late afternoon, but the night falls heavy and gathers around the slim black trunks of trees. I'm tired, I haven't shaved in days and my scruff's grown thick down my neck, but it feels nice, like I'm half hidden and soft. The road narrows, begins to climb. Timothy's dressed in a tuxedo and I'm nervous I'll be conspicuously schlubby at the party—I wore what I thought would blend in, charcoal slacks and a flannel shirt, tucked in. A tweed jacket I've had for years. Timothy's headlights illuminate the trees. He's taking the turns close, driving breakneck through the rain. His windshield's lit with night vision augments and I watch the pale green shapes of deer clustered at the edges of the woods, dozens if not hundreds of them. A miserable icy slush congeals on the windshield before the wipers push it away—if any of those deer bolt, I'll die. I'd hit a deer once, years ago, and pulled over to the side of the road. Mine had been a doe, I'm fairly certain—it seemed small when I was near, but I don't know how to tell much about deer. The middle of the night, in Westmoreland County. The deer moaned and whined—bleating, I guess you'd call it. I'd seen movies where calm men broke the neck or killed dying animals with one shot to ease their suffering, but I had no gun and I couldn't bring myself to kill it, let alone touch it. The sight of my shoe prints in its blood froze me. I withdrew a pace and simply watched the doe die. When she was silent I said a prayer over her body and left. What else could I have done? My windshield was cracked and buckled inward where the deer's spine must have ricocheted from me.

"He lives far," I say.

"But it's a nice drive," says Timothy, "and Waverly doesn't commute much. Every so often he has business in the city—"

Timothy slows for a private drive—a strip of pavement winding through a thicket of pines, footlights illuminating the drive like a runway. The drive must be heated, I suppose—slush sticks to the boughs of pines and the ground on either side, but melts into a wet shimmer on the drive.

The pines fall away like a robe to reveal Waverly's house—built on a bluff overlooking a shallow valley. The house itself looks like a haphazard stack of frosted glass cubes, illuminated. Valet parking's offered in the turnabout, but Timothy follows the driveway as it dips and curves around the far end of the house. We plunge into an underground garage large enough to accommodate twenty cars, at least.

"Usually this place is empty," says Timothy.

Timothy circles once before settling for a rear space. His Fiat rattles when he cuts the engine, the sound almost offensive among the silent Maseratis, Porsches and Ferraris filling out the other spaces. A uniformed attendant wipes the slush from Timothy's car with a white towel, never minding that the Fiat's a piece of shit. Timothy's quieter than usual—nervous, maybe.

"Don't like parties?" I ask him.

"Not much," he says.

An elevator with a parquet floor lifts us into the glass foyer. The doors slide apart and we're washed in gold light—the interior of Waverly's house is like a dream of art deco, the guests in slim-cut tuxes and flapper-style gowns shimmering like precious coins. Waverly's there to greet us—he's already flushed pinkish with drink.

"Have you fallen in love with her yet?" he says as he shakes my hand.

"I'm sorry?" I ask.

"Have you fallen in love with Albion?" he says, breath sour with alcohol. "You can't spend time with her and not fall in love, apparently—"

"Not now," says Timothy.

"I haven't," I try to say, but Timothy's taken Waverly's arm and nudges him away from me, separating our conversation.

"Drinks are in the blue room," says Waverly as we part. "We'll stream the executions in the Caraway room, I think—"

A hundred or so on the guest list, it looks like, and I'm as exposed in my flannel as I feared I would be. Pathetically underdressed. Timothy's already abandoned me, disappeared somewhere. Adware profiles hover over each guest, names I recognize from the streams, Elric Broadbent, a presidential adviser, and Michelle Frawley, from Arizona, host of the *God and Guns* stream. Actresses I recognize from Disney sitcoms and reality-stream girls, Donna from *Hello Pussy*, season 3, and the guy from *Truth or Dare*. I ping Gav to see if he recognizes anyone here and he pings that I should watch where I step and be sure to clean my shoes when I leave. Everyone's wearing those Meecham pins that were popular following Pittsburgh, her profile portrait like a cameo and twin crimson ribbons in the shape of a heart. A bit overwhelming, I suppose, but nothing I haven't seen before—I've been the wallflower at celebrity-studded parties Gavril's dragged me to, nothing terribly novel about gawking at recognizable faces. Zelda Kuhn, host of *Buy, Fuck, Sell* is talking with the Republican whip from Texas. Christ, there's a lot of power gathered here—

I drift to the blue room for a drink, the blue room easy enough to find—a dining hall with expansive walls papered in royal blue damask. I pluck sushi from a passing tray—the waitresses look like they've been bused in from a modeling agency rather than a catering company, as much a decoration here as the Louis XIV chairs and oversize landscapes in gilt frames. The dining room table's been converted into a bar and a waiter pours me a finger of brandy. I swallow quickly, cutting the edge off my anxiety. He pours another. Waverly's not playing the Gatsby tonight—no melancholia for his lost wife and daughter—he's practically giddy with his guests, if anything, glad-handing and laughing, already a bit sloppy with drink. Difficult not to notice when he corners one of the waitresses in a dim hallway and kisses her hard enough to force her head against the wall, massaging her breasts through the front of her uniform while she holds a tray of champagne flutes, trying to keep them from spilling.

One of the guests watches me—she's across the room, leaning against the blue damask, her silk gown the color of cream, her hair dyed a rich Albion-shade of crimson. She sends gentle pings my way. Vaguely familiar, but her profile's blanked and I can't quite place her. I'm meant to notice her—I feel she's like an invitation, if I want her, but I can't help but feel repelled by the gag. She's meant to resemble Albion with that red hair—did Waverly do this? Timothy? She knows I've noticed her. She accepts a drink from a passing waitress. She leaves the blue room and I'm invited to follow, but I hesitate. I finish off my brandy and go for a refill. The last glance I catch of her is so similar to Albion I'm convincing myself there's a glitch in the Adware, that maybe there is no woman here, that maybe I've spent too much time studying Albion and now I'm hallucinating her.

I leave the blue room and find her—she leads me down a frosted glass hallway lined with black statues of nude women on white pedestals. Another hall—I've lost her somewhere in this maze of rooms, the design eighteenth century in style, stuffy despite the sleek modernity of the architecture. Framed photographs are arranged on a decorative mantel—many are of Waverly as a young man, his hair a dark sweep, his eyes the same color as the sea behind him. Most of these pictures were taken on the bow of a sailboat called, of all things, *The Daughter of Albion*. I can't quite place the reference—Housman? Tennyson? Scroll through my e-library and search the *Norton Anthology*—find the poem: *Blake, William. Visions of the Daughters of Albion.* A few photographs show a woman, Waverly's wife, I assume but can't be sure. She's younger than Waverly, but not by much—handsome rather than beautiful, with a square jaw and chestnut-colored curls. She appears only twice in these pictures, glancing at the camera but never smiling. There aren't pictures of his children here, no images of the two sons I found listed in the census and none of his daughter. I roam through to another room and find the woman I was following sipping a drink lounging on a settee.

"Forget me already?"

Hearing her voice—Twiggy. "I didn't recognize you, not with the hair color," I tell her. "Twiggy, isn't it? Gavril's friend, right?"

"That Twiggy's just a stage name," she says.

"Your valentine landed me in a heap of trouble. It was heroin, for Christ's sake. A felony charge. I lost my job. You should have warned me what it was—"

"What's that you're drinking?"

"I don't even know anymore," I tell her. "Brandy, I think—"

She raises her glass to me. "Kentucky bourbon for me, straight. Cheers, Gavril's cousin. Life's on the up-and-up and I want someone to celebrate with. Come over here and sit by me—"

I take the far edge of the couch and she smiles at my hesitancy, extending her feet so her toes touch my slacks.

"What happened to the American Apparel sponsorship?" I ask. "There aren't commercials blaring from you."

"That's Mr. Waverly," she says. "He pays for commercial-free living. What are you doing here, anyway? I wouldn't have taken you for a big baller. Shopping for birds, like everyone else? You look like shit, by the way—"

"I think it's a mistake that I'm here at all," I tell her. "I came with a friend, I guess to stream the federal executions. I usually stream this thing with Gavril, because it kicks off Fashion Week—"

"Executions? You think that's why they're all here?"

"Why else would they be here?"

"Pussy," she says.

"Christ," I tell her, and finish off my brandy.

"I love how bashful you are," she says. "Look, you're blushing—"

"It's just the drink—"

"I won't need American Apparel soon, anyway," she says. "I'm having a series of brilliant fucking breaks that's lighting up my career. You ever have a run of luck like that? What is it Plath says? 'I took a deep breath and listened to the old brag of my heart. I am, I am, I am.' I fucking am, that's what my heart's screaming right now—"

"Someone hire you for another ad campaign?"

"I'm Theo Waverly's favorite girl," she says. "Steady work until I'm too fucking old, that's what that means. His company placed me with American Apparel, placed me with Gav. His request for the red hair, do you like it?"

"It resonates—"

"He has me up to an eighty-three percent click-through rate in the streams, that's pretty fucking unbelievable. Chanel and Dior already contacted his company about me. Everything's happening so fast—"

"I thought you were interested in poetry," I tell her. "You texted me a while ago, asking for poetry recommendations—"

"Just because a girl gets looked at doesn't mean she can't think," she says. "I finished that Adelmo Salomar book you recommended to me, by the way. I've never been much for Surrealism or automatic writing, all that stuff. I'm much more interested in the 'Confessional School,' all that Surrealism rings heavily of bullshit—"

"Salomar was writing about the Chilean Revolution—those poets had to invent ways to write around the censors, so they readapted Surrealism. 'Tonight I write the voice of a serpent devoured by a thousand doves.' Liberation Theology—"

"Well, anyway, poetry's immortal, but beauty's devoured by a thousand doves," she says. "Plenty of time to study Chilean Surrealism once no one wants me to wear their clothes anymore—"

"I'd actually like to read some of your poetry," I tell her, but before she answers, Waverly finds his way into the room with a bottle of wine.

"There you are," he says. "Timothy was afraid you'd gotten lost—"

"Not yet," I tell him.

"Why don't you run along back to the party," he tells Twiggy.

She swallows the rest of her bourbon and leaves the glass on the end table. "Makes me shivery," she says.

"Dominic, let's freshen up your glass back at the office," he suggests. "We'll finish up our business for the night so we can relax and enjoy ourselves—"

"Mr. Waverly, I actually have something I need to discuss with you about my employment—"

"Over drinks," he says. "Not here—"

Waverly's office is in a lower tier, through another frosted glass hallway, down a flight of stairs. A techie's paradise—VR cams, an editing suite, a Bride 3120 stack with a fifty-two-inch monitor on the desk, a rat's nest of ports and Adware jacks, sets of Adware like a tangle of mesh and a workbench with a soldering iron and motherboards and spools of wires and cable. One wall's covered with built-in shelves stacked with books, leather-bound classics—Hesse,

Blake—some Baudrillard, Schopenhauer, and yellowed paperback technical manuals, manila folders of printouts. A few framed photographs are propped up among the books—some shots of the Pittsburgh skyline, more of Waverly sailing on *The Daughter of Albion*, another of the woman I take for his wife, sitting on the lawn of the Frick near a rosebush in bloom. One of the photographs is a group portrait, Waverly with other suits—they're clustered around a young Meecham, a radiant blonde electric with her pageant-trained smile.

"You've met her?" I ask.

"I know Eleanor very well. Let's see—that must have been taken fifteen years ago or so," he says. "We were at a campaign event in Canton, Ohio—at the McKinley Grand Hotel. This was during her first presidential bid—"

"You were with her from the beginning of her career, then?"

"She was just a stray before I adopted her," he says. "I'm sorry, that sounds harsh, but Eleanor wasn't realizing her full potential. She was shallow, but we saw potential in her. She was articulate—we knew that from the pageants—intelligent when she wanted to be. Compassionate. Much of politics is simply manipulating broad symbols. Here was a beauty queen who grew up not far from Pittsburgh, conservative politically, a Christian. She was what the country needed at the time. Still does—"

"Timothy says you've figured out how people will behave, can manipulate the outcome of their free will—"

"I see no reason why Eleanor Meecham would ever lose an election," he says. "The ammendment passed with enthusiasm, and the votes are there—"

Another photograph. "I recognize this picture," I tell him, of a view of a house in Greenfield, in Pittsburgh, a part of the neighborhood that cuts toward the river called the Run. A clapboard

Victorian huddled with other houses in the shadow of the 376 overpass, worn out and unpainted, odd because of a whitewash cross and a Bible quote slathered in white paint on the broad side of the house: *Verily, verily, I say unto thee, Except a man be born again, he cannot see the Kingdom of God.* "We used to call this the Christ House—"

Waverly sits at his desk, tinkering with wires that have been pulled from a miniature motherboard—in his slumped posture, I think I see what he may have looked like as a young boy, lonely, I'm guessing, or maybe I'm reading too much into what an old man looks like when drunk.

"It's a church," says Waverly, "or was. You remember that house? I guess with the lettering, it doesn't surprise me it's somewhat infamous. Tact and lying low were never that congregation's strong suit. My wife's congregation. Speaking in tongues, that sort of thing. An old farmhouse. Most of the rooms were used as a Christian women's shelter. That was my great-great-grandfather's first house in America. My family came from nothing. My great-great-grandfather came to Pittsburgh for the mills, and eventually my father owned the mills—Pittsburgh, Birmingham. I bought back that house, and when Kitty asked for a place to start her shelter, a place for her congregation to meet, I signed it over."

"You don't have any pictures of your daughter—"

"No," he says. "I don't. I don't display any pictures of my children here. They all passed away in Pittsburgh, all three. I prefer to keep my past and present separate, private—"

I find another photograph of Meecham—taken shortly after Pittsburgh, during what must have been a tour of one of the FEMA camps in West Virginia they set up for people like me, the refugees and homeless.

"I was in a bar in Weirton when she was elected," I tell Waverly. "Did you take this picture of her at the FEMA camp?"

Waverly nods. All the liquor's gone to my head and I'm feeling loosely emotional, feeling my words sliding through my usual restraint: "I want you to know that we believed in her back then, when we had nothing left—I voted for her. She came from western Pennsylvania, she was one of us, and when the networks projected her as the winner, I remember I was crying like everyone else in that bar with me. I was—thinking, stupidly thinking, that her election would somehow bring everything back, that everything would turn out all right. She described the Kingdom of Heaven and told us that the dead were held in the palm of God's hand, all that bullshit—that they had found peace, telling us the world continues because the love of God continues—"

"I think those words were meant more for the rest of the nation, Dominic, people who hadn't gone through what we'd gone through, but who were still scared, who wanted comfort. I don't think the consolation was ever meant for us—"

"I need to talk with you about our arrangement, Mr. Waverly. There's just—"

"More money? We can make arrangements with my secretary. Timothy's informed me about the excellent work you've been doing—"

"There was a man who confronted me in the City-Archive. He threatened me. He threatened to take my wife from me if I still worked for you, and I—"

"Who?" asks Waverly. "What man? What's his name?"

"I don't know his name—he says it's Legion, so it might not be a man at all, it might be a collective—"

"That man's threats are meaningless. I've had others in the

Archive before you, Dominic, who've encountered this man. He's a paper tiger. If you can ID him, I'll pay you triple—"

"I can't risk losing her—"

"What are you saying, Dominic?"

"I appreciate what you've done for me," I tell him. "But I can't risk losing Theresa—I'll return to rehab, Mr. Waverly. I'll return the iLux—"

"I'm disappointed," he says. "Stay for the party, of course, and I'll still transfer what I owe you for the work you've done. I'm very disappointed. You, in fact—you were working out well for me—"

"There are plenty of people who do this kind of research," I tell him. "You could poach an actual librarian from the Archive with the money you're paying me. It doesn't have to be me—"

"Take a few days to think things over," he says. "I understand what you're telling me, that you feel threatened. I can protect you, of course—"

"You couldn't protect Albion—"

The guests gather in the Caraway room, the Caraway a basement-level game room with amphitheater-style seating. The heads of antlered stags decorate the walls. Streaming, the Caraway room's become a replica of the Capitol Building interior, live feeds of senators and the Joint Chiefs of Staff and the Supreme Court justices integrated seamlessly among us. The nine federal prisoners wear black robes that echo the robes of the justices. They're shackled and on their knees.

"Madam Speaker, the President of the United States—"

Meecham walks among us in her Porta gown like a Valkyrie, something shimmering. Some senators cheer—they actually cheer and kneel to her, reaching out to touch her as she passes in the aisle. A petal-pink lace blindfold matches her gown and gloves, an approximation of blind justice, I suppose. She pauses before each prisoner, studying each body like a consumer pricing meat. She offers each prisoner a chance to recant, to swear their allegiance to the United States—but no one speaks. I'm not on the political fringe, but even I can't stomach these executions—the pronouncements and prayer, the humiliation masked as honor, Meecham placing the black hood over each prisoner. They'll be presented one by one and she'll sign their execution warrants with a silver pen. They'll be shot point-blank in the temple. Their bodies will be draped in black flags. There will be torrents of pornography derived from these executions, there always has been—of classic Meecham sex vids spliced with death shots and the prisoners bleeding out. I don't want to be part of this, to hear her speech to the Senate, using the memory of the dead as justification for these public killings.

"Seen enough?"

Timothy's found me. His jaw's clenched like he's keeping himself from screaming through sheer physical effort. I've never seen him lose composure like this—his eyes bloodshot, brimming with tears. He smiles for my benefit but the effect is horrific, and for a brief, terrible moment I think he will lean over and bite me.

"I have—I have seen enough," I tell him. "I'm ready to go—"

The weather's turned. Timothy's venting his aggression, speeding the hairpin turns on the slick woodland roads, the Fiat's windshield augs flashing snow caution and marking his triple-digit speed in red. I lean back, swimming drunk and letting myself believe that it would be all right to die if Timothy skids on ice and we wrap around a snow-laden tree. Believing it would be for the best . . .

"Mr. Waverly tells me that you're quitting," he says, breaking what felt like an interminable silence. I'd been thinking of Albion and Twiggy and staring at the dark blur of pines.

"Your treatment schedule is under review," says Timothy. "I don't believe you're making the progress that I'd hoped you would. I may have made a mistake about you, and may have to recommend a more intense schedule to retrieve you—group therapy, work restrictions. I don't think it's out of the question that a stay at the psychiatric institute might be very good for your recovery. The Correctional Health Board may even find it necessary to intervene—"

"Don't do this," I tell him, understanding the threat implicit in what he's saying, knowing full well he could snare me in bureaucracy if he chooses to. "I'm not quitting my treatment, Dr. Reynolds, and I'm grateful for the special care you've given me, but I just can't continue with Waverly—"

"You have no idea how important your work is—"

"Why 'Albion'?" I ask him. "Mr. Waverly named his boat *The Daughter of Albion*. He named his own daughter Albion—"

Timothy says, "There's a common misconception about Christ—"

I don't like this turn, I don't want this conversation, but I don't know how to stop it, either—the snow's fallen heavy, the roads white except for a smear of tire tracks, but Timothy drives heedless. A real sense that I might die settles over me, a lightness of being, a surrendering of control. All I say is, "Slow down—"

"When I talk with people who are suffering," says Timothy, "they often tell me that they're comforted because Christ associated Himself with sinners. Prostitutes and taxmen. Drinkers. The thief who was crucified with Him. My patients often tell me that they're comforted because no matter how depraved their lives, no matter what damage they've done to themselves or others, Christ will still save them. *Christ will still save them.* They think they will somehow transcend the world, somehow continue sinning but find a spiritual perfection when the time comes because they believe their soul is pure so it doesn't matter if their body is corrupt. I tell them that Christ doesn't accept us as sinners. We might be sinners when Christ calls us, but *He doesn't accept us as sinners.* He demands that we abandon our lives to follow Him, to become like Him. That doesn't mean turning our backs to the world—it means just the opposite. He demanded the twelve abandon their lives in order so they might fully embrace the incarnation. He *demands* this of us—"

"It can be difficult to change—"

In the light of the windshield augs Timothy's eyes bore through me like I'm no longer a man in need of professional assistance or even personal grace, but more like I'm something already lost. I can't bear the weight of his eyes. I lose myself watching the snowfall. This must be what it feels like to be caught in the tide—wading deep water and feeling suddenly tugged, my feet pulled from beneath me. Whatever I'm involved in, I realize, goes beyond therapy and paperwork and work permits. Timothy drives faster in our silence. Headlights approach, at first just pinpricks of light but growing into the elaborate quad headlights of a rig—how easy it would be, I think, for Timothy to flick his wrist, to swallow us in those lights, and I wonder if he's contemplating how sometimes it feels easier to die than to live. I close my eyes, preparing.

2, 3—

BUY AMERICA! FUCK AMERICA! SELL AMERICA!

This is CNN.

A police checkpoint on Connecticut—queue with the others, waiting my turn through the scanner. *Nip-Slip for Ri-Ri with upskirt dessert*, traffic's backed up for blocks, *click here*, District cops leading drug sniffers car to car, random inspections, pulling some drivers out for the scan, bypassing others. *Raw feed of a New York woman pushed in front of subway, click here.* I ping Simka: *Checkpoint, I'll be late.* The usual paranoia that I'm carrying brown sugar or some other shit so I check my pockets, but I'm clean—I'm clean.

Simka pings: *I'll pick you up, stay by the checkpoint—*

The District cops wear opaque visors and train their weapons on us, but we're all complying, no need for intimidation here. There are three of them, enough to keep the peace. One of them waves me through the scanner archway. Yellow lights flip to green. I'm pulled aside—arms extended and feet spread shoulder width while another cop passes the wand over me. They perform an Adware sweep and my anti-malware catches, but I click *allow* to get this over with. Yellow lights flip to green. Stand against the brick wall while another cop snaps my photograph. My e-signature states that my identity matches the image. I'm free to go—

Simka picks me up in his Smart City Coupé. He shakes my hand and pats my shoulder.

"Cut your connection," he says.

There's a pock on the back of my head where the skull begins its slow eggshell slope toward my neck—an off switch. I push it and my Adware shuts down, the augmented reality blinking off, leaving me with a sudden, startling blurriness of vision without the retinal lenses.

"We can talk," I tell him.

Simka keeps to the right lane on the Beltway, his cruise control set a shade under the speed limit as other cars flash past.

"When you contacted me, you said you're having some problems with Dr. Reynolds?" he asks.

"You think he might listen through my Adware?"

"Possible," says Simka. "Some psychiatrists use that trick to eavesdrop on their patients' habits. Now, tell me: What's going on?"

"Timothy threatened me," I tell him. "He threatened my recovery schedule, he threatened me with incarceration at the health institute—"

"For what?" he says.

"Because I quit a job I was working. Because I quit helping this man Waverly with the Archive. I quit—"

"And he threatened you? That's bad, Dominic. No, no—that's illegal. I can write to some colleagues of mine—"

Simka lives out near Chevy Chase, on a solitary lane that borders Rock Creek, in a type of house common in Maryland: an oblong box, two-toned with brick along the bottom and white siding around the top. I was here once before, for a Christmas party he hosted, back when I was healthier—I was the only patient he invited. I met his family, his wife and twin sons. His boys were just babies the last time I saw them, but now they're kids—brutal in their youth, toys and the debris of toys scattered throughout the living room, but still polite when I enter with their father. They don't recognize me, of course, but they tell me their names and shake my hand before running off to another room, shaking the house with their wrestling. Simka's wife Regina's a few years younger than he is, her curly hair still jet-black—she hugs me like I'm a long-lost son, remembering my name, and begs me to sit at the kitchen table for something to drink. She takes my coat and brings me root beer.

We eat dinner together. I haven't eaten so well in quite some time, the boys wearing Redskins avatars, filling in whatever gaps and silences exist among the adults with chatter about the play-offs. Regina's made Wiener schnitzel, caloric information displaying in the *Good Eats* app, her recipe displayed in *Recipe Swap*. Dutch apple pie and coffee following dinner. Simka shows me off to his boys like I'm someone successful, like my education makes me someone important. His boys ask questions about *The Adventures of Tom Sawyer* that I'm able to answer, and it feels good—great, actually. I tell them the whitewash scene is a founding document of American-style capitalism, and they look at me, befuddled. Simka tells them it's just a clever trick, a funny story. He asks me to spend the night—a comfortable bed, away from my anxieties.

"Sure," I tell him, "I have nowhere to be—"

We drink cognac in his office, his desk windows facing a woodland backyard, chatting for an hour or so while we drink, deliberately avoiding the topic at hand, wondering what the novel by a man named Lear was. He explains, "If you spell his name l-e-e-r, then it would be a dirty story about a dirty man, Dominic. But Freud would be interested in the pun, even if you do spell his name like the king—"

I'm left alone to freshen up while Simka and his wife put the boys to bed.

"Put your coat on," he tells me when he comes back downstairs. He leads me outside through the mudroom door, down a path of pavers through his wife's garden. He's holding a lantern ahead of us, we walk in silence down a grassy slope into the woods and around to a barn he's renovated as his woodshop. He flicks on the lights—rows of fluorescent tubes—and tells me to come inside. He uses a long match to light a black woodstove in the center of the room.

"I could use electric heat," he says, "but I have so many scraps and besides I like the smell of smoke—"

I sit at one of the bench seats at the massive table near the stove. Simka's brought a thermos of coffee.

"We can talk freely here," he says. "I feel like my woodworking helps me with clearing my mind—like Zen, in a way. When I converted this barn into my shop, I insulated it with rolls of firewall. I didn't want to be interrupted with pop-ups out here. This is a quiet zone. It's peaceful—"

The furniture he's made is elegant, really. I've seen the furniture in his waiting room, back at his office in the city, but his shop here is like a showroom. Bureaus and dining room sets, chairs and tables, all in a Craftsman style. Visible wooden joints and beautifully stained. Simka pours me a cup of coffee from the thermos before pouring his own cup. It is quiet, here—I realize I can hear the distant murmur of Rock Creek. It's a sound I haven't heard for years, the sound of water dribbling through a creek bed—probably not since I was a kid, hiking with my parents in Ohiopyle.

"Something went wrong between you and Dr. Reynolds," he says. "You mentioned he threatened you—"

"Timothy's too close to a man named Waverly," I explain. "It's almost like the only reason Timothy was interested in my case was to recruit me for this work helping to track Waverly's daughter Albion in the Archive—"

"Theodore Waverly is Dr. Reynolds's father," he tells me, the connection between the two men slithering down my spine. Registering my shock, Simka says, "I've been doing some research for you. You called the other day on my landline—I thought it odd until I realized you were probably trying to keep our meeting private. I have a friend, a very close friend, on the Correctional Health Board. I asked him about Dr. Reynolds. I had to convince him—"

I open up to Simka freely, speaking comfortably to him, an old friend. Simka jots notes on a yellow legal pad, as is his custom when listening to me speak. I tell him about Albion, about Mook. I rehash Timothy's threats against me.

"Dr. Reynolds has his own troubles," says Simka. "I don't know why he wanted your case specifically. Maybe it was because he had you in mind for Waverly, I don't know. My hands were tied when you were arrested in Dupont Circle that night—the Correctional Health Board demanded changes because of the felony drug charge. I tried to keep you under my care, but Dr. Reynolds lobbied hard to have you transferred to him. I don't know why—"

"What troubles?" I ask him.

Simka opens the folder he'd brought with him. "Dr. Timothy Reynolds's file," he says. "It's relatively common for people in my field to undergo therapy once we start practicing, as sort of professional oversight to make sure we're not adversely affected by the work we're doing. Timothy and I both saw the same doctor for a number of years. This file represents the information our doctor kept about their sessions together—"

"How did you get his file?"

"Like I said, I called in favors from some influential doctors," says Simka. "The doctor that Timothy and I both saw is a mentor of mine, a very old friend. I explained the severity of the situation—"

"You don't need to discuss any of this with me," I tell him. "I don't want you to feel you have to, if you'll get in trouble—"

"Sharing patient information goes against everything I believe in as a doctor," says Simka. "But I'm worried—"

"What's going on, Dr. Simka?"

"Reynolds is not his real last name," says Simka. "When these files start, he goes by the name Timothy Billingsley. Before that he was Timothy Waverly. He has a history of spousal abuse, he's been in and out of legal trouble—"

"Spousal abuse? Did he hit his wife? Timothy told me he wasn't a very good husband, but I never thought—"

Simka leafs through the contents of Timothy's file before saying, "I want you to look at these—"

He unfolds sheets of newsprint—drawings, the same type of memory maps I made with Simka, but these drawings are exceptional. The first several are of the Christ House, the house Waverly had donated to his wife's congregation—that home for women. Timothy as Waverly's son, living in that Christ House, his mother running the place. All of Timothy's Christian bullshit starts coming into focus.

Simka finds another drawing and spreads it open on the table. The drawing's a reimagining of a Rossetti, of a woman brushing her crimson hair.

"Albion—"

"Reynolds struggled with violence and depression," says Simka. "Survivor's guilt, after Pittsburgh. He was addicted to pornography, hard-core stuff. Violent. He and his therapist talked about this problem extensively. The treatments ended abruptly—the final report says that Timothy called his therapist from the hospital. He says he was born again—"

"He tore out his own Adware," I tell him. "He told me all about it—"

"Almost killed himself," says Simka.

Simka lets me leaf through the other drawings in the file, there are several here—all extraordinarily realistic, made with colored pencils or charcoal. Simka paces his shop, cleaning up odds and ends, keeping his hands busy, obviously troubled that he's breaching his oath of patient privacy. Timothy's old doctor had arranged these drawings in groups: several of the Christ House, several of Albion. The third group grows startlingly brutal. A woman chained by her wrists in a dungeon. Two women handcuffed in bed. A woman drowning in what looks like bog water, surrounded by swamp grass. Another of a woman buried in river mud.

"Jesus—"

It's her, oh Christ, it's her—

"What is it?" asks Simka.

Nine Mile Run drawn accurately. A woman's body half buried in river mud, abandoned down a steep slope from the jogging path that worms through the park. The river's drawn in like a black ribbon. Staring at this drawing, the scene recurs to me—kneeling in the cold mud, seeing the white flesh and the grime-darkened hair. Hard rain must have rinsed away the shallow burial, or the river rose, exposing her body—tugged by currents, the face of the woman I've been tracking, drawn here.

"This is Hannah Massey," I tell him. "This is the crime scene. This is the body, it—"

"Are you sure?" asks Simka. "Are you absolutely sure? I'll call the police—"

"No, no, that's not the best for this," I tell him. "I'll get in touch with Kucenic. There are protocols to follow for something like this. Jesus. The regular police don't care about crimes preserved in the City-Archive, and will only muck it up. Kucenic will know what to do—"

I tell Simka I need to think. He says he's planning on staying up, combing through the minutiae of Timothy's files to see what else he can uncover, if he can find any information that can help me. Nearing one in the morning, we return to the house through his wife's garden. Simka makes up the guest bedroom for me, two comforters, in case I get cold.

"It's a drafty house," he says. "We can talk more in the morning—"

I climb into bed, the cooling grip of crisp sheets. My mind races. Staring into darkness, listening to the unfamiliar pops of the settling house. Autoconnect to Norwegianwood, Simka's Wi-Fi. Thinking—

Maybe Waverly never intended me to find Albion—

Maybe there is no Albion, maybe there never was—

Albion the name of Waverly's sailboat, nothing more—

Waverly and Timothy, father and son, bringing me into the fold because I found the body of Hannah Massey. Maybe they brought me in because they want to keep me under tabs, figure out how much I know, what to do with me—

Tangle me up in the fiction of Albion, keep me distracted—

A sickening certainty of comprehension, but some things don't click: Albion exists, of course she does, because Timothy drew these pictures of her for his old doctor, years ago. And why would Waverly, a man like Waverly, need to go through all the bother of having me search for Albion just so he can keep tabs on me? He could hire someone to follow me, or . . . or something could be arranged—I wouldn't be missed for long. Quivering with the thought, the panic in my nerves breaking down my disbelief—I don't believe Waverly will have me killed, or Timothy, or try not to believe, but those drawings of women's bodies are like confessions and the possibility of death grows around me like ice.

I ping Kucenic that I need to see him. Messages wait from Timothy in my in-box, vague warnings about my treatment—he seems to know I'm with Simka right now. Kucenic doesn't respond so I ping him again.

Two a.m. I register for a chat session at the World News Catalog's twenty-four-hour reference desk. An e-librarian joins me, some AI interface with a Hello Kitty avatar.

How may I help you?

I request a search in the hard archive of the *Pittsburgh Post-Gazette* for the name Timothy Billingsley—the results are immediate. Timothy's face. Thinner years ago, with a scruffy beard hiding his thin lips, but the eyes are his. I read. Domestic disturbances, arrests. I ask the AI to run a face match without limiting the news source and the bot returns hits from the *Times-Picayune*—under the name Timothy Filt, arrested for the murder of his wife, a woman named Rhonda Jackson from the Ninth Ward of New Orleans. She was found in her apartment, her head caved in from the strike of an aluminum baseball bat. He'd been pulled over for a broken taillight and connected with the crime. Blood in the car, a DNA match. Scheduled for the death sentence but never executed—political influence and an eventual pardon from the governor of Louisiana.

Filt became Billingsley. He surfaces in Georgia on another domestic violence report, now married to a woman named Lydia Holland. *Lydia*—she's the woman Timothy told me about, the woman he'd cheated on, his wife during the end. They lived in Pittsburgh but must have moved there from Georgia—Timothy told me he and his wife were traveling through the South when Pittsburgh ended. I request a search for the name "Lydia Billingsley." Only one hit—as a volunteer at a Rotary pancake breakfast in Greensburg, PA. Timothy told me that he and his wife had divorced, so I search for her maiden name, "Lydia Holland"—the name appears in the *Times-Picayune* in the February issue, four months after the end of Pittsburgh. Her body was found bound and gagged, submerged in the Honey Island Swamp. A fisherman found her, didn't know what he'd found at first. Her face was cut up and bloated in the water, a slash across the neck so deep she was nearly decapitated. Her hands had been removed.

A message hits my in-box and the chime in Simka's silent guest room startles me from bed. I sit up, my account glowing in the darkness. From someone named Vivian Knightley, with the subject line: Aubade. I open it—*You wanted to read my poetry, so here's something. I hope you aren't full of shit that you're interested because I don't show these to everyone. Love, Twigs—*

She's sent me a manuscript, the length of a chapbook—thirty pages or so. The aubade that starts the collection is just one line:

I reached for you this morning but you were gone.

I can't stay here. I schedule a cab and spend the next fifteen minutes leaning over the guest room toilet, staring at my reflection in the water, concentrating to hold down the vomit my nerves are sputtering up. Did Timothy kill Hannah, I wonder, or did he just know where she was discarded? The house is silent—Simka must have finally gone to sleep. I move out to Simka's front stoop in the numbing early morning chill, watching my breath billow out, shaking my legs to keep warm. When the cab pulls up, I hurry over so the driver won't honk and pierce the predawn skin of silence. I tell the driver Kucenic's address. I think of Hannah's body filthy from silt. I think of Albion—but thinking of Albion is like staring at something for so long that it begins to disappear.

2, 4—

Kucenic lives on G, just off Barracks Row on 8th, in a Federalist row house that cost him a couple million, easy, despite the street parking and the odd stone-paved patch that serves as his front lawn. Dawn's breaking, but the streetlights are still on.

I press the doorbell and chimes ring through the quiet house. "Kucenic?" I pound on the door. "It's Dominic—"

His Explorer's parked out front, one tire on the curb. Although the curtains are drawn, I look through a slit and find his usual living room mess from the night before: Chinese takeout boxes, half-finished two liters of Mountain Dew—Kucenic's typical cuisine for late nights of coding.

"Kucenic, open up. It's Dominic. Kucenic—"

The whispering hum of accumulating traffic circulates on nearby, busier streets.

"Kucenic, open up the goddamn door—"

I hear him shuffling around inside, now. The dead bolts fall away and Kucenic opens up. He's wearing what he must have worn since yesterday, blue jeans and wrinkled flannel, his cigarette-ash hair a wild puff of bed head. His thumb and forefinger smooth his beard from his lips—a nervous tic he has when he's thinking, when he's not quite sure how to respond to a pointed question.

"Dominic," he says.

"I've turned off my connection—"

"Come in. Come on in. I'll make us some coffee—"

The Kucenic Group operates from this house—meetings in the

living room, staffers lounging on the couches or recliners, eating cheese curls and Coke while Kucenic writes on the whiteboard. I've actually never been here without the rest of the group—the place is strangely empty, the only real sound the click and hum of servers lining the front hallway, caged in cherry-red storage lockers. Kucenic leads to the kitchen, struggling with a pronounced limp.

"Coffee," he says, and the coffeepot purrs to life. "Do you want any of this pecan roll?"

"Tell me about #14502," I tell him. "Hannah Massey, that State Farm insurance dispute I was working on when you let me go. Who's working it now?"

"No one's working it," says Kucenic. "That case doesn't exist anymore—"

"Bullshit," I tell him.

"Check with State Farm if you have to," he says. "Their bid skips from 14501 to 503—"

"You can't just fucking ignore this," I tell him. "That girl was murdered, you son of a bitch. When you fired me, I trusted you to follow through with her. I fucking trusted you. She deserves better than this—"

"Dominic, I have a lot to lose," he says, diminished, cowed, his usually elfin eyes now like a coward's pleading eyes. He turns from me, cuts a slice of the pecan roll, heats it in the microwave.

"You tell me what the fuck's going on," I tell him.

We eat at the meeting table, the paperwork of open cases spread haphazardly around the room, notes in red marker on the whiteboard—historical notes about Pittsburgh, timelines. Working on the Union Trust building collapse, it looks like, framed animated printouts of the building on sheets of e-paper are spread across the table.

"What did Waverly tell you when he first asked about me?"

"You mentioned that name earlier. You pinged me, said you'd met with a man named Waverly. You said there was a hard sell. I never met with anyone by that name—"

"Theodore Waverly—"

"Jesus, Dominic, do you know who that is?"

"He said he talked with you, interviewed you as a reference check. He said you told him about my drug habits, my work habits. He said he was checking background to hire me for a freelance job—"

"Dominic, I never met him—"

"Tell me what you know about Hannah Massey—"

"Only what you'd presented to me. When you found her body in the Archive, I reported the case to State Farm and the FBI. An agent from the field office contacted me, said they'd been in touch with State Farm—I've worked with this agent before, many times. I explained we were still researching the case as part of a claim, but that we'd present any relevant information to them. This is all strictly paperwork for the FBI, low priority—a bot actually does the work for them, it's just a formality. No one expects the FBI to follow up or bring charges to anyone over something in the Pittsburgh City-Archive. This kind of interaction is just a checklist we go through—"

"So what's different about her case?"

"This was shortly after your—incident," he says. "You had that meltdown in Dupont Circle and I had to let you go. You were a repeat offender and this was a felony, I had to. I reported your termination to the Employee Assistance Program and was told that you would be taken care of, that your case would be handled by the Correctional Health Board—"

Kucenic's tearing a napkin into confetti. He rubs his knee and so I ask him to tell me about his limp.

"Dominic, you're in some serious trouble—we both are. These cops showed up shortly after I terminated you—they just knocked on my door one night, around eight or eight thirty, told me that they had to talk to me about you," he says. "There were three of them, District soldiers—I never saw their faces. Those black masks, the armor. Their badges were blacked out so I couldn't ping their profiles or badge numbers. I figured they wanted to talk to me about your arrest, maybe your background, have me sign some more paperwork—"

"But they wanted to know about Hannah Massey—"

"They wanted to know everything about our involvement with that case," says Kucenic. "Who researched her? Who saw the files? How you found the body, where you were looking, why you were looking there, what you were working on. They took all the files related to that case, corrupted my copies with a worm. They wanted to know everything about you. Were you a good worker, how involved were you with the firm, everything—"

"And you told them?"

"I told them what they wanted to know, of course I did, but they knew everything already, Dominic. They made it clear to me that case #14502 no longer existed—that it would be erased, and that I shouldn't work on anything even remotely associated with it, that I would be monetarily compensated for the loss of workload. They told me they'd take care of communicating with State Farm, that no questions would be asked. They said they appreciated my cooperation, and that if I continued to cooperate I would be safe. That's what they said, that I would 'be safe.' They said that you might try to contact me, but that I was not to respond—"

"You're with me now," I tell him.

"I'm going to report this the moment you leave," he says. "I'm going to call the District police and tell them that you've been here—what else can I do? You just showed up—"

"Did they hurt you? I asked about your leg—"

"A parting gift," says Kucenic. "I shook their hands, told them I would cooperate. I followed them to the door—and that's when one of them turned back to me. He pulled his nightstick and punched me with it, here in my chest. The hit knocked me over, and the man struck me twice in the knee—"

"Jesus. I'm sorry," I tell him.

"It's all right, Dominic," he says. "Just—you don't know what you're involved in. Just do what they want you to do, whatever they tell you. Just get clear of this thing—"

2, 5—

I want to see Hannah again—

Paths through Nine Mile Run—someone documented all this and re-created it here, every footpath and every bridge over every muddy creek, the trees and the undersides of leaves. Plenty of JSTOR footage fills in the gaps where people never filmed, acres of this area important to environmental scientists studying the long-term effects of brownfields. Theresa and I walked here in autumn, late autumn arcing toward winter, just a few weeks following our miscarriage. We never fought, like some couples we knew, some of our friends slipping into skirmishes following a few drinks or harried days of work. We only had a few significant fights in all the years we knew each other, most of them about nothing, nothing at all, but I hurt her once here in these woods and I'm unable to walk here now without reliving the pain I caused her. Theresa loved this park—the other city parks were beautiful, but too manicured for joggers and families with strollers. Nine Mile Run remained untended in spots, spots where she could wander off-trail and find flowers growing in patches of sunlight. Despite the countless other strolls we'd taken through these paths, my memories wander back to this single afternoon and the shame of hurting her. Layering, the trickle of nearby water. Layering, birdsong. Layering, cool shade and the smell of soil. Wind in the leaves. I remember Theresa wearing a cardigan the color of tree bark, her hair the color of the golden leaves dying on their boughs. We're holding hands, her fingers cold. She was distracted, looking over her shoulder into the woods and the shadows gathering there.

"Maybe—I don't know, maybe there's a silver lining to losing her," I remember saying. "Maybe we're better off without having kids. All the hassle—"

She slumps instead of screams, collapsing to the trail like her lungs have been pulled from her.

"I'm sorry," I think I remember saying, stammering something, trying to comfort her but failing. I still don't know why I said those words, and every time I think of them my chest tightens in nauseous self-recrimination. A jogger runs past without stopping and I wait until he's long past and disappeared from view before speaking again. "Are you all right?" I ask her.

She stays on her knees, her head bowed into her hands, saying, "No, no, no," until the light fails and the damp seeps like dead fingers through her clothes and she lets me help her to her feet and walk with her.

We walk here now, in patches of late afternoon sun, to the creek to watch the dying light lie like scattered diamonds on the surface of the water. We were alone that evening, coming to terms with our loss, with a miscarriage just like the thousands of other miscarriages that occur every day, every year, but ours so unlike the others because it was our daughter, our child that never was.

Night gathers. I leave Theresa on the path, her cries about our child filling the spaces between the sounds of the woods. I use low-hanging limbs to keep my balance as I scuttle down the slope, down near the watershed. I'm looking for the body. The Archive resets to late April, the clock resets to a little before seven in the evening. I find Hannah half buried in mud and watch her white body as the sun sets and night falls. I adjust my light filters, continue watching.

Think.

Load notes for case #14502 and resume my research where I'd left off for Kucenic and State Farm, tracking Hannah during her final hours before she was reported missing—on campus, at Carnegie Mellon, a few weeks before spring semester finals.

She's slept in late this morning, the night before a raucous double rehearsal for her acting troupe's Spring Carnival performance of *Spamalot.* Hannah's role is the Lady of the Lake, and in these final hours in the Archive she trudges through a late spring dusting of snow still singing the music she'd learned the night before, full-voiced despite the relatively early hour. In a few weeks, her troupe will stage *Spamalot* without her, dedicating the show to her, the missing girl, the stage festooned with flowers. The programs will feature her high school senior portrait and a tribute written by her friends, and after each performance the actors will stand among the exiting crowds taking up a collection to aid in the search efforts. But now, this morning, Hannah sings "Diva's Lament," a freshman

Psych major in Barbie-pink boots and a camel hair coat, blonde waves tumbling from beneath her knit beret. She's effortless, burgundy sweatpants and a plaid sweatshirt, comfy stuff for a day shuffling between the library and her semester's remaining few classes. I've followed her this morning before—

Before, though, I'd followed her to determine if she perished in the bomb or perished sometime earlier, an insurance dispute—but now I need to see who killed her, to make sure Timothy killed her, to link them together if I can—or discover who killed her. Save the evidence somewhere safe, somewhere I can access and disseminate if I have to—leverage against Timothy to protect myself until I can figure out what to do. Hannah has a quick breakfast at the University Center, of coffee and a cinnamon scone—she flips through *Vanity Fair*'s spring fashion issue. I canvass the University Center while she eats, checking the faces of the people around her, of everyone with visibility of her, but there's no one threatening here, no one paying particular attention, just the faces of dead students and dead faculty and family, most likely everyone perishing in the burn when they returned the following semester for the resumption of classes. Following coffee, Hannah can't make it across campus without being stopped every few feet by friends—other actors, girls on the track team, classmates, dorm mates, professors she's friendly with—it takes her nearly forty-five minutes to make the five-minute trek to her Psychology lecture in Porter Hall. A freshman survey, eighty or so kids filling out the seats.

I settle in a rear seat, several rows behind Hannah but where I can still see her—I've sat through this lecture with her before, have already studied Hannah diligently taking notes, have already seen her checking her phone for messages, suppressing yawns but generally paying attention. The lecturer enters a few minutes late, swirling into the room in a charcoal overcoat and tartan scarf, dropping his leather satchel on the lecture hall's front table—I've seen him enter several times before, have seen the students snap to attention at his presence . . . but this time when the professor enters, my stomach feels like it slides down through my bowels. The professor for this class, who I'd seen in the background of Hannah Massey's life before but never recognized until now, is Waverly.

He looks different from the man I know—his hair here is a salt-and-pepper black and left longer than the silver hair Waverly has now. I didn't know who Waverly was when I was researching Hannah for Kucenic, he didn't mean anything to me then—but now I notice his ravenous blue eyes fall on Hannah while he speaks, I notice his eyes linger over her a few moments longer than he looks at the other students, an older professor noticing the prettiest girl in his class, nothing more sinister than that, I must have thought. He's lecturing about artificial intelligence, about how Focal Networks sims human cognition, how they've created algorithms that can replicate human thought and how they can make predictions about human behavior based on his models.

"Our choices aren't really our own," says Waverly. "We are putty hardwired with biological imperatives. A very few number of us will gain the wisdom needed to overcome our material limitations, but the number is very small—my business depends on that number being extraordinarily small. You know, when I started out, when I was just your age, an undergrad, I pursued my research hoping that one day hospitals would adopt technology so that impersonal diagnostic kiosks could be replaced with a truly interactive, almost-human bedside experience that could be used for the First World and Third World alike, but my first million came in my senior year when I was approached by the Real Doll industry. The Creator modeled us using materials prone to lust and hunger. Do we have individual souls capable of overcoming the base nature of our being? Perhaps . . . but my paychecks depend on very few of us overcoming our impulses, and I'm a very rich man—"

The class ends, early afternoon. I've watched Hannah after this class before—as she mills around for several minutes to see the professor but becomes resigned as other students cluster around him first, asking clarifying questions. I'd always simply assumed Hannah waited after class because she also had some question about the lecture, but now I wonder at a prior relationship between the two, some other reason she may have waited to see him. No matter—Hannah gives up the wait, leaves the lecture hall. This is the last known hour of Hannah's life.

The ground will be frozen through much of April of that year, maybe why she was buried shallow enough that the spring rains could wash away her grave. Snowing, now—a swirling powder. I don't know why Hannah cuts across campus toward the athletic fields rather than heading up Morewood to her dorm in Morewood Gardens, or to the library or another class, or even to the University Center for a late lunch. Rather, she skirts around the front end of campus to the parking garage on Forbes. She enters the parking garage and disappears—the archival deletion yawning enough that even State Farm picked it up on their cursory analysis of her extended family's insurance claim. Hannah will miss a three o'clock class that day, and will miss a rehearsal for *Spamalot* that evening, her friends trying to contact her but failing, her friends reporting her missing to campus security, initiating a search that will burn intensely for weeks but peter out over the summer months, when everyone will leave Pittsburgh for home. By late summer, when everyone returns to campus for their own October death sentence, Hannah will already have become just a specter, mostly forgotten.

I scan the exception report again, the listing riddled with ContinuityExceptions, time-consuming to track, tedious. It took me months to find her body, but could take as many months more to track exactly what's happened here—

But I don't have to work like this—

I can work backward now—like solving an equation by working from the known solution. Hannah's with Timothy, or will be—I reset the City, run a Facecrawler on Timothy, including older images I'd found of him as reference points for the search, limiting to this parking garage. Facecrawler hits on security cam footage of the driver of a Ford Mustang SUV leaving the lot shortly after Hannah disappears—tinted windows, but he'd rolled down the window to swipe his debit card at the gate. I zoom in on the face: Timothy—*got him*. The gate raises, the SUV leaves the lot.

I follow—

He drives through Squirrel Hill, cuts through Schenley Park, Greenfield Avenue sloping downhill until a sharp switchback called Saline brings us beneath the interstate. We're in the Run. He parallel parks on a side street that runs behind Big Jim's—a neighborhood bar only a short half block away from the house whitewashed with the words of Christ. Timothy's recognizable when he steps from the car, despite his beard and thinner frame, but Hannah's been altered with a simple face swap—an easy enough trick to throw off basic Facecrawlers. Grace Kelly's face, but the body is still Hannah's, the clothes. Timothy takes her to Big Jim's, and I follow.

Big Jim's is sculpted from security cam footage—no sound, a monochrome environment. Timothy and Hannah in a corner booth, eating spaghetti. I wait for them outside, pacing, agitated by the adrenal rush of ferreting information from the Archive. By the time they leave the restaurant it's already dusk. The neighborhood's quiet, cones of streetlamp light illuminate the snow. Andy Warhol worshipped here in the Run, down the street at the Saint John

Chrysostom Byzantine Church, metallic onion domes shimmering in the lights from the overpass. Row houses here, or houses separated by the slimmest gaps, shot-and-beer bars still sooty from the mill days almost a century gone. Timothy stays parked where he is. He and Hannah step through a gap in a chain-link fence and cross a field strewn with broken bottles and beer cans, overgrown with stubby grass and weeds. A floodlight shines on the side of the Christ House so the white cross and the whitewash-slathered quote are always visible, day or night. The lawn's mud, the front steps long since rotted and replaced by ascending cinder blocks. The front porch moans with wet rot. The door hangs open.

Timothy stands aside, lets Hannah enter the house first. He follows her, closes the door behind them. I try to follow inside but there's a barrier in the simulation. *Private Account* hangs in the doorway in green Helvetica.

"Override," I say and a keypad appears in the continuity of the doorway. I enter my access code, press Enter. *Log-in Failed.*

I think I remember Kucenic's code, so I type in his number string and the barrier disappears like a discarded veil, but as I cross the threshold I hear a rapid series of mechanical ticks. I'm not certain where the flame originates, but I see it expanding from the front door, a spreading orange light like liquid roiling midair. The concussion a heartbeat later, like a mule kick. Weightlessness before the earth swings upward to meet me. *Fuck.* I try to stand. *Fuck. Fuck.* Can't quite. Ears ringing. My breath's knocked from me, a scalding cramping in my lungs gasping the winter-frozen air. A bomb? I've bit my tongue and blood pours from my mouth, snapping me briefly from the Archive, bleeding onto my shirt and bedsheets, but I force myself to stay immersed, to focus on the City, *focus on the City.* iLux keeps me here. The Christ House, burning. Fire streams from the windows and sweeps up through the gaps in the siding. Fire belches from the front door, swathing the house, casting stark shadows the color of char.

What's happening? This house never burned, not that I know of, not until the end—

A special effect, I realize—clever, the blistering heat layered in as a sense impression, just as realistic as the coffee I drink in the Archive or the touch and scent of women here, the firelight enough to make me squint but perfectly safe. Safe. I could walk through this fire, enter this house—could still follow Timothy and Hannah—but as I'm pulling myself from the ground, convincing myself that the wind hasn't been knocked from me, that it's just a shrewd trick, someone stumbles from the front door, screaming. I can see his black body like a burning worm cocooned in fire. The man stumbles toward me, waving his fiery arms, trailing a curling vein of smoke, a fireball, and I want to escape but am paralyzed. The man seizes the front of my coat and puts his burning face close to mine. I can smell his melting skin, feel the waves of heat.

"I'm very disappointed to see you again so soon," he says, flames pouring from his mouth like writhing tongues as he speaks. "You're using the name Kucenic now—"

Mook.

"I told you to leave well enough alone," he says.

"I don't understand," I tell him. "I quit Albion. I told them I quit. I quit—"

"Mr. Blaxton, I'm acting to uphold the Fourth Amendment of the United States Constitution. I believe that part of the right to privacy is that everyone has the right to control their own image. Did you know there are sex tourists who come through the Pittsburgh Archive looking for other people's memories? Perverts, you understand—complete perversion. Would you be surprised to learn that people have immersed in Pittsburgh and have lived out your memories of sex with your wife? It's happened, Dominic. There's an industry of people who search out private sexual encounters that have been archived here and sell them. The user's sensation is just as wonderful as it is for you. How do you feel about that, Dominic? Wouldn't it comfort you to have someone like me protecting your memories, the image of your wife? My client has a right to keep people away from her image, and I intend to protect that right—"

"Your client? Who's your client?"

"You're a thickheaded young man," says Mook. "Your wife is dead now—"

The iLux net security flashes red—*malware detected*—a progress bar fills too quickly to even consider ways to protect myself.

"That's the worm," says Mook. "Reissner-Nordström—"

"What are you doing?" I ask.

"You pressed me to do this because you wouldn't stay away. You wouldn't listen to me. You did this to her. I've unlived your wife, but I can resurrect her. Remember that, Dominic. Be a good boy, and I can reward you one memory at a time—"

Mook blinks out of existence, the house fire's extinguished, the oceanic silence of the snow-filled night is painful to my ears. What has he done to her? Sift through my memories—I search for Theresa, but she's nowhere. Through snow, Christmas lights hang from the branches of barren trees. The Spice Island Tea House. Layering, curry and candle wax. Our table, but Theresa's seat is blurred, smudged like a corruption in sight.

"Theresa—"

She ran some blood work, she will say. She will tell me about the advanced amino test, our little girl, but the only sound I hear is a mumbled deformity of speech emitted from the empty blur, nothing at all like Theresa's voice, nothing at all. She's deleted now—Mook's deleted her—every memory of her, every trace, every piece of her life that I clung to here, blotted and smeared.

Our apartment, the Georgian. Paisley carpets and walls stained the color of tea. Room 208. There is nothing left here, *nothing*—the foyer empty, only shadows remain.

"Theresa?"

My voice echoes in the emptiness. No one in the living room, no one in the kitchen. Our bedroom's empty. I lie in bed and wait for her, wait for Theresa to undress in the half-light of the hallway light, to lie with me. I close my eyes to remember her body against mine, to wrap my arms around her and feel her, Theresa, oh God, Theresa, to feel the soft movement of her body, and I reach out my hand and feel her body but when I open my eyes I only see Zhou.

2, 18—

"Slow down," says Gavril. "Are you all right? Tell me what's happening—"

"Fuck, man. I'm fucked—"

"Where are you? Can you make it over?"

A Metro bus—*connected*. Layering, basil curry and candle wax. Forget about everything but my memories of Theresa, but already my memories of her seem thinner. The connection's weak and the bus jostles and I'm in DC instead of Pittsburgh. *Reconnect*. The City loads and I access my memories of Theresa but see Zhou. *Zhou*. I can't remember my wife anymore. I buzz up to Gavril's, expecting Twiggy, but another woman opens the door, a pixie with a hentai faerie avatar—pinkish hair and jiggling cartoon breasts. "Upstairs," she says, sparkling faerie wings and purple lipstick that stinks like grape Kool-Aid. The living room's filled with Gavril's models playing a space shooter on the sim, following the Amis guide *Invasion of the Space Invaders*, storming the terrain of Mars—the apartment's cast the color of rust. Other models are in the kitchen, snorting lines of cocaine, their faces hideous in the Martian light, one girl's nose raw with a trickle of blood, but everything's hilarious and they're shrieking with laughter. The hentai faerie ignores me for the cocaine, and I wander back to Gavril's darkroom.

"You look like shit," he says.

"I don't know," I tell him. "Sugar—"

"Ah fuck, man," he says. "It's been ten years, brother—ten years since you lost her. Give this up, Quixote. You can stay on my mother's farm for as long as you want. Clear your head. Or come to London with me when I go. I'll pay. Let's put all this shit behind you—"

"I need to fucking—I just need, Gav, please, you don't fucking understand—"

"Fuck you, then—"

Two pills of brown and I swallow them whole. "Take it to the kitchen," he says, "I'm working right now." Ignoring the coked girls who've fallen in a giggling heap beneath the kitchen table, I sit in the corner, on the cool tile, the warped-space sounds of their video game interfering with the immersion—

Autoconnect to Gavril's Wi-Fi, the burn hits and the Pittsburgh tunnel's like swimming lights, I'm rushing through and hold my breath until the tunnel ends and I'm hovering midair above three black rivers. I swim down through the air and touch the surface of the river—I pull myself through the skin of water into the dark, descend through the depths to drown. The river swallows me, the water covering over me but I can still breathe, of course I can still breathe—it's not real, nothing is real. Nothing is real. Looking up at the City through the rippling surface of the river, the lights of Pittsburgh waver like it's the City that's been drowned. I close my eyes. I want to die, but the City isn't set up for suicides, and so when I open my eyes I'm standing in Shadyside, in summer. I'm here—

Vibrancy of the drugs—Jesus Christ, it's all so real. The Uni-Mart—aisles of Doritos and Ruffles and Fritos and Combos. The faces of the cashiers are immortal here, the boy with a neck tattoo taking my money and handing me rumpled, sweaty cash from the drawer. I thank him and stuff the bills into my pocket. Walking home with a gallon of milk in a plastic bag. Nearing midnight, insects swarm the streetlights. A midsummer swelter. Our apartment was never air-conditioned, but box fans beat in the open windows and make a comfortable-enough draft. I take my shirt off in the foyer, sweating in the dark midnight room. Theresa's already asleep—I remember Theresa asleep, but when I go to her now, the body in our bed is Zhou's.

"Theresa," I say, and Zhou turns to me like she recognizes that name.

"Where did you go?" she says, speaking words I remember Theresa speaking.

"Picked up some milk so we can have cereal tomorrow—"

Theresa's things are still here. Her container gardens on the windowsills. Framed Audubon prints of mourning doves and flamingos. The book she was reading is facedown on the coffee table—*Zoya*, Danielle Steel.

"Theresa—"

"Come to bed," she says.

I open the refrigerator door to put away the milk and squint into the harsh white light. My eyes are still adjusting to the darkness when I come back to bed and for a moment I see Zhou as Theresa, Theresa's body lit by the moonlight, but as my eyes adjust to the darkness, Zhou's body returns and Zhou's face fades in. I crawl into bed and close my eyes, trying to remember Theresa here, trying to force my memory of Theresa back into this place. Zhou sleeps with me just like Theresa would have slept with me, her body nestled into mine, her legs crossed over mine.

"Theresa," I say, but Zhou answers, "Yes—"

I wake.

Gavril's moved me to the bathroom, stretched me out in the tub, propped my head up with pillows. Cottony, my mouth—I've vomited down the front of my clothes. Face aching like someone's punched me. I stand—shaky. He's left a clean T-shirt for me, a yellow jersey—*Washington Redskins, est. 1937*. iLux lights to the jersey augs and Agatha, the Redskins cheerleader who implanted my iLux, flashes in the bathroom with me, a cheer routine from her vids, spandex high kicks disappearing through the bathroom ceiling. "Off, off," I tell it, wincing at the stadium lights and reverbed crowd noise. She flickers out. Splitting goddamn headache. I splash water in my face. Whispers of bruises have formed under my eyes and blood's dried on my nostrils. The apartment's emptied out, Gavril's party paused for the time being. Gavril's in the living room, watching soccer. He turns when he hears me.

"Christ," he says. "*Šípková Růženka*, I thought you were going to fucking die—"

"I didn't—"

I sit with him, head pounding but dull. I grab a handful of Fritos from the bowl but just hold them, stomach flopping at the thought of actually eating one.

"You started screaming in the kitchen—the girls got scared," he says. "You were, like, slamming your face against the wall. Freaking the fuck out. Fucking blood everywhere—"

"Gavril, I'm all right—"

"I voiced your doctor friend, Simka—Once you started snapping out of it, I voiced back and told him not to bother coming and so he cussed me out for a half hour because he says I enable you. He still wants to take a look at you, but I never told him where I live—"

"I don't think I've ever seen your place so quiet—"

"A few girls are coming around for work a little later," he says. "Crash here as long as you want. I don't think you should terrorize the streets in the shape you're in—"

"I'll just collect my head a bit," I tell him. Gavril gets two bottles of Gatorade from the fridge and hands them to me, telling me to drink both. Even the thought of swallowing Gatorade is enough to make me gag—but I sip and let the liquid slip over my tongue.

"Drink up," he says. "Hydration. I mean it, brother—"

"Gavril, I have some things I need to tell you—"

"Say anything—"

"That job for Waverly's gone sour," I tell him. "The woman I was tracking. Everything's fucked up—"

I tell him about Mook, about the Christ House in Pittsburgh where I followed Timothy and Hannah Massey. I tell him about Timothy's drawings of dead women and the cops that assaulted Kucenic. I tell him that they've taken Theresa from me.

He's stunned by everything I'm mixed up in. He rubs both hands over his bristly head and the shag of his beard stubble, pacing the room.

"You're in serious shit," he says.

"Listen to me, Gavril, this is important: I've put together a collection of evidence linking Dr. Timothy Reynolds to the death of Hannah Massey. If anything happens to me, you need to get it out to the streams—"

We set up an anonymous drop box using faked contacts, encrypt it with a mirror site, share the password—easy to trace documents I put into the drop box, but impossible to trace who retrieves them. I copy the files about Hannah's murder. Gavril pulls a bottle of Sorokin vodka from the freezer and pours himself a glass. He offers some for me and laughs when I recoil at the idea of liquor.

"Sorokin will resurrect you, no matter how dead you feel," he says.

"I should be dead already," I tell him. "They're going to fucking kill me, Gavril, because I found that fucking body but it wasn't my fault, it wasn't my fucking fault—"

"You won't die," he says, "we can figure this out, figure out what to do—"

"I already know what to do. I need to recover Theresa so she can live on in the Archive. I need to help Hannah—"

My Adware's a different region code than the soccer broadcast on Gavril's *Praha* stream, so the play-by-play's like excited gibberish. He finishes the first glass of vodka before pouring himself a second.

"Dominic, you know I love you," he says, "but you piss me off sometimes. You're thinking about that dead girl, thinking about your wife. You're obsessed, Dominic. You've always been fucking obsessed with grief. Let them go, Domi. Let them go, steer clear of this. We'll lay low until these people forget about you—"

"I can't just let her disappear—"

"Is that all you can fucking think of right now? That's what all this shit boils down to?" Gavril's eyes swim with a sudden buzz from slugging down his vodka. "Theresa's dead, but you have a life to live. I'm here for you. You have a family. We have lives to live, with you—"

"I know," I tell him. "I know—"

"No, you don't fucking know," he says. I've never seen him quite like this, fraying at the edges. He pours himself more Sorokin and his hand shakes, splashing vodka on the table. "You almost fucking died in my kitchen," he says. "From a fucking overdose. And now you fucking tell me you're mixed up in this bullshit? What the fuck have you been doing with your life?"

"That's enough," I tell him.

"And now you're dragging me into it," he says. "Giving me files about a dead girl that might get me killed and all this fucking means for you is that you can't mope about your dead fucking wife or some dead fucking girl you don't even know—"

"Fuck you—"

"No, fuck you, Dominic. Fuck you. That shit was ten years ago. Enough. Open your fucking eyes. You can work for me, you know that. Anytime you want, I'll set you up with a plum job, working with beautiful women all day, every day. But what do you do? Get involved with these fucking people because they promise they'll let you live in the fucking past—"

"It's more complicated than that," I tell him.

"Go to the fucking cops," he says. "It's not more complicated—"

"I already told you why I can't go to the cops. I told you what those cops did to Kucenic—"

"All the cops? They're working with all the fucking cops?"

"Gav—"

He grabs me by the shirt and I hear fabric rip, setting off all the jersey's augs—the Redskins cheer squad splays through the room like a crimson and yellow Busby Berkeley kaleidoscope of legs and breasts and smiling teeth and flowing hair and shimmering golden pom-poms.

"I don't want anything to fucking happen to you," he screams.

"At least give me a different shirt before you kick my ass—"

"Shit," says Gav, laughing.

He gives me a cardigan that covers up the jersey augs. He tells me he knows people who can hit the streams with my evidence if it comes to that, people in the tabloids who trade in true crime and the gruesome deaths of young women, but we both know this gambit of threatening to go public with the scant evidence we have is only short-term protection, that it escalates the situation rather than tamps it down.

"You need to find Mook," says Gavril.

"Fuck him. Mook took Theresa from me—"

"Think rationally," says Gavril. "Think: from everything you've told me, he's not working with Timothy or Waverly. He might know how to protect you, how to hide from them—or at least he might have a few ideas to fuck them over. 'I know hate and ice is great,' or something like that—whatever Frost said. Right? Right?"

"That's right," I tell him.

"If you can track him down—what's the word—it's, um, *rošáda*, um, in chess—"

iLux catching up, the translation apps presenting options: "'Castling,'" I tell him.

"That's right," he says. "Better attack options through defensive movement. Castling—"

"And if I find Mook, I can also get Theresa back—"

Gavril cracks his knuckles, collects himself with a deep breath. "Maybe that, too," he says.

Gavril asks for details about what I've told him—he wants me to rehash everything for him. He wants to know about Zhou. He asks me whether Zhou is always the same when I encounter her, or if she's different each time. Different hairstyles, different clothes? He wants to know if I'm able to add up all the hours I've experienced with her, specifically "unique hours," he calls them, where she does or says things differently from the last time I'd encountered her—different gestures, different scenes.

"I can't even guess," I tell him. "She's always different. She's not just a cardboard stand-in, if that's what you're asking—"

"Quick scenes?" he asks.

"Hundreds of hours, but I've already tried tracking her. There's nothing in the exception reports—"

"She's a stream girl," says Gavril. "Either a model or someone's program. If we can find out who she is, we can track Zhou to Mook—"

"I already ran a Facecrawler on Zhou and I'm telling you there's nothing—or, there's really too much. Someone ghosted her, probably Mook—"

"I don't know what that means—"

"Someone, let's say Mook, compromised the data points that facial recognition software would use to match her face to other images of her face. Made the sign point to an incorrect referent. Mook basically made her invisible to third-party software. No exact matches so Facecrawler starts pulling results for approximate facial matches, Asian women—billions of hits. I guess I could just start sifting through the results—"

"No, no—you don't understand what I'm telling you," says Gavril. "This woman, Zhou, is the kind of woman I work with all the time. She's either a fully realized simulation or she's an actress. If she's a sim, think of all the hours to program her—not just what she looks like but all those little unique things she does. If she's an actress, think of the hours to film her. My guess is that she's an actress—but either way, a professional's involved. This bullshit you're caught up in is someone's full-time job, even if it's under the table. It won't be impossible to track her down. Show her to me—"

I show him. He downloads Three Rivers Net and the City-Archive app and we synch, Gavril's soccer match receding to a point of light as western Pennsylvania coalesces and we plunge through the mountainside into the tunnel. He tells me that he's dreamt about this tunnel, this entranceway into Pittsburgh from the airport, that it reminds him of winter flights and snow-covered midnights, of childhood Christmases spent far from home visiting his cousin and aunts and uncles in America. I want to ask him what he remembers about those Christmases at my grandmother's house, the midnight masses at Prince of Peace, the Pittsburgh Slovak Folk Ensemble dancing in the church basement, girls in white knee-highs and burgundy dresses, their hair in braids, their thighs flashing. Gav and I couldn't understand a word each other was saying back then, but we didn't need words—all we needed to know about each other was that we both wanted to melt away in those beautiful girls but were both too shy to talk with them. I want to ask him if he remembers his first year visiting, when we each unwrapped Optimus Prime, huddled together beneath my grandma's dinner table, but the tunnel ends and the City unfolds around us, the streets and rivers and bridges like a dazzling crosshatch of light.

I take him home.

The paisley carpet, the gauzy curtains at the far end of the apartment hallway. An Exit light flickers above the fire doors. Room 208. Gavril had met Theresa, only once—we vacationed in Prague for a week with Gavril as our guide. I expect him to seem dazed or dismayed when I unlock the apartment door and find Zhou greeting us instead of Theresa, but Gavril only looks her over and says, "Her, right?"

Odd seeing him here, in my living room. Gavril pulls Zhou aside and asks her to take a seat on the couch. She's wearing my wife's plaid pajama pants and Donora T-shirt and I feel protective of her, in a way, but as she takes a seat, doing what Gavril asks her to do, the environment snaps from the gauzy sentimentality of my personal memories—with Gavril here, I can see the apartment as a built environment, an illusion, nothing more.

"Serial number?" he says, but Zhou looks at me and asks, "Who is this man?"

Gavril lifts Zhou's T-shirt above her abdomen and checks a spot on the underside of her right breast, checking her like a doctor might check for lumps. He lets her T-shirt fall and touches her near her collarbone.

"What's your serial number?" he asks again and Zhou says, "Please—"

"A woman, not a sim," says Gavril. "Sims are registered, trademarked. Even pirated sims have telltale signs of the engines they've cribbed—little codes or abraded markings beneath the breast area where the serial numbers are required to go, or on the collarbone—up here. There's nothing like that on Zhou—"

"So she doesn't have markings—"

"The people who create sims, the good ones, spend more of their budgets outthinking software pirates than they do in creating the sims in the first place," he says. "It's difficult to get rid of a bar code—"

"There are workarounds. Or custom—"

"Maybe . . . but do you realize how much fucking money it would take to create a sim this lifelike running on a custom engine?" he says. "Not only the work involved but the red tape, the laws. We're talking megacorporation money, or state-sponsored money, if even then—but it's not just a question of money. Look at Zhou—look at how she interacts with the environment, with us. She's so perfect—so realistic. No one creates stuff this realistic, that's why human models still have work—"

"Waverly has significant resources, maybe Mook does, too—"

"You aren't listening," says Gavril.

"We're assuming Mook is the one inserting Zhou into the Archive, but it might be Waverly," I tell him. "Waverly could have access to a lifelike, custom sim if he needed one—"

"I know who Waverly is, and he's rich as fuck, but let me give you some context. A few years ago I was brought in as a consultant for PepsiCo after they'd fucked up their marketing—their idea was this whole virtual worlds component to their branding, so you could drink a Pepsi and enter this PepsiLand of the mind. They wanted the place populated with gorgeous women, of course, so they hired programmers to create sims. They wanted women created from scratch—they thought it would give them more control, more branding opportunities. The campaign was a disaster, though—we're talking a marketing directive from a major corporation with a team of top-flight programmers and all the women they created looked like—like gum. Fake. They brought me in and the first thing I did was recommend they scrap the sims and vid real women but the suits wouldn't let go of their brainchild so they stuck to their guns and the whole thing crumbled. Look at Zhou, though. She's perfect—there's nothing fake about her. Your Zhou's a model or an actress working somewhere, you can be sure of that. Let me see more of her—"

At the Spice Island Tea House, Zhou's revealing that the doctor ran an advanced amino test and told her we're going to have a daughter. Gavril checks the tags of her clothes. "Bullshit H&M," he announces, noting what she's wearing and requesting a catalog match through the Adware. Coming home from Uni-Mart, in the sweltering night when Theresa and I sat in the wind of the box fans, Gavril looks over Zhou's clothing, and in Albion's apartment Gavril watches Zhou in her loop, infinitely preparing for her party, adjusting her earring as she crosses the room. Gavril follows her from the shower to the bedroom, observing her as she dresses and undresses.

"Something called Dollhouse Bettie," he says, after inspecting the lace of her lingerie.

He examines her mantis-green dress, first checking for a tag, then tapping into the copyright and Consumer Protection Act information, strings of serial numbers he seems able to read.

"House of Fetherston," he says, after helping Zhou zip up the back of her dress, then helping her undress as the loop repeats. "Look here, at the stitching. And this embroidery around the hem. That's fucking trademarked—"

Gavril's seen enough. I take him to the 61C Café in Squirrel Hill, an old haunt, finding a table in the courtyard on a summer night, the courtyard edged with sunflowers, strings of lights suspended above us. Gavril multitasks a patch in the Archive so he can stream the end of his soccer match, Dukla Praha scoring just as we're settling in, making this one a rout. He tells me he knows people who work with House of Fetherston, that he's already seen their newest collection but doesn't recognize Zhou's particular pieces. He wonders if they're prototypes or scrapped designs, or simply haven't been released yet.

"I can find out," he says.

iLux accessing my account blends my memories into this

night—Zhou joins us, a tweed skirt and knee-high boots, a cardigan over a Phipps Conservatory T-shirt about the African Grape Tree that reads *I'm Not Dead . . . I'm Dormant!* She sits with us, dipping biscotti into her chai. Gavril studies her.

"She's here because I'm remembering nights when Theresa and I sat here—"

"I understand," says Gavril. "She's welcome—"

"Mook could have done anything to Theresa," I tell him. "He could have made her a horror show, or he could have deleted her and left all the gaps—but he's inserted Zhou so that I can't track him. Skillful insertions make it difficult to track—"

Gavril's not listening. "Don't get me wrong," he says, continuing some conversation he was having with me only in his head. "I'm sure your wife was very stylish for someone from Pittsburgh—"

"I guess so—"

"But whenever you show me Zhou substituting for your wife, she's wearing clothes like these, generic things, things she could buy from Target or H&M or wherever your wife shopped, clothes probably pulled directly from your memories and filled in by the Archive's corporate sponsors for historical accuracy. When you show me Zhou substituting for Albion, however, she wears unique clothes. She's wearing high fashion, very interesting pieces—"

"What does that tell you?" I ask him.

"Let me make a call," he says.

2, 24—

Waiting at the gates, Dulles International. Gavril's flight to London departed on time earlier this morning but my flight's delayed because of weather, an unexpected squall that's iced the wings. The passengers are glued to the feeds, waiting to be seated, streaming CNN.

Buy America! Fuck America! Sell America!

CNN cuts to rolling blackouts in Quebec, a Wisconsin teacher gangbanged by her eighth grade class, elderly men dying in Mississippi floods, NASCAR burns into trackside crowds.

Gavril invited me to drinks the other night. I told him I didn't want to go out but he insisted—he rarely insists. He told me to meet him at the Wonderland Ballroom. Our table cluttered with beer bottles, cartoons on the label augs, buzzed and feeling snapped on a microdose of brown sugar. A chemical giddiness stripping back layers of depression—laughing at almost everything Gavril said, everything around me. Face-pinned club kids and their girls inked in augged tattoos, dolphins arcing from ocean sprays and fairies fluttering in glitter. Gavril said he wanted to get me plastered. I told him I was already plastered.

"More plastered," he said.

A waiter arrived with a bottle of absinthe and set our table with glassware and sugar cubes.

"You'll think I'm a fucking genius," Gavril told me. "House of Fetherston's headquartered in San Francisco. Dollhouse Bettie is a boutique line of lingerie also designed in San Francisco. So I called a friend of mine on the West Coast, an editor at *Sick*, this L.A. fashion zine. I told him about Zhou and Dollhouse Bettie and these outfits that looked like unreleased House of Fetherston designs. I sent him images of Zhou. He got back to me in an hour. Here, have a drink—"

Gavril held the bottle of absinthe to me—teardrop-shaped, the augged label interacting with my Adware, the branding Mucha-inspired, art nouveau swirls around a lesbian orgy. The women kissed, stroking one another, writhed—and there, in the middle of the group, her hair like black tendrils of ink intertwining with the stylized frame of the design, was Zhou.

"Shit," I said. "Holy shit—"

"She's an actress in San Francisco named Cao-Xing," he said, pronouncing it Sow-Sing, saying, "she's American, born in Kansas, moved out to San Francisco. Goes by Kelly Lee. Small-time gigs. She's hardly appeared in anything, but she's registered with a couple different agencies—"

Gavril lent me enough money for a ticket to San Francisco and a hotel, with plenty left over for an extended stay if it comes to that. He told me he's flying to London early, to lie low until our situation settles down. There's a crush at the gates—nearly six hours to work my way through the queue. Staring into the streams: another murder in DC, another woman, her head and hands cut from her body. She was found in a dumpster trashed outside the Fur Nightclub. Despite six DJs and a raucous party, no one saw a thing. A flight attendant scans my Adware, checks my flight pass. The Channel 4 stream says that despite the lack of fingerprints or dental records, District police have identified the victim from a DNA match using her blood—she was living in DC from Manchester, England, on a student visa for Georgetown. The woman's name was Vivian Knightley. A part-time model to finance her studies, the streams flash American Apparel adverts of an ethereal blonde in a soccer jersey belted like a dress and knee-high tube socks—Twiggy.

"Oh, God—"

"Is everything all right?" says the attendant.

"It's horrible," I tell her.

I file toward the rear of the plane, searching for my seat, Twiggy's death reverberating in my mind and hovering in my eyes. Christ, I'm near tears. Twiggy's crime scene pics illuminate my sight, headless, her arms severed at the forearms—red hair, that Albion-red shade of hair dyed for the party—I'm nauseous, remembering her. This dead woman, pictures from England, her modeling stint. She was a poet, they're reporting, e-zine servers crashing from gawkers interested in her work, they post she was a genius fucking poet and she's already a front-runner on *Crime Scene Superstar*, with the highest instant-fuckability score the show's ever seen. Every passenger on this plane's streaming tabloids, mouths gaping in titillated shock at Twiggy's body, at performance vids of Twiggy masturbating while reciting "I reached for you this morning but you were gone," staring out the windows over the wings and the runway at Twiggy's face, every passenger consuming this young woman, this beautiful young woman, oh God, oh God. Primary school graduation pictures. Pictures of Vivian with friends in Paris. CNN streams fuck-vids sold by ex-boyfriends, Twiggy the top story, millions worldwide watching her fucked and be fucked, watching footage of her body pulled from the dumpster, laid out in the alley, streaming autopsy photographs, gray-skinned, flaccid breasts, nipples the color of stone, veins visible, the stump of neck and stumps of arms, death shots and money shots, shots of her smiling face, streams of American Apparel ads, giving head, lesbian fucks with other models, behind-the-scenes photo footage, set for superstardom, they report, what a waste, what a waste, oh God, I collapse into my seat and close my eyes, I close my eyes to it all, to block it out, and I can no longer see but I still see her in my mind, the image of her face burned into my mind's eye, her body beautiful, her beautiful hair like light, but in my mind I see her hair dyed that Albion color of blood, all that blood-red hair, and see her body cut apart, another missing woman, see her lips and eyes, oh God, I dig my nails into my scalp, Oh God, and want to rip it out, rip it all out, rip this world from me.

• PART II •

SAN FRANCISCO

2, 25—

Five hours in flight, nine hundred passengers staring into cells or screens embedded in the seats in front of them, in-flight streams prohibited: an entire season of *Whipped and Creamed*, a showing of *Jules and Peasley Blarf in Cairo*. Rank circulated air—mucosal breath, dirty diapers and thawed airplane meals, stale socks and the pungency of feet from people who'd kicked off their shoes. Garbage in the aisles, the crew too short-staffed to care—pushing drink carts through, serving splashes of liquor in cups of ice. Dawn, my face pressed to the window as the San Francisco sprawl cuts beige and concrete black against the blue ocean. The fractal coast becomes mundane the lower we descend. The sprawl comes into focus—strip malls, traffic-glutted highways, housing developments. The runway appears beneath us. The wing flaps adjust and rattle the cabin. *Seat belts on, electronic devices off.* Screaming kids, a cloud of body funk. The plane thumps as wheels hit concrete. A smattering of applause when the Adware blinks on and most of us reboot, autoconnecting with SF.net. We taxi, nearly everyone standing, anxious to leave, heads bent awkwardly beneath the overhead bins. People pulling jackets and luggage from beneath their seats, elbows forcing position in the aisle, a chemical waft from the bathrooms—urinal cake and diarrhea and disinfectant. It's been a while since I've flown. The stewardesses tell me to enjoy my stay.

Hannah.

Twiggy.

Albion.

Shuttle buses to the terminal, Delta security performing a first ID scan on the way in, sponsored hotels showering us with cheap rates. *BayCrawler* recommends an economy room in the Bayview–Hunters Point Holiday Inn, a Daily Deal. I go ahead and book, the terms and conditions scrolling in half-light. *Accept, Accept—Accept all.* Hours in lines twisting through cordons, everyone sitting on their suitcases, eyes glazed watching streams. Adware kicks in a flickering jangle, competing currency exchange rates for foreign travelers, taxicabs, yellow cabs, that old woman Paris in gold leggings begging me to switch my booking to Hilton, Days Inn with cheaper rooms and HBO blinking in the overlays, Holiday Inn blasting reminders that my reservation is *nonrefundable*, women in towels offer spa services and city tours. *You'll find a happy ending in San Francisco!*

Gavril's contact is an agent at Nirvana Modeling named C.Q. I ping him but he doesn't respond. I ping again with a friend request and Gavril's attachments, but still no response. I text: *Dominic, a friend of Gavril's. Looking for a model you might work with. Did Gavril get in touch with you?*

Armored National Guardsmen with submachine guns slung over their shoulders stalk the security line. German shepherds tethered on leashes sniff each of us, sniff our bags—I leave my backpack on the floor and the dogs surround it, running their noses along the seams. Praying they don't sniff out residue, but sober enough to have left my brown sugar back in DC. Another ID checkpoint—soldiers with handheld bar code readers scan my passport and retinas. Robotic voices chime: "Never leave your bag unattended. Remain with your luggage at all times. Never leave your bag unattended. Remain with your luggage at all times—"

A young woman ahead in line answers questions. She struggles with English, but a TSA supervisor, white-haired, pockmarked, finally stamps her passport and waves her through to the scanner. Strict policies arriving or departing for flights—we've been through this before, all of us, when we boarded the plane, but TSA makes us go through these security points again and again. I watch her hike up her shirt a few inches and slide her belt from her blue jeans. She unbuckles and removes each boot and places everything in a plastic bin. She speaks French, I can hear her now, but she doesn't understand anything the customs agents are telling her—translation apps struggling to keep up in the anemic Wi-Fi. The screener, a slight man in blue vest and gray slacks, holds his arms out to his side, each hand capped by a blue latex glove. The French woman understands now and imitates him—holds her arms outstretched. The man frisks her, running his hands along the back of her thighs and up over her like a bored lover, patting the interior of her thighs, cupping her genitals. The woman's embarrassed, but complies—she stands still while the man fondles the undersides of her breasts and runs his fingers along the underwire of her bra, what else can she do?—and when the customs agents instruct her to step through the body scan, I look with the other men to the crowdsourcing security screens placed where we all can see. We're curious—and there she is, like an etching in green, layers of her, her skin and underwear, demure, the fabric of her clothes. The buttons of her jeans and the underwire of her bra display pale green, almost white, her Adware displays like a lace doily sitting on her brain. The screeners have poker faces, playing their part of professionalism, but as I watch the screening, Adware girls overlay my sight, offering to bounce me to pay sites full of leaked airport scans—porn stars, celebrities, amateurs, perfect tens all scanned for national security, all leaked to the streams.

Passport stamped, I'm frisked and asked through into the scanner. My body is projected in green on the black glass—the travelers can see, but I wonder if anyone bothers to look.

Acid jazz over electronica—an unrecognized ringtone. *Check profile: Colvin Quinn, Nirvana Modeling, editor. Add to address book?* Yes—and Colvin's profile fills my vision as I sit on a bench to put my shoes back on. He's texted: *Gavril's friend? You're the one looking for a model?*

Cao-Xing Lee. Gavril said you know her?

Yeah, Gavril's question—that's Kelly, he writes. *Real name's Cao-Xing, but she goes by Kelly. She's one of mine, yeah. Are you booking her, or what? You can book her through the agency.*

I need to talk to her.

What do you have in mind? She's an actor, does some print work. Terrible at celebrity impersonations, but she'll work private functions if you're paying her.

I just need to talk to her.

If you book her, it goes through the agency. No freelance bullshit. But I can set up a meeting, as a favor to Gavril. She has a shoot on the first. You can visit her on set. Sound good?

Perfect—

I'll send you details—

Leaving the airport, I'm warned I'm leaving a secure green zone and have to "accept" before the warnings will blink out. Yellow cabs line the curb—*BayCrawler* displays user reviews of the drivers, the drivers standing curbside shouting at us, trying to convince us the one-star reviews are false, were posted by bitter, jet-lagged people, that they'd cut rates for a fare. Criminal record pop-ups halo most of them. The driverless AutoCabs are parked together, but *BayCrawler* flashes a scare piece about drug cartels tracking tourists in driverless cabs, forcing them off the road and murdering them for their luggage and cash. Too many warnings of pricing scams. I queue for the commuter train, downloading SF.net's top free travel apps and augs while I'm waiting. The commuter train's a maglev bullet cutting through suburban slums, empty station to empty station—storefronts blur, abandoned strip malls, cars stalled out and feathered in tickets, whole sections of outer communities burned, the wood char left to rot in the paradisiacal sun. I lose Wi-Fi until we're closer to the city center, office towers and skyscrapers coming into crystalline view. An autoconnection to City.SF.gov—a ping from a Nirvana Modeling intern waiting in my in-box, the subject line: Kelly. I download a press packet and scan through publicity shots along with tomorrow's shooting schedule. Unmistakably Zhou. Video clips from *Our Town*, *Long Day's Journey into Night*, *Gem of the Ocean*. She's not a bad actress, but most of her credits are from liquor commercials—a nude Kelly dripping with red syrup for Absolut Strawberry, in a minikilt for Dewar's. A fashion shoot tomorrow—the Nirvana Modeling intern gives the address and mentions that Kelly's been told to expect me.

We skirt the city center and enter Hunters Point. Retinal scans for fares, the station scrawled with Meech-HAM graffiti and swastikas—a graphic Meecham death's-head with hair like a corona of blonde fire. The neighborhood's shit, but the Holiday Inn looks passable and I check in through the kiosk, gathering the key cards that pop from the slots. I reset the dead bolts once I'm in my room—the economy-size little more than a closet with a sofa and toilet. Jet lag's catching up with me—but I wander out to find a grocer on the next block for a few apples and Greek yogurt, a two-liter of Pepsi and a box of Ho Hos. Men loiter on the corners here, in oversize T-shirts and baggy jeans. Someone shouts out to me, asking for money. "A quick loan," he says. I keep my head down. I lock myself into my room. Ho Ho after Ho Ho, watching the flat screen bolted to the wall—I've tried the streams, but the Holiday Inn router is spotty, blinking in and out. I try to visit the City, to visit the empty spaces, but the connection's lost.

Paying for a few minutes of sat-connect, I call Simka.

"Dominic, where are you? Are you okay?"

I open my room curtains and look out over the third-floor view of Hunters Point so that he can see what I'm seeing, an empty apartment tenement slashed with graffiti and lewd tags meant to implant viruses in unprotected Adware. There are fires somewhere distant—three columns of dark smoke mar the horizon.

"Where are you?" he asks.

"Paradise," I tell him. "I'm all right—"

"Your call says San Francisco. Dominic, are you really in San Francisco?"

"I landed a little while ago," I tell him. "I'm feeling ill, Simka. I'm feeling so bad right now. I don't know what to do—"

"You'll be fine, Dominic. Remember to breathe. In and out, in and out—"

"I've gotten mixed up in something," I tell him, not sure how much to say.

"I'm worried about you," he tells me. "What's going on? I haven't heard from you since we talked about Timothy. I can call the police if you're in trouble, Dominic. Tell me—"

Hearing his voice is like a balm on wounds I didn't quite realize I have—lonely, I realize. "I'm realizing how fucked up I've been," I tell him. "After Pittsburgh, once winter came, they used to run these PSAs about radioactive snow, do you remember? Those commercials used to stick in my mind—I'd dream about them—that person walking through snowfall. Everything serene, snow piling on trees, over lawns, on houses, before we realize that all the snow is poisoned with radiation. They'd list these symptoms. Tell us about Caesium-137. That's what my depression's like, Simka—I can't really quite explain it, I guess. When the depression settles over me, it's like I'm walking through that radioactive snow, that no matter how fast I run or try to cover myself, the snow will keep falling until I'm buried under—"

"I remember those commercials," he says.

"I'll forward my hotel information, in case something comes up, some emergency—"

"Of course," says Simka. "Dominic? You're not alone, do you understand that? Whatever you're going through, I'm here for you, I'm with you. If you're in trouble, come here. You have a home with me—"

My sat-connect runs out and I decline approval for another session. Cramped, here, in this cheap hotel—claustrophobic. I crack open the window, I want to take a walk, clear my head—just like Simka always suggested, that exercise might lift my spirits—but I can hear the braying of dogs outside and people shouting nearby. I read a paperback I brought with me, Ed Steck's *The Necro-luminosity of Pink Mist*, drinking Pepsi with hotel ice until my eyes droop closed and I sleep, dreaming of greenish drifts of ice, poisoned snow. I sleep through until morning.

3, 1—

Adverts scroll the bathroom mirror, shimmering through shower steam: *Popeyes Fried Chicken, Grand China Buffet,* accept the ten-dollar surcharge to book a cab through the mirror, using the touch screen as I brush my teeth—these things never work and I have to push twice, wondering if I've paid twice. *Wharf Central, Bay Company, Anchorage* coupons grid the ceiling and walls, skewing into pixelated distortion whenever the Wi-Fi hiccups. Local streams: cop killer guts four, VoyeurTube catches spy vids in J.Crew changing rooms. Gavril's lent me a Caraceni suit for my meetings—he told me I wouldn't be taken seriously if I showed up anywhere dressed like I usually dress and told me to know the brand in case anyone asks. *Caraceni.* I feel fake, wearing this thing—but the fit's nice, it feels nice. He told me to leave the top buttons of my shirt unbuttoned, but I can't pull off that look, exposing the upper triangle of my pasty chest, the scrawls of hair, so I button up to my neck. The coupon grids shift: *Redwood National Park bike tours, lodging,* collagen ass implants turn your sag bag into a beautiful bubble. Coffee at the House of Bagels vending kiosk in the hotel lobby. I wait for my cab outside—the weather's gorgeous.

The cab's an AutoCab tricked out for tourists—driverless, its silky voice crackles through the speakers.

"Destination?"

"Fort Point," I tell it, checking the shooting schedule I have for Zhou.

"Destination?"

"Fort. Point."

"Calculating," it says, synching with my profile before sliding into traffic. "Welcome to San Francisco—"

The topography of this place is sun-blanched ruinporn, an economic gutting—city block after city block of housing projects, slapdash QuickCrete construction jobs, acres of storage container housing sites stacked in corrugated sheet metal towers. Apartment building units with window slits. Beige patches of dead grass. A car's been pushed to the center of a playground and set on fire, the smoke and gushing flames like the oil fires they streamed from Iran and Iraq following the Israeli War. iLux catches my position, pushes notifications through the streams—warns me travel delays are likely.

"What's causing the delay?"

The cab searches, broadcasts relevant headlines: *. . . this morning, an explosion on a Muni bus . . . Several dozen feared dead . . . Thirty-six reported dead, twenty-one wounded, the death toll expected to climb . . .*

"Jesus Christ—"

"Travel delays are likely," says the taxi.

I pin the news report to a city map, overlay with the cab's route to Fort Point—it looks like we'll be passing the scene. Stuck in traffic, the air gritty, or maybe just soured by the chemical stink of the car fire we passed. Headlines swim in my eyes: a pipe-bomb explosion on the Double Rock route, the wreckage gumming up traffic for miles. *Gang-related*, crowdsourced news feeds, *Cartel dispute*, I go ahead and set up a user account with AutoCab while we're inching along, buying a week-block fare instead of paying by the meter. We reach the first police barricade and I can see the bombed-out bus ahead on our right. Cops direct us through their pylons—the scene's grisly despite the extinguished fires, the skeletal remains of a double-long bus, blown-out windows, bodies lined up on the sidewalk wrapped in sheets, some of the bodies' social profiles still lit, rapidly updating profile statuses despite being dead. Ambulances and fire trucks are on scene, but the paramedics stand around with a couple of SWAT officers—everyone's laughing now that there's no one left to try to save.

The taxi threads into a single lane. Three white cops with shaved heads and Ray-Bans hold a black teenager to the ground, his wrists zip-tied, an arsenal of automatic weapons spread along the sidewalk, baggies of cocaine and bricks of brown sugar on the hood of a Camry. Labels hover over each gun: *AK-47, FN SCAR Mk 17, M72 LAW.* The Adware's augged the cops: *Espozito*, *Stewart*, *Klein*, badge numbers and service history, real-time charges as they're levied against the kid. Already the comment fields are blowing up, CitizenWatch, SFAnti, 4thState, SFLibertarian, complaining of racially motivated violence, tagging each cop with civil disobedience accusations and filing citizen review complaints—the cops' records display in the Adware, every complaint, every charge processed, every official review. Crowds have gathered, watching disinterestedly.

"Every measure will be taken to provide for your security," the taxi says. "I've calculated a safe route—"

A few blocks past, the traffic picks up speed—emptied storefronts, boarded-over windows, abandoned cars tagged with phrases: *Slinks all the fcuk* and *187 $-T* and *God si Love*. We pass through an intersection and the city improves, like I've entered into a different city entirely, SmartTags on the businesses, coupons offering free samples of eggnog lattes at Fourbarrel Coffee, Einstein Bros. bagels, BOGO deals at Burberry and the Gap. The street narrows like we're driving through a canyon of gold, Bulgari and Louis Vuitton and Gucci, women wearing little more than string bikinis with max socials broadcasting their availability. I squint up into brilliant blue sky where a gorgeous face smiles, a model for Bovary's saying, "Everything you've always wanted." The Golden Gate Bridge looms ahead just like the innumerable pictures I've seen of it, the red spires and swooping cables vivid in the sun, almost unreal how crisp it seems. The cab pulls through Fort Point security checkpoints into a turnaround.

"Enjoy your afternoon," says the taxi. "Find your happy ending in San Fran Cisco!"

A sloping hillside, a copse of pines. The ocean spray scent of the bay. Cars are double-parked in the lots, joggers and dog walkers crowd the sunlit paths that lead downhill to the fort at the base of the bridge. The fort comes into view, a sort of squat-box brick building tucked beneath one of the bridge's behemoth arches, and NPS.Gov/Fort Point pop-ups bubble up toward points of interest in the masonry and link to articles about the Fort: Castillo de San Joaquin, 1865, the CSS *Shenandoah*, blinking for donations to fund preservation efforts and future expansion of the museum. Wandering the interior of the fort's like wandering catacombs—stone corridors and arches, the roar of the ocean and the cries of gulls reverberating across the repeating architecture, blending into a deafening echo that robs the place of any beauty. Signs guide me downstairs, to underground halls that have been roped off for the fashion shoot. A production assistant waits on a folding chair. Once she sees me, she explains that I've entered a restricted area.

"I'm here to see Cao-Xing," I tell her. "I think she knows I'm coming," but the production assistant's face doesn't brighten until I say, "Kelly Lee—"

"Sure," she says, scanning my profile against her list. "Dominic?

John Dominic? Go ahead and follow along the hallway here. They're in the middle of the shoot, so hang back until they break. Kelly's down there already—"

The air of these corridors is stale and the bricks are cold. The outer sounds of ocean and gulls and tourists have been suffocated, the only echo in the corridors is the sound of my footfalls and what I imagine to be the beating of my heart reverberating off the bricks. I'm nervous—to see her, like meeting someone I've known intimately from a distance. Will I even recognize her? I walk until I hear the whispering shutter whir of cameras and hushed voices. The corridor curves and I come to the shoot—they've set up in a cell, studio lights aimed at the curved ceiling push unnerving shadows across the walls. Massive chains hang from bolts in the stone and lay coiled. Only a half a dozen or so work the shoot—adjusting lights, stationed at a makeup table they've set up inside a pop-up tent, working a computer rig almost identical to Gavril's back home. The photographer's on his knees, a young kid, searching for angles. Zhou's here—*Kelly*—modeling with two women, the three of them painted gold, nude except for a lace of gold chains, their bodies detailed with finely drawn gold-leaf lines. Their eyes are brushed black with smoke-colored paint. They lie in the dust and in the chains, intertwined with each other, watching the photographer scurry before them like they're demons interrupted from ancient sleep. The women open their mouths as if to swallow him, the interior of their mouths and their teeth dyed crimson.

"Break. Let's pick up again in fifteen—"

One of the assistants switches on a trio of portable heaters, another offers the women sips of water through a straw. The photographer's editing his images on the monitor. He's criticizing aspects of the lighting, claiming the scene won't render when they sculpt this environment for the streams. I make my way to Zhou.

"Excuse me—Kelly?"

She smiles. "Yes?"

An odd sensation, talking to her—I'm so used to seeing her as a stand-in for Albion that I wonder if Albion's here, or has been here, that if Kelly turns away quickly enough I might see a flash of hair that matches the crimson of her mouth, like there's another, truer, world covered over by the one we're in.

"I'm—um," I say, swallowing. "Excuse me, I'm—my name's John Dominic Blaxton—"

"Oh, Mr. Blaxton," she says, "I'm Kelly Lee—I'd shake your hand, but my fingers are caked with this stuff. Four hours this morning in the makeup chair to get this applied—"

She holds up her hands so I can see they're gold. The other two models have fallen into a conversation about sushi while a makeup assistant sprays metallic paint to smooth out their sheen.

"That's all right," I tell her, our Adware updating friend statuses and synching connections—the closest we have is through Nirvana Modeling's link to Gavril and once Kelly notices I have friend status with him, she says, "You're actually friends with Gavril? Oh my God, I flag his blog on my *Lucy* account. He does amazing work—"

The photographer says, "Start wrapping it up—"

"How can I help you, Mr. Blaxton?" says Kelly. "Nirvana probably forwarded you my portfolio, but I have other work samples to send if you'd like to see more—"

Everything about her is familiar from the City, but only familiar in the way a dream of an unfamiliar place can seem familiar.

"I have reason to believe you can help me find a man named Mook—"

"Mook?" she says.

"You've worked with him—"

"Look," she says, "I really don't have time for this—"

Her body's gone stiff, her demeanor sour.

"The man has taken everything from me," I tell her, trying to keep calm.

"If you want to book me for work, go through the agency," she says. "I only work through the agency—"

"I can pay you for your time," I tell her. "I don't have much, but I'll give you everything I have if you can help me. I need to talk with him—"

"I really can't get involved in something like this," she says. "I thought you'd be interested in my professional work. I'd be happy to send you my portfolio, if that would help. If you want to book me, go through the agency—"

"Please stand to the side," says the photographer and I back out from the ring of light.

"We're really going to need you to leave," says one of the assistants.

"Just call the cops. He's trespassing at this point—"

"I don't want any trouble," I tell them. "I can get you in touch with Gavril. Kelly—what do you want? I know he's working on Anthropologie right now, I know that. I just need to know about this man. Please, I can set it up for you—"

"Talk to me after," she says. "I don't want to fuck up the job I already have—"

"Fine, sure," I say. "I'll—after the shoot. I'll wait outside—"

I back out of the cell. There's a burst of laughter from the models—about me, I suppose, to cut the tension. I'm washed over with a wave of shame and hate and cold sweat. *I've fucked it up*—Theresa, *I've fucked it up*. Ascending from the fort the aura of the shoot disappears and once I'm in the bland sun, buffeted by wind rushing in from the bay, I feel like I'd left the chamber of a goddess but fumbled my chance for grace. Three hours waiting on a park bench beside a two-hundred-year-old cannon. The Fort Point information pop-ups ping me so often I almost miss Kelly's ping when it comes. She asks if I'm still around and tells me to meet her. She flags herself and I follow hovering arrows in the Adware, pointing my way to her.

The moment you see me, she texts, *disable your connection—*

I find her sitting on a park bench. She's still painted gold, the lines of gold leaf flashing in the sun, but she wears a red wool coat. A few tourists ask to take her picture and she smiles hesitantly but lets them. I disable my connection.

"I'm sorry about the scene I was causing," I tell her. "Back there—"

She stands from the park bench. Nearly as tall as I am, but thin. She lights a cigarette and asks me to walk with her toward the water. We don't talk, and I'm aware of the attention she elicits from the crowds we pass—she must be used to being noticed, anyway, but painted gold she looks like an alien among a lesser race of beings. Most don't stare, not obviously—though I do spot a few people baldly ogling her, probably recording her with their retinal cams. There are pay streams, things like *Candid Candies* and *Real Girls*, full of vids just like these would be, of women unknowingly filmed and served up in the Adware for men in their privacy to swallow whole. At the water, Kelly takes another drag on her cigarette while I gape at the Golden Gate Bridge above us, stretching to distant hills, wondering at its immensity and trying to imagine how men in a different century than my own had constructed this thing, let alone dreamed it.

"Mook's not his name," she says.

"I don't know his name. I don't know anything about him—"

"That's good. We'll call him Mook, then. The work I do for Mook is all private stuff, off the books," she says. "If my agency knew about it, they'd drop me and I can't afford that. They own my image. The stuff for Mook is a different deal—"

"I understand," I tell her. "I shouldn't have barged in like that. I should have told you up front what I needed—"

"It's all right," she says. "If you would have told me up front, I would have told you to go fuck yourself. We're here together now, though. And if you're hooked up with Gavril, in some way, if that's true, then you're legit—"

"He's my cousin," I tell her. "I'm not in the industry—"

"I don't want to talk with you here," she says. "I don't want anyone from the shoot starting rumors about who you are. I want them to forget the word *Mook* and forget about this afternoon. I'm serious—if word gets around that I'm working jobs outside the agency, my career is fucked. I only have a few years before I'm replaced by younger girls, so I need to float all the work I can. I can't fuck this up—"

"I didn't mean any trouble," I tell her. She takes a final drag before tamping out the cigarette and saving the rest for later.

"Fuck it," she says. "Here's what you can do for me. Get out of here. Tell my agent that you met with me and liked what you saw, that I was agreeable and have the perfect look, that you're interested in hiring me but will get back to him—"

"I can do that—"

"As for you and me," she says, "book me with Gavril. Have Gavril present my agency with a contract. If I'm going to risk my work with Mook, I'll need something better to take its place—Gavril will give me that. If the contract comes through, I'll ping you and let you take me out to dinner. We can talk then, okay? I'll ping you—"

I don't want to watch her leave—I want to believe I'll see her again, that I'll learn everything from her, so I look out over the water, watching waves crash against the buffers, watching kids run from the white sea spray, laughing. In the AutoCab I leave a message with an administrative assistant at Nirvana, relaying what Kelly had told me to say—that I liked what I saw, that I was interested, that I'd be in touch. I try to call Gavril but he doesn't answer, so I write him an e-mail with everything that's happened.

Chicken McNuggets for dinner, watching an old *Battlestar Galactica* marathon on TV when I pay for a few minutes of satconnect to check my accounts.

Gavril's responded to my e-mail: *Love is an irresistible desire to be irresistibly desired—*

3, 7—

Kelly has a few things to take care of first. She says she wants to meet in Jackson Square, so I head over in that direction early, to wait in City Lights. *Poetry is the shadow cast by our streetlight imaginations*, carved into the sidewalk. *Ferlinghetti*. Chessboard floors and room after room of books on wooden shelves—rare, places like these. Coming here's like a pilgrimage. Posters of glowering geniuses ring the walls, Ginsberg among them, wild-eyed and ink-stained—Ginsberg, whose work I once memorized and chanted at 2 and 3 a.m. on empty Pittsburgh streets. I was a teenager then, loving the feel of his words in my mouth, loving the shock and lucidity of his imagery. It's been too long since I've felt like that—I pick up a copy of *Howl and Other Poems*. They stock titles here the streams never promote, titles never on bestseller lists and never with the full weight of marketing departments hyping them on daytime talk shows or blurbing them through bookseller apps—European novelists, dissident writers, established writers I'd lost track of in the past decade, like J. Constantine, Picard, Lucille Hash, all with new volumes, a new edition of the collected works of Bob Dylan and Grace K.'s new translation of *Beowulf*. I pick these up, buy an armload of books—gouging my Visa for thousands more than this trip is already costing me, but worth it to buy this paper, to hold the weight of these books in my arms. The cashier wonders if I've depleted their poetry section and I laugh. "Maybe I have," I tell her, "maybe—"

Kelly pings, *There in fifteen—*

A few blocks to the restaurant so I walk, cradling my paper bag of books in both hands so the bottom won't rip, sweaty and wheezing when I reach her. Kelly's waiting on the sidewalk, wearing a baby-doll dress she once wore to impersonate Albion in the Archive, elegant in a cloche hat and all that creamy lace.

"I've already taken care of the wait," she says. "I know one of the cooks and he's saved us a quieter table where we can talk. There's a coat check room—"

"I've got it," I tell her, readjusting the sack in my arms. "Books—"

"Gavril voiced earlier," she says. "I was flustered at first, hearing his voice—I admit I thought you were full of shit about Gavril, and I was surprised to actually talk with him. We came to an understanding. He says he's going to change my life with the work he's giving me. He says he'll use me for Anthropologie, fly me out to London with him, but he made it clear that everything depends on how much I can help you. I'm not sure what I'll be able to do for you, but I'll tell you about my work with Mook, if that's what you're interested in. You don't understand how big of a break this is for me.

You should have heard my agent when the contract came through. I'm yours tonight, Dominic. Anything you need is yours—"

"Good," I tell her. "Let's start with the food—"

The restaurant's called Ambergris, a seafood place—intimate booths and smoked glass lit by candlelight. Kelly leads me through. The dress doesn't cover much of her legs, her patent leather heels add inches to her height and her socials flash her modeling work, flicking vids of runway shows and behind-the-scenes clips of lingerie shoots. I feel everyone's eyes on us as we pass. Our booth is set off from the others, private—the kind of table that might usually get bad service, but perfect for us tonight. I shove my books beside me. The smell of curry, of citrus, smoked fish. Zhou across the table's disorienting—*Kelly*. I have to remind myself that this is Kelly, that her name's Kelly, that she's not an illusion in the Adware. She orders rum for us both once we've settled in.

"To getting what we want," she says for a toast. We click glasses and I take the shot, the dark rum vanilla smooth and warming.

"I fell into some trouble back east," I tell her. "I got mixed up with some powerful men but I have reason to believe that Mook can protect me from them. I have other reasons to find him, too. He took something very valuable from me—"

"*Mook* rhymes with *book*," she says. "Not *fluke*—"

"You said that 'Mook' isn't his name—what is his name? What's Mook?"

"Are you a gamer?"

We're interrupted by a soft swell of music from the tabletop touch menu, a gentle, impatient, reminder—I order mahimahi and Kelly a salad with sushi. Another round of rum.

"Mook finds political allegories in the video games he plays," she says. "You've played first-person shooters, haven't you? At least know what they are? You're given a point of view and you murder everything in sight. All those nameless, faceless waves of enemies you murder are called mooks in gamer parlance. He's adopted the notion of mooks for his theories about the state. He believes that one day the mooks will kill their killers—"

"He's a communist, then? Mooks are the proletariat, is that it?"

"Anarchy," she says. "Actually, he'd bristle at any label you applied to his pet theories, but he's enthralled by the communist mythology, despite himself. He believes in the overthrow of the bourgeoisie and the dissolution of the state. When you hear him talk about this stuff, you'd think he's telling you about the End Times—"

"Who is he?"

"A terrorist," she says. "An artist. I really don't see how he can help protect you, though—"

"Tell me about an image he uses of a woman walking two other women like they're dogs. He pulled it from an Agent Provocateur printbook—"

"Oh, sure, he calls that one *The Dog Walker*. He once told me that image is personal to him, that it's meant to rub pepper into the eyes of his enemies," she says. "He articulates his political thought through imagery. He's underground, off the grid—He once told me that Blum & Poe offered to sign him, offered to make him rich, but he turned them down because he's against the capitalist ethos. Death's-Heads, Dog Walkers, Blood Diamonds. He tags everything—some people tear down walls and billboards to collect his stuff. I was at a party following a shoot and the guy, this producer, had the side of a Corvette Mook tagged hanging in his living room. The side of an entire red Corvette just because it was painted with a Meecham death's-head—"

"Graffiti on walls? Mook's tech savvy. I'm surprised he sticks with paint for his art—"

"He doesn't. He started with paint, but he didn't get famous until the geocached installations—"

"Explain those to me—"

"Short films that will only download and play when someone's Adware hits the exact coordinates he's established. About a year ago, he set up an installation in front of City Hall—when you reach the last step leading to the building, the exact correct spot along the stairs, a stream downloads to your Adware, whether you consent or not—it's a pornographic stream of then mayor Costa fooling around with two underage girls, snorting cocaine off their asses. It hijacks your vision until the film ends. The installations can't be removed because they're broadcast from satellites he's hacked. Understand?"

"And he has these installations all around the city?"

"All around the country. There are fans of his who try to track them down, catalog them—but Mook says only about twenty-five percent of his installations have been discovered so far."

"Are they all antigovernment?"

"Not all of them," she says. "Most are love letters to Meecham. He's obsessed with President Meecham. You should hear him—he sounds like an American flag–bleeding capitalist patriot in one breath, but in the next he'll curse the mere notion of government and calls capitalists the scum of the earth. He once showed me this painting he made called *The Worker's Paradise* but it was only this weird portrait of Meecham painted all in gold. He hates government but loves Meecham. He says truth lies in contradictions, so he expresses his belief system through images because images contain contradictions without becoming contradictions—"

"He once implied there are others he's working with. He said he was Legion. Does that mean anything to you?"

"There are others, but I wouldn't know what he's referring to. Sometimes he's grandiose—"

"How about a woman named Albion Waverly? Have you ever met her?"

"I know the name Albion," she says. "I thought Albion was just the name he called me—"

"What's the job?"

"Strange things," she says. "I don't quite understand the specifics. He has a suite over at the Brocklebank he uses for a studio. He's fitted out the place like a soundstage. VR cams, sculpting engines. He has a Hasselblad with 3-D and tactile capture, a shoulder mount. I've worked on plenty of shoots and VR work, but I've never seen anything like his studio—all top-of-the-line gear. He's heavy into the equipment he uses. When I show up for our meetings, he has clothes already picked out for me, gorgeous clothes, and has instructions for me to follow—"

"Like the clothes you're wearing now. They must be from one of your sessions with Mook," I tell her. "I recognize it—"

"House of Fetherston," she says. "I couldn't afford this otherwise. He tells me what to wear, what to do. He shows me vids of women and has me re-create them frame by frame, sometimes it's like a dance. He's making a series of short films. Usually I'm re-creating vids of a woman he calls his collaborator. He pings her, sometimes, during our sessions—"

"Albion," I tell her.

"He's careful not to say her name—"

"What does he ask you to do?"

"Lie fully dressed on the bed. Bend my legs a certain way. Sit in a certain position while reading. Fix my lipstick while looking in the mirror, adjust my hair. Prepare a salad—no, cut the lettuce like this. Greet people as if I'm in a boutique or a gallery. Smile, shake hands—"

"Ride in an elevator, flirting with another woman—"

"The blonde," she says. "You know all this work? If I perform an action slightly off, I have to do another take until he's satisfied—"

Our food arrives, elegantly plated—minimalist. Kelly picks up a quivering piece of sushi and bites into the pink flesh, closing her eyes to savor the taste. I fork off a bite of my mahimahi and realize my dinner's already a quarter gone.

"How did you get involved with him?" I ask her.

Her real love is acting, she tells me—it always has been. She tells me about her business partner, another actress. "We've already performed Mamet's *Boston Marriage*," she tells me, "and Genet's *The Maids*. Our most recent work was a staging of Bergman's *Persona* set during World War II, but spare. I played an actress, Hui Zhong, a survivor of the Rape of Nanking, who's interred at a mental hospital in Lijiang. My partner Tía played the nurse, Miao Tian.

"Mook approached me one night after a performance. He complimented my acting—gushed, really. He asked if I had regular work and asked if I would work for him—some acting, some VR sculpting. He didn't introduce himself or tell me what I'd be doing, but he flashed the kind of money he was willing to pay—"

"Can you introduce me to him? I need to talk with him—"

"I figured you'd want to meet him," she says. "Listen, I don't know who you think he is—Mook's just a weird guy. He's very talented, maybe a genius, but he's just a lonely pervert who trumps himself up in the streams. People who've heard of him want to take him seriously as an artist, but he avoids that scene. I'll sell him out in exchange for Gavril, but I don't want him to get in real trouble over this—"

"Mook took my wife from me—"

Expedient not to tell her about the body of Hannah Massey, but I mention Timothy and Waverly and tell her what Mook's been doing to them. I tell her a little about Albion. I tell her about Zhou—Kelly seems shocked to hear this, like she truly didn't know what her work with Mook amounted to. I tell her why she's important, that Zhou's the only thing I have left of my wife.

"Fuck it," she says. "I didn't know what Mook was doing. I don't know why he ruined the image of your wife. I'm so sorry—"

I pay our bill and accompany her home—she lives close, so we walk. Kelly's profile's a mood display, astrology charts synched with a real-time map of the night sky. She's haloed in diamond stars and animated illustrations of constellations. We weave through cliques of club kids and drag queens, side streets like carnivals, but I'm the odd one in my Caraceni suit, clutching and struggling with the weight of my paper sack of books. We walk through a pop-up market, a row of booths—Kelly stops at a street vendor selling homemade perfumes. She spritzes her wrists, sandalwood vanilla on one wrist, lilac on the other. She holds her wrists to me and tells me to breathe.

"Lilac," I tell her.

"Do you want to experience one of Mook's installations?" she asks. "You're near one, actually. There's one near here he calls *The Apotheosis of American Innocence*, or something like that—"

Kelly leads down a cross street, mostly residential—until we reach a parklet, nothing more than a few trees and a single bench, some places to chain bicycles. She points out a dogwood tree.

"You should use this tree as your marker," she says.

"How does this work?"

"Put your back against the tree, then walk forward in a straight line toward the street—"

I do what she says. One step away from the edge of the parklet, my Adware's commandeered by sat-connect—my anti-malware blinks but is useless and soon my vision's hijacked by a vision of Eleanor Meecham, long before she was president, back when she was a model for American Eagle Outfitters, just fourteen or fifteen. She's not wearing anything, but drapes herself with an American flag like a robe. She walks through honey fields of wheat. I can almost taste the fresh air. Her hair matches the fields, the sunshine glows golden on her skin. The mountains ringing the horizon seem lavender. The installation is a perfect moment of serenity, but only lasts thirty seconds before I'm plunged back into the San Francisco night.

"Sometimes they're beautiful," says Kelly.

We reach her apartment and she says she'll ping me once she hears from Mook about their next appointment, that I can meet him if I show up in her place.

"I'm expecting to hear from him tonight—"

I wait to see her safely inside before leaving. Alone on her front curb—like dreams I've had of finding myself alone on city streets I know should be crowded. By the time a cab answers my call I'm as hungry as if I'd never eaten, the mahimahi feeling like little more than an appetizer.

"Destination?" it asks as I buckle in.

"How about some barbecue," I tell it. "Maybe just sort by user reviews, I don't have a specific place in mind. Take me to the highest rated—"

Back in my hotel room, Memphis Minnie ribs from a Styrofoam tray and a slice of chocolate cake in a plastic cup. I flip through the books I bought, but don't want to stain the pages with barbecue sauce fingerprints so I loop Kelly's commercials from her portfolio, aroused by liquor spots where she's dripping with strawberry sauce and vodka. I scroll through her production credits, looking to link to her version of *Persona*—instead I find her version of Genet's *The Maids*, and watch her in her mistress's clothes, playing out the roles of domination and submission with her sister maid, the women tiptoeing toward sex and blood. Watching the women onstage, bathed in the blood of their masters, the actresses kiss each other and I think of Kelly's wrists spritzed with lilac perfume—I could have kissed her wrists, delicate wrists. Theresa. I've undressed and lay huddled beneath the blankets, the room lights off but the coupon grids on the ceiling and walls bathing everything in an artificial multicolored glow. I don't know if the coupons are real, if they're really lighting my room, or if the coupons exist only in my Adware and the light I see is nothing but an illusion. I check the sat-connect rates and even though they're peak right now, I accept—

Schenley Park where we walked together. Winter in Pittsburgh. Snow sits heavy on the canopy of branches and sifts down in sudden, gentle gusts. Panther Hollow Trail, creek beds dried out leaving black rivulets of mud skimmed with ice, snowfall on the stone bridges. Adjust the tabs to summer and watch the ice melt to flowing water, watch the trees thicken with dark leaves, the paths obscured by shadow. This is loss. There was never a funeral for Theresa, for anyone—just the mass cremation.

We'd lose ourselves in those long walks through the park following our meetings with Dr. Perkins and Dr. Carroll, discussing options—Lupron, Clomid, Serophene. Remembering how difficult it had been to conceive. In the summer, at home, we'd escape the swelter of our second-floor unit by walking through Shadyside until 2 a.m. or later. These were the nights she'd dream of our lost child. She wondered whether something was wrong with her—afraid to use fertility drugs because she worried about God, oddly fatalist those nights and terrified about bleeding. We'd come home in sheens of sweat and strip naked and sit on our couch drinking ice water while the box fans propped in our windows churned the humid air.

I go there now—

Through the foyer—but it's Kelly waiting for me in our living room, the box fans pushing moist air around the room. Zhou. I wake in my hotel room in the middle of the night with a leaden ache through my chest that I wish I could grab with both hands and pull from myself.

"I'm so sorry, I'm so sorry," I pray, but I don't know who or what I'm praying to—nothing answers my prayer, nothing ever will.

Nearing 3 a.m., Kelly pings: *Brocklebank, Room 2173; shoot scheduled for 3 p.m. the day after tomorrow. Gavril called. I'm off to London, a red-eye. Ciao!*

3, 9—

The victim of urban renewal, it looks like, Nob Hill looped off from the rest of the city by a ring of sheer one-way streets called the Downtown Connector—box stores lying dormant, storefronts choked off and vacant. The city's done well retrofitting nineteenth-century architecture instead of tearing it down, but everything's dingy and boarded up. Poor whites meander the streets, obese women in spandex herd groups of kids on leashes to dollar stores and men clutter the liquor stores and QuickCash. The AutoCab announces we've arrived at the Brocklebank, but the building looks nothing like the pictures online. A famous building, once—

Wiki pop-ups flash Technicolor vid snippets of century-old films that were shot here, but the building's changed, the stonework façade's been effaced, updated with smooth white weather barrier that's already cracked and streaked with filth. Hovering billboards advertise *Pussy squirts and cum lovin', Adult Books and More*. I ask the cab to wait for me in the turnaround.

"I shouldn't be long—"

There's a kiosk in the lobby, but no attendant and everything's off-line anyway. A bank of elevators with scratched metal doors and buttons with broken lights. I don't really know what I'm doing here, I don't really have a plan—I'm nervous . . . nervous to see Mook—a bit manic, toe-tapping to Bruce Hornsby and the Range over the speakers, "Mandolin Rain." I lean on the elevator wall and force myself to breathe, to breathe, to regain myself. He'll recognize me, I realize, but I won't recognize him—I've only seen his avatar, assuming the droopy-old-man bit is an avatar. What the hell was I thinking by coming here? I should have handled this differently. When the elevator doors slide open, I pause in the second-floor hallway, figuring out what I'll say to him—but my mind's gone blank. Tell him Kelly sent me here? Twin vases filled with fabric flowers arranged in front of a smudged mirror. I'm moving without quite realizing that I'm moving—first the wrong way, down the wrong hallway, the unit numbers increasing, so I swing the other way and count down until I find 2173, a corner suite. A white door with gold numbers. The door's already inched open.

"Hello?" I say, knocking, nudging it farther open. Odd odor from the room, rancid metallic. "Hello? I need to talk with you—"

No answer, so I slip inside. The fetid metal stink's dizzying, but it's not the smell that overwhelms me—I scream when I see him, the dead man half flopped on the sofa, his toes dangling to the carpet, blood on the ceiling and walls in sloppy looping arcs like someone's sprayed the wall with blood from a hose. I fall. Backward, against a television and knock it from the stand. Screaming. Or I must have wanted to scream, but the stink of blood fills my mouth like a filmy coating when I scream so I choke it off. Mook—here he was, the legs in trousers, the head scalped, the face wearing a veil of blood, the crown of his hair a few feet away on one of the throw pillows as if he'd sat up from a nap and left it there. My Adware's flashing a *red* strobe, attempting to call 911 but I keep overriding the emergency settings, the software scanning nearby buildings for an AED, flashing directional vids for performing CPR, overlaying the dead body with bright white medical graphics, pointing out exactly where I should lay my hands and push. Chest compressions, breathing. Check for breath. I shut it off, shut everything off. I shut the door and set the chain and dead bolts and slump quivering to the carpet, thinking.

Ping Kelly, the police? No, no—keep quiet. I've never seen a corpse before, not in reality, not like this. Ten or fifteen minutes or more before regaining some sense, before my breathing evens, even though my heart's still pounding like a rabbit's heart. This was his studio—this suite, every piece of furniture cleared out except a sofa and the television. There's a kitchen, a bedroom off the main hall. The rest of the space is white, blood-spattered now, with an array of cameras that have been toppled over and broken apart. There's a green screen setup and a white stage, the stage set with buckets and clotheslines and fabric that's been dyed purple hanging to dry—my God, replacing the trace of Albion in Peyton's apartment, that first trace I'd found. Opening the window, I feel like I'll get drunk on the fresh air—I throw up on the balcony and spend another few minutes with dry heaves before I bring myself to look again at the body. Whoever did this had attacked his face—the face is zebra striped in blood and cuts, like he'd been hacked at with a flurry of crisscrossed razor blade swipes. The neck was gashed open and dug out, the head nearly decapitated. So much blood, Christ, so much blood, the comforters sopped like wet paper towels, the carpet squishy. His hands are cut off at the wrists. Sawed off, but the hands are still folded on his lap. Like Twiggy's body—Timothy did this. I try to avoid the blood but it's already on me—my pants, my shoes. The top of Mook's head has been removed—the top of the skull's been cut open and the brains scooped out. The brain is smeared across the armrest, at least I think this is the brain—the Adware gone. The eyes have been cut apart, the retinal lenses sliced out.

Fuck, fuck, fuck. The presence of mind to use the clean bath towels to wipe off as best I can, to wipe off the bottom of my shoes and my hands, and everything in the room I've touched, hoping the police, when they find the body, won't be able to trace me here. Wiping down the walls, inadvertently smearing Mook's blood. Just stop, *just stop*. I drop the towels in the tub. Rinse the blood I've already stepped in off the soles of my shoes and leave them near the door. The blood on the carpet seeps through my socks, sticky cold, but I keep my shoes off so I won't leave bloody shoe prints through the halls when I leave. I've been here almost twenty minutes already—too long. Concentrate, damn it. Theresa. I'm here to find Theresa or information about Hannah Massey, or Timothy, or Waverly. Information would have been in Mook's Adware, if anywhere, but the Adware's gone. I try the bedroom. Clothes in the bureau, a desk scattered with papers and a computer but the computer's been smashed open and gutted. I look over the papers—bills, drawings, things I can't understand. There's nothing I can find here about Theresa or Hannah Massey, nothing about Timothy or Waverly, nothing. I'm shaking—I need to get out of here. Back in the main room I fear Mook's body might breathe and stand up on its own. I stare at it almost willing the dead to stay dead. There's nothing here, nothing.

That's not quite true—

A series of framed watercolors hangs over the sofa—six of them, of uniform size and barnwood framing, on cream paper, maybe two feet on a side. The paintings are finely drafted but raw, a mixture of ink, charcoal and watercolor, all depicting facets of the same house—the house down in Greenfield with the words of Christ painted on the broad side. The house of Waverly's wife, of Timothy. Thinking of Timothy's memory maps that Simka showed me, the draftsmanship—are these paintings Timothy's? No, the style's too different. The artwork emits despair and ruin, each drawing a skewed, cubist detail of the architecture—of a wrecked cornice, a sagging overhang, a window frame without a window, a rotting cellar door. The whitewash words of Christ fold in on themselves in the collapse, unreadable if I didn't already know what they said: *Except a man be born again*. These are drawings of a ghost, made by a ghost. I push the couch with Mook's body a few feet from the wall so I can sidle near and pull down the paintings. Too heavy to carry a stack of six framed pieces, so I slide the artwork from the frames, hands shaking, smudging bloody thumbprints on the first two pieces until I'm more careful and pull the rest out clean. I roll the pieces together and tuck the tube into my suit jacket. Fingerprints on the framing glass? I wipe them down and leave the frames in the tub with the bloody towels. I put on my shoes, feeling Mook's blood on my feet like I've been walking on water.

The AutoCab's where I asked it to stay and I tell it to drive, suffering another bout of dry heaves, the image of the man's body recurring.

"Destination?"

"Drive. Just drive—"

"Destination?"

It's not a warm day but I'm sweating. The hovering flash billboards advertise luxury watches but the rubies in their faces look like spots of blood. "Shit." I can't think. "Just—take me back to my hotel, where you picked me up. I don't know the address—"

The AutoCab pulls from the building. I left the windows open—up there. *Fuck, fuck.* Thinking of ways they can track me—vomit on the balcony, shoe prints in the blood—the AutoCab's route is saved, they can tell I was dropped off and picked up from the building if they check the AutoCab records. They must have security cameras. I must have left fingerprints, or hairs, or something—they'll find those. Did I wipe off the window that I opened? Did I wipe off the handle I'd used to open it? No. Did I wipe off the door handle? No—*No.* I should ping the police, tell them everything. Ping Kelly. I'm innocent. Innocent in this, I should—

"Drop me off over here—"

A few blocks from my hotel. A Payless shoes—I buy a pair of Adidas for cheap, pay with a retinal scan. My old shoes and socks in the Payless bag and thrown out in an alley dumpster. *Think.* It dawns on me: three District soldiers approached Kucenic, intimidated him. Three District soldiers stopped me at a checkpoint shortly after I quit Waverly—they downloaded something, I remember. Some quick thing I accepted. *Fuck.* There's a Cricket Wireless storefront across the street—the place smells like marijuana smoke and Burger King. The clerk's a few minutes slow to wander from the back room. He seems surprised to see me waiting at the counter.

"I need you to tell me—how I can fix—I think there's someone listening in on my thoughts, following me around through my Adware—"

"Come into the back," he says. "You're either paranoid or hacked. Either way, happens all the time—"

While the clerk's running a malware scan, he cleans his tools with an alcohol-dipped cotton swab. He whistles as he applies the local anesthetic, tells me my brain's loaded with spyware, tells me not to worry—he'll take care of it. He cuts open my head. He digs out my receiver, replaces it. He tells me I might have some performance issues because the Cricket parts are Euro imports, nowhere near the quality of the Chinese iLux gear—but the iLux processors will still work and without the malware everything will speed up anyway. I switch connection plans, picking up a Cricket pay-as-I-go.

"You're a new man," he tells me, bandaging my head. He writes out a prescription for medicinal cannabis for the postanesthetic pain. "Brand-new—"

A quick trip to Walgreen's for Tylenol and Advil and a pack of THC cigarettes. At the hotel I shower twice, the water scalding my fresh scalp wounds. I ball up my bloody clothes in the paper bag from City Lights and pitch it in a dumpster outside. The Cricket clerk's done a shitty job and when the anesthetic starts wearing off my skull feels like a plague of fire ants—I check beneath the bandage and my scalp's puckered with his careless incisions. Fuck, it *burns*. Swallow the pills and light up and start to numb—numb for hours as I watch TV, waiting for the police to charge in, thinking they might do it like cops in the streams, with a battering ram to splinter the door and SWAT agents rolling me to the ground, tasing me. Voter ID laws passed twenty years ago—I remember registering my fingerprints and DNA with the government when I renewed my voter registration card. Was it constitutional for the police to check the voter ID rolls without cause? I think there might have been a court case—

Television's no good, so I pay for sat-connect to lose myself in the streams. *Cricket* appears in block green font, iLux in gold cursive, Holiday Inn in retro-1950s lettering. Shitty offers and add-ons before I reach the streams. Mook's body whenever I close my eyes and a barren sickness at reliving his zebra-slashed face. Prime-time listings—*Chance in Hell*'s on tonight, the season finale. I hit the vending machine for a dinner of cherry Pop-Tarts, Ho Hos and Pepsi. Walking the hotel hallways, I feel the dead body's somehow still present with me—like it's a black spider I've seen slip from view behind the furniture but know is still there. It's there, across the city, but it's there. Gwendolyn Tucker on *Chance in Hell*, two-time CMA performer of the year, eighteenth birthday announced on the *Grass on the Field* blog. Eating the crusts of the Pop-Tarts first, then the middle, streaming Gwendolyn Tucker as she fucks her "Regular Joe," a roofer from Tennessee. Recaps of how the Regular Joe entered the *Chance in Hell* lottery on a whim while buying hot dogs and coffee at an Exxon, of how he survived the initial Internet and text message voting, and the elimination challenges, Jesus Christ, I've dealt with images of the dead for so long I thought I'd be numb to something like this, but I've never seen a ruined corpse so close, never had to smell something like the tang of all that blood. Camera crews highlight the Regular Joe's hometown, a hardscrabble cluster of trailers and ratty ranch houses, and show him working his job, hammering shingles with a crew of guys, rolling from house to house in his Ford F-250 Super Duty. A Republican, a good American. He's married, his wife's a spitfire brunette—*Chance in Hell* shows her laughing, uncomfortable. "I feel sick about it in a way," she says, "knowing my husband will be having sex with Gwendolyn Tucker and all, but this is *Chance in*

Hell so I'm real proud of him and Lord knows we could use the money and I'm such a huge fan of her anyway." Everything's confused when I try to sleep, Mook's body and crime scene images of Twiggy—Timothy's here, Timothy's *here*—headless and handless, of Hannah Massey lying reposed in river mud. Take it as a matter of faith that nothing exists and maybe never has. I wake up screaming—

Dr. Reynolds,

The moment you contact me, or the moment you contact my friends or family, I will release all evidence in the Pittsburgh City-Archive linking you to the death of Hannah Massey. If you leave me alone, Hannah will stay buried—

—JDB

3, 18—

Simka would call it PTSD. The past week and a half holed up in my hotel room, thinking every cleaning lady that pounds my door is Timothy pounding my door—thinking every car in the lot outside my window is Timothy's car, every headlight flash is Timothy's headlights. I spend hours peering through a slit in the curtains, taking notes about the cars pulling into the lot, parking, leaving, trying to figure which one might be his, if any. No one to turn to. A police cruiser circles through every afternoon at 3:30—it's some schedule, some patrol routine, but I break out in cottony-mouthed panic that they've tracked me here. Two in the morning, three, I want to confess to the murder, confess that I murdered Mook just to end this waiting, end seeing Mook whenever I try to sleep, fitful sleep, the blood scent of his room stinking up my room when all this place really smells like is pizza boxes and coffee. I finally let the cleaning service take care of things—the room smelled fresh for about a half an hour after they left but that blood scent's seeped into everything again. It's all in my mind, an hallucination of blood, that's all, that's all.

I spend most nights talking with Simka, but all we talk about is the past—I haven't told him that whoever killed Mook will kill me, too—Timothy—that I'm waiting for my death sentence in a Holiday Inn.

I talk with Gavril. Zhou's been staying with him—Kelly—he's sent pics of the two of them in London, bouncing around like tourists in love at Trafalgar Square, Westminster Abbey, the London Eye. I tell him I've tried to ping Kelly, to explain what's happened, but she won't respond.

"She thinks you killed him," he says. "I told her that's ridiculous, but she's scared—"

"I didn't kill him. Tell her I didn't kill him—"

Despite Gav's swagger I know he's terrified. He tells me he's already been in touch with some producer friends of his, a stringer for TMZ and another at CNN, who are interested in the footage of the murder.

"I've teased the story—high-profile businessmen, college girl sex, murder, cover-up. I told them it's breaking fucking news about one of the richest men in America. You give the word, the story hits the streams—"

Gavril's reviewed what I'd sent him about Hannah Massey—and now the weight of her murder bears down on him, too, I can tell, like he's carrying a bit of radiation close to his heart. Gavril's world is beauty and fluff and light, or should be—but he's feeling the threat against him now, knowing that he's been drawn into this mess because of me, because of his association with Kelly.

"Maybe you should come out here," he says. "Maybe we can hide out for a while. I have contacts in Brazil, maybe we could head down to São Paolo together, wait this out on the beach—"

"I don't think I can wait this out," I tell him. "Timothy's been waiting this out for a decade at least—I can't last like that. You can't. Gavril, you can't just disappear—"

"Fuck that, brother. I'll transfer you cash and you can buy a ticket to Heathrow. You could be here by tomorrow. We could take the train to Prague, wait at my mother's farm—"

"I shouldn't have mixed you up in this," I tell him. "Christ, I'm so sorry. I didn't know what was going on—"

"I think I'm falling in love with her," he says long after midnight.

"Kelly?"

"I think once we're finished with the shoot tomorrow, I'll try the Lady Chatterley thing with her. Out in the fields—"

"Christ, Gav. You're supposed to be channeling Robert Frost—"

"This business can be cruel to the ones we love—"

When his voice ends, the early hour silence is oppressive so I turn on the TV and classical music on KDFC and stream and piece together the traces I've saved of Albion. Albion. Every night I wait for Mook's body and Hannah Massey's body and Twiggy's body. I close my eyes—and it's like they're lying in bed with me, these ghosts.

Waverly once asked me to track a ghost for him. Albion. I unroll the paintings of the Christ House and spread them out on the sofa—scan them and search the universal image cache. There are hits, but only low-res matches on San Francisco art blogs, unmarked and unlabeled. E-mail the bloggers through contact pages, inquiring about these images.

I pick up a magnifying glass at Walgreens and spend hours studying each painting—obsessively detailed, the wood grain's drawn on every board, veins drawn in on every leaf of weeds. Are these Mook's? No signatures—the style's much different from Mook's usual work, more like a cubist version of Andrew Wyeth than the graffiti agitprop he's known for. Timothy? I saw Timothy's memory maps in Simka's office, and even though they were good, they weren't this detailed, this perfect. I may have found a partial fingerprint in the charcoal dust of the drawing of the front porch. Studies of a single house. Fetishizing the house. Only one of the six paintings seems to be an interior view, a view of a window with hints of trees, a faint representation of a fleur-de-lis, partially erased, the planks of an unfinished hardwood floor, but the point of view of the painting is torqued, disorienting.

I pull the comforters over my head, carving a small tunnel through the blankets for fresh air. I load the City—the pay-as-you-go's much slower than the iLux contract-plan, so the Fort Pitt tunnel buffers and the City skyline breaks apart in a digitized blur, *buffering*, before the stream catches up and the City resolves. Greenfield loads, the Run, Saline Street to the vacant lot near Big Jim's restaurant—I'm outside in winter, seeing my breath. I skirt the vacant lot and approach the Christ House from a side street, *Verily, verily, I say unto thee, Except a man be born again, he cannot see the Kingdom of God*. The house is smoke-charred from the fire, some sort of special effect still lingering here.

The porch smells like damp soot, the front door burned black. I use Kucenic's override codes and brace myself for another bomb blast of heat, but it never comes—just a yawning, moist smell of rot as I step inside. The house is spare. Cold. No furniture in the living room, only soot streaks and blackened ceiling beams. There's a fireplace in the corner that had been converted to an altar, a burned wooden crucifix intact except for the missing arms of Christ. A dining room, a cut-glass chandelier melted black. I kick through ash as I walk. A kitchen without appliances, just plugs and hookups, gas lines protruding from the floor. Between the dining room and kitchen, a stairway descends to the basement. The smell that rises is dank, but that's just my imagination feeding this place, just impressions in the iLux—I flick the light switch, but it doesn't work. Everything is darkness. Running the length of the wall is a pipe meant to be a railing. I hold on and descend the stairs, following through into impenetrable basement darkness until my foot touches concrete. I inch ahead—water running somewhere, a trickle sound somewhere nearby. My foot touches something and I reach out—porcelain. Wet porcelain, a leaking toilet at the bottom of the stairs. I feel along the wall, concrete blocks furry with mold. I find a utility sink and a drain. I hear sounds—breathing—from somewhere in the dark.

"Albion?"

The breathing's coming from a root cellar, but when I open the door, the room is empty. The sound of breathing is silenced. I close the door and hear the breathing again. Whoever's here in this basement room hasn't been archived—just her breathing.

The rooms on the second floor haven't been burned—bedrooms up here, the fleur-de-lis wallpaper I recognize from the watercolor is faded and peeled but intact. I find Albion in the second bedroom on the right. She and Peyton Hannover lie together in a queen-size bed, their bodies gaunt and white, naked together, wrists tied with twine to the bedposts, their ankles blistered and rubbed raw from twine binding their feet together. I work to untie their wrists, but this is not real, they're not real, and just as I untie the knots, the Archive resets and the rope is retied.

Footsteps in the hallway—Timothy. His face is much younger than the face I know—gaunt, bearded. He unbuttons his shirt and undresses, he slides naked between the women, but the moment he touches them, their heads transmogrify into pigs' heads. Maybe that's why Mook was here, maybe that's why this house is burned—maybe Mook mangled these archival scenes so no one could relive them. I look at Peyton's and Albion's eyes, and despite their pig faces, their eyes are still women's eyes, terrified, wounded. Timothy gropes them, but they just stare—Albion at the ceiling, Peyton at the far wall. Timothy groans, barking almost as he licks their breasts, biting their nipples and caressing them. He kisses between Albion's legs, then thrusts into her, using his hand on Peyton. The two women turn their eyes toward each other, almost willing each other to endure Timothy's assault. Peyton whimpers. Jesus—what am I seeing? This is preserved in the Archive—which means Timothy must have filmed himself doing this. Albion clenches her teeth to keep from crying out. I kneel beside her and look up to the ceiling where she looks. I arch my head back just as she arches her head back, and I see out the window above the bed that she can see out of—the point of view is torqued, but I can see hints of trees. The watercolor of the interior depicts this view—the paintings of the house were made by Albion.

Albion disappearing from the Archive means she was alive when Timothy and Waverly thought she had died with Pittsburgh. Who is she? Waverly claimed she was his daughter—

Albion is Mook's client—Albion hiring Mook to delete her from the Archive, to delete scenes like this from being eternally relived—

Waverly hiring me to distract me from Hannah Massey—

Waverly hiring me to find Albion and Mook—

Tie up their loose ends—

Albion, Peyton. The explicit violence of Timothy rutting women with pigs' heads—I can't figure out what I've seen. Albion and Peyton were lovers, but here they are with Timothy. Think through: Timothy's history of abuse, of murder. Is Albion Timothy's wife? Peyton? That doesn't make much sense—but they're his victims, like Hannah Massey was his victim, maybe, like other women he's killed or tried to kill, or wanted to. Peyton's documented as dying in the blast, but Albion—maybe she escaped from him somehow. Maybe she escaped, but Timothy thought she was dead until she hired Mook to delete her. Maybe the act of her disappearing was enough to signal she'd never disappeared. I need to find her—

I voice House of Fetherston studios, but no one's ever heard of Albion Waverly. I explain to the receptionist that I'm looking for someone who works there, who'd have access to clothes that haven't officially been released—I describe what Albion looks like. I'm bounced around, office to office—soon, someone asks who I am. I try to explain why I'm calling, who I'm looking for, but she says they've given too much of their time already and disconnect. I search the San Francisco white pages but no Albion Waverly—no hits for *Albion* at all.

Track the artwork: a Google search is useless—too many art galleries in the greater San Francisco metro region. Thousands of red flags pinned to Street View when I search "San Francisco AND art gallery." I get a sense of which neighborhoods might have the most galleries—Lower Haight, gentrified parts of Hayes Valley, maybe around Haight-Ashbury, the Mission District, maybe the Castro. Two of the six paintings have smears or spots of Mook's blood, so I leave them rolled in the hotel but I bring the other four paintings with me. I try art galleries almost at random, taking an AutoCab to a neighborhood and just walking wherever GPS points me. Some galleries are of obvious no help, dark holes foul with body odor and antagonistic scenesters on the streams that can't be bothered to even acknowledge my presence. Other galleries are more professional, try to be helpful. Refurbished spaces with white walls and paintings hung with price sheets available. Chic young women who don't recognize the paintings I brought with me, can't identify the artist but show me other work about "the Pittsburgh theme," as they call it, artists with no true discernible connection to the city, using the end of Pittsburgh as a metaphor for whatever pet cause they want to indulge in—governmental control, military culture, religious intolerance, capitalism, the spiritual death of the modern age—or using the Burn as nothing more than a pretext for depicting bodies and cities in flames, faux-visionary apocalypses. Artist Statements written entirely with mock-theoretical buzzwords, incomprehensible, about the *deconstruction* and *defamiliarization* of Place, the *ambiguity of Identity*, the *Monologism of History*, the *Society of the Spectacle*, the *Articulation of Desire*. Of artists co-opting our sorrow, of how artists "respond" to the oblivion of a city, as if their "response" was somehow profound or even necessary. No one I ask can identify the paintings I've brought to them.

4, 10—

I change hotels to an EconoLodge a few blocks away from where I'd been staying. There's hardly any staff here, only a maintenance guy in charge of the sweepers that troll room to room. I check in under the name Wallace Stevens—no questions asked.

Mook's death hit SF.net two and a half weeks after I'd found his body and the story goes viral—crime scene photographs stream for tabloids, blog posts memorialize the death of a rising street art star, Blum & Poe reports the price of Mook tags salvaged from billboards and mailboxes ballooning four hundred percent even though most people had never heard of "Mook" until now. User commentaries theorize Mook's death was a CIA assassination. Zebra-striped face and hollowed-out eyes. Maxing out credit cards with my hotel room rate and AutoCab fares—I didn't expect to stay in San Francisco this long. Whole Foods for groceries but I spend the days canvassing galleries. KRON4's been reporting on Mook's murder every evening newscast—the killers were caught on video, but their identity's unknown. Plenty of HD footage of three men in police SWAT uniforms, their faces hidden by black visors. They seemed to know where every security camera in the Brocklebank was located. Their visors loom close to each lens before the cameras go dark—deactivating security camera to security camera all the way to Mook's room. The news reports that these police officers are imposters and not members of the San Francisco PD, warns of imposter cops at traffic stops. The San Francisco People's Org advertises their PD ID app to identify legitimate members of the SFPD by badge number and career profile. I download the app. The streams report the motive appears to have been simple robbery—the victim's Adware was stolen, the Adware more than likely already hacked and wiped and impossible to trace.

SFMOMA praises Mook in press releases, announces a retrospective to be held in the spring of next year. The streams tell us he was a visionary artist, a genius of the modern age, but the general public yawns—nothing but a juvenile-minded vandal and the sale of his artwork should reimburse property owners he'd victimized. His name was Sherrod Faulkner but he'd gone by Mook since he was a teenager in Wichita. He moved to the West Coast to attend Harvey Mudd, majoring in VR environments and game design, but dropped out. He drifted to San Francisco and worked as the day-shift manager at a Denny's on the corner of Mission and 4th for over fifteen years. I took myself to breakfast at his Denny's a few days ago and ordered big but didn't eat much. I asked my waitress about him, saying I was an old friend from school and was sorry to hear what had happened. She said, "Sherrod doesn't work here anymore—"

The streams pull apart his life. His work as Mook is encrypted, hidden, but his IP addresses as "Sherrod Faulkner" and his search histories are hacked and broadcast. Right-wing and Fourth Amendment websites and a taste for hard-core porn—a thing for redheads, erotica, decadent art—links to the e-texts of Ayn Rand and Julian Assange, user accounts with the Anarchist Loose Collective and a fan club member of the band Eat Christ. Some of his personal papers were hacked and published—fanfic written in the form of epic poetry imagining graphic sexual encounters between John Galt and President Meecham, about their child slipping from her like a bolt of lightning. The tabloids uncover his family back in Kansas, upper-middle-class parents and a sister in Chicago. His father makes a statement about the death of his son, begging the news streams to let them mourn in private, to respect their privacy. Mook's avatar as Sherrod Faulkner was a picture of Alfred E. Neuman that will chortle, "What, me worry?" in archived comment streams and chat rooms until the world goes dark.

Iced coffee at a Starbucks in the Mission, late afternoon. The baristas recognize me for being in here so much these past few days, taking breaks here in between art gallery inquiries—they tell me "see you tomorrow" when I slurp the last of my venti and trash the cup. Already four thirty in the afternoon, most places will be closed by the time I get there, but I have time to swing by a gallery called Cell. The front room's a lounge with worn-in couches, a few paintings hanging on the walls of dollhouses inhabited by foxes. The attendant's neon-pink bob's like a pom-pom floating above her PVC bodysuit. Her lips are painted oxblood, and silver studs bullet her eyebrows and tongue. She tells me they're closing in ten minutes but I show her the paintings anyway. She recognizes the images. When she brings out a portfolio from the flat files, I know I have her. The attendant slides out a stack of ink and watercolors, the paintings hand-stitched together in groups of six, each leaf separated from the one below by a sheet of acetate.

"She calls these her fascicles," the attendant explains.

The attendant handles the paintings like she's handling sheets of gold leaf. Images of gray wood, rotten, of architectural details out of context, several of the house's front door, porch columns, the words of Christ painted in whitewash but folded in on themselves, a coal chute, the interior of stairs, hardwood floors, cracked paint, stripped light fixtures in inks and charcoal, the bed where Timothy kept her, several of the bed. Only a few paintings show the house beyond these few details. One painting's of the root cellar door—and looking at the image I can almost hear the sound of breathing I'd heard in the Archive behind that door.

"Who did these?" I ask.

"A local artist," says the attendant. "Dar Harris. She was part of one of our group shows two years ago—"

"Dar Harris?"

"Darwyn Harris," she says. "She's Pittsburgh—or had friends there. She works in fashion. One of the big houses, I think. Fetherston, maybe—"

Darwyn—that was Peyton's hometown. Darwin, Minnesota.

"What's she like?" I ask. "Who is she?"

"You notice when she walks into the room, if that's what you're asking," she says.

"I've been searching every gallery in San Francisco, but no one's heard of her—"

"It depends on who you've been asking. Dar keeps to a certain scene—she only participates in group shows with people she knows well. I approached her once about having a solo here, but she seemed uncomfortable with the idea. I let it drop—"

"Why?" I ask. "Her work's incredible—"

"She keeps to herself," she says. "She's not a recluse, but I don't know. I don't think she wants too much publicity. I remember she refused to be photographed for the promotion we did for this group show, which is fine except she looks like a model. Would have brought more people to the gallery if they knew what the artist looked like. I don't get it, but I respect the decision—"

"You know her well?"

"Well enough," she says. "She sells each fascicle as a whole, but I see you have two separate works there. They should be kept together—"

"I have the others. I bought them already separated—"

"Where did you buy them?"

"From eBay," I tell her. She's interested in who was selling, but I beg off, vaguely worried that these paintings may have been reported stolen and she might be fishing for information. I tell her I'll come back the next day, to look over the collection. A Spicy Chicken meal at Wendy's before sat-connect at my hotel, scouring the streams for mentions of Darwyn Harris—she's easy enough to find now that I have her name. She has a Facebook page, without a profile pic. Her About is brief, without a mention of Pittsburgh. Scroll through her site's slideshow—image after image of the same ruined house, each bound together in fascicles of six. There's another series of paintings as well, as obsessively detailed as her renderings of the house, but these are paintings of a blonde, the tone not unlike Wyeth's Helga images if shattered and reformed by Picasso or Braque—the same muted colors she uses for the house, but lighter, hay-colored blonde, the cream of pale skin, darker hair in curly tufts and the pink of lips and nipples and interior folds, the blue of her eyes. I look at slideshows of several of the fascicles before I realize the woman she's painting is Peyton. House and blonde. Some fascicles feature the woman and the architecture echoing each other, but most of her small books keep to their own unified themes.

Listings under *Events*. Group shows throughout the winter, into spring—she's busy even if she's trying to stay relatively anonymous. I check the dates—in a few weeks, for the "First Friday" Mission art crawl, a show opens called *Paper Covers Rock*, all works on paper at a space called the Glass Dome.

I talk with Gavril late into the night. He asks when I'll be through with this and I tell him I don't know. "Soon, maybe—"

"I would love to see San Francisco," he says. "I've always thought I would like to see the Redwoods. Drive a car through a hollowed-out tree trunk—"

5, 3—

An art crawl tonight, openings at thirty-three venues throughout the Mission, places like Artists' Television Access, Project Artaud, the kind of grant-funded spaces Theresa and I used to visit during crawls back in Pittsburgh, the Xchange, Intersection for the Arts, the Mission Cultural Center and the Glass Dome—free downloads with walking tours, exhibition highlights, artist bios, the most hyped show a display of Day of the Dead masks made by the Latino Art League. I eat an omelet for dinner at a café called Kahlo and buy fresh-cut fries doused with vinegar and ketchup from a street vendor on Dolores. Mexican folk buskers and exhibitions of salsa dancing in the closed-off streets—gallery assistants cut among the crowds passing out handbills for after parties. The streets and sidewalks are already carpeted with their handbills and postcards, most augged with Day of the Dead death's-heads, ornately painted skulls with crimson eyes and flashing grins that float illusory in 3-D and break apart as I step through them. Hesitant among the crowds, trying to figure my move—a gnawing doubt in my guts that I shouldn't meet Albion at all, that I should let her be, let this all drop and run, but knowing Timothy and Waverly won't ever let me disappear, knowing that Hannah Massey will disappear forever. A drag queen procession's just getting started, a Tina Turner mash-up Sousa march—the pageant queen's dressed like Meecham, a Stars and Stripes ball gown and a pig skull mask.

The Glass Dome's street-front windows are lettered *Paper Covers Rock: New San Francisco Works on Paper*. Electro house emanates from inside, vintage Deadmau5, a riot vibe fueling the dance party erupting in the streets. I shoulder my way through the crowd at the door—an acute claustrophobia hits me, like instead of a narrow space crowded for an exhibition I'm in a cave packed tight with bodies. The Glass Dome's a tapered space, like a hallway without doors—it reminds me of Pittsburgh galleries: reclaimed buildings left raw with exposed tubing and knotty braids of wiring. Pittsburgh was ringed with dead mill towns, ghost towns almost, ripe for art collectives and nonprofits to rent on the cheap, whole neighborhoods that would have died out and disappeared except for artists that wanted to rent a sense of authenticity and grit.

I grab a can of beer from a leaking kiddie pool filled with ice. I stay to the sides of the crowd. I make my way to Albion's fascicle—this one unstitched, the six pages displayed in a line, hung with pins. A portrait of the blonde—Peyton—and despite the suffocating crowd, the inadvertent knocks and nudges in the congested room, the changes in music and the greater pitch of conversation as the party deepens, everything might as well be silent as I stare at the artwork and realize that what I'm looking at isn't the fetishized limbs of a young woman, but an entire portrait broken into six planes as if I'm looking at the reflection of a nude in six shattered mirrors, or reading her body in six chapters. Only two of the six show her face, her head arched rearward in a limp frenzy, her expression like *The Ecstasy of Saint Teresa,* and I realize that her entire body, obscured though it is in Albion's cubist disjunctions, would echo *The Ecstasy of Saint Teresa* without the impish angel, without the touch of God. An attendant places orange sticker dots next to each painting, denoting that they'd sold. Two other artists show their work—cuttings along one wall of urban scenes, the other a set of phrases, *Dispositif,* or *Panopticon,* painted in black Times New Roman on white paper, simple things.

She's here.

I miss when she comes in, but notice the tone of the room shifts, when everyone present despite their fashion and cultured posing seems suddenly dim and wan, suddenly insignificant. I see her over the heads of others, her hair dyed raven black. Her friends flock to her, and watching her hug women she knows is like watching the bride embrace her bridesmaids. She wears a white dress tied at the waist with a black ribbon, but her shoulders, her elegant neck, the length of her arms are almost paler than the white lace. Her skirt has two large pockets, each pocket filled with a bouquet of daisies. I shrink against the wall—irrelevant now that she's here, all my troubles and all my desires suddenly the concern of a minor character that's barely made the page. The first thing Albion does is find the other two artists in the exhibit with her, two men who look like schoolchildren meeting a woman for the first time when she gives each a bouquet and congratulates them on their work. Taller than the others here, she leans over to hear them talk, her body swanlike. She laughs easily.

Admirers cluster around her most of the evening. She drifts from one group to the next, people congratulating her on her work. I overhear them asking her to explain the woman, but she talks about technique and style instead, avoiding mention of who this woman is. I hear people calling her "Darwyn," a few, who must be closer friends, call her "Dar." A few hours pass, the crowd's thinned out but Albion remains. I wait until she's alone, a break in her conversations, when she's in line for the drink table.

I wait in line behind her. She wears her hair up, like a wave of silk. She's near enough I could touch her—feel her here in the world with me, no longer an illusion. The shape of her neck flows into her shoulders in a perfect line, like she's been carved from marble. Is she real? Am I hallucinating now? A scatter of freckles

flecks her shoulders, near her collar. Wisps of hair on her neck grow a chestnut red. I don't know what to say, so I say, "Raven and Honeybear—"

She flinches from me like I've struck her.

"I'm sorry," I tell her, as if I might be able to take it back, approach her in some other way—but it's too late. I feel myself blushing and shiver with sweat. There's so much I want to say to her, but all I can say is, "I'm sorry—"

She recovers, like someone falsifying dignity after a public humiliation.

"That was a long time ago," she says, her voice touched by an accent—West Virginia, maybe, or rural Pennsylvania.

"Albion?" I say.

"Are you the one who killed him?" she says, losing her composure. A cry escapes from her, almost like a guttural, barking laugh, an ugly sound that the crashing music can't cover. A friend asks if she's all right. She clenches her jaw. She's trembling, her skin grown somehow paler, losing more color except for scarlet blotches on her cheeks and neck. She wipes at her eyes with a cocktail napkin. "I'm okay," she says, "I'm all right—"

"No," I tell her, "it wasn't me—"

"Then what do you *want* from me?!" she says. "I've done *nothing* to you—"

"My wife," I tell her. "I want my wife back. I want her back—"

The words temper her hysteria. She's staring at me with bloodshot eyes, nearly panting, trying to figure out who I am, what I mean, why I'm here, why she's been discovered.

"I'm sorry?" she says.

"You took her from me. Mook took her from me. I want her back—"

Trembling, now, my voice cracking, I also start to cry—heavy

sobs. Telling this woman that I no longer have my wife is somehow like admitting for the first time that I lost Theresa ten years ago, that I've been alone for all these years. I've never felt Theresa's absence so acutely, I've never admitted to myself that even if I found her now, there's nothing left to find.

Someone asks her, "Do you want me to call the police?"

"No," she says. "We're all right. We're all right here—"

"Please," I tell her.

Albion gazes around the room, at the artwork and the people surrounding her—bewildered, it seems, but more like someone emerging from a pleasant dream into a harsh morning, knowing that all the pleasing illusions surrounding her are on the cusp of fading, trying to take them all in, to absorb them, before she wakes.

"I'm so sorry," she says to the two other artists, to her friends, who've gathered around us like we're actors playing a scene. "I'm mortified for interrupting your show, please forgive me. I'm so sorry about all of this. This gentleman and I have some things to discuss—"

She leads me to a quieter corner of the room, the others warily watching us. She studies my face inquisitively—it's unnerving, like I'm being dissected.

"Don't I know you?" she says. "I think I recognize you, but you were different then. Didn't you—you were a poet, weren't you? I think I've seen you at readings—"

"I don't know," I tell her. "I think, maybe—"

"What's your name?"

"Dominic—"

"You're full name," she says. "Tell me—"

"John Dominic Blaxton," I say. "I was married to a woman named Theresa—"

"Theresa," she says, testing the name, weighing the sound of it. "I don't remember a Theresa, but I remember you. You look different than you used to, but I can see you now. I was at a reading once, at ModernFormations Gallery in Garfield. Twelve years ago, at least—isn't that right?"

"That's right," I tell her. "A small-press festival. I was Confluence Press. The *New Yinzer* was there, Copacetic Comics, Autumn House—"

Saying these names to someone who remembers them is like remembering how to speak a coded language invented as a child.

"Caketrain," she says, "City of Asylum—"

"I remember standing onstage, the other poets on couches behind me, looking out across the audience but I couldn't see any faces because of the stage lights so I looked down at the sheets of typed poetry I brought with me, and was surprised to see my hands were shaking—"

"I loved your work that night," she says. "I bought two of your books—"

"*The Stations of the Cross*? The blue one?"

"That one, and another one," she says. "You'd brought a chapbook with you, of love poems. Those were my favorites—"

I'd forgotten about that chapbook, something I made to sell along with *The Stations of the Cross* when I gave readings, little love note sketches I'd given to Theresa over the years and collected together.

"You wouldn't happen to still have those, would you?" I ask her.

"Everything was lost," she says.

We've drifted farther away from the others and are standing beneath a white sheet of paper with black words that say *fucking in a car at 85mph running into a brick wall.*

"I don't remember you from that night," I tell her. "But I know you were there—I saw you in the Archive, but I wasn't sure if I saw you. I thought I would have remembered meeting you before—"

"There were a lot of other people there that night," she says.

The gallery's filling in again as people drift through from other parties. Albion suggests we take a couple of drinks and head outside for fresh air. She gives assurances to her friends that she'll be all right, that I'm an old friend. She promises she'll voice them, to check in later. The evening's grown cold and I offer her my jacket. She turns me down at first, but later accepts to keep from shivering. The front windows of the Glass Dome gallery have fogged over, the people inside like specters through the glass. We walk a few blocks in silence until she sits on the front steps of an antique store that has closed, lost in the shadows of the awning. I join her. Laughing people passing by don't notice us—it feels like we're invisible, here.

"Tell me about your wife," she says.

"Theresa Marie," I tell her. "Mook deleted everything about her, just like he deleted you. He warned me off from looking for you in the City, but he killed her anyway. I need you to bring her back—"

"I can't bring her back," she says. "I can't. Maybe he could have—"

I lean into the shadows, watching my breath billow out from my lungs like it's my soul that's escaping. The familiar depression settles over me, blacker and deeper than I'd ever felt it before—I want Theresa, I want her back, I want to kiss her, I want to hear her talk to me, I just want to see her again. Albion lets me regain my composure. She's patient. I imagine swallowing the steel of a gun barrel, aiming into the roof of my mouth.

"Did he send you here?" she asks.

"Waverly?"

"Is that who sent you? I was thinking it would be Timothy—"

"Timothy, too," I tell her.

"Is he here, then? Is he the one who killed my friend?"

"I don't know—"

She nods. She's considering who I am.

"Are you working for him? Are you going to tell him where I am?"

I explain everything. I tell her that I'd started for Waverly thinking I was searching for his daughter but kept looking only because I thought she and Mook could protect me from Timothy, help me disappear. I tell her I was hoping she could recover my wife.

"Are you hungry?" she says.

"Yeah, I actually am," I admit. "I only had an omelet earlier—"

"I'm starving," she says. "All I've had was a salad for lunch. Do you like Thai?"

We leave the antique store stoop, emerging from beneath the awning. Albion sees a few friends heading to the show. They ask if she's coming along and Albion smiles, a brokenhearted smile. "I'll be along," she says.

We walk together. "You don't mind if I keep your jacket on?" she asks. "You won't be too cold?"

"It's not too cold," I tell her, but she says she's freezing. She knows a place called Thaiphoon that's too busy to get a table, so we place takeout orders and she offers her apartment, just around the corner. She says we'll be able to talk there. We wait at the counter, thinking of things to say—organizing our thoughts. I pay for our food, and once we're outside I ask if she made her own clothes and she says that she did.

"You probably know a lot about me," she says.

"Not a lot, no," I tell her. "Some—"

"Sherrod told me about you," she says. "I wouldn't say he was worried, but he said you might be able to find me. He said you worked in the City-Archive, that you knew how to research and could see through his methods. He figured you might—"

"You have to believe me that I didn't know he would be killed. I never knew what was happening, what is happening—"

Her building's run-down. Floral wallpaper in the elevator, peeling along the seams, exposing the brown metal beneath. We ride in silence, listening to the mechanics and pulleys until we drift to a stop and the doors screech apart. She unlocks the dead bolts to her room and leads me in, flicking on the light switch as we pass through the main hall. Her apartment is a loft, a lot of space but there's not much furnishing other than twin sofas and a coffee table. Most of the space is set up as a studio, outsized canvases propped up against the brick walls, rolls and bolts of fabric, two sewing machines, oversize art books bowing shelves homemade from boards and bricks. She has a drafting table near the window with pens and ink and brushes in ceramic mugs, and several pads of paper.

"Is this where you make your fascicles?" I ask.

"Over there, yeah," she says.

"The canvases?"

"I bought those a while ago, thinking I might try something different," she says. "I haven't, yet—"

A lace curtain's thumbtacked to the doorframe that leads to the kitchen. She says, "I'll make tea, if you'd like—"

"That sounds perfect—"

I follow her into the kitchen, asking where she keeps her plates. I work around her, dishing out our Thai food while she fills her kettle with tap water and lights the stove.

"Earl Grey?" she asks.

I take our plates to the main room and set them on her coffee table. She's hung one of those cheap *We will never forget* souvenir clocks of downtown Pittsburgh. The water of the three rivers, through some trick, looks like it's rippling—it's the only reference to Pittsburgh I can find. It's already after ten. Albion brings in the tea on a tray and sets it next to the food.

"You should have started eating," she says. "It'll get cold—"

She pours each cup—she's been crying again, in the kitchen. She puts on music, Etta James, and we eat largely in silence, listening to the music. Her radiators cough and sputter and eventually heat the room. She asks about DC. I ask about San Francisco and she says it's a paradise that has seen better times. I tell her DC's much the same, except it was never a paradise. After dinner I wash our dishes while she makes a pot of coffee. She sets out a box of lemon cookies she's had in her cupboard and pours me a cup, setting out sugar and milk. I indulge in both. I take a sip of coffee.

"I've found some information about Timothy that has put my friends and family in jeopardy," I tell her. "I don't know who they are, really, or what their connections are to you—but I know that Timothy and Waverly are dangerous—"

"Yes," she says.

"I need you to help me," I tell her. "That's why I've found you. I need you to tell me about him, so I can put together a case, put together some protection from him—"

"You can't protect yourself from them," she says. "Nothing I can say will protect you—"

"Who are you?" I ask.

She speaks:

5, 3 *IBID.*—

"My name was Emily Perkins," she says.

"What about 'Albion'?"

"Dr. Waverly is influenced by William Blake. There's this poem called *Visions of the Daughters of Albion*. I believe he named a sailboat after that poem," she says. "He ran a house in Pittsburgh that took in lost girls and once you agreed to stay on, you adopted a new name to signify the beginning of your new life. He suggested I take the name Albion—"

"Down in Greenfield?" I ask. "The house with the words painted on the side?"

"We were affiliated with the King of Kings parish, but all the financial support came from Waverly. Mrs. Waverly ran the house—"

Talking like this dredges up heartache for Albion, I can tell—she brings her coffee to her mouth but holds it there, shivering without sipping.

"How young were you?"

"Young," she says. "I never knew my parents. Foster homes all my life—eventually Mrs. Waverly took me in. When I was fifteen, sixteen, I was homeless—I did pills back then and meth, this was with a bunch of kids I fell in with, we'd take drives down into Washington County and West Virginia to these old houses we'd squat in for weeks just blown out of our minds, sometimes in old barns or just camping out in the woods. I was picked up for drug possession and pled guilty but was still a minor so was referred to child services. I lived in a halfway house but started cutting myself—they said I was a suicide risk. I turned eighteen and was moved to a different facility, part of Western Psych. I was recommended to psychological services and that's when I met Timothy—"

"He was your doctor?"

"We'd have these sessions once a week. The first time I met with him, he just looked at me—he has those blue eyes. It was like he was sizing me up, forming a whole opinion of me in just those few seconds. I told him I didn't try to kill myself, that I didn't know what I was doing, that I just cut into my arms, and he smiled and said, 'It's all in the past now, it's in the past,' and I felt forgiven. Just hearing those words—

"Two years in detention like that, but seeing Timothy once a week and then three times a week when he started prepping me for a GED. He shared an office and whenever we'd meet he'd tell one of his colleagues before closing the door.

"There was only once he locked the door and after he did, he just sat there like he was deciding something. He said, 'Emily, what I'm about to tell you could get me fired. I could lose my job—my entire career. But I need to say this, and my need to say this is greater than my need for employment. I want to tell you about Jesus Christ—'

"I forget what I did—rolled my eyes, maybe, I don't remember. All I remember is Timothy grabbing my neck and squeezing. I couldn't even scream. I felt the edges of my vision blacken and he must have seen my face turning because he let go and let me breathe, but he was gasping for breath harder than I was. It took him a minute or two before he calmed down and apologized.

"'I shouldn't have done that,' he said.

"He told me he still struggles, but he knows that his soul is pure, that we all have pure souls that are untouched no matter how much we've abused our own bodies. He told me that despite my own failings—how I cut myself, the drugs—that Christ could save me as well, that I could transcend my limitations because the body is corrupt but the soul is pure. He told me that we're born into sin, that our bodies trap us in sin, but to never forget that our souls reflect the true God—

"He presented a Bible to me, a printed Bible with a blue leather cover that had my name embossed in gold. He told me to read the Gospels. He pointed them out to me. He told me to pay attention to the words printed in red. This was part of the new curriculum, he told me. He unlocked the door and told me that he'd see me the day after tomorrow.

"I could have said something to the guard who escorted me back to my room. I could have told one of the nurses at dinner or check-in what he'd done to me, but I didn't. I was terrified. I was terrified that whoever I told would ignore me or wouldn't believe me and that it would get back to him. I kept quiet.

"That night I read the Gospels out of fear but felt a change—I felt what I believed was the grace of Jesus touching my life—at least that's what I thought it was, because the feeling was so glorious. I'm far away from that time now, but when I first read Matthew and Mark, and when I read the account of the baptism of Christ in Luke, I felt my life—felt like my chest just melted, like I'd been made of ice but some incredible warmth had broken through. I fell to the floor of my cell and knelt at the side of my bed, not knowing how to pray so I just said the words, 'Jesus, help me, Jesus, help me,' repeating His name in a hysteria, and with every word I felt His love overwhelm me. I was converted, that night. I felt protected by a power beyond myself. I reread the Gospels, then began in Genesis and when I next saw Timothy I confronted him about what had happened and told him that I'd report him if he ever touched me again, but his entire demeanor had changed. He smiled and laughed like he, too, was lit with an inner light at seeing me saved. At the end of our session we held hands and said the Lord's Prayer.

"On his recommendation I was released from the facility and he placed me at Mrs. Waverly's house. He thought that I might like living there in a community of faith. He introduced me to Mrs. Waverly, who we called Kitty—

"I realize, now. Kitty was the leader of the house but Waverly controled everything. He gave sermons about evangelism. He told stories about mission trips to Haiti and showed slides of past groups of girls in dusty villages. The people living at Kitty's house were young, mostly college girls, girls who'd moved to Pittsburgh from other cities and other countries, lonely girls brought together because they were searching for fellowship. We were encouraged to socialize with one another, to recruit more people to our congregation but to limit our contact with people who weren't interested in our faith. We took long hikes and trips to Ohiopyle. I was in love with it all, with the community. Eventually I adopted the name Albion and Timothy called me his sister in Christ—

"It was a Saturday afternoon when Timothy and Waverly visited me in the upstairs room. We prayed together, and Timothy explained what would happen. I still remember how calm his tone of voice was. Waverly crawled into bed and lay there while I went through with it. He kissed me like he was drinking me but fucked me like I wasn't there at all. I wish I could tell you why I went along with it—but there is no why, that house was my life back then, my entire life. Even now I'm disgusted and relive that afternoon and wish I'd somehow taken control, had somehow done something, run screaming or refused or something, but I didn't. I went through with it. Timothy took his turn and that was the first time he touched me since trying to choke me back in the center—he took me like I disgusted him. Afterward they prayed over me, these men. To heal me. The diseases in me. Asked God to be lenient with me.

"They visited every Saturday afternoon, and before they started they called me especially beloved, like the disciple 'loved by Christ,' but afterward I had to endure their prayers on my behalf and Timothy waiting for Waverly to leave so he could finish. Waverly was quick, but Timothy was violent and some nights I couldn't help him finish until he hit me. He said he could get me Percocet—he never failed to bring pills and I don't know if you've ever used Percocet but those sessions became the trigger for pills. After, he'd send Kitty into the room with me, to sleep in my bed with me, to make sure nothing happened while I was using. She'd spoon me and hold me like I was her child, sometimes stroke my hair or cry with me. I remember she smelled like ointment and hair spray and I could feel the abrasive skin of her legs touching mine as she curled her toes up close to me. But she would talk to me, whispering to me while we lay together. I learned from Kitty that Timothy had another family, that he was married. He was married again even before that. He had some sort of troubles in his past—"

"When did you move to the apartment in Polish Hill?" I ask her. "That's where I first started looking for you—"

"Timothy broke my arm," she says. "Dr. Waverly asked me to move out of the house because of it. He rented that apartment for me, paid for my classes at the Art Institute. Timothy still visited me—there was a café downstairs from the apartment and we'd have coffee, just talking. He apologized for what had happened. He told me he needed to clear up a few things about his life. He stayed late at my apartment almost every night and I let him. He would berate me if I was late coming home or if I was supposed to see any of my other friends—"

"Peyton?" I ask.

"She was the reason he broke my arm. He didn't like how close we were, said I was trying to make a mockery of him—"

"What happened?"

"There was a morning I didn't have classes and Timothy made breakfast and told me that he wanted to marry me. He said he was going away for a little while, that he was taking a road trip down south with his wife and that he would return to me a stronger and better man, a free man. We would live together through Christ when he returned, he said. I asked where he was going, but he wouldn't tell me. All he said was 'far.' 'A week or two, that's all,' he said, 'and then I'll be back for you—'"

"You're Timothy's wife?" I ask her.

"The world ended first—"

5, 4—

"I died that day," she says.

"I died with everyone I knew and loved.

"I was downtown. I had a fashion photography class that morning, working with lighting. The weather was beautiful like a spring day even though it was October, and standing on the corner of the Boulevard of the Allies, I remember thinking that Timothy had left, that there wasn't anything I needed to rush home to, no one expecting me, and wanting to go to the Galleria, to the South Hills—to some of the boutiques in Mount Lebanon, anywhere but just home to my apartment, anywhere. I was interested in vintage looks at the time and Mount Lebanon had a location of Avalon that I didn't get to as often as the Squirrel Hill store. A beautiful afternoon, do you remember? I could spend all afternoon just walking, if I wanted to—

"I had a quick lunch at the Bluebird Kitchen. I remember figuring out which bus to take because I hadn't made the trip all that often and wasn't familiar with the route. I remember catching the bus and remember the bus was crowded that day. It was almost too crowded, and I remember second-guessing whether I should even go. I was fearful of what Timothy would think if he found out I didn't come straight home after class—but I'd already paid my fare and had already worked my way through the crowded bus aisle, threading among people's legs and backpacks and shoulders until I found a free space to stand. Holding the nylon strap, swaying with every turn. I remember everything, every detail of that bus ride. We inched corner to corner through downtown, more passengers boarding, crowding me farther toward the back. The faces of the passengers are seared into my memory. I have dreams about them—even now I dream I'm still on the bus with them. At the time I remember wondering why so many of them weren't at work—I remember wondering where they were going. I've ridden that bus in the Archive. I feel a desperate need to see those people again, to visit them, to remember them—and they're there, perfectly preserved because of the bus's security camera. I see myself among them and wonder why, wonder who they were and what their lives had been before they boarded the bus that afternoon.

"We left downtown—no more stops until the far side of the tunnel. An old woman in front of me was clicking her tongue for a child in front of her. Most people kept to themselves, looking out the windows or into the streams or at their cell phones. I remember riding across the Liberty Bridge, the Monongahela flowing beneath us like a ribbon of mud, the downtown skyline receding behind me. I remember Mount Washington looming like a great and expanding shadow. I remember plunging into the Liberty Tunnel, the smooth tube of concrete cutting through the mountain. The sunlight is cut off, replaced by an unnatural fluorescent glow. The taillights of cars are exceptionally bright. The sound is odd—a reverberation of wind and engines, like a cocoon of sound. The smell is motor oil and stale air. It's twilight here. It will always be twilight here.

"This is when the world ends. This is when a man opens his suitcase. I remember falling. The mountain heaving. The bus flipped over. The metal screamed. The tunnel had collapsed and the sudden stop was padded by bodies. A jumble of bodies in the aisles, in the seats, finding my face pressed against window glass, my neck bent. So many people died right then—most of us were dead. I don't know minutes from hours. The terrible pressure. The dark. Movement against my shin—someone else was alive, but the movement stopped. Blood rushing to my head, the pain intolerable. Screams in the darkness. Moaning—like animals moaning, panicked, not like the sounds people make.

"A few who were alive turned on their cell phones and held them out like flashlights. There was room for some of us to move, a few of us who were unhurt, who started picking through the dead. I remember panicking then—it was the only moment I panicked, understanding that I was buried in dead people. I screamed but my screams sounded distant, like I was under water and listening to someone else scream. I remember hands grabbing my legs and pulling me free. I remember screaming until a man's face appeared in the bluish-white glow of a cell phone and calmed me.

This man's name was Stewart—I can still see Stewart's face hovering in blue light when I close my eyes. He asked if I was hurt and when I said I was, he asked how bad and where. I told him I thought my leg was broken and his response was, 'Then you can still help us—'

"We separated the living from the dead. Working in the dark for what must have been hours, reaching out and touching a cold hand, cold faces. Only eight of us lived. We worked until we could no longer hear the voices and didn't dare to speak until the distant cries from people we couldn't reach fell silent. The bus was crumpled in a way that left enough room to huddle together near the steering wheel. The glow of cell phones—faces so covered with blood that I couldn't see who these people were. Stewart told us to turn out the lights, to conserve the batteries, but in the dark the dead crawled around us so we kept the lights on. Someone had a radio, but all we could hear was static. An increasing stink of gasoline. A woman named Tabitha screamed for God to kill her. She dug out her eyes and chewed on her tongue. We watched her bleed to death in the faint glow of our cell phones. The batteries on the cell phones ran out one by one and we lost our lights. Another man, Jacob, began to sing—a rich baritone voice that was like a thread in the dark. We were left with nothing but our voices. I heard Stewart—he was rummaging through what backpacks and bags he could reach, trying to gather together whatever we could eat or drink. He divvied what we had, rationed it out to us. He tried to convince us all to go to the bathroom in the same corner—in a shallow pocket you could crawl to on your belly between two bodies, but no one listened to him and soon our little space was fouled. Stewart was certain that someone was digging through the rocks to find us and we'd listen and hear slides and shifts in the stones and convince ourselves that help was coming, that if we could just hold on we would be rescued. He begged us to be intelligent, to conserve our energy, to conserve our water. He talked about his daughters and his wife and tried to get us all talking about who was waiting for us, to give us all hope. At some point we stopped hearing Stewart's voice.

"Time dissolves. I'd sleep and I'd wake up but I don't know for how long or how often. I'd stop hearing someone's voice or someone's breathing and I'd think they died only to hear them say something or hear them shift and know they were still alive. There were six of us, after Stewart and Tabitha. We hung on by playing games—word association games. I wondered where the old woman who clicked her tongue was, or the mother and her child—they would have been right near me in the crash and so maybe they were alive, too—and I'd scream and start pulling at the bodies around me, trying to dig through to them, thinking someone else might still be alive, but the others would say, 'What do you think of when I say the word *sunshine*?' And I'd say, 'a park,' or 'the ocean,' and then I would have to say, 'Jacob, what do you think about when I say the word *ocean*?' and Jacob would answer until we were telling each other about the beach and we weren't buried alive at all but were in the sun, or in a park having a picnic, or swimming in the ocean.

"It was only later—long after we'd eaten through our sack lunches and drank through all the water and bottles of pop and thermoses of coffee, long after we grew thin and agonized from hunger and after burning thirst made us desperate—that we gave up hope of a rescue and began tearing at the bus walls with small bursts of our failing energy, listening to the shifting of concrete and stone, hoping we would die in a sudden rush of weight. Instead, a path opened. One of us, a woman named Elizabeth, felt a slight breeze that she thought was one of the dead men breathing, but when she reached out her hand through one of the broken bus windows, she found that her arm could fit through the unexpected gap in the stone. She climbed out the bus window. When she spoke her voice was distant and we thought it was a trick of our ears, but she said there was enough room to crawl. Too narrow for a few of us to fit through—they tried and plugged the hole, wriggling back into the bus, but I was thin, I was one of the ones who could push through the broken window, slicing open my breasts and my abdomen and my thigh on a shard of glass. Once I crawled through, the narrow path opened wider. There were only three of us who could fit through—Elizabeth ahead of us, and a man named Steven in front of me. I was the last. I remember hearing the others screaming after us when we left them. They cursed us. They damned us. They begged us to come back, to stay with them. Pitch-black rock, scraped and bruised, gouged by rebar in the shattered concrete, bleeding. I remember crawling, what seemed like hours of work to only move an inch or two inches. I remember thinking that one of the people we'd left behind would catch up with me, that I would feel their hands grab my foot and pull me back, but no one touched me and eventually their voices faded. We crawled like worms through the earth.

"Elizabeth led us, picking our path. We slept several times. We found a car that had been buried, the windshield broken in. Steven found a bottle of Mountain Dew in the cup holder and we drank—the sweetest I've ever tasted. We slept together near that car, but Elizabeth woke us and picked a new path. Eventually I felt heat rising and felt that the stones were becoming smooth. A sharp, noxious odor of soot and char. I heard Elizabeth scream—a sound that in the dark was like the voice of horror but I now know as the sound of joy. I saw daylight. From the mountain down across the lake of fire where the city had once been, fields of fire and black tumbles, a landscape of ash. Loosely standing skeletal husks that were once skyscrapers, a leveled landscape. We didn't understand. We crawled down the mountainside, keeping ourselves from tumbling by holding on to the roots of trees. We made our way down to the river and drank the poisoned water. We ate the poisoned mud on the banks. We slept huddled together on the shore.

"We lived like this for three days, but it rained on the fourth and we stretched our faces upward gasping for the water. The rain tempered the fires and turned everything sodden. Others who'd lived came out of their shelters for the rainwater, small hovels or miraculous buildings that hadn't collapsed. We met a man named Ezra who brought us with him back to his shelter. It was only a matter of time before someone came to pick us up, he told us. They knew we were there—there were drones zipping about the place, filming the survivors, so they knew we were still alive. He was living in the basement of a building in the South Side. There were vending machines with food and bottles of water and more water he'd saved from the toilets. He gave us all something to eat—bags of peanuts and animal crackers. Ezra told us about the bomb. We listened to the radio. I realized that everyone I knew had died. I realized that the destruction was so swift and terrible that whoever I had once been could have died with the rest of what I had known. I felt like a dragonfly that had been trapped in amber and suddenly freed. I was new—

"Ezra planned our way from the city, packing up as much as we could carry—four of us shouldering the load would give us a better chance at surviving, he figured, but it never came to that. We heard the sound of helicopters. Men in protective clothing airlifted us to a hospital in Ohio. We were kept in separate rooms, but I know that

Steven died from radiation poisoning. I don't know if Elizabeth died or not. I was in the hospital for nearly a year, a sickness so overwhelming that I figured each day might be my last, but I lived. I lived—"

5, 4 *IBID.*—

Dawn by the time we say good night. She shuts her door as I leave, soft enough I hear the click and dragging sway of her chain lock and the heavy fall of the bolts. Crimson hallway carpet the color of pomegranates, early morning light the color of wool. The scent of her apartment lingers in my clothes—coffee, oil paints, container orchids and soil. Leaving her feels like a mistake, somehow, a critical lapse now that I've found her—but last night Albion said if we hesitate here we both will die.

"Why? Who'll kill us?" I asked. "Who are they? The men who killed Mook—"

Just after 3 a.m. when she brewed a second carafe of coffee. We sat facing each other on her couch, where we'd been all evening. Albion tugged on her earlobe—a little nervous tic when she's thinking.

"I really wasn't sure who they were until you found me, but now I'm certain," she said. "Waverly's brother, Gregor, and his sons. Rory and Cormac. Rory was just a teenager when I knew him. Cormac was older. He was married—I remember he liked showing us pictures of his two little girls. The brothers used to come up to the house during hunting season for weeks at a time and Waverly's brother would stay for even longer stretches. There's something odd about him, the brother—I don't know if he can take care of himself fully. Sometimes he goes catatonic for hours at a time. They're from Birmingham, in Alabama—"

"Timothy mentioned Alabama," I said. "The first time I met him he told me a story about driving through Alabama and passing roadkill in the middle of the night. Miles of roadkill. He said he was with his wife—"

"If Timothy brought a woman to Alabama, then she's dead," said Albion. "He took her to his uncle's farm—"

"Jesus," I said—already assuming that Timothy had killed his wife, but the blunt image of his uncle's farm still jolted me. Barns and sheds, maybe—decapitations and hands cleaved away, imagining what might be hidden in those fields. "Lydia Billingsley," I said. "Timothy's wife was named Lydia Billingsley. Her body was found in Louisiana. There are other women, too. Actually, I wanted to ask you about a specific young woman Timothy had a relationship with—"

"I'm sorry, Dominic," she said. "I can't help you with that—"

"Anything you know will help me. Anything you can tell me. I understand talking about Timothy will be difficult—I don't want to take that for granted, but I believe he may have killed the young woman I've been researching—"

"Let her go," said Albion.

"What?"

"Let her go," she said. "The dead deserve their rest—"

My feet feel hammered flat from the walking I've done, blisters like water balloons between my toes. Starbucks for coffee and oatmeal—a window seat where I watch the traffic gather and clot as morning thickens into the rush hour commute. *Click through* offers for a free latte if I fill out a customer satisfaction questionnaire, but all I can think of is Albion and Waverly's family and the desire to disappear. I need to think. Redraw my lines of inquiry into the death of Hannah Massey. Hourly forecasts, cloudless and radiant. Albion told me to let the dead rest and in the moment I assumed she meant Hannah Massey, but realize now she may have been referring to herself. I wick headlines from my line of sight—there's a gas station across the way and sunlight glinting off windshields and chrome distracts me.

I notice the error message first—

Red text and a faint notification ping: *identification failure.*

The SFPD app I've left running in the background keys on a police officer at the pumps across the street but fails to identify him; 3× zoom, 9×—he's wearing SWAT armor, without a helmet, an oily slick of hair and porcelain-fine features; 12× zoom—thin lips, like Timothy's, and smallish eyes. I store his image. The app locks onto his badge number but again fails identification, reporting *invalid* as checked against the existing roll.

Call 911 for immediate confirmation?

What would happen if I called the cops on him? The car he's filling is a San Francisco PD cruiser—steel cages over the fenders and slim-profile lights along the roof. Worst-case scenario: Waverly has police cooperation, they track my 911 call, flush me out, find Albion.

"Dismiss," I tell it.

Fuck. I schedule an AutoCab pickup and receive a ping just a few minutes later when a cab pulls into the Starbucks lot. I nestle into the rear seat and decline when the cab prompts me to load my personal account.

"Cash," I tell it, scrambling in my wallet for enough to cover the fare. I tell the cab the hotel address and decline options for a scenic route or self-guided city tour. A last glimpse through the rear window as the gas station recedes into the distance: he's still at the pumps.

Call Albion.

Her avatar's an image of a sparrow.

"Dominic?"

"You have to leave—you have to get out of your apartment right away. I'm in a cab right now on my way back to my hotel and I saw him, one of the men who killed Mook. I think it was one of them—"

"Slow down," she says. "Tell me what's happening—"

"There's a Starbucks near your apartment, with a gas station across the street. A Shell, I think. I think I saw one of the men who killed Mook. Only one of them—dressed like a cop. I don't know where the other two are. He's right by your apartment, he might be coming for you. You have to leave. Now—"

"Dominic, are you safe?" she says.

"I'm okay," I tell her. "I don't think he saw me—"

"Go back to your hotel and wait there," she says. "Call me when you get there. Be ready to leave. Lock the doors. Don't open for anyone, do you understand?"

"You need to leave," I tell her.

"I will," she says. "What hotel are you staying in?"

I forward her the hotel's address and she disconnects.

"Can I interest you in discount events at Candlestick Park?" says the cab.

"Cancel," I tell it, but the voice drones on, BOGO deals and spa retreats for the women in my life, cycling through its litany of offers. I scan out the rear window and spot the police cruiser, a lane over and two cars behind. We turn the corner onto Oakdale Avenue, an open stretch of smooth concrete glaring in the harsh sun. Wide lanes lined by pastel houses and apartment buildings on either side, like art deco dyed for Easter. Trees dot each block, leafy puffs on thin trunks. The police cruiser's immediately behind us, now, drawing closer. A siren squawk. It flashes its lights.

"Don't pull over, for Christ's sake, keep going," but the cab says, "You are instructed to prepare your driver's license and valid state ID. You are instructed to place your hands on the headrest in front of you—"

I try the door but the safety locks are engaged. *Fuck, fuck.* Squealing breaks as the cab pulls over through the bike lane to the curb.

"Cab, what's the badge number and name of the officer who's pulled us over?"

"Working . . . Working . . . Your patience is appreciated . . ."

"Cab, call 911. There's an emergency. Call 911—"

"Great news!" says the cab. "The police are already on the scene!"

"Son of a bitch—"

The cruiser pulls behind us, about two car lengths away. There's still only one officer, the one I saw at the pumps.

Call Albion—but she's not answering.

"No, no, no—"

Oakdale Avenue's streaming with traffic, cars flashing past too fast to flag someone down from the backseat of the cab, although I try—but even cars that rubberneck are just blurs of color sweeping past. He could shoot me here—locked in the cab, he could shoot my brains all over the backseat. The officer waits for a slight gap in traffic before he steps from the cruiser. He makes his way toward me along the edge of the street.

"Call 911. Unlock the fucking doors. I want to talk to a fucking human. I want to speak with my account representative—"

"Holding . . ."

The cab's front windows slide down. The officer leans in the driver's side. Moussed strands of hair have come undone from the rest of his slick. He's pale. His lips are bloodless. He's chewing, or maybe just grinding his teeth, and for a moment I let myself wonder if he's as nervous as I am.

"Are you John Blaxton?" he says, his voice silky with a southern accent, a little higher than I would have guessed.

"What do you want?"

"I think you and I have some things to discuss, don't you?"

He's not nervous at all—all that chewing must be some sort of restraint, or the anticipation of shredding me with his teeth.

"I don't have anything to discuss with you," I tell him, my life dwindling to a series of limited moves before an endgame. "I was working for a man named Timothy Reynolds," I tell him. "If you need to discuss me or my work, you can talk with him—"

"Get out of the car, John," he says, reaching inside the cab to override the locks. I know I'll die, but even so I obey him, simply obey him—shifting my bulk across the backseat, conjuring enough nerve to spring from the opposite side of the cab, to put the car between us and break for the pastel houses, but I'm already jelly-kneed and know I couldn't run. He could instruct me to fall to my knees so execution would be easier and I would obey, I would obey him—every clench of self-preservation already gone craven, paralyzed. Out of the car, I realize how tall he is—taller than me—wiry and athletic. He rests one hand on the handle of his nightstick.

"What do you want from me?" I ask him.

"Walk with me to the car," he says. "Ride in back. I'll be your chauffeur—"

The man's hands are white, white like they've never felt the sun, with long fingers and distorted knuckles that look more like bony protuberances than proper knuckles—one hand rests on the nightstick, but he's holding the other to his chest, drumming little rhythms against the smooth metal of his badge.

"What's your name?" I ask him.

Along the edge of the street, not on the sidewalk. An intersection's up ahead, but the traffic streaming past is heedless, the posted limit's forty-five but these cars are blowing past that. I can smell the man's aftershave or cologne—despite the breeze I can smell him and I wonder if this is what Mook smelled when he died.

"Did you kill Hannah Massey?" I ask him.

This draws a reaction—a puckish sneer like he'd cracked the vault of something sacred and defiled what he'd found. A little over 280 the last I weighed myself, but that was years ago when I was slimmer—I must outweigh him by a hundred pounds or more. Almost without thinking, certainly without considering many outcomes, I step into him—pushing with both hands and shouldering, leveraging my weight into a headlong thrust. He keeps his balance, but stumbles several feet into the nearest lane. I can't tell the make of the car—but I'm sure the driver never sees this man suddenly in the street. Driving into the glare of the sun. There isn't a shriek of breaks or even tires squealing away in a tight swerve, only the plastic crunch of the car striking him, the fender cutting him at the knees and plowing through his leg and hip. The man pinwheels onto the hood, back bouncing against the front windshield and buckling the safety glass. His body flips away from the car and straddles the center lane. The car slides to a stop. Other cars stop. Distant horns. Someone screams. The man isn't dead—I can't tell how injured he is, but he isn't dead. He's already on his hands and knees, spitting blood and vomiting. I run.

Across four lanes, through the intersection—between houses,

cutting across lawns, odd artificial patches of neon grass. I slip to my knees. I collapse. Facedown in the cool grass. *What have I done? God, I killed him, I tried to kill him.* Sirens, approaching sirens. Fear paralyzed, winded: the man's body buckling the windshield, all that blood splashing from his mouth. *Fuck, fuck.* One knee at a time. I stand. I stand and run. Onto another street, a cross street. Sides stitched, cramping, so I walk as fast as I can, stitches of pain coursing through my chest, my arms. A bus approaching. Is this a heart attack? I lift my arm at the corner and the bus pulls over, the door folds open.

"Hey, mister—Are you okay?"

I collapse into a front seat, searching my pockets for bills to pay the fare—the bus already pulling away from the stop, turning a corner. The air-conditioning's like a frigid suffocation. I can't catch my breath. I don't know where I am, where I'm going—focal points on my Adware disoriented, useless. Two bills to pay the meter. A police car screams past in the opposite direction. A woman across from me holds her groceries to her chest like she thinks I'll steal them. I'm trying to catch my breath.

"Are you all right?" says the driver. "Do you need a doctor or something?"

"I'm good," I tell him. "Just a few blocks. I'm okay—"

They must think I'm having an aneurysm—fat drops of sweat roll off my face. I settle in, slump, *I tried to kill him,* headlines scroll but I'm too agitated to read, TMZ's going viral with a vid of a girl who's lit herself on fire—suicide-dare.com. The girl douses herself with lighter fluid like she's at a wet T-shirt contest; she lights a match. The video's playing out, millions of hits—she ignites in a blue flash, then runs screaming around her bedroom, bouncing against the walls, burning alive. Someone's overlaid 8-bit Nintendo music over the vid and it's like she's writhing to the music. #Suicide-

Dare trends in the global feeds. Coupons for Dunkin' Donuts, coupons for McDonald's. I try to call Albion again, but she's still not answering.

I don't know where I am. I hop off the bus after twenty minutes and request an AutoCab pickup. It's a different cab from the one I'd had before so I have to decline the chorus of offers as I ride. Apartments and strip malls, gas stations and traffic. I ask the cab to pull over across the street from my hotel and approach around back—no police cars, nothing unusual. I keep the lights off in my room, calling Albion while I pack, rolling up my Steelers hoodie and sweats, changing into my Adidas. I pack up my new books and Albion's artwork.

She calls.

"Dominic? Where are you?"

"At my hotel. Are you all right? I've been calling you—"

"Look for a green Prius. It's light green, almost silver—"

I find her in the lot, idling near the entrance. The backseat and rear hatch of the Prius are filled with suitcases and garbage bags stuffed full. She must have been packing when I tried to call, taking whatever she could gather in just a couple of trips, leaving everything else behind. She rolls down the window and says, "Get in—"

Awkward, my suitcase between my legs, my knees splayed out so I have to cringe to the side in order for Albion to shift gears—she drives fast, rolling through stop signs and pushing intersections, rarely stopping. Her posture's prim, her hands kept at 10 and 2—she leans forward, scanning the traffic for spaces to slip through, aggressive. I hold my hand to the dash and see my fingers still shaking—I can't quite calm down.

"I tried to kill one of them," I tell her. "I pushed him—he was hit by a car. I can't believe, I, almost I—"

"Who was it?" she asks. "What did he look like?"

"A young guy," I tell her, flashing the image I captured. "He looked like a stoat. Pale—"

"Rory," she says. "Did you kill him? Is he dead?"

"No, I don't think so—"

Albion cries as we cross the Golden Gate Bridge—a self-controlled sobbing that amounts to little more than tears in rivulets down her otherwise stoic face. Hallucinatory women float like angels in the Adware, singing daily deals and half off admission to tourist traps. Auto-Toll with Adware registration but Albion waits in line to pay with cash, paranoid our connection might have been hacked. I stare out over the bay, at the white flecks of sailboats and gulls against the expanse of impossibly blue water, the phantom weight of the man's body against my palms as if I'm still pushing him—*He's not dead,* I tell myself, *it's all right, he's not dead. I haven't killed anybody.*

"We wasted too much time," says Albion, panic edging her voice. "We should have left hours ago. We should have left the moment you found me—"

She has a checklist for disappearance—her first few steps scripted years in advance. Up 101, distant folds of mountains and grass verges and overpasses, medians lined with skinny pines. She pulls over at a McDonald's in Novato, one she'd picked out because the parking lot's hidden from view of the road, transferring her checking and savings into a floating account. She stops again just outside of Santa Rosa at a place called Good Stuff Auto and trades her Prius for a used Outback and five thousand in cash—she's bilked on the deal, but adamant that the Outback is featureless, no GPS, no OnStar, Adware hookups only to the stereo, no other account access. She signs her papers using a Washington state ID that lists her name as Rose Callahan. The salesman knows the ID's bullshit, but he's happy to deal—even helping us repack our luggage in the new car before counting out a hundred crisp fifty-dollar bills. We grab burritos from a roadside grill before backtracking south down 101.

"Now tell me who you are," she says. "I need to know why you're here, how you found me—"

"I told you last night—"

"Do better than what you told me—"

"Are you taking me back to San Francisco?" I ask her. "We're heading south—"

"We'll pick up I-80 toward Nevada. There's a town called Elko," she says. "We'll figure out what our next steps are from there, but I need to know more about you before I decide what to do—"

By four o'clock, the afternoon's turning syrupy, hours of driving already behind us. She pulls over at a rest stop so we can stretch our legs, use the restrooms. Pepsi and cheddar cheese Combos from the vending machine.

"I've been keeping a journal," I tell her when she's back at the car. "It's the best I can offer to tell you about myself, why I found you, how I'm involved in all this—I'll let you read it. It will tell you everything—"

"Go ahead and start," she says. "Read it while I drive—"

I read from the beginning, "'Her body's down in Nine Mile Run, half buried in river mud,'" but Albion stops me after only a few pages, once I've read about my session with Simka, when I told him the name of the body I'd found.

"I knew her," she says. "I remember Hannah—"

Albion's connection to Hannah, or their potential connection, never occurred to me until now—beyond their separate relationships to Timothy, to Waverly. Albion always sliding away from me toward her disappearance, Hannah Massey always emerging, someone I'm excavating. Thinking of them together unsettles me.

"Did you know her well?"

"Not very well," she says, speaking to the miles of highway in front of us more than she's speaking to me. "Waverly was interested in her. He was a lecturer from time to time—he said it kept his mind elastic to be around so many intelligent young people, that it helped keep his work fresh for his company, Focal Networks. I remember when he told us about Hannah—there were about eight of us eating together that night. We'd just said prayers when Waverly said something about finding a flower growing in a barren field. Anyway, he was enthusiastic about a student in one of his classes, and asked me to get to know her, me and Peyton—"

"Is that how it worked? Did you recruit women to live at the house?"

"Recruit might not be the right word," she says, "and Hannah never lived with us. We introduced ourselves, spent time with her. She was an actress and was interested in modeling, so there was a natural connection with me and Peyton. She was impressed by Waverly, impressed by us. She came to the house for prayer group, sometimes, but never lived there—"

"Do you know how she died?" I ask, but the question closes her off. I know I've bungled something, though I'm not exactly sure what—maybe the bluntness of the question, maybe scratching at a wound she thought had healed years ago. After a few minutes, I say, "Albion, I'm sorry. I shouldn't pry. I didn't mean to sound so callous or direct about someone you knew. I don't mean any disrespect to her—"

"It's all right," she says, but turns on the radio and eventually the oldies ease us.

We arrive in Elko late and check into the Shilo Inn, a stretch of white motel with the feeling of an emptied swimming pool. Once we drop our bags, she takes me to a sports bar called Matties and tells me to bring my journal. After midnight. We sit in a corner booth far from the windows, scanning the front door whenever someone new drifts in. Terrified and anxious about the faces we might recognize. She asks me to start my journal again from the beginning. She listens carefully, stopping me every so often to clarify something I'd written or to ask me to fill in details about my life. I read until two, when Matties is closing and we retreat to our rooms at the Shilo.

A few days in Elko. We spend most of it at Matties or wandering slow laps around the Elko Junction Shopping Center, lost in conversation or sitting for hours in the food court while I read my journal to her, only retreating to our hotel rooms once everything's closed and the streetlights blink yellow. I read to her about Theresa, and Albion supposes she may have known her—that she once took a class on container gardening at Phipps. "The teacher was kind of quirky," she says. "Longish hair, blonde? I liked her. I remember she liked to tell jokes—"

Matties lets us linger for hours—we're picking at chocolate cake and sharing a pot of coffee when I read her my description of how we met, the moment I first saw her in the gallery in her white dress, her pockets filled with flowers. I close the journal, set it aside, finish the cake.

"There's a house in New Castle," she says.

"New Castle, Pennsylvania? Is that where you're heading? Near Pittsburgh?"

"We'll be safe there," she says. "Sherrod helped me buy it anonymously a few years ago. It's meant to be a safe house, someplace to hide. It could work for a little while—"

"When they killed him, they took his Adware," I remind her. "They'll know what he knew—"

"Sherrod was careful," she says and I want to say, *Not careful enough*, but let the obvious slip past.

We leave Elko the next morning, sharing the drive to New Castle—we eat Bob Evans or IHOP for every breakfast, pushing through the days and staying at whatever Express hotel we come to when we're each too tired to drive. Albion loops audiobooks through her Adware to the stereo—she prefers centuries-old books, Longfellow and the like, Tennyson and Shakespeare. We make it through *Jane Eyre* twice. We listen to old French music as the evenings descend—acoustic jazz and folk, Carla Bruni and Boris Vian. When she's asleep I shut down my Adware and just listen to the radio, country twang through most of the country, or stations filled with evangelism, but I listen to that promise of God's love because even those preachers' voices are easier to take than the silence, when all the death I've been hounding coalesces and hangs in my thoughts like butchered meat.

Night by the time we drive through Ohio, the landscape changing to something as forgotten but familiar as my mother's voice—flatlands giving way to the warp of fields and the hills that will become the mountains of what was once Pittsburgh. We cross into Pennsylvania. We reach New Castle late—I pull in the driveway and cut the engine, the sudden lack of sound and movement dragging Albion from her reverie. I switch off the headlights and we sit looking at the place—the aluminum siding, a dead crab apple tree in the front lawn, untended bushes close against the front porch. No electricity and no heat, so we bring flashlights and set up camp in the living room. Albion paces the hallways. I hear her footsteps on the hardwood, hear her footfalls creaking upstairs across the ceiling, hear her coming back down the rickety stairs. She screams, but by the time I run to her she's already laughing—she trains her flashlight to the kitchen wall just above the electric stove, illuminating a smiling pig's face that had been spray-painted there some time ago, loopy eyes and a lolling mouth, the words *Welcome home!* scrawled in a speech balloon.

· PART III ·

WESTERN PENNSYLVANIA

8, 18—

New Castle, Pennsylvania—about an hour, maybe an hour and a half, outside of what the EPA maps out as the Pittsburgh Exclusion Zone. PEZ, it's called. New Castle was a mill town once, the industrial machinery and warehouses sprawling along the bank of the Shenango in disuse now since Pittsburgh. The houses sag and are worn like cardboard boxes left in the rain. Downtown must have been vibrant once in a long past decade, the newest building now a Sprint wireless store, but otherwise we're left with a Giant Eagle, a Dollar Blowout, a Kentaco Hut, a Dairy Queen only intermittently open. There are rumors we'll get a Walgreens sometime soon. Just down 65, a little closer to Pittsburgh, is PEZ Zeolite, but the money from all those government cleanup contracts hasn't flowed to New Castle—most of it's gone up to Youngstown, far enough away from the exclusion zone for the cleaners and engineers to settle their families. There's a Walmart not too far away in Ohio, and on weekends we have a farmer's and flea market in the school parking lot. Albion's house is on the outskirts. She bought the place for cash—she said it only cost the equivalent of a few months' rent of her loft back in San Francisco. A two-story Victorian with claustrophobic rooms and warped hardwood floors. I bought a bookcase for Albion but had to prop up the front with folded towels because the living room sags so deeply down from the edges to the center. The kitchen's a work in progress with mildewed wallpaper to peel, cabinets to repaint, a floor that needs a fresh layer of sticky tiles or maybe just stripped back to the hardwood. I've tried to paint out Mook's graffiti pig with several coats of primer, but the damn thing still shows faintly through. There's an acre or so of patchy yard before the neighbor's fence. We have a garage made of cinder blocks and a few pines in the back.

Tracking Albion in the Archive gave me a wildly inaccurate impression of the woman I've come to know—now I realize that all her interest in fashion and design, which I took only as something artsy, is a symptom of a larger rage for order and self-reliance. She makes all her own clothes, by and large, and cooks every meal—I haven't had takeout for weeks, but she'll go to Dairy Queen with me for sundaes. She jogs several miles before dawn and by the time I get up and pour my first cup of coffee, she's already out tending her garden, a twenty-by-twenty patch of vegetables we use for cooking. I sometimes wander out with my coffee and sit on a folding chair to watch her, helping only when she wants help. A few months ago she'd washed out the black dye she had when I first met her in the gallery—her natural hair's no longer the startling crimson I'd known from the Archive, but a chestnut shade of red that seems brown in the dim but like changing autumn leaves in the light.

Every Sunday morning Albion drives us south into the wildlife refuge and we walk for hours along the trails—muddy paths and creeks cutting through underbrush, ugly reedy groves and metal signs warning not to drink the water for fear of radiation or animal contamination, scum-skinned lakes with mucky swathes meant as beaches. Miles and miles, the kind of woods I grew up with—nothing majestic, just Ohio and Pennsylvania scrub, but Albion finds charm here. She knows birdcalls and identifies flitting shadows I'm never quick enough to see. She's a good hiker, she drives our pace—I often fall behind, heaving for breath and sweating, and when we hit upward slopes my knees crackle like damp sticks breaking and I figure I'll need to lose even more weight or my joints will just give out some day, but I'm happy to try to keep up with her.

Sometimes I lose patience with my trepidation and broach questions about her past. "You once mentioned that you and Peyton were sometimes sent out to recruit other girls," I say on one of our hikes, working to keep my wind, to match her gait.

I never know if I'll push her away when I ask questions like these—I've lost entire days to her silence when I've overstepped—but over the past few months I've come to believe that Albion wants to talk about the raw areas of her life, only it's difficult for her. She's guarded herself with strict boundaries, and seems to weigh each exchange she has with me against her vulnerability. I've learned that talking at the house about anything other than our life together is off-limits, but that she's much more willing to talk candidly when we're in these woods—I don't know if it's because she feels protected or removed out here, or if she feels a sense of grace in nature that turns her confessional.

"We were loosely affiliated with the King of King's parish and if we ever spoke with members of that church, we talked about ourselves like we were a foster home," she says. "Some of the girls came to us through that church—but Kitty was particular in who she would accept for residence. You're right, though, there was recruitment involved, especially on campuses. One or two of us would make friends with the same girl and invite her to worship with us. We'd try to make contact with her every day, usually more than once a day, and eventually we'd try to preempt her other friends. Every so often one of us would be too aggressive and we'd lose her, but usually young women on their own want to meet other women. We picked foreign exchange students or women who were already looking for a community of faith. We'd go to prayer services on campuses and watch for girls who came alone—"

"Hannah didn't seem vulnerable," I tell her. "She had plenty of friends—"

"We wouldn't have been successful with Hannah in the long run," she says.

"But this was something you were actively involved in?" I ask her. "Meeting girls and bringing them to back to the house with you—"

"I was very religious," she says. "I don't know if you'd understand if you've never been religious, or if you've never felt something so strongly that you think it's God. I thought I was helping those girls—"

When I don't answer, she says, "You know, I really fucked up my life. I can't have that back—all those years of shitty choices. It wasn't until after I was free of Timothy and Waverly and that house did I feel the weight of what I'd done to those women—it's like a panic, whenever I realize what I helped do. I didn't know what would happen to them, what Timothy and Waverly did to them—all that time I thought I was helping bring them closer to what I called Jesus. I was deluded and still feel sick, physically sick, when I think of my part in that house. I had to stop believing in God before I realized what it meant that we all bear the weight of the cross. I had to stop believing in God before I wanted to atone for what I'd done in His name—"

Albion pushes the pace and I fall behind—I can't keep up with her when she picks up speed, but I also realize I'm not meant to, so I slacken my pace and let her pull away. Whenever we come to a creek or some vein of running water, she pauses to listen. She once asked me if I was a Christian and I told her that I wasn't, that I don't believe in God.

"You believe in love," she said.

The New Castle Farmers' Market and Super Flea, perfect for plums. Saturdays the worst for crowds, aisles difficult to thread through, vendors in tents or wooden-framed booths draped with tarps. Steelers jerseys, Confederate flags, bootleg MMA sims, strawberries—I still need strawberries. Strawberry rhubarb cupcakes for Albion, if I can figure out the recipe. *Scroll, scroll:* one-quart saucepan, heat strawberries, rhubarb, sugar, flour, butter. Four of five stars, but sounds easy. Do we need butter? Ping Albion and ask, *Do we have butter?* Rhubarb, ten dollars for a bundle from Tuscarawas Farms—*SmartShopper* says I can do better.

Good on butter, pings Albion.

I purchase a package of plums. Booths of jarred preserves, bell peppers in plastic wrap, gourmet marshmallow cubes, dark honey of Ohio. The aisle's capped with a booth for the handmade ginger soap Albion likes, so I grab a few bars and pick up a dozen bananas Foster marshmallows. Trust *SmartShopper* when it flashes *BEST BUY* on a package of rhubarb sprigs.

I buy groceries from lists she writes and she prepares our dinners. She has me on a vegetarian diet. With our walks and what I've been eating, I've lost weight—I feel trimmer than I have in years. I try to dress up for our dinners, sometimes even wearing Gavril's suit if I know she's making something special. I pour wine and set the table, just the small kitchen table, and she serves our food. Albion still likes the act of prayer, to remember what her life was once like and what it has become, but says she doesn't know what or who she prays to any longer. I bow my head and clasp my hands and say "amen" when she's finished but spend my time thinking over what I've lost but also what I've found.

I clean the dishes while she works in her studio. I tidy up the place as best I can. Around nine I brew tea and around nine thirty she joins me on the sofa and we talk. Most nights we talk about art. She shows me her designs and sometimes I read to her. At some point it became tacit between us that Albion would leave behind making images of the house in Greenfield if I started to write poetry again—that we would help each other move forward. We go to bed nearing midnight and every night I wonder if we'll kiss good night, but we never have. She uses the only bed. There's a mattress on the second bedroom floor and an antique trunk she found for fifteen dollars at a Goodwill I use for my clothes and books. I lie on my mattress staring out the window into the dark tops of our pines until I no longer hear the soft sounds of Albion readying herself for bed. I can't sleep until she's asleep.

I can never have Theresa back.

She's been deleted and Albion believes that even Mook couldn't have brought her back, that Mook's work is thorough. She asks how we met.

"It's not a romantic story," I tell her.

"It's romantic to me," she says.

"So, there was a conference every year about social networking tools called PodCamp," I tell her. Albion wants to see the moment I met Theresa, so we immerse together—strolling downtown Pittsburgh like tourists in a foreign city lost to time. The City's working through its infinite loop of weather, the sky a leaden ceiling, snow and rain slurring into an intolerable frozen mush that grays out the buildings and dampens everything. From certain angles, there is a beauty to these downtown streets, even on days like this, when car windows fogged and people huddled in grotesque wet coats, using umbrellas and slipping on the sidewalks. It's November in the City. Windshield wipers brush away globs of snow. Albion and I duck into the Courtyard Marriott where it's warmer, and sit together in the lobby drinking hot cocoa. Despite the weather, dozens of people arrive for PodCamp—designers, students, young professionals, all dressed better than the rest of us wading through the muck outside. I scan their faces, recognizing people whose names I've forgotten.

Albion and I wander the hotel hallways together, looking behind room doors at televisions playing to empty rooms and out-of-town travelers inadvertently filmed as they fetched ice from the vending machines or went to the pool or checked into their rooms, their images trapped in the Archive like ghosts haunting wrong, unfamiliar places. Throughout the morning the PodCamp attendees settled into folding chairs to listen to PowerPoint presentations and take notes in PodCamp binders, but after lunch the sessions became more specific. The room was called Partitioned Conference Room B, and the session was "Generating a Realistic Income with WordPress and Affiliate Marketing." There were only six of us registered. Theresa came in just after me—a peach blouse and blue jeans, a suede jacket, her hair longer then. She doesn't come in now. She sat a few seats away, I remember, and I stammered when I introduced myself.

"Theresa Marie," she said, and I remember that hearing her name was like hearing a rare and sacred word, but all I could come up with was, "Aren't you Elvis Presley's daughter?"

"Itching like a gal on a fuzzy tree," she said, "but I think that was Lisa Marie—"

We talked—about statues of horses in Washington, DC, for some reason, I don't remember why, some sort of small talk, but we talked. What one hoof lifted from the ground meant, what two hooves lifted meant—I think I asked her what four hooves meant and she said "Pegasus."

Partitioned Conference Room B is set up with folding chairs when Albion and I visit here, a dry-erase board in the center of the room. We watch John Dominic Blaxton, and Albion says that I was cute back then, that no wonder Theresa fell for me, but I don't like seeing myself—skinny and young, full of unearned confidence. I see in that young face a total ignorance of everything that will happen and I both admire and hate him for it. The others filter into the class and take their chairs for the session, just like I remember they did—but Theresa never comes into the room and I watch myself speaking to no one.

"Please, let's go," I tell Albion.

I remember standing outside in the thickening slush waiting for my bus after the conference, nearly heaving with excitement like my lungs were bursting into sparks and might leap from my chest singing. I wanted desperately to somehow keep talking with her, so I tapped out an e-mail on my cell, saying how great it was to meet her, how I would love to keep talking about WordPress with her, and accidentally hit Reply All and so for the next few days heard from just about everyone from the conference except her. People trying to set up a follow-up meeting about WordPress, even the WordPress lecturer wanted us all to meet at the Panera in Shadyside. I figured I'd embarrassed her, or that she was politely unresponsive because she had a boyfriend, or just wasn't interested, or genuinely thought I was interested in WordPress, but after three days she responded: *Drinks? When are you free?*

Albion and I go there now—to Cappy's over on Walnut, only a block away from the apartment where Theresa and I would live in Shadyside. I look for Theresa here, Adware pulling memories of this place, but she's nowhere—instead, Albion and I sit at the same table Theresa and I shared, near the front windows, watching the increasing snowfall and the snow-laden shoppers on Walnut Street. Theresa and I talked for over three hours that night. She was a botanist, working for Phipps Conservatory. I told her about my Ph.D. program and my poetry. She loved music and talked about bands she loved—the Broken Fences, Joy Ike, Life in Bed, Meeting of Important People, Shade—bands I'd never heard of become suddenly important to me. We said good night and I offered to see her home, to ride the bus with her to the South Side where she lived, but she refused the offer so I waited with her at the bus stop, shoulders piling with snow, until the 54C appeared through the mist. She boarded and I watched her in the lit interior of the bus—her hair covered in wet flakes of snow. She waved as the bus pulled away and I walked home—the city quiet, everything shrouded in a profound white silence. I was so happy that night—an ecstatic contentment in that silence, a feeling like I'd come home, like I'd discovered where home was. I remember singing "Maria" from *West Side Story* at the top of my lungs, but not knowing the words and replacing "Maria" with "Theresa." A few minutes later she texted and told me that she had fun, and asked if I was free that weekend. *Yes,* I answered, *yes.* I texted her for a playlist and she wrote back in an hour with a list of bands and tracks—my homework. I spent the next several days memorizing everything I could, every band, learning to love what she loved.

Albion and I are there now, at the bus stop watching the 54C pull up through the snow, its wheels leaving muddy tracks, the driver asking if we need a ride, but the bus feels like a ferry for the dead and we refuse. Albion and I walk through the snow together holding hands. She says she misses the winter, living in California so long. She sometimes forgets how beautiful it was. We walk through the serene Shadyside streets to Ellsworth Avenue, to the apartment

I shared with Theresa, through the courtyard to the lobby, shaking snow from our shoes and the shoulders of our coats. We walk to Room 208—I'm here. Theresa, I'm here. Albion kisses me, a slow, tender kiss, our lips cold but warming. The kiss is perfect but doesn't exist in the real world, it only exists here and I understand that, I understand the gift she has given me. I open the door to Room 208 but in Theresa's place we see Zhou. This is the first time that Albion has seen what Zhou is in my memories, that Zhou is here where Theresa should have been, and she begs my forgiveness and I tell her that it's all right, it's all right—

Albion's taken me on her bus. We ride together and I brace her against me as we enter the perpetual twilight of the tunnel. I watch the old lady in front of us clicking her tongue at the child in front of her. I find Stewart, that first voice of her hope, a handsome man in a Pirates ball cap—he must have only been in his thirties, about my age, his kids that he wanted so much to see again must have only been toddlers. Albion points out every person on the bus and tells me what she's been able to find out about their lives. She points out Jacob, the singer, an overweight black man with ashen hair, and hopes that he's forgiven her for leaving through that thin path in the stones, leaving him behind. She points out Tabitha, the woman who tore out her own eyes—she's dressed in nurse's scrubs and reads Joel Osteen. We brace for the explosion, for the bus to wreck, but I only experience the initial concussion of the end because that's when the footage stops and we're left in total darkness with the Archive asking us in floating bronze text if we'd like to visit somewhere else. Sometimes Albion and I ride that bus several times in a row, looping back to the moment when she boarded and riding until we die, until I finally say, "That's enough, Albion, that's enough," and we retreat together to somewhere else, usually to Kelly's Bar in East Liberty to sit in a shadowy corner booth on the vinyl seats, listening to rockabilly on the jukebox, drinking cocktails and eating baked mac and cheese, trying to forget together what we desperately want to remember.

Kelly's in East Liberty has become important to us, a bar neither one of us had visited often when we were both in Pittsburgh but perfect for us to discover together now.

"Tell me about Mook," I ask her, one night over drinks in our usual booth. "Sherrod, I mean—"

"Sherrod was troubled," she says. "I feel sad when I think of him—"

I ask how they met and she tells me they met at Denny's. "I was out with friends from Fetherston," she says. "We went out and ended up at Denny's in the Mission—two or three in the morning. The waiter, this guy, he was hitting on us, kind of flirting with the entire table, when one of the cooks came from the back. Baggy jean shorts, a 49ers jersey, a white apron. He was short—only five feet tall, maybe, or maybe a touch over—and deformed, in a way. Hunched. He walked with a limp, though I think the limp was an affectation—once I knew him a little I realized that sometimes he forgot to limp. Cauliflower ears, this wet mouth that sort of hung open. Squinty eyes. He smelled like grease and cigarette smoke but he sits right in our booth, right with us, and asks if we were interested in an orgy. My friends laughed at first, some of them, but I didn't—not my type of humor. I remember he noticed I wasn't laughing and he just glared at me until I acknowledged him. Unnerving. 'I have access to a hot tub,' he said, and I think he called me Red.

"I can't remember what I said to him, something dismissive, and so he started telling me everything about my previous life—he knew my real name, knew about Pittsburgh, knew parts of my past that no one had the right to know. He knew about Peyton. He told me obscene things about myself. My friends didn't know what was going on, thank God, but they could pick up that things had taken a turn. We left right away—I was mortified. I didn't even know what the Archive was at the time, but once I figured it out, I realized that my past life was living itself again and again and again. I wanted it erased. I went back to Denny's the next afternoon, found Sherrod at the start of his shift. I went back to the kitchen and screamed at him, just—I really broke down. All those cooks looking at me. He realized he'd crossed a boundary when he dredged up those things, that he wasn't being cute or clever but had overstepped. He was contrite. For all his tone-deaf bluster, he's actually principled. He's sensitive. I can't quite call him a gentleman . . . but he said he could help me and I accepted. I didn't know who he was until much later, I didn't know about his art—"

We never talk about how he died.

We take walks in the afternoons, sometimes, back around the garage and the pines into Albion's garden, sometimes taking longer walks through the neighborhood, but Albion feels conspicuous—passing our neighbors on their front porches, women Albion's age already three or four kids deep into families, old women and old men on lawn chairs in front yards smoking cigarettes, young girls circling bikes on the street or the teenage girls in cutoffs and tank tops—it's obvious that Albion doesn't belong here. Besides, I think most of our neighbors are keen enough to spot a woman in trouble. After our walks, Albion will disappear into her room or lose herself in a charcoal drawing and I'll head outside to the front porch and voice Gavril—we usually talk at least every other day. After dinner one night, sitting out on the porch, Gavril asks about my psychiatrist.

"Timothy? What about him?"

"No, the other one. The one you had before—"

"Simka?"

"You didn't hear about him? He was stripped of his credentials—it was in the *Post*," he says. "He can't practice anymore. Some scandal—"

"What scandal? What are you talking about?"

"Selling painkillers to kids," says Gavril. "You haven't heard about this? Three or four girls accused him of trading sex for oxy. They were on the same tennis team, came forward together. The whole thing broke open—"

"No. No, that didn't happen—"

"It's all over the *Post*," says Gavril and I tell him I have to go, to read about what's happened. I scan DC Local feeds and find something on the *Washington Post* blog, allegations that Simka sold painkiller medications to teenagers, some of his patients. *Cock Doc Writes Oral Prescriptions*—cached streams show vids of his arrest, District cops leading him from his office in cuffs, carrying away boxes marked "evidence." I try to ping Simka, but no answer. I write him an e-mail asking what happened. Details are sketchy—a follow-up post explains Simka's painkillers led to the deaths of three young women who'd gone missing after nights on the DC club scene, surveillance footage of coke and liquor and pills, overdosing on Simka's narcotics before disappearing. Some of the victims are underage, but hacks have posted pictures anyway, prep-school blondes in burgundy blazers and plaid skirts, photographs of them in tennis whites. *Bullshit.* He sold to anarcho club kids who sold on campuses, a drug ring centered on Simka's office. *I can't believe this.* Simka's lawyer, state-appointed, maintains his innocence, but in the interim the state board has stripped him of his license and has incarcerated him. When Simka finally responds, it's through e-mail: *I don't regret helping you.*

I tell Albion while she's painting and she hugs me, holds me until I stop shaking. She asks if I need anything, if I need to go to DC.

"I don't think so. I don't know what good it would do—"

My other e-mails go unanswered, and when I reach out to his family I receive a form e-mail from an *unknown sender*, signed by their lawyer, requesting not to be contacted. Restless sleep, obsessing over Simka—at night when I'm thinking of him, he's so present it's like he's here with me, like I can smell his aftershave and coffee breath or reach out into the dark of my room and touch his hairy arm, convince myself he's right here with me, chuckling about some joke he'd heard, ready to dispel my gloominess by asking about the Beatles.

Albion wakes me early, says I was shouting—having nightmares. Over grapefruit, she asks if I want to go camping and we drive to the wildlife refuge. She checks the park guides for different trails to explore, but we've hiked them all. We rent a fifteen-dollar site to pitch our tent and stow our gear and walk familiar, light trails. I bring bottles of water, hummus and pita and a bottle of wine. We hold hands as we hike like friends who might someday discover they're lovers. We take naps in the afternoon and hike again before dinner, coming back to the campsite to cook mushroom burgers and fry potatoes and drink our second bottle of wine.

We stay up around the fire and Albion asks if everything's all right.

"No," I tell her. "Everything's not all right . . ."

"Tell me," she says.

"His family doesn't answer—they don't want my attention. They don't respond to me, and I don't know where he is. I haven't heard from him since that first night. There's nothing I can do for him—"

"Simka?"

"He's married, he has a family," I tell her. "Simka was one of the best people I've ever known—compassionate. There's no way he's involved in something like this—"

"You think he's innocent?"

"I know he's innocent," I tell her. "I don't believe he was selling drugs to kids, not after everything he's done for me. About my own problems. I don't believe it. They're ruining him, his entire family—"

"Sometimes people disappoint us," she says.

"Enough of that," I tell her. "Enough. He has two sons who no longer have a father. We're not just going to keep ignoring the obvious—"

"What's obvious?" she asks.

Is she going to make me say this? "Someone's doing this to him," I tell her. "Someone's fucking up his life, probably because of what he knows about me. Maybe they lost us and they're trying to provoke me, to flush me out—"

"Waverly?" she asks, her voice tentative, breathy, like she has trouble forming the word.

"You tell me—"

Albion doesn't answer and I don't care if I've somehow hurt her, and after a few moments she leaves the fire, dissolving into the outer darkness of the woods. Bruised anger catches in my throat that she's run away, but I'm more upset at how abstruse she is, at the lines she's drawn around herself, withholding even when others are suffering. Simka—*fuck*. That furniture he'd made and his house cradled by the creek and the woods, roughhousing with his sons—gone, gone, and I want to scream but I sit staring at the fire, impotent and cold.

I hear Albion's tread in the woods and when she comes back into the ring of firelight, she sits next to me instead of across from me. She puts her hand on my knee and leaves it there for a moment before pulling a marshmallow from our pack. She skewers it on a stick, lights it on fire. She holds it up to watch the glowing cube before puffing it out. The air's filled with the scent of caramelized sugar and Albion holds out the marshmallow until I eat it.

"Dominic, I can help you," she says.

"Help me? Or help Simka?"

"I don't know if we'll be able to help Simka," she says, "but there's something I can show you that we might be able to use—"

"Use how? What do you mean?"

"I've kept things hidden for far too long," she says. "I was mistaken, Dominic. I want to face this, I want to help end this suffering—"

Something's different about her, something opening—a complex comfort grown between us, present in a way that I hadn't yet felt, less diffuse and fragile, like we'd been describing a relationship to each other these past few months but suddenly find ourselves together in one.

"In a day or so we have to go on a hike. It will be harder than the hikes we've been taking recently," she says. "You should rest up, rest your feet. I'll need to buy some gear we don't have—I might need to drive for it, maybe as far as Cleveland. I'll go tomorrow morning, but I shouldn't be gone more than a day—"

We share a tent together. We're in separate sleeping bags but she reaches for my hand and holds my arm around her. My body feels like liquid fire holding her and I pull her close but we never kiss. Instead, I let my face rest against her hair like I'm lost in a veil of flowers. It's rained in the night. I wake up earlier than Albion and watch her sleep. I slip from our tent. Gray light hangs throughout the forest. I hear a tread and stop—a tawny deer twenty or thirty yards from me looks up. He's unconcerned, and lopes away through the fog.

Three days pass, we wake in the darkness before dawn.

"Good morning," she whispers.

Adware at half-light, the dashboard clock flips to 3:47 a.m. Albion's sitting on the edge of my bed, silhouetted by the hallway light. "Are you awake?" she says.

"I'm awake—"

"Coffee's brewing, and I'll make some eggs."

Albion's only packing prewrapped food for our trip—protein bars, dehydrated meals, enough for a few days if needed, even though we're planning on being home by tomorrow afternoon. We've divvied up the weight of our gear, but she says my main job is to lug water—we can't stint ourselves on water, she says—so my frame pack will carry the bulk of our supply plus a ClearSip purifier. I load the Outback while Albion brews a second pot of coffee and fills two thermoses. When she joins me, she hands me a bouquet of flowers cut from our yard—dahlias, it looks like, deep violets, bundled with sprigs of yellow and miniature sunflowers.

"These are for Theresa," she says.

We leave before dawn and watch the sunrise break violet as we drive, burning the ridges of clouds like they're waves of fire, pink and tangerine. Coming down 65 toward Pittsburgh, running alongside tracks cluttered with the iron hulks of trains, graffiti-bright boxcars and flatbeds loaded with heavy equipment—hunter's-orange bulldozers and excavators—and car after car strapped with canisters of radioactive waste. Canisters filled with glass, if I understand the process correctly—by-product hauled off for burial in reinforced cement sarcophagi, sites dotting Pennsylvania, West Virginia, Ohio. Our road follows the tracks, the tracks hugging the course of the Ohio River, past the first of the tri-state purification plants straddling the water—zeolite dumps built beneath one of the steel-span bridges, the water churned and pumped, filtered. The facility looks like a shopping mall.

"Will I see her body?"

"No, you won't see her," says Albion.

"I don't know what to expect—"

"There aren't bodies, if that's what you're imagining," she says. "You may see some remains specifically where I'm taking you, but there aren't bodies anymore—"

Of course, she's right—staring out the window at the ripple of hills, remembering sensationalistic streams that leaked after the blast, of bulldozers rolling bodies and other debris into mass burial ditches. The authenticity of those streams was disputed—I don't know if any of that was even true—but I've always imagined Theresa's body rolled with those others, imagined her body somehow still whole, buried in a shallow grave, naked with the naked corpses of strangers, but I know it's not true, it's not true.

"There were no funerals," I tell her. "I think sometimes—when I imagine how many people died, I can't help but think of their bodies—"

"It won't be like that at all," says Albion. "Even right after the blast, right after I came from the tunnel, my memory isn't of bodies—"

"Where did they go?" I ask her.

"The way they died," says Albion. "Most were cremated—by the blast, I mean. There was so much ash, at first—buildings, trees, people. I remember being covered with ash. Ash in my hair, my eyes. Breathing ash. I still remember the taste of ash. Anyway, even if there was a body, it's been ten years, Dominic. No, most of what we walk through will look like very young woods—or heavy growth like weeds and wildflowers. You'll probably recognize some things—"

Twenty minutes or more before we pass another car on this road, a white pickup with flashing yellow lights heading in the opposite direction—we don't see anyone else until we come to an intersection with a BP and a McDonald's, the McDonald's already bustling, a few cars queued in the drive-through and several tables filled. Jingles in my Adware, spinning hash browns and Egg McMuffins. I don't know what I was imagining the approach to PEZ to be like, something anonymous, maybe, something private. The McDonald's is absurdly bright, like the architecture's made of light—Albion sees me looking over and asks if I need to stop, but I tell her I'm all right.

"Who are all they?" I ask her.

"I'm guessing they're connected with the cleanup crew," she says. "Independent contractors. PEZ Zeolite—"

"I've never been back," I tell her once the McDonald's has disappeared behind us and it's easier to believe we're the last people left on earth.

"What we're doing is illegal," she says. "And, anyway, there are only a few places to access PEZ. You have to have an idea of what you're doing. People don't just come here to visit—there aren't any memorials, not yet. There was no reason for you to come back until today—"

This stretch of 65 used to be desolate, oddly active now because of PEZ Zeolite—makeshift signs line the road: WARNING. SLOW. CONSTRUCTION VEHICLE ENTRANCE. We pass PEZ Zeolite's main campus, buildings that look like small airplane hangars and administrative offices, enough piles of what looks like sand to make it seem like we're passing through acres of dunes incongruously planted in Pennsylvania. Heavy machinery plies the dunes, yellow trucks with tires as large as our car, the whole place a dust haze of sand. Albion runs her wipers with fluid to smear away powder from the glass. Belches of fire in the distance—the vitrification plants. We get stuck behind a convoy of dump trucks, each one mounded with that grayish sand.

"This is going to slow us down," she says, and I see her eyes scan, searching in her Adware for alternate routes. Eventually we turn off 65 onto a winding side road overgrown with trees—Camp Horne Road, bracketed by long-defunct houses, chapels and schools, many of the structures partially collapsed, windows broken. The pavement's cracked, huge gaps devouring our tires. We come to a checkpoint, the first we've seen. Nothing but an abandoned kiosk with a crossbar lowered across the road. A sign's posted:

MILITARY ZONE

DANGER

TRESPASSERS WILL BE PROSECUTED

Albion pulls off the road, tires sinking in soft grass. She drives around the crossbar and pulls back onto the road. We pass another military checkpoint, this one with a raised gate—Albion says the only checkpoints that matter are the PEZ Zeolite checkpoints on direct access roads closer to the city. The military abandoned this place years ago—after cases of thyroid cancer spiked among the soldiers stationed here. We pull onto what was once a major artery into the city, 279, but the road is extremely poor—rolling bramble and chunks of tar, swathes of shredded blacktop and greenwood trees and waist-high grass. Albion pulls off the road and parks in a thicket of brush so our car won't be too obvious if someone were to pass through.

"This is good, I think," she says. "I think we're close enough. The last thing we need is a blown-out tire trying to park a little closer—"

I wander into the street, look around—the day's overcast, the sky marbled steel gray, the light murky and depressive. My body's refusing to wake because of the early hour and the weather—moist, heavy air that's already gummed up my sinuses.

"You said we're close enough?" I ask her, considering the vast expanse of emptiness and flatland and scrub surrounding us, thinking we must be nowhere near the city, not yet, that we must have miles still to drive, until it dawns in my gut that ahead, in that emptiness cradled between slopes, should have been the city skyline—yes, the city skyline should have been there, right over there, skyscrapers leering over the tops of trees. There's nothing now—just space.

"Oh no, oh God, no, no, no," I say, the corners of my vision darkening, everything tunneling into black—I don't exactly faint but sit down gingerly, like too much blood's rushed to my head. "I can't do this," I tell Albion. "I don't think I can do this—"

Albion opens the hatch of the Outback, unpacks the car. She separates our gear before making her way over to me. She kneels, waits until I raise my face and look at her.

"Are you okay?" she asks. "Physically, I mean. Are you hurt?"

"No, I'm okay," I tell her.

"Then get up—"

We prep—Tyvek coveralls over our clothes, layered with rain slacks and hard shells. Smurf-blue PVC-coated gloves, a military-grade first aid kit in case one of us falls or is somehow injured.

Flashlights and a compass in case our Adware blinks, a nylon rope and a SHIELD severe-weather-graded tent. Albion tucks her hair beneath her Tyvek hood and tugs the drawstrings tight. She yanks my drawstrings hard enough to collapse my hood over my face. She laughs, and when I work my hood open she kisses me, a chaste kiss—she smells like hardweather lip balm.

"You've gone beet red," she says.

"High blood pressure," I tell her, feeling my flushed face. "I'm just having a heart attack or something, nothing to worry yourself about—"

"Do you think you can handle all this?" she asks. "This will be difficult—and I don't mean the emotional toll. Some areas are still very radioactive, others aren't. We'll have to monitor our levels. I know how to hike, even in extreme weather, but I've never done anything like this, so I might make mistakes, too. The surfaces will be uneven so there will be plenty of things to trip over. We should rest often. We can still head home right now—"

"I want to do this," I tell her.

Albion unravels a necklace with a heavy plastic badge and places it around my neck, tucking the badge down beneath my Tyvek so it rests against my T-shirt.

"That's your dosimeter," she says, wearing one as well. "It starts out clear. We'll check again in a little while—if it turns red, we'll need to leave right away. If it's black, we leave and go to an emergency room—"

We wear gas masks, the same type the cleaners from PEZ Zeolite wear on their shifts—rubber-shelled, insectile, with bulbous filtration systems that hide our faces. Difficult to talk with these things, so we ping text messages to each other, go over our checklist one last time. I bring the bouquet of flowers, thread them through a loop in my pack.

Albion holds my hand as we start—we're wearing our gloves, but I savor the weight of her hand, the feel of her long fingers cradled with mine. I'm assuming these gestures of hers are meant to succor me through the dead land, but hoping, in a way allowing myself to hope, that we're falling somewhere deeper. We don't make it ten minutes before the first drops of rain.

Springtime in Pittsburgh, she writes.

Uncomfortable in all this gear—already sweating. I figured this trip wouldn't be much more taxing than one of our strenuous hikes through the wildlife refuge, but our water sloshes in my backpack with every step, throwing my weight off-balance, and the paths are uneven through here, knotty with weeds and brambles and pits and pocks of the road, potholes we step over or around. The rain picks up. I load Compass Rose, the graphics vivid against the bleak sky, true north marked, the direction we're heading—SSE—marked with a flourished green arrow, latitude and longitude displaying in real time. I load the Archive, and the City appears like a transparency glowing in brilliant colors, layering over the blighted landscape. There should be two churches here, side by side--I can see them in the archived landscape, vanished from the true landscape—and there should be houses and bars lining the hills a little further to the west, the tower of Allegheny General. There should be hills. There aren't hills anymore.

Do you know where we're going? I ask her.

I'm following directions Sherrod left, she pings. *He's been this way before—*

Another military checkpoint and a barbed-wire fence meant to keep people like us from trespassing. The checkpoint's long since abandoned, the kiosk littered with Mountain Dew bottles and used hypodermics, Snickers and Mounds wrappers and old condoms. A boot, a bird's nest. Albion leads me along the fence until we come to the GPS marker Mook once set at his entrance point—supposedly a spot where the fence had become unmoored, where someone could peel back the chain-link and slip through. Everything's been patched, though. Albion spends twenty minutes or so mining PEZ forums, sifting through discussions from people who claim they've gained access to the city—thrill seekers, conspiracy theorists, journalists, looters—until she finds solid references to another entry point, another breach in the fence somewhere nearby. Another forty-five minutes to find the gap, nothing but a corner section of the fence that's been cut away. We push our packs through, then take turns crawling on our bellies—muck slicks our chests once we're on the other side. Compass Rose reorients and the Archive resets—a ghost image of the Veterans Bridge spans the sky but the actual bridge is nothing more than rubble and rebar scattered on the slopes running to the riverbed.

Sherrod's directions say the 16th Street Bridge is passable, Albion pings.

We pick our footing along the Allegheny into a strong headwind, the fabric flap of wind against our hard shells like the beating of birds' wings. We skitter down slopes and find a passable trail across the flats of what was once the North Side, nothing but wildflowers now and saplings sprouting among the guts of incinerated buildings. I have vague memories of the architecture here, but even checking against the Archive, I can't quite place what was left behind by what's left—a rectangle outlined in bricks, exposed basements filled in with rubble, a doorway without a door. Most things here have simply disappeared. There used to be a camera store somewhere over here, the last place in the city that would develop actual film—grass, now, as far as I can tell.

The 16th Street Bridge is relatively intact—still standing through some fluke in blast pattern. The span whines in the wind and the sound is like a chorus of infants crying. Cacophonous, steely-pitched, unnerving. As we draw closer I notice that the winged horses and armillary spheres decorating the tops of the bridge columns have scorched and melted, the horses now like blackened hellhounds. The screaming of that bridge as we cross—all I think of is my own child dying with Theresa, that I'm hearing our child among the others, but this is melodramatic, I know, hysterical, but still—my child burned in a concussion of fire, layers of skin, the system of her nerves and of her veins, her profile, hair and eyes, ten fingers and ten toes that I would have counted. Stop it, *stop this*. The river passes below us, a poison stream flashing silver. I pause halfway across to search out downtown. The Archive layers in where the city once was—nothing, now. Plumes of dust. At the end of the bridge we find a lone brick wall casting a black shadow so we rest for a moment, lifting our gas masks long enough to take swigs of water. Albion's eyes are ringed red—she's been crying, and I wonder what tormented her as we crossed that bridge, who she heard screaming, but I can tell by her tenseness that I shouldn't pry, that she'll deal with this pain on her own terms, on her own, like she's dealt with every other pain. The rain sweeps through again, cooling even if it is turning our footing to mud. Albion checks her dosimeter—still clear, so she slips it back beneath her suit.

We skirt downtown, still following Mook's old route—threading single file along a thin path, Albion about ten yards ahead of me. I don't know what would have caused a path like this—animals, maybe? Deer, or something? I'm almost on top of a snake when it uncoils and glides away from the path. The thing startles me and I stand quite still, holding my breath, giving it plenty of time to leave before I start clomping again along the trail. Amazing how quickly nature has reclaimed this space, only ten years and everything's covered with grass and weeds, vines curling the mortar—

Albion gets my attention and points ahead: about a hundred yards down the trail, a herd of deer feeds among the concrete stoops of the vanished courthouse, tawny shapes in the distance. Oddly, not every tree that was here perished in the blast. Older trees still stand, but their bark's been shocked red.

In the Adware, the 10th Street Bridge flutters golden in the rain, its hesitant art deco styling even more like a phantom image of a lost age than it used to be. The mouths of the Armstrong tunnels still gape out of the side of stone, and I suggest making our way a little into the tunnels to duck out of the rain.

I'd rather get pneumonia, Albion pings.

Rather, she points out a verge of Second Avenue that ascends beneath the 376 overpass. She suggests we make camp up the slope, to scramble up where enough of the old road still forms a natural roof. The rain hasn't let up and climbing the mud's almost comical, slipping every few steps, but we find enough footing on a scatter of rocks, pull ourselves up with shallow-rooted weeds. The place where Albion suggested we camp is bone-dry. I help her pitch our tent, a cherry-red narrow tube that snaps into form like fabric flexed into concrete. Albion takes off her mask, checks her dosimeter—still clear. We've been hiking for over five hours, now, and this is our first real rest.

"Are you hungry?" she says.

"Starving, actually—"

I don't remember lying down, let alone falling asleep, but Albion's sorting out silver food packets when I startle awake.

"You were out," she says. "Snoring—"

"How long?"

"Twenty minutes, maybe. Not too long. Do you want Tuscan-style veggie lasagna or roasted red pepper fettuccine?"

"Oh, ugh. The lasagna, I guess—"

Albion pours water into the foil reservoir in the dinner packets, cracks the spine along the ridge—a heating element—and stirs. She hands me the steaming lasagna and a wooden spoon, almost like a miniature little trowel.

"This is for you, too," she says, giving me rehydrated chocolate pudding.

"Delicious," I tell her. "You're a great cook, adding water to this stuff. Actually, this pudding's not too bad. I'd just eat this stuff, normally. We should have some of this around the house—"

Albion wants to finish the last leg of our hike before dark. "Another couple of hours there and back," she says, "then we can relax until we head out tomorrow morning. How are you holding up?"

"I'm all right," I tell her. "More humid than I thought it would be, and everything aches. My feet. I think I have blisters on my blisters—"

"Just a little longer," she tells me.

We continue along Second Avenue—Albion hasn't told me why we've come here, why we've come back to Pittsburgh like this, but this far along Second it's clear she's leading me to the Christ House, that she wants to fold me into something private there. We hike underneath the old rail trestle at the end of Second and take the switchback at Saline, entering the Run. Streets are still here, or the outlines of streets, frames of some of the houses—a few of the houses. Albion leads me through a field, tromping through grass that's grown knee-high. The wind breathes through the grass—it sways like green waves.

"Here," says Albion.

I may have missed this place on my own—the Christ House vanished except its outline, cinder blocks and brick and slabs of foundation, but even the outline's obscured by grasses and the wild growth of weeds. I load the Archive to gain my bearings and the

Christ House appears translucent—the charcoal gray wooden siding, the words of Christ slathered in whitewash, *Except a man be born again.* The last time I saw this place, Mook made the house appear as if it were burning, but even now without the fire the house seems ignited by some inner blaze—something burning cold and black, inexhaustible. I click away the Archive, but now even the field seems damned by what once stood here—the grass seems oily, ill, and the remaining bricks and cinder seem like they'd be corpse-cold to the touch. I walk the perimeter, the house easy to trace.

"Watch your footing," says Albion.

After a thicket of overgrowth, the earth drops away into a concrete pit, maybe an exposed section of the house's basement. I'm glad Albion warned me—someone could easily misstep here, the plunge at least ten feet to concrete. The pit was once a series of small rooms, it looks like. Coal rooms? Root cellars? They're connected by a hallway that still tunnels underneath the main body of the house—I could scuttle down, I think, and still enter the original basement. I once walked that basement, in the Archive, I walked through the darkness, feeling my way along the dank walls and heard the sound of breathing. They kept people down here.

Albion's removed her gas mask and taken down her hood—her hair's vivid red in this storm light, blown about, the weeds are lush and gaudy green. She's standing over in what would have been the house, tracing rooms in her memory.

"Over here is where we sat for prayer meetings," she says. "Bible study. There used to be a fireplace about here—you can still see the chimney base, those bricks. We set out folding chairs in a semicircle around the fire, but Peyton and I always took a love seat over about here. Whenever Peyton came to these things—"

"She didn't live here with you?" I ask.

"Peyton was a critical thinker," she says. "She didn't like this place, she hated being here. After Bible study, when we were alone, she'd look over my notes and tear apart whatever Waverly had told us. She only came here because of me, whenever she needed to help me—"

Albion crosses the grass to the other side of the house and points out a slab of stone.

"The stairs were here," she says. "There were two bedrooms downstairs, built as additions out back. We had the second floor divided into six bedrooms, with another two rooms in the attic. It was a big house. Kitty had the master bedroom to herself, but we doubled up in the other rooms, sometimes three to a room. My bedroom was on the second floor, second to the right—"

Albion paces forward, trying to figure the location of her bedroom, one story above the grass.

"About here. Sometimes Peyton stayed with me so I wouldn't have to be alone—"

"Peyton protected you—"

"We were able to endure things together that we might not have been able to endure apart," she says. "She couldn't protect me but she never abandoned me—"

"We can leave," I tell her. "You don't need to put yourself through this—"

"I haven't shown you yet," she says.

Albion leads me around to the exposed section of basement, to a place where a minor cave-in has created a series of earthen steps.

"I can't go down there with you," she says.

I scramble down into one of the chambers—a minuscule room, only about six feet to a side, if that. There's a concrete slab—maybe a bench, or maybe it was supposed to be a bed. Jesus. I find my footing along what would have been the connecting hallway to a doorway veiled by wisteria—through the flowers, a hole leads underground. I glance back at Albion—she's watching from the edge of the precipice. She helped bring people here, she and Peyton—whatever else happened in their lives, they recruited women to come here, they helped fill these cells. By the end of the city they lived in their own apartments, playing dress-up with each other and modeling, pursuing fashion design and art, Raven + Honeybear while women suffered here. This is hell. I'm walking into hell.

I pull aside the flowers and vines, plunge through the hole into the dark of the basement. This place smells like soil and rot, the sweet rancidity of things that grow in death. I have the flashlight—click it on, sweep it over the room. This place is preserved. A worktable with tools. Hammer, lathe. Circular blades hung on pegboard. A washing machine, a dryer. Sooty floors and sweeps of ash that must have blown in through the weeds. Above me, the ceiling boards moan and crack with every gust of wind like a cave-in is imminent—*run, I should run from here*—but whatever Albion wants me to see is down here somewhere. Other cells sprout off this main section of the basement, hidden behind wooden doors. One of the doors is painted with a stencil of a woman walking two other women on leashes like they're dogs. There.

The door's stuck, but jerks open once I pull with my weight. Musty, cold. Another concrete slab for a bench or bed. There are bones in the corner. There are human bones lying intertwined in the corner. Two skulls, like whoever these people were held each other as they died—or maybe the bodies were just stacked here, somewhere out of the way. Losing myself, feeling the need to vomit—but what pours from me is a scream, a harrowing, sorrowful scream. I collapse to the bench, and when I do, a stream launches in my Adware. The stream's swift, sweeping past anti-malware and firewalls. Mook. This is one of Mook's geocached installations—the stream triggered when my Adware synced with the right coordinates. This basement, this cell, this bench.

My eyes fill with recorded memory: I'm still here in this basement room, but someone flicks on a light and Timothy and Waverly are here, bathed in greasy orange from a naked bulb. There are others here, too, three others—one of them, the youngest, is just a teenager, lanky and pale with feminine eyes and long black hair. Rory. This must be Rory, the one I pushed into the path of traffic, but he's so young here—a camo Pussy Hounds jersey and boots worn without laces. I've never seen the other two, but they must be Waverly's brother, Gregor, and the other son, Cormac—Cormac's the one Albion said was a family man, the one she remembered showed pictures of his daughters—he's broad shouldered with a barrel belly, midtwenties here or probably older, his sloping chin covered in a reddish scruff of beard. Gregor Waverly stands apart from the others, his posture stiff, like he's wearing a brace or some sort of body cast, arms hanging limp at his sides. His natural expression's a horrific pout, the purple underside of his thick lower lip curling outward and down. His hair's bone white, close-cropped, his ears like meaty, ragged flaps.

Timothy grips me by my hair, forcing me to stay close to him—all that crimson hair spilling over my shoulders, he's looped it around his wrists and holds me by it. Albion—this is Albion's memory, recorded through her eyes.

"You don't have to suffer," says Waverly.

Timothy pushes me farther into the cell and I see her: Hannah Massey. She's imprisoned here. Gaunt, naked—only a specter of the young woman I'd tracked through the Archive, case #14502. She's kneeling on the bench, gazing up through the ceiling at—

what? Is she praying? Her eyes are like dead eyes, distant. Her ribs and breasts are striated violet with bruises. Rory and Cormac, the brothers, pull her from the corner and stretch her out between them. I realize, now: by leading me here, Albion is showing me how Hannah Massey will die.

The men take turns with her, Waverly first. Rory and his brother. Gregor. I scream—or is it Albion who screams? My innards turn to water and I slump, my legs buckle. Hannah doesn't struggle—she's endured this before and endures this now like her body's already dead. Her head falls to the side and she looks through me. When our eyes meet, her eyes tremble. "Please," she says, "please, please, please—"

I want to help her, but can't because Albion can't help her. All Albion offers are her screams, and so I scream.

"Why are you screaming?" says Waverly. "Albion, why are you screaming? What is causing this fear in you?"

"You'll kill her," Albion says—I say.

"And what if she were to die?" says Waverly. "Look at her—all of you, look at her. What do you see? You see a body—but what is a body? A body is flesh. A body is not the spirit. Don't weep for this woman's body. When you look at her, remember that you're looking at nothing more holy than roadkill is holy. What you see is not her spirit—her spirit is immortal. You can't see her spirit. When you see her, see the beasts you've seen dead on the side of the road. Roadkill, that's all she is. Remember, there is a God above God—"

Timothy's young here, thinner—I recognize him from the newspaper photographs I'd researched, when he went by Timothy Billingsley or Timothy Filt. His beard's just a stringy strip outlining his chin, his arms reedy, his paunch a soft sag.

"You can save her," says Timothy to me—to Albion. "I'll forfeit my turn with her if you take her place—"

Albion's hyperventilating. Hannah turns away. Albion says nothing.

I think of Twiggy. I think of Timothy's wives. I think of Albion and Peyton. I think of the farm in Alabama and these basement cells, of the countless, faceless others as Timothy takes his place between Hannah's knees. He strips off his clothes and the two bodies are absurdly white in the dim cellar room. He takes his turn with Hannah, or tries to take her. His movements aren't the bludgeoning of the other men but a frantic, vicious scrabble until he yells, "I can't, I can't," and strikes her in the stomach. Hannah groans, doubles up, but Cormac and Rory pry her legs apart and brace her between them. Timothy's father hands him a chisel from the basement workbench. Timothy doesn't finish until he stabs Hannah through her breasts, his arm pumping, gashing quickly, pulverizing her. Timothy moans at the eruption of Hannah's blood. He's whimpering, spent.

Albion's memory ends, resets to the beginning.

Jesus. Oh, Jesus Christ, please, oh Jesus, please.

It's the closest I've come to prayer.

I don't know how long I stay hidden in this darkness, but I exhaust myself crying, hoping for comfort in this utter black but finding none. I reload the stream and record everything I witness. I send the file to Gavril's drop site with a message: *Do not open or view. Save for me, please.*

Deep twilight when I emerge from the basement. The rain's cleared out for the time being—the stars are thicker here, without the pollution of city light. I climb from the pit, walk the perimeter of the house, around farther back to lush weeds. Albion's sleeping on a bed of grass. No—she's not sleeping. Her eyes are flickering, almost like she's dreaming—but she's not dreaming, she's not asleep. I lay with her, load the Archive, find her.

It's daylight where she is, in the garden of the Christ House. The Christ House casts a shadow across the lawn, but the garden is bathed in sunlight—archived sunlight from some distant past. The brightness of this place offends me—it's too warm here, like the world is sick with fever. Albion's tending to sprigs of calla lilies. She's wearing a sundress pattered like a painting by Rousseau.

"I never want to come back to this place," she says.

"I won't ever ask you to," I tell her.

"I used to work in this garden every morning," she says. "This was my bliss—being out here. Calla lilies for Peyton because Peyton once mentioned she liked them—they remind me of her. I learned to cook because of this garden. I'd grow food out here and cook for the girls in the house. There's rosemary and pansies, fennel and columbine and rue—"

"How many died here?" I ask her.

"I don't know, Dominic—"

"But there were more, weren't there? Jesus Christ—"

"I brought them," she says, "I helped bring those girls here, I brought them here, I brought those girls—"

I watch as her emotion boils, as every humiliation and shame she thought she'd buried rises in her, as the horror and guilt at what she'd done brims in her eyes. When she cries, her sobs seem like pleas for forgiveness, but I can't absolve her, nothing can. "I can't get rid of it," she says. "I can't—"

I hold her, try to comfort her. "It's all right, it's all right," I tell her, knowing it never will be. I cradle her head to my shoulder, but when my hands touch her hair I realize that's where Timothy's hands were—the comfort I want to give curdles, I don't know how to comfort her or whether I even should. The garden's gorgeous here, full of garish flowers that thrive in the sweltering heat.

"Timothy used to tell me the only reason I was alive was because he loved me," she says.

"What could you have done," I ask, not really a question.

The stream was visceral, and the complicated residue it's leaving feels like a sinkhole in my stomach. I look at Albion, now, in her sundress standing among blooming flowers in her absurd garden, archived here, and just as I hate her for recruiting girls, for playing at glamour to bring girls to Waverly, I remember the burning grip of Timothy's fists in her hair and can't blame her for what happened here, I can't, I can't. Now that I've seen how Hannah Massey died, I'm not sure what I can do with the information. Anyone piecing together what had happened at this house so many years ago would figure out Albion's involvement and might not be as forgiving as I want to be.

"That stream will be here forever," I tell her, "or at least until every satellite fails and falls. Eventually someone will come through here, eventually someone will see—"

"I asked Sherrod to delete everything, every moment I appeared in the Archive, but when he came across Hannah, he refused—he wondered if I was using him to bury her. We argued but came to an understanding, and when he came through here to buy the house for me in New Castle, he made his way to this place, installed this stream. He said he created this space so no one would forget what happened here—he called it a memorial. He didn't want the house to simply vanish, he didn't want it to be buried over in a mound of zeolite and disappear, rebuilt as something new in a city with amnesia. He wanted anyone drawn to this place to know what happened here—"

"But you're implicated—"

"I kept quiet when others were suffering," she says.

We close the Archive, step into the night wind and find our way back to our campsite by moonlight, sweeping our flashlights over the broken road to spot our footing. We climb the mud hill to our tent. We eat protein bars around a campfire and find that the coffee we brought with us in the thermoses is still warm. We undress from our rain gear and our Tyvek and slip together into the tent—the only living creatures in miles of dead lands, the desolate moon bathing everything in silver. We stay up late, remembering Pittsburgh together, recalling the patterns of streets we'd known like we're plotting a map between us—discovering where our courses may have overlapped.

"I want life," she says.

We immerse together. The Spice Island Tea House in winter—and although Zhou is sitting at the table Theresa sits at in my memories, Albion and I stay. We choose a table far enough away so we can't hear Zhou's voice endlessly circulating the words my wife is supposed to say. Layering, the scent of basil, the scent of curry.

Albion and I linger over chai. I tell her, "Tonight—the one we're reliving here at this restaurant—was the happiest night of my entire life. Theresa and I tried for years for another chance to have a child, but couldn't—but tonight, Theresa told me that she was pregnant, that we were going to have a daughter, and I knew everything would be all right for us. I've never been happier. After this night the future just opened wide—"

Snow's on the ground when we leave the restaurant and strings of lights hang in the barren trees. We walk from Oakland to Shadyside, through the college campuses and Craig Street, the restaurants and cafés and bookstores populated with ghosts, forever frozen in their past lives. I bring Albion back to the apartment, to the Georgian. When we're in the lobby, she kisses me.

We make our way upstairs, through the paisley-carpeted hallway, to Room 208. I don't engage the room through my own account, because I don't want to see anything other than Albion tonight—I don't want Zhou, I don't want memories of my previous life. I want Albion. An empty blueprint of rooms with generic furniture. We leave the lights off—I lead Albion into the bedroom where we kiss again.

"Let me help you remember," she says.

I untie her dress and she unbuttons my shirt and we lie together. None of this is real, but it is real—there are consequences here, even if we don't speak them. Albion is beautiful, certainly the most beautiful woman I've ever seen, but what I'm seeing isn't her, it isn't really her, and when I hold her or kiss her breasts, what I'm feeling is the closest the iLux and imagination can convince me that I'm feeling. This isn't Albion, even though I'm with her here—it's all so close, but it's all just a beautiful lie.

Albion pauses. She separates from me, leaving a gap between us.

"I'm sorry," I tell her. "I'm so, so sorry—"

"I can't do this," she says. "I'm just not ready to be with someone, not yet—"

She lets me hold her. We listen as a train rushes past the window and she says, "I don't hear trains much anymore," but it's just the sound of the wind battering our tent as we wake.

Dominic—

Two thirty in the morning when I wake from a dream of Theresa. Fine rain taps the mud around us. I'm sweating in my sleeping bag. Wide awake, concentrating to recapture details of my dream, but the only thing I remember clearly is Theresa speaking my name. I'm uncomfortable, fidgety. Albion sleeps beside me. I hear her even breathing. I slip from our tent.

I don't bother with the Tyvek, but *hourly forecast* displays rainfall throughout the night so I dress in rain slacks and the hard shell. Peckish, but I'm not sure where Albion's packed the pudding and there's little light to search by, only the overcast moon and the last of the fire sputtering whenever raindrops hit it. Careful down the hill, lighting my way with the flashlight—the only other thing I've brought with me is the bouquet Albion picked from our yard.

I ping Albion: *Went for a walk. I'll be back by breakfast.*

I remember a set of stairs at the mouth of the Armstrong Tunnel that hugged the sharp ascent of the Bluff, topping off at the Boulevard of the Allies—the stairs were concrete and steel, maybe shielded from the blast by the Bluff itself, and when I check on them now, shining my flashlight over the steel rails and cracked concrete, I'm relieved to find the stairs are relatively intact. The moon hangs like a silver smudge as I climb. Sweating by the time I reach the hilltop, but cold in the haze of rain—I'm sure I'll get sick clambering around out here in the mist, maybe catch pneumonia. Feverish already, shivering. Scorched cars and the ruined faces of houses through what were once the streets of Uptown, splintered wood and sheet metal, tendrils of wire and rubble.

Burial mounds warp the earth of what was once Oakland—the radioactive scrap of museums, row houses, lecture halls, bulldozed and interred under heaps of chemical sand. Heavy machinery's parked here, excavators and dump trucks—Oakland must be PEZ Zeolite's focus right now. Layer in the Archive to gain my bearings and Phipps Conservatory shimmers in a distant field behind the burial mounds, the greenhouse like a Victorian dream of white steel and glass, gardens and lawns. This was Theresa's, this was hers—I used to come here from campus to visit her in her office, we'd have lunch together in the café. There's nothing here, now—

nothing but the poisoned dunes. The air's tanged with the stink of burning plastic.

I follow makeshift roads gouged from the ruins by PEZ Zeolite, threadlike stretches of slippery gravel vaguely milky and luminescent by moonlight. To Shadyside, to Walnut Street where she died. Layering the Archive over this place, boutiques and sidewalk sales, outdoor tables at cafés. Layering, the scent of roasting coffee, of baking bread. Layering, J.Crew and the Gap, United Colors of Benetton, Banana Republic. I find the store where she died, Kards Unlimited, layering in the T-shirts she was looking at, *It's a Neighborly Day in the Beautywood*, but she's not here, not here. Timesearch the moment of the blast: light flares over the west and everything blackens, the bodies around me spark to flame, then shrivel to cores of ash, then vanish. In the moment of the blinding flash, Theresa's reflection appears in the store's window, just for a heartbeat I see her face. The buildings ignite and vanish. I'm left with ash.

A breath of ash.

This is not the Archive, this ash. On hands and knees—crawling through ash made muddy with rain. I grasp at handfuls of ash. This is Theresa. This is her body, my child's body. This is all she'll ever be, this ash, this is all I have left of her.

This ruination in the moonlight looks like shattered marble and lunar dust, broken statuary, shadows.

I reset the Archive to the moment just before her death, layer in Walnut Street and watch for Theresa's split-second reflection in the moment of blinding light.

This time, however, following the flash and her fleeting reflection in the window, Theresa's here with me as if she'd never been deleted, as if I haven't lost her. She's turned away from me, looking into other store windows. There is no fire, there is no ash. The sidewalks swarm with upscale shoppers living lives that were never given to them in life—they should have died, they should have all died in the fire, but there is no fire. Is this some trick of Mook's? Some other geocached installation of Pittsburgh as if it hadn't burned? The day is crystalline blue and crisply tinged with fall. Theresa is full-term, and women who pass her on the sidewalk stop and ask when she's due, tell her she looks beautiful, a glow of health, wish her well. I want to see her, I want to hold her and feel the movements of our child. *This can't be happening—this never happened, this isn't her.* I follow her.

"Theresa?" I say, but she can't hear me—she doesn't turn toward me. She walks down Bellefonte, a side street running off Walnut that terminates at Ellsworth, our apartment. Layering, cool tree shade. Layering, a distant lawn mower and the scent of mown grass. *This can't be.* This never existed—the bomb should have detonated five minutes ago, all these places should have burned—but we're here, we're here. Everything about this is wrong.

"Theresa?"

I run to her, place my hand on her shoulder. She turns to me but she is faceless, just a gray oval where her face should be, featureless, a blank avatar. I recoil. The images end—the Archive crashes, collapses into a point of light, then blinks away, day flips to true night, the desolation of the world as it is. She's led me home.

Broken earth, the sky arcing toward dawn—sunrise still an hour or so away, but the horizon bleeds gray into the dome of black and the stars are dim. The Georgian Apartment still stands, much of it, anyway—the western-facing wing collapsed, either in the blast or in the years of dereliction following, but much of the far side of the building survived. The front stairs are nothing now, just a splay of mortar and brick, weeds and soil. I scramble across the front lawn, past where Grecian urns once spilled over with peonies, through the cracked front portal into the lobby. I'm here. The checkerboard tiles singed black, the brass mailboxes lying twisted across the floor. Shattered glass. Burned-out couches. Everything's glistening from rainwater leaking through gaps in the roof—puddles and wet wood, pungent soot.

I run upstairs.

I'm here.

Theresa, I'm here.

Room 208.

I open our door—but there is no Room 208, not any longer. The rear of the Georgian's collapsed, Room 208 nothing more than a few splintered floorboards and an expanse of air, a twenty-foot drop onto a slide of bricks below. I look out from the cliff that was once our home. There's nothing left. Nothing.

I don't know what I was hoping to find—

I should never have come here—

I drop the flowers, watch them fall.

"Mr. Blaxton?"

I turn from the emptiness. A man stands in the hallway wearing black fatigues and a gas mask.

"Are you John Dominic Blaxton?" he asks, his bass voice oddly muffled in his mouth, like he's speaking through a side of raw beef. Another man stands a few feet behind him—a bear of a man, also in a gas mask. *I'm going to die.* I'm at their mercy, whatever mercy they'll show me. Increasingly faint—this apartment will be the last thing I see.

"What do you want from me?" I ask him.

A third man has trailed us up the stairs, blocking any exit I'd hope to have. Rory, it has to be—he's also wearing a gas mask. The one who's speaking must be Gregor, Waverly's brother.

"Waverly knew that once you saw your wife you'd come running here," he says.

The bear, Cormac, unsheathes a nightstick and advances swiftly. I flinch, but he strikes me across the side of my head, the blast like a bright light of pain that explodes my ear and breaks my jaw. Ringing, but like I'm hearing underwater—my Adware's music shuffles, Albion's Boris Vian jazz sputtering from inside my head, skipping. *Error—*

A second strike, this one across my right knee—and I crumple, my leg broken forward. I see bone gore through my skin. My right shin and foot flop like they're made of cloth, unattached, when a third strike lands across my face. Adware rebooting. *iLux*. Blood sprays from my mouth. Teeth. Two more strikes, one against each hand—bones snap, fingers shatter. I scream—

My Adware blacks out again, reboots a second time. *iLux*.

"I saw you," I tell them. "What you did to her. I saw how you killed her—"

Blood pulses from my mouth when I speak and I don't know if they've even understood what I said. I'm swimming in blood and darkness, but I concentrate—I can't black out, not now. *Think*. This isn't going to be quick, what they do to me. I need to get out of here. *Christ, Christ—*

"Rory, he's all yours," says Gregor. A dark, swift shape kneels over me. I see his eyes through the gas mask lenses.

"An eye for an eye, brother," he says.

He pulls a serrated hunter's knife and I feel the blade slide cleanly into my shoulder, snagging on muscle and bone as he pulls it out. The knife slides into my chest, rips me as it comes out. I can't breathe, but don't realize I can't breathe—I can't scream, but still try to scream, my breath like a fog of blood. He swipes his blade across my face like he's a calligrapher writing something sacred into my skin. Pain flares through the right side of my face, a deep pain—like he's reached into my skull through my eye socket. I wonder at all the blood—is this all mine? It doesn't seem possible—

I'm lifted.

It must be Cormac who lifts me.

I'm falling—

They've pushed me out, over the ledge. Falling. The apartment recedes from me—

"Dominic—"

That voice.

I recognize that voice. From where? I try to open my eyes, but can't.

The camphor scent of coagulant and the cottony rank of blood and gauze, but also the smell of dirt and something like milkweed and grass.

"You need another dose of morphine," says that voice.

Open my eyes—

Everything's blurred—no, everything to my left is blurred. Darkness to my right. I'm blind to my right side. It's like a charcoal cloth covers everything to my right but if I close my left eye the world goes dark. Daylight—I can see well enough to know there's daylight.

I lift my head but the movement cramps through my chest, an

agonizing soreness, and I collapse back down, panting. Every breath is pain.

"You're awake," he says. That voice.

Timothy.

"Where is she?" I ask him.

"Do you remember what happened?" he asks. "Do you know where we are?"

I'm here. Theresa, I'm here—

"You're at the site of your apartment in Pittsburgh. Three men attacked you," says Timothy. "Do you remember? You fell. I haven't moved you—"

Rory Waverly carving me with a knife.

"I can't see very well," I tell him. "Come over here where I can see you—"

He blocks the sunlight when he stands near, but I still can't see him. I hear him kneel. A damp towel touches my face. He wrings water over my eyes and wipes gently with the towel—once I blink away the water, I can see him, but it's like I'm looking at him through a scrim of steel wool. He's examining me with those pitying blue eyes. I want to ping Albion, ping Gav, someone who can help me, but the virtual interface I'm so used to seeing isn't here.

"You're very injured," he says. "I did what I could, but it's been a long time since I've had to practice emergency medicine—not since school. I stopped most of the bleeding. I'm so sorry, Dominic. I didn't intend for this to happen—"

"Did you kill her? Did you kill Albion?"

"She's safe," says Timothy. "She'll be here soon—"

My body's numbed from coagulant and painkillers but whenever I move, profound pain ripples through me. Something plastic's draped over me as a blanket—a tarp, maybe—the corners weighted by bricks. My head's cushioned by a rain jacket—Timothy's, it looks like. He's wearing a T-shirt and khaki hiking pants, but nothing to protect him from the radiation or the rain. His backpack's nearby, cherry red. What will happen here? Where are the others? Why didn't they just let me die?

"Did you kill Twiggy?" I ask. "Why? Why her?"

"I didn't kill her," says Timothy. "My father knew you'd be interested in her—he'd studied your Adware, knew your tastes. He hired her, made sure she'd cross your path by making sure your cousin worked with her. My father paid her to give you hard drugs so that once you were arrested on felony drug charges I could commandeer your case from Simka. We knew we had to get close to you, one way or another, to find out what you knew about the woman's body you discovered in the Archive—"

"Hannah," I tell him. "Her name was Hannah—"

"My father thought he'd taken care of that mistake years ago, but when you found her in the Archive, he panicked. He wanted to have you killed—he thought killing you would solve these problems from the past. I had to convince him to let you live. I told him that we should figure out how you found Hannah, what you knew—what else you might know about us. I convinced him that you might be able to help us with another problem we were having—"

"Albion—"

"The dead don't stay dead," he says.

"Albion wanted to stay dead. She wanted no part of this—"

"We didn't know Albion was alive until she disappeared from the Archive—she wanted to disappear, but that's what exposed her. Albion vanishing was like a dead woman rising to life, and then you found Hannah's body. My father was haunted by these Lazarus women. He met with his brother and told him he wanted Albion dead. My uncle and cousins remembered Albion. They wanted to kill her, they've always wanted her . . . but I couldn't let them. I can't let them—"

The door to Room 208 is at least two stories above us, leading into the scorched hallway—I remember falling, but don't remember hitting—I'm so numbed I feel like I'm hovering inches above my body, like I haven't quite finished the fall. I glance around—the flowers I'd brought for Theresa are all around me.

"Are you going to kill Albion here?" I ask him. "Kill us?"

Timothy's incredulous. "I'm saving her," he says. "I've tried to save you. This whole time, I've been saving you—"

"Bullshit," I tell him. "I saw what you did to Hannah. I saw everything, you sick fuck. I saw everything—"

"I've saved you three times," he says. "When you found Hannah, I saved you from my father. I saved you a second time after my father's party—when you quit working for him, you ceased having value to him, but I convinced him that we could still follow you to Albion. I saved you a third time just a few hours ago, when my cousins were scrambling down here to mutilate you, Dominic—"

"You don't want me to live," I tell him. "You're luring her here because you don't know where she is—"

"The first night I met you I told you that I'd been saved—"

"When you tore out your Adware—"

"I was Saul on the road to Damascus," says Timothy. "I lived with the shadow of my father—that Adware, those images that filled my mind, were him. They were *him*. I slit myself open and tore out my Adware and it was like I was tearing him out from me. I knew I might kill myself but tearing out that Adware was like tearing sin from my soul—"

"Twiggy didn't have to die—"

"No," says Timothy. "No, she didn't, but once she served her purpose, my father saw her as a liability. He gave her to his brother and his sons. Killing her was a mercy, by the time they were through with her—"

"You keep saying 'my father.' 'My father.' You keep saying, '*They* did this.' *You* did this—"

Timothy's not listening—something's caught his attention and he stares out over the ruins into the far yard, intent like a hunter who fears his movements might scare off the prey.

"She's here," he says. "She's here—"

"Albion?" I try to scream, but my breath's frail. "Get out of here. Run—"

I follow Timothy's eyes and see her. She stands at the base of the slide of bricks. Something formal in the way she stands. She's come to meet death.

"Dominic's up here," says Timothy. "I promised I was with him—"

Albion scales the bricks like she's scaling a slant of a shallow pyramid, picking a circuit that will keep her wide of Timothy.

"My God," she says when she draws close to me, "what have you done?"

"He would be dead if it wasn't for me," says Timothy, voice edged with—not quite glee, but something proud, catlike, like he's gifting his owner the body of a bird.

Albion doesn't cry at the sight of my body—she's blanched white, but studies each of my wounds like she's cataloging them, keeping tally for some future reckoning. She sits next to me, takes my hand. Having her so close is like a balm—the scent of her hair, the feel of her as she caresses my face. "Poor Dominic," she whispers as she touches kisses to each one of my eyes, "poor, poor Dominic—"

"Leave," I tell her. "They're coming for you. Run—"

"How did you find us?" she asks.

"My father ruined that doctor, Simka," says Timothy. "Drugs for sex with high school girls, bullshit he knew would hit the streams. My father snared Dominic's accounts, sent him an e-mail—it was supposed to look like it came from Simka's lawyer. When Dominic opened the e-mail, my father could track him. We came to New Castle, found your house, but you were already here—"

"What have you done to him?" she says, her voice like someone grown weary of a long and brutal prank. "Timothy, what have you done to him?"

"Gregor," he says. "Rory and Cormac—"

"Why did they do this?" she asks.

"They were preparing to do much worse when I stopped them," says Timothy. "They wanted to open him up, collar to belly—they were going to hang him by the ankles and let him bleed out. I told Gregor that you were the one we wanted, but that you'd run if Dominic was dead. We needed him alive to get you—"

Albion takes the news stoically, like someone used to absorbing sudden horror.

"Are they here now?" she asks.

"Gregor and Rory are waiting for you at your house," says Timothy. "I told them I'd bring you there. Cormac is at our camp here, waiting for me. We won't have much time to get out of here before he comes looking for us—"

Albion removes a compact mirror from her pack and holds it up for me to see my reflection. Although she doesn't angle it so I can view my entire body, I see enough—my chest wrapped in bandages and gauze, blood seeping through. My forehead had been slashed, almost torn from my skull, a ragged gash running from just above my right eye up across my scalp. Sloppily applied coagulant coats the stab wounds and slashes, a cloudy gel that's hardened into a medicated carapace. My eyes are ringed with bruising, my mouth swollen. My right eye socket is crushed inward, the eye almost black with blood. She removes the mirror.

"Why are you helping us?" she asks.

"I've changed," he says. "Alby, I've changed—"

"They won't let this rest," says Albion. "They'll kill you. They'll kill all of us—"

"There is a way out," says Timothy. "I need to convince my father and my uncle that you're both dead—"

"Don't listen to this," I tell Albion. "This man is a murderer. You showed me what he's done. I've seen what he's done to you, I've seen what he's done to Peyton—"

Albion flinches at Peyton's name.

"Albion," says Timothy. He slides a flat white box from his backpack. He lifts the lid and reveals my Adware resting in a cushion of folded cloth. It looks like a tangle of golden wool, stained by flecks of my blood. "I removed this from him. It's the only way—I need to send this to my father. I'll tell him that I killed Dominic, disposed of him—as long as I have this, he'll believe me—"

"That won't be enough," says Albion.

"No, you're right—this won't be enough," says Timothy. "He'll hire people to check my work, to look for Dominic's body. He'll want proof after proof of his death. He'll want access to his account information, all his passwords. He'll need to be certain that any shred of evidence that Dominic has found against him is eradicated. Dominic will need to get out of here. Out of the country, preferably—"

"Don't listen to him," I say. "Don't listen to any of this—"

"Dominic needs to go to a hospital," says Albion. "He'll need money. You're asking him to start a new life—"

"Money won't be an issue," says Timothy. "I've prepared everything—"

Albion turns to me. "Dominic, we can do this. There's another place we can go, somewhere far up north—"

"You don't understand," says Timothy. "I can convince my father of Dominic's death by giving over this Adware, but Dominic never mattered to him like you do. Convincing him that you're dead without presenting your body to him will be much more difficult. I need to take you away, Albion. I need to hide you somewhere I know my father can't look. I have a cabin in Washington State—it's a private place. You'll be comfortable. I'll take you there, tell them all I killed you and disposed of you like they taught me. We'll come up with something to show him, some images, as proof. Alby, come with me—"

"You killed her," I tell him. "You killed her and you're killing her again. Albion, what he did to you—"

"I remember everything," says Albion.

"Listen to me: God changed me," says Timothy.

"You're wrapped up in all this death," I tell him. "You're trying to convince us of Christ, you're trying to convince yourself that you've changed, but all you want is to take her away again, to keep her for yourself. Look at you. You're desperate. You don't look like a man who's found peace—"

"I was never offered peace in this world," says Timothy. "Every day I live with the weight of what I've done. I was never offered anything remotely like peace, but I am offered grace. I want to work to earn God's grace—"

"Grace isn't God's to give," says Albion. "Grace is ours to give."

Timothy's eyes are quavering pools, his face fatigued. He's several inches shorter than Albion and watching them is like watching a supplicant before a queen.

"Let Dominic rest," says Albion. "Timothy, we should talk. There are arrangements we need to make—"

Timothy injects me with medication from a clear bottle. Albion kisses my forehead, my eyes, my lips. I feel numbness beyond the numbness of the medication, like my soul has dropped through the darkness of the earth to slumber in the soil. I listen to the ringing in my ears like listening to chiming bells, straining to hear what Albion and Timothy are saying to each other, their voices at first just whispers but swelling into a clipped argument. I can't distinguish their words—I try to listen, but the numbness swallows me just like it has swallowed every other pain.

• PART IV •

DOMAŽLICE

MID-SEPTEMBER—

Beige walls and a television stuck on *Riot*—Japanese horror shows and loops of backyard accidents ending in horrific injury—smashed groins, face-plants. I saw a water-skier's legs chopped apart by a motorboat. I saw a guy decapitated when he flipped over the handlebars of his Quad. *Whipped and Creamed* marathons play late every night.

The highlight of each day comes around ten when Brianna, one of the nurses, wheels the breakfast cart onto our floor. "Morning," she hollers to every room, her phlegmy cackle reverberating through the halls as she makes her rounds. She's missing her bottom front teeth and lets her dentures dangle from her mouth when she asks, "Hotcakes or omelet, honey?" I learned early on that hotcakes are the only viable option, the omelets rubbery and so banana yellow they seem to taste like Yellow No. 5. Brianna likes *Riot TV*, so she sits for a few minutes beside my bed under the pretense of helping me with my breakfast—she unpeels the foil lids from the coffee and orange juice, something I'm grateful for because I can't manage with my hands the way they are, and cuts apart the hotcakes and sausage links. She's riveted by *Riot* and laughs great belly laughs whenever someone's hurt—cheerleaders landing on their necks, kids' teeth broken by pogo sticks—actually crying because she's laughing so hard.

On my second day awake, Brianna told me I'd been lying here for five days already.

"Where's here?" I asked her.

"Saint Elizabeth's," she said. "Youngstown. Do you know where Youngstown is?"

"Ohio—"

"And I thought you'd say heaven—"

I've been in this hospital for a little over five weeks. I'm in the uninsured wing, with street people and drug addicts and howling lunatics housed three or four to a room, the kind of clinic I floated through not long ago when I was hooked on brown sugar. Compared to the others here, though, I'm in comfort: one of the administrators told me I was in a private room because my bill's already been paid in cash—mystifying, though Timothy did say he'd take care of my medical expenses. When the administrator asked for my name and social security number, I told her I couldn't remember, a response that must be somewhat typical here because of the way she breezed through the rest of the form without cross-examining me.

"Will you give us permission to run a face scan or DNA match against the national database?"

"Not if I don't have to—"

"Most people don't," she said. "I'll just write *unidentified, uninsured, male,* on the forms—"

"That's accurate," I told her.

At midnight the channel flips to infomercials selling bulk discount gemstones and I think of Albion, usually remembering her standing above me on that pile of bricks, her hair loose in the wind. I can no longer remember the color of Albion's eyes, but when I think of them, they're the gray of storm-wracked skies.

When I finally drift to sleep, I dream of Hannah.

The doctors keep me updated—there's a trio, one in Boston, the other two in Mumbai, faces on HD screens mounted on a roving turret. A doctor rolls into my room every other day or so, but since the turret webcam's loose on its mounting, the doctors rarely face me when one of them speaks.

"Whoever healed you may have saved your life, but they didn't do you any favors," says Dr. Aadesh.

"Why's that?" I ask.

"Bones not set properly. Ligaments in your knee aren't healing correctly. You've lost your right eye, something that may have been avoided if you were brought to the hospital sooner. Severe radiation exposure, near lethal, you were lucky there was enough blood supply for the transfusion—"

The doctor reads through my litany of injuries, asking how I feel about each one—the Re-Growth splints in eight of my fingers, the splint and cast for my obliterated knee and the compound fracture of my right shin. Chemosutures for the knife wounds on my face, shoulders, hands and chest. The sensor in my glass right eye wired to my visual cortex. I'm supposed to wear specialty glasses, now—thick lenses in bulky black frames meant to assist my left eye in tracking the same focal points as the sensor in my right.

"Very good," says Aadesh. "Dr. Hardy will check on you the day after tomorrow. Do you have any questions for me?"

"I do have a question," I tell him. "I think the glasses might need an adjustment on the prescription—they wear out my good eye. I have to take them off every so often or I get headaches—"

"I apologize," says Aadesh, "I can see you clearly through the monitor, but I can't hear you. Can you try to adjust the volume? Or, no, I'm seeing here the volume is set at high. The audio must be out. Please go ahead and submit your question to the on-call nurse and she'll contact our company directly—"

The turret spins in place, roves from the room—I hear it progressing down the hallway, like someone's driving a remote-controlled car out there.

Brianna's got to be closer to seventy than sixty, but her hair's smoothed and dyed a bright blonde and her eyes are young. She leans in when she's talking, touches your arm.

"You don't have Adware," I mention one morning while we're watching *Riot*.

"What do I need that for?" she asks. "My kids' kids have that. I saw this man at a fair, had magnets inside his fingers, actually under the skin so he could just touch a piece of metal and hold it. Said he kept erasing his credit cards. Shivers, honey. Look at you, with that fake eye plugged into your brain. I don't need that shit inside my body—"

"You could watch *Riot* all you want," I tell her. "You could sit back and make it seem like you're right there with them—"

"We're watching the follies of man," she says. "Why would I want to be closer than I am now? Besides, I got better stuff to do, like teaching you to piss for yourself—"

When I can stand with crutches, Brianna walks with me down the hallway to the toilet near the nurses' station and waits out in the hall until she hears the flush. She walks me back and sees me back into bed.

"Rehab," she says. "Keep walking, you'll be all right—"

Toward the end of the fifth week, I'm scheduled at the attending doctor's offices on the first floor. I crutch myself down, even managing the stairs between floors 3 and 4 where the elevator's out. The attending doctor's taciturn, uninterested in small talk—I'm just one of several people who'll pass through her office that day. She examines my body using a checklist of injuries sustained—hand-scanner X-rays, cold rollers over my chest. She's especially concerned about the knife wounds and my right eye. I do a sight test for her, trying to read smallish letters from across the room, failing miserably—they all look like the letter *D* to me, or maybe *E*. She sends my glasses off to the lab downstairs for a better prescription and at the end of our appointment signs my papers.

"You'll be discharged this afternoon," she says.

The hospital administrators present me with a hoodie and sweatpants from the gift shop, recompense for the blood-soiled clothes the doctors had to cut from me when I was first brought to the ER. The sweatshirt says *St. Elizabeth's, Youngstown, Ohio*—only an XL, but once I put it on I'm swimming in it and realize just how much weight I've lost in the weeks since I've been here.

Brianna brings in two bags along with my lunch—my backpack from the zone and a duffel bag I've never seen before.

"I sprung these for you," she says. "Ain't looked inside, ain't nothing missing—"

My last lunch at St. Elizabeth's is a soy burger with limp fries and an aluminum can of Pepsi. My fingers never healed correctly, just like Dr. Aadesh said, all five fingers on my left hand reset in a twisted, knotty mess. Difficult to pop the tab on the Pepsi, I can't get a grip even with my right hand and I don't have as much strength as I should, but I manage.

"I've worked here for forty years, just about, and I've seen bodies wash up, all kinds of people wash up here. No one knows who they are or where they've been, but I ain't never seen nothing like you," Brianna says.

"What's that mean?" I ask her.

"You know how you came here? Someone called 911 and said where you were, didn't leave a name. Took a medevac out to find you, and there you were: half dead in the middle of Pittsburgh, for God's sake, with these two bags and an envelope full of cash. Cash, mind you. Nobody told me how much cash, and I hear about most of everything around here, but it must have been enough, if you've been here this long. Never nothing like it before, in forty years. But you can't remember none of that, can you? You can't even remember your name, you can't remember nothing—"

"I remember a few things," I tell her.

"I know you do, honey. But don't worry, we ain't snitches here. Nobody here will say we saw you, once you get from here. We never saw you, all right?"

Once Brianna leaves, I look in the duffel and find stacks of bills—twenties and hundreds, there must be thousands of dollars in here. In a manila envelope, there's an Iowa driver's license and a passport with my picture but the name Glen Bower, the birthplace Dubuque, Iowa. No notes, no instructions.

My journal's still in the backpack, that's the main thing—otherwise there are just water bottles and a flashlight, nothing important. My dosimeter's in there, black as death. I dump the gear and stuff the duffel into the backpack so the money's easier to carry. I leave a stack of hundreds in an envelope marked *Brianna*, I don't know how much—a few thousand, at least.

I catch a cab out front of the hospital and tell the driver I need to go to a store, a Target or a Walmart, whatever's nearby. Youngstown's been cleaned up since I'd last been here about fifteen years ago, maybe all that money from the presence of PEZ Zeolite. Downtown's a mini arts district with small shops and flower baskets hanging from the streetlamps. Just past downtown, an old mill's been redeveloped, anchored by a Target and a Dick's Sporting Goods. The cab waits as I buy a pay-as-you-go smartphone under the name of Glen Bower—the registration's valid. I take the cab out to an EconoLodge on the interstate, pay for a room in cash.

I sleep for several hours, order a pizza for delivery and watch TV while I eat. I set up the cell and call Gavril once I have my connection, using Translator to speak with him in pidgin Czech.

"Dominic? Oh, God," he says. "Oh, thank God, Dominic—"

I tell him what's happened. I tell him I'm all right. I tell him I don't know what to do. He asks whether I'm able to buy a ticket to London, if he needs to come to get me or if I can meet him there.

"I think I can make it on my own," I tell him.

10, 21—

October twenty-first—

Eleven years since the end—

Gavril met me at Heathrow—I'd bought a one-way ticket from Youngstown-Warren to London with cash, a purchase that ruffled the TSA screeners. The ersatz passport left in the duffel bag of cash worked well enough, though—scanned in Youngstown-Warren, Cleveland and Atlanta, then again at customs in London without a hitch. Flocks of baggage-laden travelers sprinted through Heathrow's labyrinthine corridors to make their connections, but I stayed well to the edges to let them pass, taking my time, strolling those ramps and walkways gingerly with my cane. Gavril didn't recognize me at first, I'm so much skinnier now and the injury to my eye skews my face, but when he heard my voice at baggage claim he hugged me and cried, refusing to let me go even as other passengers scrambled around us. Kelly was with him—I'd been nervous to see her, thinking of Zhou, but she'd cut her hair into a platinum bristle of pixie spikes, looking nothing like the version of herself in the Archive.

Six days catching up with Gavril and Kelly in their Chelsea flat before he purchased three tickets from Heathrow to the Václav Havel airport in Prague, and rented a private car to Domažlice to his mother's farm. We arrived at dusk, the floods illuminating the unpainted plank wood of my aunt's barn, the house lights lit, the surrounding fields red-gold furrowed with black. My aunt waited for us on the front porch in an ink- and paint-stained smock, her hair a springy bush of graying corkscrews. She hugged me and cried, just like Gav, then fed us dish after dish she'd made throughout the day, pork chops and cabbage, potatoes and spinach and apple strudel. Kelly picked at her food, but Gav and I ate like we'd been starved in exile, finishing with coffee and then cognac out on the front porch, watching night coalesce over the fields. The back den was made up as a guest room for me, with a foldout sofa bed and a small desk. I slept, comfortable and feeling safe, my body releasing the shock of the past several months—I slept through two full days, only blearily emerging to use the bathroom before crawling back underneath the covers, curling back into bed. By the time I woke up, Gavril and Kelly had already returned to London.

The doctors here in Domažlice tell me I'll limp for life without further surgeries, but even then there aren't guarantees. I take walks every other day, usually around the perimeter of the fields, to build strength and get used to my limp and the dull ache of my weight.

My aunt takes breaks from her work usually by the time I finish up one of my longer walks, so I'll often hitch a ride with her into town, a twenty-five-minute drive through the countryside before the narrow flagstone streets of Domažlice. The buildings here sit in long rows tight against the edges of the streets, ancient architecture from the twentieth or nineteenth centuries, maybe earlier, each facade painted a different pastel shade—pinks, yellows, light greens, blues—that make the town radiate cheeriness even as the weather turns bleaker toward winter. My aunt tends to park on Náměstí Míru to run her errands, checking in on artist friends for tea or the owner of the gallery she works with. I make my way over to Petr Bočan for a pilsner, sitting under the yellow awnings when I can or moving inside if it's too cold. The place is a sports bar, and even though I'm not interested in soccer, I find the background noise helps me turn inward—I'm exotic here, an American, but no one cares as long as there's a game on. Once my belly feels warm, I make my way over to the Bozen public library to check out one of their tablets and access the streams. I try to keep up with Simka, to follow what's happening to him. I've gathered what information there is about his arrest and trial—but there's nothing much, nothing truly substantial. When she's finished with her errands, my aunt finds me in the library—sometimes we'll swing back to Petr Bočan's for pork chops, or we'll just head home where I help her cook.

I keep a filing cabinet for all the printouts I've made at the library—cached streams about Simka's case, commentaries from DC legal analysts. I bought a whiteboard just like Kucenic's that I've filled with starting points, suppositions about what might have happened, how I can prove that Waverly framed Simka, but I can't figure it out—there's nothing, no leads. Without Adware, I've taken to writing Simka letters, actual letters, addressing them care of his prison—I don't know if he receives them or not. I never write a return address, I never specify who I am and am careful to leave out details of my life. I write about my recovery, mostly, that I use a cane when I walk, that my hand never healed correctly.

After one of my walks around the field, I pour myself coffee and cook up toast and a scrambled egg. My aunt joins me, splits her grapefruit with me, and asks if I'd like to go out to the studio with her.

"You want to see?" she asks, her English much better than Gav's.

"I'd love to," I tell her.

My aunt's converted the barn into a print shop—nothing too fancy, just drywall and space heaters, a raised floor in case there's ever a leak, fluorescent tubes like a lattice of light suspended from the roof slats. She opens the wide double doors for fresh air, but even so the place smells like ink and astringent chemicals, old wood and wet hay. Gavril used this barn as his studio when he was making art, and some of his things are still here, stashed in the corner—televisions, speaker parts, old computers still in their boxes. The rest of the barn is taken up with my aunt's printing equipment—several presses of different sizes, cabinets filled with a rainbow of ink.

"Over here," she says, leading me to her worktable—a massive wood slab with benches suitable for a mead hall. She's a woodblock printer primarily, and her worktable's covered with carving tools and wood panels for different steps of the layered printing process. Her work is fanciful, hyperdetailed, lush—mostly children's book illustrations. She's working on a series for a new Czech translation of the Brothers Grimm.

"I'll use you as a model for the good prince," she says. "He loses his eyes in the brambles, no? So I'll model him after you, put your troubles with your eye to some good use—"

"All right, but my modeling work doesn't come cheap—"

"I know, I know," she says. "Strudel. More strudel—"

She's especially interested in showing me a press she calls her "jobber," a cast-iron old thing that looks like an overgrown typewriter.

"Letterpress," she says. "For your poetry. You can work when I work—"

My aunt hands me two keys on a ring, the smaller key for the type-case drawers, the larger for the cabinet stocked with her expensive paper. "Here," she says, pulling a drawer from the type case and setting it on a secondary worktable near the jobber—the drawer's filled with metal blocks, each bearing a letter in a different font, capitals and lowercases.

"Easy," she says, showing me how to fit each letter into the composing stick, how to tie off the galley. She spells out *John Dominic Blaxton lives here*, then shows me how to ink the letters and run it through the press.

"For your door," she says, handing me the print. "Now you try. Something simple for first one—"

I rummage through the typefaces, picking out metal blocks—difficult with my hands the way they are, but my aunt helps. The heft of letters in my palm is comforting, somehow, like language become sculptural, tangible. I'm drawn to a blocky Cloister Black font, picking out uppercase letters. I'm not sure what I'm trying to spell until I collect the first two letters, *M-O*, then find the others, *O-K*.

MOOK.

"What's mook?" my aunt asks once we've finished the print, that single black word in the middle of a bone-white page.

"I'm not sure," I tell her.

I have trouble sleeping, so I spend the dead hours sitting on the front porch bundled in a quilt, staring into midnight and drinking brandy and milk, probably drinking too much, but I can't relax until I've nudged myself into a dull buzz. I think about Mook. What he must have thought when I started finding those traces, tracking Albion like I was following a thread through a labyrinth, unraveling all the work he'd done to hide her. He knew about the Christ House. He knew about Timothy and Waverly and he knew about Hannah's murder, maybe of other murders. He was recruited into this terror just like I was, and didn't know what to do when he peeled away the surface story and found Waverly's legacy of dead women, just like I don't know what to do now—so he made that monument in Pittsburgh, the geocached installation of Hannah's death because he couldn't turn away from the evil he'd uncovered but he was too afraid to expose it, was too invested in helping Albion disappear, maybe he loved her. Will I just let this pass? For all his threats, for his deletion of Theresa, Mook was probably terrified of me—he probably thought I was one of them, one with Waverly. I hate him for what he did to me, for what he did to Theresa, I hate him—but I understand, too. I finish my brandy and milk and pour another finger from the bottle and wish Mook was here with me to help me think this through. I wish he was still alive.

Monuments to the dead—

The next time my aunt drives to Domažlice I check out a library tablet and log into my old e-mail account—someone's been through my in-box, it looks like, some recent messages have been opened, others deleted. Risky to log in like this, in case Waverly's monitoring the account, so I make it quick—sifting through old message folders until I find the poetry manuscript Twiggy once sent to me. I print out the thirty-five pages of her work.

My aunt works early in the morning, but I don't make it into the studio until the afternoon. I bring her a fresh thermos of coffee. She pauses in her work to help me get started with the jobber and answers my questions, gives me advice about printing technique. I only make small edits to Twiggy's manuscript, fixing typos or correcting obvious mistakes, then design each page for the letterpress by stacking every letter in the composing stick until I form her words. I begin my printing. I start with the first poem of hers that I read:

I reached for you this morning but you were gone.

My plan is to produce a limited-edition chapbook, no more than a hundred copies of her work. I'm slow at this, but I find the process calming—assembling the text, inking the letters. It takes me a full day to create two pages, sometimes a few days for a longer page of text. I pull each sheet and hang them to dry on lines that crisscross the barn, the studio starting to resemble a ship with sails unfurled.

11, 11—

Gavril and Kelly have flown in for the week. My aunt showers him with kisses. "Ma, Ma," he says, wiping wet smudges from his cheeks and forehead.

My aunt's warm with Kelly, but formal—still measuring each other, I suppose. They can't quite connect, is all—Kelly a little too urban sophisticate, my aunt a hayseed hippie. They do their best bonding over food, Kelly a health-food obsessive and my aunt a champion of the farm-to-fork movement—they're making plans for a trip into Prague, to try a raw-food tapas bar a friend of my aunt's opened a few months ago.

I pull my cousin aside. "Gav, I need to talk with you—"

"Sure," he says. "Can we go for a walk?"

I use the translator app on my cell, holding it to my ear whenever Gavril talks—regaling me with tales of London nightlife, his contract negotiations with *Vogue*. He waxes rhapsodic over his love for Kelly. "I want to marry her," he says. "Think of the cute little Gavrils we could make—"

The dropping temperature's affecting my leg, cramping me up quicker than usual. We walk the driveway, turn left along the edge of the road. When we reach the forsythia, an unkempt riot of browning leaves and branches, Gavril says, "I think I still have some *Playboys* buried in Tupperware over here. We can try to find them—"

Gavril digs around beneath the bush for ten minutes at least before he starts worrying that his mother might have found his *Playboys* and thrown out the issues.

"It's all right if she did," I tell him. "You're a grown man—"

"Hm," he says, resuming his search, using a stick to poke deeper into the frigid clay. "Maybe I'll come back in the summer when it's not so hard to dig—"

"Listen, Gav, I have something I need to ask you—"

He stops digging, wipes his hands on his coat. "Sure, Domi. Anything—"

"You said you have some people who'd be interested in that stuff I sent you? The footage about the young woman who was killed?"

"Absolutely," he tells me. "Mika Bronstein, he's a producer for *Buy, Fuck, Sell America* at CNN. He was very interested—still is. In fact, he texted me about a week ago saying I'm an asshole for teasing him with celebrity gossip, then holding out—"

"I want you to release it," I tell him, not sure if this is the right thing to do even as I'm asking.

"Why?" he asks, scraping at the dirt again for his *Playboys*. "All of this bullshit is finally behind you. Why do anything? Leave well enough alone. Let it go—"

"I've been drinking too much," I tell him. "I can't sleep because I think of her—"

"The redhead?"

"No. The woman I found," I tell him. "I wake up in the middle of the night and think her body's on the floor beside my bed. Just down there, and I'm paralyzed thinking about her, not even questioning why her body would be there, just certain, absolutely certain, that if I looked over the edge of my bed I'd see her covered in ants—"

"You sound like you need another Simka in your life—"

"I want justice for her," I tell him.

After dinner, we linger around the kitchen table with beer and wine, hunks of my aunt's honey-wheat brown bread and sharp cheese. It's started to snow—icy flurries that clatter against the kitchen windows. We talk until well past midnight, my aunt still awake in the other room, working on her cross-stitch, listening to Emil Viklický's piano cover of "A Love Supreme." Kelly's gone to bed hours ago, and soon Gavril says he's heading upstairs to join her.

"One last thing," I say as he's rinsing out our glasses in the sink. "When you release that footage, I need you to tell your producer friend that you received it from a man called Mook—"

11, 19—

CNN International breaks the story, but within a few minutes other networks have picked up the footage—I'm watching on my aunt's television, drinking milk and brandy. BBC Europe, ČT24 from Prague, Sky News, Al Jazeera—nearly every channel I flip through shows uncensored video of the murder stream, of Waverly screaming that Hannah's no more holy than roadkill, of Timothy stabbing her twenty-four times. American officials say the evidence is being authenticated, that President Meecham has been briefed and is evaluating the situation. Waverly's file photo flashes on-screen. Hannah on a constant loop, zoom shots of Hannah's genitals, her breasts—zoom shots of her dying face, talking heads discussing whether or not her face expresses orgasm, whether or not her rape and murder were on some level consensual. A remix set to hip-hop of Waverly's autotuned voice, singing, "You're looking at nothing more holy than roadkill is holy." Numb with shock that Hannah's murder is going viral, that I did this to her. Hannah's life's exposed—pictures and vids from high school boyfriends, intimate after-prom footage sold to the streams, big paydays for Hannah Massey sex tapes, producers begging on-air for *newsworthy* footage. Naked. Sex tapes. Homemade. Beach vacations, headshots, ex-boyfriend spy cam footage. Interviews with Hannah's extended family in Ohio, the same people who'd filed the insurance claim I'd investigated—they've already signed off for Hannah to appear on *Crime Scene Superstar*, already thrilled to see she's scoring high in the pre-rankings, already discussing what they'll do with the prize money if she wins.

I swig the rest of the bottle of brandy, then stumble outside in the vast lawn, the alcohol lifting me but I collapse. A light snow. The grass is frozen, prickly. I can smell the earth and wonder how many millions of worms writhe just below the surface, wriggling toward the sky to feast on me if I should die. I lie facedown for hours—*What have I done to you? What have I done?* Beyond shivering, beyond freezing. My aunt finds me unresponsive but awake—I remember staring into the white sky. *What have I done to you?* I don't remember my aunt moving me inside, submerging me in a warm bath. I don't remember the EMT's visiting me, I don't remember anything.

12, 12—

Gav calls.

"Turn on the television," he says.

Eleven at night, drunk on rum—I turn on the living room television to reruns of *Takeshi's Castle Revival*, Japanese women running an obstacle course, their voices dubbed over in Czech. Snow's fallen heavily the past few days, shrouding the fields. My aunt's in the barn, the barn lights the only brightness for miles and miles.

"What am I looking for?" I ask Gav, but flip through the news channels and see what he's guiding me to: *"Breaking News. Shootout in Alabama."*

"I'm going to ping my mom," he says. "Someone should be there with you—"

Helicopter shots of a sprawling farmhouse and acres of fields. Two barns, one of them on fire. A dead body's in the yard.

"Authorities have ID'd the victim as Cormac Waverly, 36, an Alabama state trooper. At this time, Cormac Waverly is believed to have been one of the assailants in the Theodore Waverly death stream—"

"Dominic, are you all right?" my aunt asks, hurrying inside—she thinks I may have had another episode, a drunken fit or something. She's relieved to find me sitting on the edge of the couch, even if I do have a drink in my hand. I set the drink down.

"I'm fine," I tell her. "They found him, it looks like. Waverly. There's a shootout—"

She takes off her hat and gloves and after a few minutes leaves to brew us tea—a strong Earl Grey that reminds me of Albion, of our first night together. I wonder if she's there in Alabama.

Cycling the same helicopter shots: circling the compound, black smoke churning from one of the barns, the body sprawled in the lawn just outside the house. The farm is Gregor Waverly's. Diagrams of the compound, illustrations of the barn fire. The fire started earlier in the day, during the first wave of the assault, when members of Birmingham SWAT established a perimeter. There was an exchange of gunfire. A grenade explosion ignited the barn.

Nearing one thirty in the morning, my aunt makes Cream of Wheat with brown sugar and butter and brews a pot of coffee. The networks recycle the Hannah Massey footage, flashing Waverly's capsule bio. Footage detailing Waverly's relationship with President Meecham, extending far back to her earliest days in politics. Talking heads fill in the narrative of the morning's events—an FBI task force working with private researching firm the Kucenic Group built a case against Theodore Waverly and the Waverly family of

Birmingham, Alabama, following the release of the Hannah Massey murder stream.

The Kucenic Group—my old boss appears on television, his white hair and beard growing in wild tangles and braids, looking much more like an avenging prophet than the leader of a private research firm.

"We recognized initial footage as evidence linked to an unsolved case related to the Pittsburgh City-Archive and pursued this lead jointly with representatives of the FBI—"

I wonder what changed—what gave Kucenic courage enough after he'd already abandoned me, after he was so willing to let Hannah Massey slip through the cracks? Maybe the FBI recognized the footage of Hannah's body, maybe they traced it back to his case file and demanded answers. Maybe the FBI showed up at his door with a bigger stick than Waverly.

Phalanxes of Birmingham SWAT and the FBI assault team snake toward the house, advancing on foot behind armored trucks, eventually moving single file behind men holding steel shields. An explosion rips through the rear section of the house, a fireball that plumes toward the news helicopter covering the siege. Within minutes it's reported that one member of the Birmingham SWAT was injured in the explosion, an apparent gas leak in the house ignited by gunfire. A few minutes pass and the networks confirm a second death—a man identified as Gregor Waverly, his body recovered. Images of Gregor as a younger man, posed arm in arm with his brother.

Fire trucks and ambulances on scene. The FBI assault team streams into the house. Within minutes they emerge with two men in custody, Rory Waverly and Theodore Waverly, though Rory is reportedly in critical condition resulting from gunshot wounds. Thirty minutes after the arrests, the governor of Alabama holds a press conference, thanking the joint work of the agencies involved. During questions from the press, he confirms that Rory Waverly has died as a result of gunshot wounds sustained in the siege.

SUMMER—

Every so often Hannah Massey intrudes on my dreams—I follow the slope down to the riverbed and find Hannah still alive, her body still in the river, half buried in silt. I wonder if I'll be able to save her, if I can just reach her in time, but in every iteration of this dream the river current kicks up swiftly and carries Hannah away.

"Wake up," says my aunt, "it's just a dream—"

I'm fragile now, somehow—I realize that. Physically, I'm fragile and still become exhausted easily. The limping, the difficulty with my hands. Even simple things are still frustratingly challenging for me. The blindness in my right eye has broadened despite further laser surgeries—even on the brightest days there's a haze that hangs over everything I see. I have trouble sustaining my concentration, even when I'm researching Simka's case. One afternoon I realize I haven't made headway for weeks—I realize I'm letting Simka slip through the cracks, so I write to Kucenic—an appeal to continue unraveling Waverly. I describe Simka to him, describe how I believe Waverly was behind the accusations that sent Simka to prison. I figure that Kucenic won't receive my letter for weeks, or maybe months, as he's adjusting to his newfound fame—his stream appearances commenting on high-profile cases—but I know that despite the wait, Kucenic is the best hope for Simka. Kucenic will put two and two together, I'm certain. He'll realize that I'm the only one who can possibly know so many connective details about these cases, but I keep my name out of the letter. I sign as *Mook.*

General solitude, dedication to poetry. My aunt made an ultimatum—that I stop drinking or move out. She said she'd give me three weeks to make up my mind, but I told her I no longer needed alcohol or drugs, that something had broken inside of me and healed. I resurrected the name Confluence Press for my chapbooks and attend small-press festivals and art fairs, my aunt helping me with the business end of things even though my only sales goal is to break even. After Twiggy's chapbook, I solicited a Ukrainian poet I've long admired for a chapbook and again a poet from Mississippi who'd won the National Book Award a few years ago. I just received confirmation from Adelmo Salomar that I can reprint *Ouroboros* as a limited-edition chapbook for the fourth book in my line. His letter is postmarked from Chile—I've framed it and hung it near my workstation. Everyone I meet is enthusiastic about my craft. I keep my chapbooks to limited runs and have received some positive reviews, even a mention in *Poetry* magazine in an article about Fine Press books. The attention is appreciated—but I've already heard from poets I knew marginally a decade ago, people wondering about John Dominic Blaxton and how I knew him.

"An old friend," is all I have to say.

I wake one morning to news that the FBI arrested Dr. Timothy Waverly, living in a cabin outside of Tacoma, Washington, under the name of Timothy Filt. He was spotted buying groceries at a Target—facial recognition cameras matched his features despite a beard and the knit hat he wore pulled down almost to his eyes. Traffic cameras tracked his route as he drove, intersection to intersection, until a Washington state police drone locked onto his car and followed him for the hour-and-a-half drive to his cabin. Considered armed and dangerous, the Tacoma PD SWAT team led by FBI agents from the Seattle field office stormed the cabin and arrested him—there was no need for the show of force. Timothy was unarmed and surrendered peacefully.

The FBI releases a statement saying it had been determined that a woman had been staying with Timothy Waverly, the last person of interest wanted for questioning about the murder of Hannah Massey and information relating to more than thirty cases of missing or murdered women connected with the Waverly family, both in Pennsylvania and Alabama. The woman's name is Darwyn Harris, from the San Francisco Bay area. The FBI release pictures—old images of Albion that Timothy must have had with him from before the bombing of Pittsburgh. She looks so young.

Spring Fashion Week—

I don't have the stomach to watch these things, never have—but when Gavril calls to tell me that President Meecham wears a gown from House of Fetherston for the executions I tune in to see the spectacle, the irony of it all. My aunt's streaming a presentation of the Vaněk plays by Václav Havel in the living room, so I lie in bed with a glass of warm milk, watching on the smaller flat screen bolted to the wall above my bookcase.

"A crimson gown with an ivory neck ruff that halos her head," says Gavril. "Very Elizabethan. Her hair in plaits streaming over her shoulders like ribbons. She wears a black lace blindfold—"

"I'm watching," I tell Gavril. "I can see her—"

America's Queen, they call her, and she looks like a painting of ancient royalty, Elizabeth I, or maybe the Queen of Hearts. President Meecham carries out the executions in the Rose Garden, the genetically modified roses blooming into gargantuan flowers—reds, pinks, whites. Meecham will be on hand for the start of the Fashion Week runway shows in New York, flying from Washington following the garden party. The prisoners are led in, nine as always, wearing black robes. They are forced to their knees.

"Madam Speaker, the President of the United States—"

Meecham reviews each prisoner, each one charged with a crime symbolizing the ever-present threats to the country and to her presidency. A man convicted of pipe-bombing a food court in Minneapolis, killing thirteen and wounding scores of others. A woman convicted of leaking NSA secrets to the streams, endangering American sovereignty abroad. Timothy and Waverly are among the nine, each charged with multiple counts of murder in two states. I may not have recognized them without the captioning—Timothy's head is shaved, his scarring like white worms on his scalp, and Waverly's hair is different, too, shorter, all those cottony locks shorn down to a white bristle. Meecham walks the line of prisoners, inspecting them. She doesn't pause or give special attention to Waverly or his son, merely glances at them like she glances at the other prisoners—hasty, disdainful. She offers each prisoner a chance to recant, to swear their fealty to the flag.

"I should go," I tell Gavril.

"Call me later, if you need to talk," he says.

Meecham pauses in front of Waverly and offers him his chance to plead for leniency. I figure Waverly would have cause to beg Meecham to spare his life, considering his history with her—he once told me that he'd created Meecham, that he was responsible for her—but after Meecham finishes her speech and asks if there are mitigating reasons why she should look on his case with mercy, Waverly doesn't speak. He simply stares at Meecham—or rather, he seems to stare through her, like he's concentrating on something beyond her, beyond these proceedings. When his lips finally do move, the commentators suggest he's reciting the 23rd Psalm.

Timothy doesn't speak either when Meecham offers him leniency, although I want him to—I want him to confess here publicly, to recant everything, to break down and weep and beg, to ask Meecham for compassion, to give himself over to her mercy. He doesn't speak, but he's not stoic either, not like his father—his eyes well with tears and his face reflects anguish as he forces himself to keep from crying. Timothy wanted me to believe that he was working toward grace. Is this what grace looks like? All that pain—

Black hoods over their heads. Meecham signs each execution warrant with a silver pen.

I turn off the television, head to the barn and work at the press until dawn.

The last mention I hear of Albion, maybe the last mention I'll ever hear, was on the BBC, a brief mention buried amid a flurry of other, more pressing news. A Canadian border patrol agent came forward to report he had spotted Darwyn Harris crossing from Washington State into Canada several days prior—that she had used a passport and ID under the name Albion Waverly and had been driving a Volkswagen Rabbit. "Her passport didn't catch on the Do Not Cross list, so I let her through," said the agent. "Our facial ID software was off-line for a few hours that afternoon, she must have known. I didn't recognize her until later, when I was flipping through some paperwork." Collaborating with Canadian authorities, the FBI determined that she had most likely purchased another car with cash just outside Vancouver. The segment about Albion ended and the BBC turned to continuing coverage of Nina

Penrose, Page 3 girl and winner of last year's Miss Universe pageant, and her upcoming appearance on the British version of *Chance in Hell.*

I wonder what name Albion's using now—

I've contemplated new Adware, something simple, to retrace our steps through the City, to search for her—sometimes I imagine I'll find her if I just spend enough time in places that were important to us, maybe in our booth at Kelly's in East Liberty, or maybe if I ride her bus as it plunges into the tunnel just before the end of the world. She's sure to haunt those places eventually—but I realize I'm a ghost to her now, a link to a past she wants to efface. I think of her as I take my walks around the fields. I remember her. I've never been to Canada, but I imagine Albion with new hair, new clothes, behind the wheel of a car bought used just outside Vancouver. I imagine her driving on interstates, heading farther and farther north, as far north as she can go. I imagine that the roads she travels are beautiful, studded with mountains and lush with evergreens. I imagine that as the roads thin and the forests darken she feels safe, finally safe. I imagine a single road cutting through all those miles and miles of forest, all that infinite forest, a single road that someone could drive for hours, for days, and never see another human face.

ACKNOWLEDGMENTS

Although writing is a solitary act, a writer's work is never accomplished alone.

Thank you to Stewart O'Nan, whose writing is an inspiration to me, and whose wisdom, friendship and encouragement came at an unexpected and crucial time in my life.

Thank you to Jonathan Auxier, whose critical insight helped my writing, and whose friendship enriches me.

Thank you to my close friends who read early versions of this story, whose commentary and enthusiasm were crucial to the development of this book: Angela Seals, David Seals, Nicole Capozzi, Joshua Hogan, Caroline Carlson, Brother Thomas Bondra.

Thank you to Matt McHenry and Guy Bialostocki, whose computer expertise helped bring a sense of realism to the Archive.

Thank you to Pittsburgh artist Seth Clark, whose finely constructed architectural collages served as an inspiration when I imagined the type of artwork Albion might create.

Thank you to David Gernert, Andy Kifer, Rebecca Gardner and everyone at the Gernert Company. Thank you to Sylvie Rabineau at RWSG Literary Agency.

Thank you to Meaghan Wagner, my editor. Thank you to Ivan Held and Susan Allison at Putnam. Thank you to John Wordsworth at Headline books. Thank you to the hardworking copyeditors and designers at Putnam who helped bring this book to life.

Thank you to everyone at the Carnegie Library for the Blind and Physically Handicapped, true friends and a second family, who I've shared my life with for twelve years.

Thank you to my mom and dad for everything, and to Howard and Marilyn, to Jenna and James and Karen, to Tal and Jenn and Pete, and to Eloise, Amelia and Pen.

And thank you to my wife, Sonja, and my daughter, Genevieve, whose love is everything to me.